My One Love

NECIE NAVONE

Brothers OF Camelot

MAR 2021

My One Love

Book Two in The Brothers of Camelot

by Necie Navone
Copyright 2019 by Necie Navone
Cover Design by: RMGraphX
Formatting By: Duffette Literary Service & Kaila Duff
www.duffette.com
Editor: Katy Nielsen

❀ Created with Vellum

CONTENTS

DEDICATION

This book is dedicated to "YOU" the reader.
Thank you from the bottom of my heart, for your support.
I hope you enjoy this book as much as I love Grayson and Lexy and
sharing their story with you.

To Katy Nielsen for your endless support and encouragement that kept me
going and kept me writing. You're a true blessing and sweetheart.
Thank you.

PLAYLIST

INSPIRATIONAL MUSIC LIST

I'd like to give a huge thank you to all these artists for their spectacular music that would play over and over again in my mind while writing. Some would actually haunt me, every time I got in the car. The lyrics actually inspired several scenes as well. I cannot encourage you enough to listen to them and see how they make you feel. Music has always been such an escape and calming balm to me. I hope you enjoy them as much as I do.

1. I Don't Want To Live Forever: ZAYN & Taylor Swift
2. Crazy In Love: Sofia Karberg
3. Perfect: Ed Sheeran
4. Praying: Kesha
5. Ready For It: Taylor Swift
6. Thinking Out Loud: Ed Sheeran
7. All of Me: Jon Legend
8. Not All Heroes Wear Caps: Owl City
9. You Are The Reason: Calum Scott
10. Be Alright: Dean Lewis

PRELUDE

ALMOST CAUGHT

Lexy

*H*oly shit, Isabella saw me. I've got to get out of here, fast. Thank God I still have on my gym shoes. I make a mad dash towards the penthouse, hoping not to be seen by Grayson in the crowd. I don't want to bump into him for the first time in over eight years wearing leggings and looking a mess.

"Aless!" Grayson's voice calls out from behind me.

Crap, crap, crap. Up ahead, I spot the fire hydrant near the corner of the alley by my penthouse. My legs pump harder. I just hope the dumpster lid is closed so that I can get a good leap up to the balcony. Dang, I hope these large trees hide my jumping trip up there.

"Is that you, Aless?!" he calls again. My heart aches to answer, but not yet. I'm not ready.

Swiftly turning the corner, I leap up, placing my foot on the top of the hydrant and pushing off. My silent prayer that the lid of the dumpster is closed is answered when my foot connects with it. Thank you, Mother Mary, and all that is Holy.

I tug my collapsible grappling hook from the side of my backpack. I never leave home without at least one. With a push of the small hidden button, it opens completely. I toss it onto our balcony, watching the hidden coil inside unwind towards me. Grabbing it and giving it a little tug to make sure it's secure, I scramble up the rope, hoping the trees are hiding me. Once I reach the top, I swing my leg over and fall onto the safety of my balcony, letting out a relieved sigh.

"Holy Fuckin' Shit-balls woman!" Anissa yells, walking out of the sliding door. "Lexy, what the fuck? You scared the ever-loving shit out me with your ninja shit. You're supposed to warn us when you're doing that shit." She stops at my feet, looking at me laying on the floor.

"Sshhh! Grayson followed me home. I had to," I whisper, trying to catch my breath.

"Fuck, girl. Why didn't you tell me?" Reaching back into the penthouse, she grabs a pair of binoculars, which she regularly uses to check out the hot guys on the beach and boardwalk across the street. "Yup, there he is. He's just a block down the road, headed our way. Want to see?" she offers, but never stops looking into the binoculars, nor does she hand them to me.

"Damn, girl. He's looking around, obviously for you. He's even stopping and asking people. Shit, he's hot as hell, and *huge*. I've seen pictures of him on your Facebook and at a distance when we went to spy on him at the club, but damn, they *do not* do him justice."

I slowly sit up and peek through the cutout cloverleaf in the balcony wall.

"Yeah, I believe he's even bigger now than he was that last time we were together. He's let his hair grow out a bit too and has a shadow of a beard," I inform her. I'm in a trance just staring at him.

"Goddamn, that man must do squats every day. Mmm-mm, that bubble butt, I bet you could rest your drink on it.

Your poor children are going to have ass issues. What with the two-seater swing you have in your own back yard and his bubble butt, yeah, your children surely won't lack in that department."

"Anissa! Stop looking at Grayson's ass." Slapping at her legs, I move to stand up and take the binoculars from her. Grayson's still looking for me, but at least he's walking away from us. Damn, that's one mighty fine view.

"Yes, he's one gorgeous man," I sigh. "I can't wait to be in those arms again." Lowering the binoculars, I turn to my bestie. "Nissa, this proves one thing to me. He hasn't forgotten me, either. He was calling out my name. It's time to put the wheels in motion and get back into his life."

"It's about damn time. I just hope your little game of cat and mouse doesn't piss him off," Anissa says as we both watch him walk away,

"It won't, it can't. This just has to work. I do believe in the fate he talked about years ago, I just need to help it along a bit now."

1

REMEMBERING AND ADMIRING

Lexy

*I*t's been six weeks since I heard Grayson's deep, sexy-as-hell voice calling my name, looking for me. It's definitely time to see what this chemistry is between us. I've got my plan in place, and I'm ready. I just need to watch him one more time for encouragement. I'm so excited and nervous at the same time. My plan has got to work.

At 7:17am on this beautiful morning in Santa Monica, I plant myself on a lounge chair on the beach while wearing a huge floppy hat and dark glasses to hide my identity, holding my Kindle and pretending to read it, knowing that at any minute, I'll see Grayson running in the far distance. He comes in to view, and I'm mesmerized, watching his powerful stride as each foot hits the sand, just above the wet sand line. My heart starts to beat stronger as each foot-pound brings him closer to me.

His black muscle tank top is clinging to his work-of-art chest ever so nicely too. I enjoy watching each pec and arm muscle flex as he moves it forward with each stride. It is such a divine movement, full of power and strength. His very being just captivates me.

I'm sitting here actually watching the sweat glistening off Grayson's hair, face, and chest. Each huge, muscular thigh raises and flexes on its downward motion, pushing the sand up behind him. His movement and beauty are compared to no other. Spying on him like this is so thrilling, and exciting.

Blinking out of my trance, I try to make sure my breathing stays calm. I'm keeping my head down with my eyes turned up watching him through my sunglasses. I can't give away that I'm watching him. My Greek God, the man who stole my heart and turned my world upside down. Meeting him that day gave me the courage to escape and flee Italy and my crime Family. I just had to find him and see if what we felt was real.

Grayson Riggs, the man of my dreams. He has no idea what he's done for me, nor does he know that I'm days away from putting my plan in motion, to accidentally-on-purpose run into him. I've got to see if he remembers me the way I remember him, if that chemistry still ignites between us, like we felt years ago.

Since I moved to Santa Monica, not quite a year ago yet, you could say I've been researching him... Okay fine, stalking him, in a non-creepy way. Getting his pattern down wasn't that difficult. I know he lives in a very expensive condo complex down at the other end of the beach. I don't know where in the gated community he actually lives though. Some things I want to leave a mystery for some crazy reason. I want to wait till he shows his home to me himself. My friend Tony has cameras hidden somewhere and gives me updates of his comings and goings.

I know he works at Camelot Security. He and about eleven of his friends own and run several businesses. They call themselves 'The Brothers of Camelot'. Cute name, but I don't think it has anything to do with Camelot. I've seen all their pictures, both online and on that huge billboard. I'm even friends with several of them on Facebook, but they are clueless as to who I am. He's going to have a fit when he discovers I'm even friends with his sister, Sarah.

A few months ago, I even went to his club a few times and watched him flirt and leave with different Amazonian women. Never the same one twice. I had to make sure he wasn't in a serious relationship.

Tony, my IT guy, is one of my best friends from The Family, that had to escape to America before me. He has been researching all of them for over a year now. It's just hard to believe Grayson's still single. Just that regular hookup, about once a week. There has only been a couple of relationships, lasting a couple of months at most. Lucky for me, they didn't work out. Tony couldn't find out more info than that either, other than the girls wishing they could get him back.

This really could go two ways for me: Grayson could be thrilled to have me back in his life. He could grab me in his big incredible arms and share how he has never forgotten about me either and how he has been hoping and dreaming I'd find him one day. Or let's be real, he could think I am some delusional whack-job with a serious stalking problem. I chuckle to myself. I can only hope it's option one.

I have held on to his words for eight years and prayed fate would bring us back to each other. I've been wishing on stars, hoping that wherever Grayson was, he was doing the same thing. Now I think it's time I help fate along a bit.

Meeting Grayson back in that house in New Jersey where Annalisa and I were celebrating Brenda and Sarah's High School graduation was my first taste of freedom. I finally felt alive. The realization hit me on that balcony that I had to set my dream of escape into motion if I ever wanted to feel like that again.

I close my eyes and remember that moment when my heart started racing, the heat, the passion, the feeling of not wanting it ever to stop, realizing in that one moment, that my life had been changed forever. There have been times in my life where this memory has been the only thing keeping me fighting for my freedom and my right to be me and the ability to make my own choices. It was probably only about thirty minutes of my life, but to this day, it was the best thirty minutes ever. The memory of dancing with Annalisa, busting out our favorite moves...the feeling of being watched and looking up to lock eyes with my Greek God from the hotdog place...just to learn he is Sarah's older brother. The two of us getting food and going out to eat on the balcony so we could talk, the way the attraction fairly sizzled between us...it was the stuff romance novels are made of. The way Grayson picked me up like I weighed nothing and set me on the railing, the passion in his kiss, my first kiss, which got interrupted in the worst way by Stevens coming out to see what was going on...how upset I was at the thought of never seeing him again. I open my eyes, letting go of the memory. *Time to change that.*

I watch Grayson getting closer, he's only about ten feet away now. He passes me, not looking at anyone, just focused on the path in front of him. Now I'm admiring his broad shoulders from the back and the way his shirt is clinging to his every muscle... the sway of his back to the curve of his tight round ass. Yum. The man is huge! He makes my mouth water just looking at him.

He has to be at least 6'6 or 6'7, his blackish-blue hair comes just to his shoulders as it flows in the breeze coming off the Pacific Ocean. His tanned complexion and perfectly chiseled face, his ripped body... the man is perfection. I called him my Greek God when I first saw him, and damn, he still is one. I've never seen anyone like him. He still makes my heartbeat at warp speed, and my blood pressure explode to new heights.

I'm surprised there's not a row of ladies sitting out here every day just to watch him jog by. Lucky for me at this hour of the morning, it's just me and my covert spying. There are a few other runners, but none of them hold a candle to my Greek God. You rarely see anyone running in the sand like Grayson does for most of his run. Usually, they're running on the wet sand, where their feet don't sink with every stride. What Grayson does is a lot tougher. I've tried it and decided I'll stick to the wet sand too.

As he runs almost out of sight, I think to myself that it's time to get things moving. I've got one last practice with Ginger and Bonnie before the competition at the club on Friday. I know he'll be there. I'm just going to have to pray I can get him to accept my story of being Lexy now. Alessandra is no more. Not just for my safety, but for his too.

WHO IS IT REALLY?

Grayson

On Thursday night, I walk into my penthouse, tossing my keys in the bowl on the table by the door. After emptying my pockets, I walk over and put all my change in the big burgundy vase in the corner of the living room. "Madame, turn on living room TV, to the NFL channel," I call out to the voice-activated house controller that Hawkins set up for me. Gotta love that guy. He is a pure genius, and a smart-ass to boot. He refuses to tell me how to change her name recognition, so I'm stuck asking "Madame" to do everything.

"TV is on Sir, may I do another task for you?"

"Thank you, Madame. Send a message to Hawkins. Tell him he needs to make me a robot that can bring me a cold beer when I need one."

She quickly responds, "Yes Sir, your wish is my command. Message sent."

I walk over to the bar chuckling to myself and grab myself a couple of beers before I finally flop down on my overstuffed couch and allow myself to do some thinking.

First, getting comfortable is a must. Taking off my work boots, along with my socks, I then grab the back of my Camelot Security t-shirt pulling it off, tossing it to the floor beside my boots and socks. Reaching over to the coffee table I grab a beer, taking a long drink.

I gaze towards the ceiling and feel my stomach grumble. "Madame, order me my regular pizza from Benassi Pizzeria and add a Caesar salad to that, with extra chicken, cheese, and dressing. Oh, and tell them to surprise me with one of their Italian Desserts. Thanks Madame, that will be all."

"Yes Sir, order placed. It should be here in less than thirty minutes."

Damn, she's handy to have, even if I have to call her Madame.

Putting my feet up on the couch and getting more situated, I start to wonder, who's this chick that has been stalking me? She doesn't think I've noticed her a couple of mornings every week when I jog on the beach. She's always sitting in a lounge chair or on a towel. She must have a big collection of different style hats and sunglasses because she rotates and mixes them up, but always keeps her body very covered up. She's never wearing the same combinations of things more than once, but I know it's always the same girl.

Her fingernails are real because they aren't all the same length, but they are painted nicely. I've noticed the ring on her right-hand ring finger, none on her left hand, so she's single. I've also noticed the ends of her black hair occasionally showing from underneath those hats. I'm guessing it is long by the way I can sometimes see it stuffed down the back of her top.

She always keeps her cell phone facing her, standing up in her right shoe, so she can check the time I assume. They're always set neatly to her left side. Her toenails are always painted as well, but they don't always match her fingers.

Another giveaway is that she doesn't seem to swipe her

finger to turn the page on the Kindle she's holding. She just sits there pretending to read but is watching me instead. I might have to run up there to her tomorrow and say 'good morning', just to see if she takes off running. Could that be Aless?

I seriously don't think she can outrun me, her legs don't look that long. I think she's a little thing. The way she covers up so much of her body makes me think she isn't trying to catch my attention either, unlike most women. She probably doesn't have a clue I'm aware she's there. Yeah, the more I think about it, I decide it's time to give this young lady a thrill and say hello. I need to see for myself if this is Aless or not.

I'd say she is somewhere in her twenties, just by the nail polish and what skin I have seen. I'm thinking she's younger than me, but not too young, or she wouldn't be sitting on the beach at 7ish in the morning.

For the past several months, I've been having these strange feelings, like someone is watching me, and not just on my morning run. There have been a few times when I stop by for my morning coffee, and I just get this odd feeling. I wonder if it's her? Or does this girl just enjoy watching me run? I've also had someone pay for my coffee several times. It's really making me wonder.

What was it, like six weeks ago, when I met Drake and Isabella, and it happened again? The girl Isabella described to me really makes me believe Aless is out there, watching me, and hopefully trying to decide when to approach me. When Isabella pointed her out in the crowded coffee shop, she ran off. Naturally, I went running after her, but she somehow got away from me. Maybe she lives close by and made it back to her place before I could catch her. If it is her, why would she be playing this game with me?

My cell starts playing 'All the Single Ladies', startling me from my thinking. It's time to reprimand my good ol' buddy for screwing with my phone again.

"Looks like I'm going to have to kick your ass again Stevens. When the fuck did you change my ringtone to fucking Beyoncé? All the Single Ladies? Really?"

"Good Evening to you too. Come on, that was awesome! I just wish you were out in public when I called instead of laying on your couch with 'Sir Vulva-ate-her' in your hand. I thought you were having dinner with Mom Riggs and Sarah tonight," Stevens inquires, still chuckling.

"For your information, I had dinner with my mom and sister last night. I just flipped on the TV to catch up on a bit of football. And just so you know, nosy bugger that you are, Sir Vulva-ate-her isn't in my hand right now either. In fact, he has been a bit neglected recently. There have been too many complications lately. Now quit with the twenty questions and tell me why you called."

"Well, Mister Grumpy-pants, you do still have on your pants, don't you?" More chuckling. "Oh, and I'm sorry you've had to handle Sir all by yourself recently. I didn't know you were hitting a dry spell, but I'm sure there are a lot of vulvas out there that would just love for you to eat her." Stevens stops talking to laugh at his own stupid joke.

"Keep it up Stevens, and tomorrow you'll be paying for it during our workout. Just remember that," I remind him of just how painful I can make his training early tomorrow, knowing he is probably calling from the club and he's having fun drinking.

Stevens has so much fun teasing everyone about their dick names. I must say he does get quite creative with his dick gifts at Christmas. But those gifts can be rather embarrassing too, like when you're wearing a t-shirt he had made for you with your dick's name on it, and you answer your door to see some elderly ladies taking up a collection for the Food Bank. I just about gave them coronaries.

"Hey, hey, don't threaten me. We're discussing getting your dick some action. I was watching the video from last week's talent competition at the club. You know a lot of girls have been competing and doing pole routines. They're all trying to win the $5,000 prize money and the chance to be one of the regular performers for our Gentlemen's Night. Well, one of the finalists that will be performing tomorrow night is a three-girl routine. They are good, and I mean damn good. I'm very impressed with both Bonnie and Ginger's performances. But it's the girl that trained them that I'm calling you about. I could swear she's the chick you got a major hard-on over. She looks just like that Alice girl you had a thing for in college."

"Who the fuck are you talking about? I didn't have a thing with any girl named Alice in college."

Just then my doorbell rings and Madame announces, "Benassi Pizzeria has arrived Sir, should I allow them entrance?"

"Yes Madame, allow them in. I'll meet them at the door." Turning my attention back to the conversation, I continue, "Look Stevens, my dinner is here. I have a lot of research to do tonight and it doesn't involve strippers or pole dancers you think I dated in college.

"Remember we are in the middle of helping the cops with that mob conflict brewing downtown. It looks like it's a bit personal between two mob families from Italy and one from Russia. This could get ugly, real fast. We need to find out all the intel we can on all three mob families and what brings them here to our town.

"I think you need to get your mind off my dick and get your hand out of your own pants while watching pole dancers' practice for the contest. We have a lot to do tomorrow. And by the way, I just call my dick Sir."

Listening to Stevens laughing through my phone brings a smile to my face as I walk to my front door. He finally stops laughing long enough to add, "Dude, I still have to hand it to Hawkins and the way he hooked up Madame for you. You can look at it two ways. A, she is being quite the submissive always calling you "Sir". More laughter rings in my ear. "Or B, she is always talking to your dick, or calling you one. I think it's B myself. Just saying. And fine, don't check out the tape, but tomorrow night if it is her, I'm going to watch you shit yourself. Consider yourself warned." Then he hangs up before I can say anything else.

After opening the door and getting my dinner, I walk back to the couch and listen to a bit of football news while eating my pizza and salad. Stevens has me thinking. I have never dated a stripper, and surely not one named Alice. That's a horrible stripper name. I don't know who the fuck Stevens is thinking about.

Looking at my watch and realizing its fucking midnight already, I decide to call it quits on my research. I must get some sleep. But at least I've learned that it looks like the two Italian Families going up against the Russians for control. A turf war basically.

One of the major players is the Benassi Family, who mostly live in New York. They've branched out to our coast and have some kick-ass local restaurants. They're trying to get a few strip clubs opened in the LA, Santa Monica and Santa Barbara areas with the help of the Canzano family from Italy. Those names ring some bells for me. It was the Canzano family we worked with a few years ago to help stop that Russian sex trade ring. I'm going to have to have Hawkins look into this more deeply.

The Russians had taken a couple of the Canzano Family girls as well as our own country's diplomat's daughter and her friend. They had plans of hurting both the mob family and the Americans by putting them into the sex trade. They'd schmoozed up to them at a college house party and drugged them right before they left, so it'd be easy to follow them right to their houses and kidnap them. By the time they woke, they were in a warehouse being prepared to be shipped off for auction. Some of the girls there were being traded to some sheik in Dubai for his sexual pleasure. Some of them were as young as eleven. They were some sick fuckers for sure.

That was one of our first big jobs with the Feds and CIA. Thank God we were able to combine forces with them and that crime family. We saved the girls, putting a stop to those sick mother fuckers. That was also when I had that strange feeling… that maybe Aless was going to be one of the girls, but she wasn't.

Damn, I do remember that bad-ass little Italian assassin though. He was one tiny little shit, but boy could he swing from the ropes he was throwing from beam to beam like a fucking monkey, and with such accuracy. He was one of the best moving sharpshooters I think I've ever seen, either in or out of the military.

Both Stevens and I took a bullet that day and were saved by that little Italian assassin of theirs. Those bullets just added to our collection of scars. But I must have hit my head going down from the impact because I could've sworn I heard Aless's voice call out my name, right before I hit the floor.

Stevens and I were so pumped with adrenaline we didn't even realize we were hit until it was all over. Thank God they were just minor flesh wounds. But damn, it sounded so real. It must have been wishful thinking, or her voice in my subconscious, I guess. It's what made me turn around so quickly, taking the bullet in my shoulder instead of my heart. Thankfully with all 'The Family', as they refer to themselves, we were able to kill every one of those mother fuckers. Those fuckers had set off a bomb that blew the building up within minutes of us getting out. It is possible one of their SUVs got away that night, because we saw one was missing when we got the hell out of there.

The Canzano Family split so fast that we didn't get to

thank their little assassin ourselves. After we got stitched up, we were the ones left to answer all the questions for the local police and *Carabinieri*. And like we expected, when 'The Family' was questioned, they didn't know what the Americans were talking about.

So, we left Italy with our two girls, after we made sure the others we saved were reunited with their families. We were thanked privately, all around. They did request us not to share any details of the rescue with anyone. They didn't want that in the headlines.

Naturally we kept that promise, because we aren't dumb-asses and want nothing to do with that five minutes of fame. We get enough of that shit from just being the Brothers of Camelot. What we do within Camelot Security is always kept completely confidential.

It's just that voice. It haunts me. Was it fate protecting me? Was it her at the coffee shop? Is it her on the beach? My gut tells me it might be her. Maybe she's scared of how I'll respond to her. She was a shy little thing back then. Damn, I loved how she'd blush with nerves. Just remembering that wakes Sir right up to full attention. Damn. She was hot, in every way.

Reaching over to the nightstand and grabbing some lube out of the drawer, I take Sir in my hand and start stroking him. Closing my eyes, just thinking about those damn clear blue eyes of hers… I'm sure they could see into my soul. I've taken care of Sir like this a thousand times, remembering that night with her. I squeeze my cock harder in my hand, making sure to twist even tighter at the base. Just remembering how very firm and round her ass was as I squeezed it and lifted her up onto that railing, and the passion we shared is all I need to quickly reach my release.

Wow. I clean myself up and catch my breath. I still hope and pray that somehow Aless will find me. She, at least, knows my full name. I was in such a trance when we met, I never thought to ask her what her full name was. God, she has to find me. With such little information, I can't even ask Hawkins to help me with my search. I have to depend on fate. That's another reason I keep such a big profile, hoping she's looking for me.

When Mom took the job of being the head of the OBGYN department out here, dad already having offices on both coasts made it an easy move for them. They have hubs in all four major law firm cities: Los Angeles, New York, San Francisco, and Chicago. Sarah and Brenda were both thrilled to move back here and go to UCLA. It brought Mom Stevens back to California too.

Throwing the tissues away, I grab my laptop and put it on the nightstand, getting up to take one last piss before I call it a night. I can't help but wonder if Aless ever got forced into an arranged marriage. She told me her father was worse than mine. With time, mine did get a little better, and I wonder, did hers?

If this mystery girl isn't her, I'm going to have to take another trip to New Jersey and New York, in hopes of bumping into her while she's searching for me. It wouldn't take much of a search for Aless to discover I relocated to California. This mystery girl needs to be her.

Laying back down in bed I call out, "Madame, make sure the house is locked up and the lights are set to night mode."

"Yes Sir, consider it done. Goodnight to you, Sir, and sleep well."

Chuckling to myself as I lay there, I acknowledge that yeah, Stevens was right. I'm going to have to kick Hawkins' ass and make him change her name and voice. She does sound just like a kinky submissive. Thank God I've never brought a chick here. That could really be embarrassing.

3

TIME FOR THE BIG REVEAL

Lexy

*W*alking over and picking up a picture of Mom from my nightstand, I smile down at it, wishing she was still here. I've been talking to her in my mind since she was taken away from me. It gives me peace and helps me to cope with losing her so tragically.

"Mom I could really use yours, Nonna's and Aunt Elena's help tonight. I know you're up in heaven keeping an eye on me. I feel your presence at times, giving me the strength to fight on. If you could help me tonight, and ease this reunion with Grayson, I would so appreciate it. Your last words to me were to be free and get away from the Family. Well, I've done that. You also told me to find love, real love." Pulling the picture to my chest and closing my eyes, I whisper, "Mom, this could be it. If I were to tell anyone how I felt, I know they'd think I was crazy. But there is just something incredible and powerful between Grayson and me.

Even though we only spent one wonderful evening together, there was just something… magical. I've never been with anyone who made me feel the way he does. Help me

19

Mom, help fate along if at all possible." Opening my eyes, I kiss my finger, placing it on her face as I return the photo back to its place on my nightstand.

Turning away, I take one last look at myself in the mirror. Yeah, this dress completely accents my curves and brings attention to everything I want him to see and want again. This needs to take him back to that night on the deck when he changed my world forever.

"Wow, don't you look hot in that retro dress! The man is going to shit himself. With the way that thick white belt emphasizes your tiny waist and huge boobs, he'll be putty in your hands. Turn around slowly so I can see the rest of it," Anissa demands, while spinning her finger around in the air.

Giggling and shaking my head, I slowly turn around. "You do know I have to change once I get there, right? Grayson will see me in my costume first. I don't want to see him face to face until after the performance so I'm having Tony drop us off around the back. That's why I've got Ginger and Bonnie bringing all the make-up, and most importantly, my costume. So... what do you ladies think? Do you think this dress will work after the show?"

"Damn, let's hope he takes a minute to look at your face, because when he gets a look at your body in that dress, he's going to want to throw you over his shoulder and get you the fuck out of there. It definitely accents everything you want it to. I predict he's going to have some...*hard* problems," Anissa adds before going to grab her purse.

Before I can even respond to her, Shelly adds her own sassy comment. "Well isn't that the plan, you dimwit? We want him to fall flat on his face - tripping over his tongue, with a full-on face plant, in a pool of his own lustful drool. That would be an added benefit, don't you think? That would give Lexy just what she is looking for."

"Eww Shelly, that was just plain gross. Give the girl a bit of a break. I think she might be on the verge of a nervous breakdown. She's just trying to act cool for us," Dana says, snickering towards me before continuing. "She doesn't need the added stress. Let's remember that she needs to be calm to pull off her ninja stunt tonight. She'll be swinging around from that giant piece of silk, performing while wearing that barely-there-sparkling-leotard-thing. I can't wait to catch his first impressions of that on film," Dana adds, walking over and grabbing her camera equipment bags.

"Okay ladies, I've already said a little prayer. I think I've got this. It's time for my Big Reveal to Grayson. I'm still hoping he'll be understanding and accept my reasoning for being Lexy now. He needs to be able to deal with that, without asking too many questions I can't answer."

"Your Big Reveal is right. Girl, everyone will see your every curve in your costume and in that dress. I'm so excited for you and have complete confidence you're going to be great. It's a unique way of letting Grayson know you're here and putting him into 'hunter mode'. Come on, with that dance routine and then that dress? I can't wait to watch this big guy fall hard for you," Anissa adds with a reassuring smile.

"You better hope this big Alpha male of yours isn't into spankings, or you, little girl, will be getting your ass whooped very soon," Shelly says while laughing and giving me such a mischievous look. "Because he could see all of this wrong and take it as you're toying with him, and Alpha men don't much like being toyed with."

Dana interrupts and calls out, "Let's go! The clock is ticking. Lexy, you just got a text. Tony's here. He says, and I quote, 'If you don't get your fine ass down there in two minutes, I'm coming up to spank it'." She hands me my phone that she picked up off the counter. Wow, I must be a bit nervous. I was about to walk out of the house and leave my phone behind.

Taking a deep breath, I close my eyes, making myself believe I'm doing the right thing. "It's time to go in for the kill and blow Grayson Riggs' ever-loving mind. Don't forget to keep yourself out of sight too. I don't want to blow this before the show."

"Are you serious? He doesn't know us from dick. We've never laid eyes on him in the flesh, except when you had us all in disguise spying on him at The Brothers of Camelot Club. But damn girl, you give that man a decent haircut, and he's one fine piece of ass. High quality, grade A prime ass for sure," Shelly weighs in, causing us all to laugh.

"He doesn't need a haircut! He's perfect as he is. I'm just hoping he can deal with all I'm about to lay out in front of him. That is my only concern with tonight. It's going to be a lot for him to hear, from not being Aless anymore to teaching self-defense and dancing, and that includes teaching strippers. He just better not be the jealous type," I add.

"A little jealousy isn't going to hurt. I think all men need to know up front that they aren't the only one out there. He'll need to know you aren't desperate for him. It'll keep his blood pumping and keep him alert," Dana adds with a wink, as she gets into Tony's SUV.

"Come on girls, we're supposed to be keeping her calm, remember? We wouldn't want her falling from the rafters tonight," Anissa adds as she gets into the car, smiling at me.

"I can hardly wait to see what he does. I hope they serve popcorn. I see it going one of two ways: he'll either be thrilled to see you and believe that fate brought you back into his life, or he's going to be mad as hell that you didn't come straight back to him over a year ago. That's why I said he could be the spanking type," Shelly says so casually, not helping my fears at all, but it still makes us all laugh.

Tony turns around as asks, "Are you girls giving her shit too? I'm glad to hear it. I've been telling her since day one that she should just walk up and grab that big hunk of a man and kiss the shit out of him. But she wouldn't listen to me either."

"Well, hello to you too, Tony. Nice that you're trying to help keep me calm and not freak me out before the show," I inform my good friend, who's the only one who knows all of my secrets.

Tony chuckles as he says, "Come on ladies, get those asses moving. I can't wait to see this big show either. From seeing her in that outfit, to how Grayson responds is going to be great entertainment. And if Grayson spanks her, I'm taping it myself and adding it to my collection."

"Don't even go there. This is going to go great. It just has to. He'll understand that I had to make sure he was single. I wouldn't just run up to him and jump on him screaming 'I'm back'. This way is a lot better. You'll see. And Shelly, for your information, I was spanked just a couple of years ago by my bodyguard, Luigi, and I did not like it. You might be into that kind of kink, but I'm not. I'll pass thanks. I don't think I have to worry about Grayson spanking me," I hear Tony laughing as he pulls out onto the road.

"Luigi spanked you?! For what? I've seen his pictures, and he can spank me any time he wants. Damn girl, I want to hear that whole story," Anissa adds.

"Alright Anissa, we all know you're a perv and into anything a touch kinky. She didn't say he handcuffed her or used any whips or other kinky toys, he just spanked her ass. And seriously, what man wouldn't want to hit that big bubble ass of hers? And Lexy, what the fuck! Why haven't you told us about this spanking, and why he did it? That's what I want to hear," Shelly says, while Tony is trying to control his laughter.

"Hey my favorite girlies, I have the whole thing on tape. I'll come over and show you girls tomorrow morning before our Rogers' Family Adventure. You'll all get a kick out of it. Believe me, it's a memory I'll never forget."

"Tony you will not show them, or anyone, that tape. Do I make myself clear?" I give an order.

"Lex, you used to be able to give me orders and I had to

obey, but those days are over girlfriend. And come on, it's all in fun. The girls will love it," he says as he winks at me in the rear-view mirror.

Thinking back to when I wanted to get my dad's attention, when he wouldn't tell me his girlfriend was pregnant, I smirk. I went to one of the Family clubs and put on a quick pole dance routine, and that did the trick. I got his attention alright. He talked to me, but I also got my ass spanked for the first time in my life, by Luigi. I don't think I'll ever understand what some girls find hot about that. I'll never admit it to a soul, but it might have given me a hint of a thrill, or it might have been the fact he was the first man to put me in my place.

"Tony I'm warning you, I can still make your life a living hell, and you know it," I inform my good friend as he drives us to the Camelot Bar and Club.

Standing backstage a little over an hour later, I peek around the corner of the curtain and watch the last group of girls finishing up their routine. They were good, but knowing we're better gives me the confidence bump I need. As they leave the stage to the sounds of applause and whoops and catcalls, I can feel my heart pounding in my chest, not from nerves, but from excitement. I'm moments away from shocking the hell out of Grayson Riggs and coming back into his life in a big way. I can't wait.

In my head, I start the count down, the announcer's words to the audience becoming a background buzz. Stevens told us it'd be seven minutes after the last act left the stage before it's our turn. We need to get into place. I'm not nervous about my performance at all. I'm just a bit concerned what Grayson's reaction will be when he realizes it's me performing.

"I'm going out there now. I've got my pass to get back here the second your act is over. I'm going to make damn sure I get his reaction, as well as all of the Brothers' responses to you and your performance. Now you go and kick some ass, or 'break a leg'. I think that's what I'm supposed to say. But whatever you do, don't break your fucking leg with all this aerial shit. That'd piss off the big guy for sure," Dana tells me, chuckling, as she heads out of the curtain to the spot she picked out to tape the show.

"You got this, bitch. You're going to kick their asses. None of those other acts hold a candle to you flying around the rafters in a second skin of sparkling spandex while the girls are riding and swinging from the poles for all they're worth. You go do your thing and win this, while I go look for some popcorn," Shelly adds before she heads out too.

Taking a deep breath, I turn and see Tony coming up to me with his arms around Ginger and Bonnie. "We're ready, just waiting for our introduction. You better head on up to the rafters, boss." Ginger puts her arm around me and takes one last peek out the curtain as well.

"Go on Lex, get yourself into position. We don't want you missing your own cue. I'll be watching from back here, making sure all goes smoothly. Go claim your man, before I do," Tony whispers with a chuckle. "I know he doesn't swing both ways like me, but maybe one of those Camelot Brothers does." He wiggles his eyebrows at me before continuing his whispers. "They're all hot as hell. I'd take a ride with any of them. Don't worry Lex, you know I'm just teasing. Come on, I'm walking the straight and narrow with Sarah, and you know it. That woman is something else."

"Tony, behave," I snicker, shaking my head, trying hard not to laugh. Looking to Bonnie and Ginger, I try to reassure them. "We have this, ladies. Let's take home that trophy."

Anissa squats down beside some of our equipment. "I'm sitting right here for the whole performance, not moving a muscle. The second the lights dim, I'll turn on these fog machines. I got this down pat. I can't wait to see the show and watch Grayson's reaction. And damn girl, look at all those hot as fuck Camelot Brothers waiting. They are going to shit themselves when you come swinging, flipping and rolling from the rafters. If I were you, I'd drop right into Grayson's lap as a big finish," Anissa tempts me, chuckling.

"That is the last thing I'm going to do. Girls I'm going to get in place, you be ready for your cue. This is the real deal. Let's go win you that prize money and that dance spot for Gentlemen's Night for you two. They'll never know what hit them. We've got about two minutes before our music starts. Make sure all the important parts are covered, we wouldn't want to be disqualified for showing too much," I tell the girls, hoping they stay calm as well.

Taking one last peek out to see Grayson, I see he's sitting at the end of a long table, joking and drinking an amber liquid, that I'm assuming is whiskey, laughing at something Stevens must have said. All the Camelot Brothers are sitting there. They're the judges. We're the last act. This is really it. I wonder how long it will take before he realizes it's me. Looking up to make sure all my aerial silk is still hanging and looped around the rafters, I hope Stevens and Hunter don't get pissed when they see I've changed the program just a bit and added this.

I turn around and give Anissa a big smile. "This is it." I give her and Tony a quick hug. "Thanks guys. I'll see you two when it's over, in a little less than five minutes."

I take off running to the far side of the stage and get behind the curtains that line the wall. Within seconds, I hear one of the Camelot Brothers start announcing our act. I know it's only about a minute before the lights start dimming. I'm relieved when I see my rope still hanging where I left it. Reaching for it, I give a quick pull, checking that my grappling hook is still firmly attached where I hid it yesterday.

Quickly, I start climbing up as fast as I can. Just then, the lights start dimming, and my heart starts pounding. Not much longer to wait. I have until after the first verse of "I Don't Want To Live Forever" to get into place.

Standing up here on the highest beam of this three-story club, I let out a breath as I quickly make my way to my place, wrapping my silks around me. I look down and watch the girls from my vantage point. They're doing great, in perfect unison on their poles. I couldn't be prouder. This is it, time to look Grayson in the eyes, and hopefully, let fate and our magical chemistry take over.

4

IT'S REALLY HER

Grayson

*a*s the final performers come out through the fog that has now covered the stage, their skin just sparkles. That's a pretty nice intro. This is the fifth and final set of contestants, and it's supposed to have three girls in it. But so far, it's only Bonnie and Ginger. It still surprises me they both want to work the pole on Gentlemen's Night, but it looks like they have the talent to pull it off.

"Where the fuck is that Alice chick you had the hots for in college? She performed with them every time during practice," Stevens says from beside me.

"Dude, how many times do I have to tell you? I've never dated a chick named Alice. And I sure as hell didn't date a stripper with that name."

"Alice is their teacher. She isn't a stripper. As much as I tried, she refused to strip. She was incredible, showing the girls things I've never even seen done on a pole. But she flat out said she took her clothes off for no one. She also informed me that she didn't need the money."

Just as the chorus begins, the girls start swinging from one pole to the other, like they're parallel bars instead of vertical poles. Ginger swings at the top of the pole, while Bonnie swings around the middle. Now that trick I haven't seen before either. Impressive. I hear the whole room gasp, making me alert and look all around. Jesus! I get to my feet with the rest of the Brothers. We watch as a burgundy satin looking curtain comes rolling out from the top beam in the ceiling. Then I notice a very shapely chick has unfolded herself from it. Fuck, that scared the shit out of me.

"What the Fuck!" Stevens says. "She never practiced that here. I have no fucking idea how she got that shit up there! But look at her Grayson, that's your Alice." Steven starts pointing at her, not taking his eyes off her performance.

That odd feeling overcomes me. I watch as I see her long black hair blowing in the wind as she starts spinning and twisting those silks until she is in the complete splits. This is one impressive aerial silk performance. Taking a quick glance around the room, I see she has captured everyone's complete attention. I still can only see the back of her, and whoever she is, she does have one fine ass, that's for damn sure.

Now she starts twisting and wrapping the silk all around her body again and spiraling in a circle. Damn, she is good. She must have it attached to one hell of a carabiner on the ceiling beam.

Then I see her face. Holy shit! It is Aless! I feel a huge smile spread on my face. It vanishes as quickly as it appears as she starts swinging and spinning and flipping. What the fuck? She's going to kill herself with no spotters and no safety net. Fuck! Then she drops her upper body with just her legs wrapped around the upper silks and starts swinging like it is a Goddamn trapeze.

"See, I told you it was Alice. But she's changed her name to Lexy now. It fits her a hell of a lot better than Alice. Because shit, we can call her 'Sexy Lexy.' Damn, you have to admit she's good. But I still have to figure out how the hell she got that shit up there and attached it without any of us finding out. Hawkins is going to be pissed." Steven shouts to me over the crowd's applause and cheers.

I can't take my eyes off her as I respond to Stevens, "Her name was never Alice, it's Aless." I can feel my heart pounding in my chest like a locomotive. I'm completely mesmerized, watching as she climbs those silks even higher. She then wraps all the loose silk around her tiny waist and legs. As she turns and faces me again, laying down forward in what silk remains, she looks right down and into my eyes and blows me a fucking kiss, her face lighting up in a big smile. A smile fills my own face. She's so fucking beautiful, and she's found me. I'll never let her leave now.

Aless reaches her arms towards me as she rapidly starts spinning downward, timing it perfectly with the ending of the song. Holy Fuck, I'm on the stage within a split second. She lands gracefully on her feet right in front of me. My heart's still pounding, as she looks up to me with those clear blue gorgeous eyes of hers. She reaches up and places her small hand on my cheek as Taylor Swift says, 'Until you come back home'.

Heat rushes to where her hand lays on my cheek. I briefly closed my eyes, and just feel her touch permeate my entire being. Opening my eyes, I don't notice anyone or anything in the place. Not the applause, the cheering, nothing else in the room matters. Our eyes are locked onto each other's, just like they were almost eight years ago.

As I start to say her name, "Al…" she reaches up and puts her delicate finger over my lips to shush me. "No, I'm Lexy Rogers now. I changed my name a long time ago when I found out I was already an American citizen. Aless is no more. We'll talk more after I change. Okay?" she says, breaking our spell.

"Okay, Lexy. How long have you been here in California?" I ask, as Bonnie and Ginger rush over all excited.

"Lexy! Oh, God Lexy, that was so awesome!" Bonnie says looking between the two of us. "Lexy, you never told me you knew Riggs."

"We go back many years," Aless says, pulling us further out of our own world. She turns and hugs both girls congratulating them. I hadn't even noticed their performance once she rolled down from the ceiling, doing her routine with those silks.

"I see you wasted no time in your guys' staring competition either. See Riggs, you owe me. I was right, she is the girl," Stevens declares as he punches me in the shoulder.

"Yes, Stevens, it's her. Punch me again, and I'll take you out," I reply, teasing him.

I watch as three other girls and a guy come up and congratulate her, all calling her Lexy. The guy, he looks very familiar. I've seen him around here, I'm sure. They all have on backstage passes as well. So, these four must be her friends. That guy better not be anything more than one of these other girl's boyfriend. One of the girls is still taping and looking like she's interviewing all of them. Occasionally she turns her camera on me. Is she taping my reaction?

Looking back at Aless, I'm completely enthralled by the flesh colored sparkly thing she has on that shows every curve. Damn, she is built like no other. She's all fucking ass and tits and defined muscles. She's like a walking wet dream. Goddamn, I can't wait to get my hands on her. Just looking at her is bringing 'Sir' to full attention.

Shit, I don't want every guy in this place checking her out. I don't want to have to kill someone tonight.

"Your vote is for 'The Girls', the last act, right? I don't think I really need to ask by the way you are staring at Lexy," Hunter asks, pulling me out of my trance.

"Yeah Brother, my vote is for them."

"Then we have a winner, unanimous as usual. Do you want the honors of handing out the trophy, since you can't take your eyes off Sexy Lexy? It'll give you a chance to get to know her better. But good luck, you'll need it. I don't know any guys that have been lucky enough to tap that," Hunter says with a chuckle in his voice.

"Don't talk about her like that, and don't call her 'Sexy Lexy' either, or I'll have to beat the shit out of you. But yeah, I'll hand her the trophy."

"Wow, I've never seen you get bent out of shape over any girl. What's up? Do you know this chick or something?" Hunter asks, handing me the golden trophy of a pole dancer.

"Yeah, I know her Brother. We go way back. Consider her officially off-limits to all Brothers, and anyone else for that matter. We'll talk about it later. You got me?"

"Okay Riggs, I got you. I'll spread the word. Wow." He looks at me again, I'm sure he's very confused as he turns towards the audience.

"We have a winner! I'm sure you'll all agree," Hunter announces as he lifts his hand towards Bonnie, Ginger and Aless. It's 'The Girls', with their wonderful instructor Lexy Rogers, who is one of the managers and teachers down at 'A Better You' Fitness Club and Spa. I'll even give you a free pitch for that performance Lexy."

The crowds on all levels of the club are cheering, and all I can think about is getting Aless backstage so she can change and cover up that magnificent body of hers. Then we can talk. I need to find out everything, from when she got here to how she's an American citizen. And how did she find me?

God, I can't wait to taste her lips again. I've got to kiss her, and soon. My mind keeps tracking back to our make-out session on the back deck of Stevens' old house in Jersey. I've dreamt and relived those moments over and over again a million times in my mind.

"Congratulations ladies," I say, watching Hunter hand Lexy the check, which she quickly passes back to Bonnie, who is squealing with excitement. I hand the trophy to Aless, staring into her eyes again, blocking out our surroundings.

Without even blinking, she stands on her tippy toes, reaching for me. Realizing what she's doing, I bend down to meet her halfway. She goes to kiss me on my cheek, but I turn my lips to hers at the last moment to make sure I get a taste of her. A small and quick slide of my tongue across her closed lips brings the flavor of her that I remember so well back to me. I can feel my heart racing, and I can hear her breathing escalate as well. She parts her lips and returns the favor with a quick flick of her tongue on my lips, before pulling away with a smile and that incredible blush.

"Thank you. I'll put this trophy in my office." Slowly she looks away from me, "You two can divide the check like I told you before. I don't want any of the money. I got my reward right in front of me," she says, turning back around and looking at me.

"You're damn right you do. You want to go change so we can go talk somewhere?" I ask, letting her know in the politest way possible that I want to get the hell out of here.

"I can't leave, I have my roommates and a friend with me." She turns around, waving to her friends. I notice one of the girls is still taping us. "I want to introduce you to my roommates first. The one who ran the smoke machine is Anissa." She has an incredible smile, as she sticks out her hand for me to shake.

"Nice to meet you, Anissa.".

"Nice to finally meet you too, Grayson," she says, looking me over from head to toe.

"This is Dana with the camera. She takes most of our pictures and films everything for us. She's in charge of all our memories. Dana's also a professional photographer, as you could probably guess."

"Nice to meet you as well Dana."

Pointing the camera at me, she asks, "I'd like to know what

you personally thought of the show, and more importantly, Lexy?"

"You don't waste time do you? At first, it shocked the shit out of me. But her performance was more than great. It was beautiful and as captivating as she is." I put my hand on her cheek, looking at those sumptuous full lips and clear blue eyes of hers that melt my heart. "My only wish would be for her to have come back to me sooner." Bending down, I kiss her again on the lips, unable to stop myself.

"I couldn't come to you sooner. I had to make sure you weren't seriously involved with one of those Amazonian women I've seen you pictured with. I'd never step up and ruin a relationship," Aless informs me. Okay, I can understand her reasoning for staying away. That does make sense. But I was never serious with any woman, they were just hook-ups, although I guess there was no way for Aless to have known that.

Another woman starts talking, interrupting my thoughts, "I'm Shelly, the one friend you need to worry about. Warning, if you play our girl Lexy for a fool, we can and will make your life a living hell. We'll not allow her to be involved with a player." Looking around, she continues, "All you Camelot Boys have that reputation. You are one of the quiet ones, not much shit is written about you. But sometimes, the quiet ones are the ones to keep an eye on the most," she says, full of confidence and radiating attitude.

"Well, nice to meet you too, Shelly. And you don't have to worry. I'm not a player, nor do I like to be played either. I'm very up front and honesty is the most important thing to me. Go ahead and keep an eye on me, because I'll be watching all of you as well. Just thought I'd warn you too." I let her know with a smile that it goes both ways. I can damn well promise that we'll know everything about all three of Aless's roommates and her male friend too, once I get Hawkins on it.

Just then, her male friend who has to be around six feet tall and 190, with messy black hair that has the tips bleached blonde walks up and sticks his hand out. "I'm her oldest and dearest friend, Tony. Nice to meet you, again. But the last two times I met you, I was just another dude that was introduced to you. You paid me no mind, since I wasn't your normal Amazonian woman with fake tits. And I'm the one who helped her find you. Let me tell you, I accept your challenge of watching us, as we watch you. I'm the one you really need to worry about if you mess around or toy with Lex here," he says as he puts his arm around Aless, never letting his eyes leave mine.

"Nice to meet you too, Tony. I can't wait to get to know anyone who is old friends with Lexy," I say while shaking his hand very firmly. Well, he isn't flinching, so he's not a pussy.

Turning, I call out, "Jackson, Carpenter, Hunter, would you mind taking Lexy's friends up to our private part of the club? Keep them entertained, drinks and everything is on the house. Once Lexy changes we'll be up there to join you." Turning back to Aless, I ask, "That's alright with you, isn't it Lexy?"

Hearing her friends all cheering and getting excited, I smile. The ladies are eyeing up their escorts like a kid eyes the cookies in the jar. Yeah, getting information out of them shouldn't be that hard at all.

"Yes, thank you. I'll go change; it won't take me long, I promise." Turning to her friends, she tells them, "Remember to play nice, I'll be up in a minute."

Turning back and winking at me, she walks off into the changing rooms. Can't help myself from watching that fine ass of hers. Damn, the things I'd like to do to it.

Once the door is closed, I turn to watch the Brothers escorting her friends to the elevator. I'm going to have to get a message to each of them to get as much info as possible about each of her friends, as well as all the intel they can get me on Aless. I'll also send a message to Sarah and Britney to go after

35

Tony and see what they can find out. Those two just love to flirt around.

Seeing Hawkins come out from behind the curtain, he heads straight over to me. "I figured out how she got up there. She went behind the curtains to the lighting ladder that is attached to the wall. Since it is behind the curtains, it isn't visible to our cameras. That will be changed very soon. She also used a high-end grappling hook, to get up to the ladder, then attached one to the beam. Once she was up there, she lifted her things up and attached them to the beam at some point, probably during the day.

All our security cameras are facing downward to watch the crowds. I never thought anyone could breach the security and get up to the beams. That will be fixed first thing tomorrow. I'll be installing cameras up there also, so we can see anyone playing in the rafters. Riggs, do you know this chick?"

"Yes, I do. She's a girl I met almost eight years ago. She was from Italy on vacation when I met her. It was days before Stevens and I went into the army. Her name was Aless then, but she just told me she's an American citizen now and has changed her name to Lexy Rogers. I don't know the whole story, but I want to know it all. Open up an investigation, but do it on the down low. Don't let anyone know who we are or who we're looking in to.

She told me back then that she had a very controlling family and was hoping to escape one day. Her father was worse than mine. He was old school Italian, controlling everything about her life, all the way down to picking her friends, and I'm sure, her husband. But how and when did she get here? And for her to already be an American citizen and working at a health club? Sounds a bit fishy to me," I explain to Hawkins.

"It sounds very suspicious to me. Yeah, there is way more to this story," he pauses and looks around, I'm sure to make sure no one can hear us, before he continues.

"Stevens got a copy of her license when she entered the competition. I'll start there. I'll also get the word out to the Brothers that this is an info hunting expedition with her friends. Riggs, do you have feelings for this girl or something?" Hawkins asks, looking me right in the eyes, not even pausing to take a breath.

"You could say that. I've had feelings for her since the moment our eyes met in Gray's Papaya years ago. We only spent a few hours together, but the chemistry we shared changed my life forever. I opened up to her and told her things that I don't share with chicks. And that went both ways. She told me things I'm sure she's told no others. This stays between us for now, okay? I'll call you later tonight and update you on everything from back then and what I can get out of her now."

"Got it. I have a strange feeling about this one. Be careful Riggs. Something else is going on here. That little pint sized hottie is a lot more than just a dancer that works at a health club, I'm sure of it. I'm going up to the security room, and I'll be working from here for at least the next 24 to 48 hours."

"Thanks Hawkins. We'll touch base soon," I tell him with a slap on the back. Getting a head nod from him, he heads straight to our private elevators. He lasted longer tonight down here with all of us than I thought he would. I think having Isabella back in his life has been very good for him. With the return of Aless, he has something new to keep his mind occupied, which is a very good thing for him.

Leaning up against the wall just waiting for Aless to come out, I can't believe she's back. Calling her Lexy is going to be tough. It makes me wonder why the hell she changed her name to Lexy Rogers. I need to figure all this shit out and get as much info as I can out of her without scaring her off. Because the way she makes my body react, I'll be damned if I ever let her leave me.

5

JUST ENOUGH INFORMATION

Lexy

*O*pening the dressing room door and seeing Grayson waiting for me is such a wonderful and exciting feeling. Looking at him leaning up against the wall texting someone, I can't resist teasing him. "Texting your girlfriend and making up excuses as to why you're going to be late tonight?"

"Hell no! I was just texting Stevens and threatening him with bodily harm. Wanna see? I definitely don't have a girlfriend, and I'll always be open and honest with you, just like I told your friend. I mean that." Just as he turns his phone around for me to see, it dings with a text from Stevens. I read the message, 'I'm not scared of you! Bring it you big pussy licker. Just wanted to know if Sir Vulva-ate-her is planning on eating some Sexy Lexy tonight? LOL'"

With what I'm sure is a look of shock on my face, I crack up laughing. While trying to compose my giggling, I inform him, "Wow, I don't think Stevens is scared of you at all. And to say he is a wee bit nosy and blunt would be an understatement."

"Stevens is scared shitless of me. He's a texting tough guy.

Just watch and see." Grayson turns the phone back to himself and reads the text, busting out laughing. "Emm, I can explain that message if you like?" he says, while his eyes roam my body.

"Damn baby girl, you look hella fine. Love the dress too. It makes me want to explore your every curve." Looking me up and down for a second time, he grabs my hand and pulls me beside him, putting both arms around me.

"Hey now, none of that. Aren't you supposed to be taking me up to my friends?" I tease him with one eyebrow raised.

He moves but still keeps one arm around me and leads us towards the elevator. Then his hand slides down to my bum, giving a good squeeze. "Damn, have I told you how much I love your ass? And by the way, that dress should be illegal and not allowed to be worn in public. With an ass like yours, it's too tempting for a man like me. And I'd rather spend my night getting to know you better rather than kicking someone's ass for checking out your assets, if you know what I mean," he tells me with a wink and another squeeze to my bum.

"Excuse me, but if you keep squeezing my bum like that, you might find yourself slapped, or with a knee somewhere you might not appreciate it." Looking up at him, I smile, taking the sting out of my words as he moves his hand back to the curve of my waist, tugging me closer to his side. "Thank you for behaving yourself. And as for the way I am dressed, this dress doesn't expose anything. It's just fitted. And I cannot help that I have more 'assets' as you put it than the average girl. But no one tells me what I can and cannot wear," I say looking into those deep blue eyes, wondering how he'll respond.

"I'm not going to say you're welcome, because I'd rather have my hand on your ass. But I'll respect your boundaries... for now," he replies with a chuckle as we reach the elevator, not saying anything more about the way I am dressed.

He places his full palm, fingers extended on a screen about

the size of an iPad. You can see a green light bar go up and down his palm, scanning his hand, before the elevator doors open. It looks like his security is as good as my own.

"I'm guessing this is an employee elevator?"

"You could say that. Any of the Brothers can get into any location within our facilities with our full hand scan. High ranking employees have a code number to enter after their hand scan, but they are only allowed in certain areas.

We run a very tight security system in all our locations. In fact, your little surprise performance tonight pissed off the head of security. Hawkins had to go around and figure out how you did it without any of us knowing. You can bet he'll be adding more cameras tomorrow and tightening up security," Grayson adds with yet another deep chuckle, a sound that gives me a welcoming shiver, as the elevator doors close behind us.

"Grayson, I'll let you in on a little secret. During the day, your men are a little lax. All it took was my friends being a little over friendly and showing a bit of extra cleavage, and they didn't notice me going to the bathroom with a gym bag and coming back fifteen minutes later without it." He shakes his head, making me laugh.

"Oh, you'd better tell me the employee's names so I can kick their asses for staring at your tits and not doing their jobs," Grayson says, pulling me completely into his arms, so I'm facing him. We're so close we're sharing breath, just looking into each other's eyes.

"I just told you, it was my friend's boobs, not mine. I purposely came in overly covered up, with my hair up and big sunglasses. I'm sure he thought I was their short and pudgy friend and didn't pay me any mind, as you would say."

Grayson smiles down at me and asks, "Now that you mention big sunglasses, I have a question for you. Have you been the one watching me on and off for the past couple months during my morning jog, and paying for my coffee?"

I try to hide the look of surprise I'm sure must be on my face. "Who me?! I don't know what you're talking about. What! Is there some young lady stalking you while you run? She must be awfully shy. But come on, you can't blame her one bit. You must be a sight to remember jogging on the beach. I say what a way to start the day, watching you jog on the shore as the sun rises." Winking at him, I know I'm blushing because I can feel my face warming.

He pulls me into his chest, chuckling at me. As I inhale his vanilla woodsy smell, he says, "Busted! I did kind of think it might be you. I was fully aware of the collection of hats and glasses you had. Why didn't you ever just wave or say 'Hi' then?" He pulls away and looks down at me, using one finger to lift my chin to look deeper into my eyes. Every time he does that, I feel like he can see into my soul.

"I was a bit scared and nervous. I didn't want to look like a whacked stalker. I needed to make sure you were single first, and that you even remembered me," I whisper, just as the elevator dings and stops.

"Aless, I never forgot you. I've relived our brief moments together in my mind countless times. I think that memory alone helped me make it through my military days. I never gave up on you somehow being able to find me. I couldn't look at the stars in the night sky and not wonder where you were and if you remembered me, like I remembered you. Since I was a dumbass back then and never asked your last name, I didn't know how to find you. But believe me, I tried."

"Really?!" standing there feeling overjoyed at his admission, we ignore the doors as they open, just standing there looking deeply into each other's eyes again.

"Well, we just made a wager on this." Looking towards the bar, I see it's Stevens calling out. "Hey, Clay! Look who decided to join us. You just lost fifty bucks Brother." As Stevens starts laughing, he turns back to us and we walk out of the elevator.

Stevens comes over to greet us, putting his arm around Grayson's shoulders. "Riggs, I was beginning to think you might have taken her upstairs to our apartments, to give 'Sir Vulva-ate-her' some much needed attention. I mean, you did admit you were having a dry spell," Stevens teases while walking with us towards the tables.

"Shut the fuck up Stevens. And there better not be bets going on already. Come on, dude. I just saw her for the first time in years. How could you be taking bets already?" Grayson pulls away from Stevens and pulls me to his side with his arm around my waist as we continue to walk.

I'm just laughing at the two of them. I still can't get over 'Sir Vulva-ate-her'. What does that even mean?

"Excuse me, but what is a 'Sir Vulva-ate-her'? I mean it is quite funny. But is this a guy language I know nothing about? I feel like such an outsider right now," I ask.

"Lexy, I'll tell you. 'Sir Vulva-ate-her' is Riggs' cock's name," Stevens says so matter-of-factly.

"Stevens, I said to shut the fuck up!" Riggs tells Stevens, while punching him hard in the shoulder.

"Fuck, Brother! I was just answering the girl's question, since you turned into a pussy and wouldn't answer her," Stevens whines while rubbing his shoulder. "That hurt like a mother fucker, you bastard."

"Wow, do you two toy with each other like this all the time? I would think you were real brothers," I say.

"Come on my little one," Grayson says, in such a soft deep voice, pulling me closer to him, making my heart turn over. Heavens, that is what Uncle Louie calls me. "Let's go join our friends and grab a drink. Have you had dinner? Don't pay any attention to the crybaby."

He looks over to Stevens, "Brother, I didn't even hit you with my full force. Keep it up and next time I will." Grayson gives such a stern look it 'causes Stevens to raise his hands in surrender.

We walk over to a round table where my friends are all sitting, talking and flirting with Grayson's friends, or as he calls them, 'Brothers'. Tony has Sarah with him, and I think Britney is flirting with him too. I sure hope none of them are planning to hook up tonight. That could really complicate things, because I'm not sleeping with Grayson tonight.

"Lexy girl, you're late. We've already ordered dinner. Grayson's friends have been great company. I really like these guys. If we make everyone scoot over some, we could probably squeeze around and pull up two more chairs in for you if you'd like," Anissa says, always looking out for me.

"That's okay, Anissa. Lexy and I will just sit over here to have our dinner and catch up, if that's alright with you?" Grayson asks, looking down at me with pleading eyes.

"Sounds wonderful." Turning to my friends, I say, "After dinner, we'll all hit the dance floor if everyone still wants to bust a move."

"Perfect! That'll give you two time to catch up anyway, without all of us listening in. But if you need me, I'm here," Anissa reminds me with a wink.

Nodding, I watch as all the Brothers sneakily watch me. Grayson escorts me over to a booth about ten feet away from them. I guess he did want a bit of privacy. Here goes, I have to make him believe me and not ask too many questions.

"Aless, I mean Lexy, what would you like to drink? A cocktail or wine?"

"I'd love a nice glass of red wine."

Grayson calls over to the bar, "Scott, bring my lady over a glass of Barolo, and me a glass of Woodford Reserve, and send a waiter over too. Thanks man."

He places his hand on the low curve of my back and motions for me to sit down. I slide into the small round private booth that has very comfortable burgundy leather wrapped bench seats. Grayson quickly slides in beside me, our legs touching.

"May I ask you why you changed your name to Lexy, of all names? Aless was so unique and beautiful." He doesn't waste any time, getting right down to the questioning. Placing that one finger on my chin again, he turns my head to once again look into my eyes. I know I have to start answering him.

"I couldn't keep Aless here in America, it's too unusual, so they used part of my real name. In Italy, I had a very long name. It was just shortened to be similar to my grandfather and grandmother. My grandfather's name is Lexington Rogers, and my Nonna on my father's side, was Alexa. I stayed with my mom's parents soon after I moved to America. They live in Santa Barbara with the rest of my extended family. See, I didn't know about them until right before my grandmother passed away."

"I'm so sorry to hear your grandmother passed away. I remember how important she was to you. Hopefully, your Uncle is doing well. And how is your father? I remember how we both shared about how controlling our dads were. Mine actually got a little better. We still bump heads regularly, but he at least gave up trying to run my life," Grayson adds, giving a little squeeze around my shoulders.

"Thank you, my uncle is doing very well. I miss him greatly. But life goes on, and so many things have changed through the years. He married my nanny when her sister and brother-in-law died in a house fire. They had two small children that my uncle and his wife are now raising together. But he's the only one in the Family I stay in contact with," I answer, knowing I have to tell him more to get this line of questioning to end.

"So, I guess things with your father didn't get better. Is that why you escaped and don't want to talk about it?" he asks, lightly caressing my shoulder.

"I know you want information Grayson, but I'm here, I was able to escape. I cannot let that side of the Family find me. I'll be honest with you, but this is the only time I'll say this, and then this subject is closed. Do you understand me?" Looking him in the eyes, I make damn sure he knows I mean it.

"Aless, I mean, Lexy. Sorry, it'll take me a little time to get used to that name. I understand it must hurt you. I'll respect your wishes and won't bring it up again, for now. I just need to know you're okay, and how you were able to escape and become a citizen."

He looks so concerned. I know I have to tell him something more. He does need some answers. I just need to make sure he will be satisfied with the information I do give him. I need to tell him just enough, not everything. Just then, the waiter brings over our drinks and menus, giving me a minute to compose myself and plan.

"Thank you for the wine, and Grayson, I'm not like your Amazon women and live on lettuce alone. I'm a big eater. I didn't get this ass of mine by dieting," I inform him, causing him to laugh out loud.

"Good to know! Eat as much as you want. I love the fact you aren't a dieter. I love to eat as well. I already told you how much I love that ass of yours, let's keep it that way."

I swat my hand at him playfully. "Okay then, I'll totally mix things up. I want to start off with a Caesar salad, that is with chicken, and I mean plenty of cheese. Not a cute little sprinkle of it, I mean I barely want to see lettuce for the cheese. Then I'll have a filet mignon with linguini and fresh vegetables with extra cheese on them as well, just like the salad. Make sure to bring the bread and can we get a little side of olive oil with blended basil, garlic and butter for dipping it into? Thank you."

Grayson throws his head back and laughs so hard that everyone looks over at us. "I so love that my woman can eat. I'll have what she's having, but give me the largest cut of filet mignon, medium rare, and add some marinara sauce on that linguini and veggies for me. Thanks"

"Sorry, I never order anything right off the menu. I just order what I'm hungry for, and I barely ate lunch. I guess I was a bit nervous about how you'd react."

"Nothing to ever be nervous about with me. And as I said before, honesty is the most important thing to me," he says, as he runs one finger over my shoulder. He should have just said 'hint, hint' with that. Taking a deep breath, I decide now is as good of a time as any.

"I get the hint, Grayson. I'll tell you what happened and how I became an American citizen so easily. My mother was an American and married my father when she was very young, in Italy. She, my Italian grandmother and Uncle, while on a shopping trip to America when I was just an infant, went to the American consulate and got me an American birth certificate. My grandmother and uncle kept it a secret from me for many years. They never even shared that with my father either. He would never have allowed it. He has no idea that I know anything about my mom's side of the family.

I had no idea I was half American as a child. My mother came to Italy when she was a little girl, with her family. Her father worked in an international accounting firm and taught at a well-known university. She went to school, had friends, and there were no clues while I was growing up that she wasn't Italian too.

But after we met, when I got back to Italy, my family threw me a huge birthday party, as they always did. A guy I knew tried to kiss me. I was brought up to defend myself, so I kicked him in the family jewels and was about to do more damage to him, but my father walked up and saw it. He thought I was kissing the guy. I didn't have the chance to explain what had happened to my father. He accused me of acting like a whore and beat the ever-loving shit out of me that night. I mean busted lips, black eyes, I couldn't leave the house for over a week. It was bad.

But what made it even worse was that he flat out told me

he owned me and my virtue. He let me know he, and he alone, would be picking out my husband and controlling my entire life, down to what I wore. He even picked who my friends were, what I'd study in university, I mean college. He was a complete dictator over my whole life. I was just a shiny possession to him, to use as trade.

My uncle could do nothing at that moment to protect me. My grandmother came in during the beating and told him if he ever touched me again, she'd shoot him. That was, I guess, when we all secretly started to plan my escape. After my grandmother passed away, my uncle and bodyguard helped me to do just that. I'm sure my father is still looking for me.

Please Grayson, respect my wishes and never bring it up again. It's too painful. My life is here now, and it has been that way for a long time. Can you do that? Can you allow this subject to stay buried for me, please?" Looking straight into his eyes, I'm praying he can see the pain just talking about this causes me.

He finally nods, "Okay, baby. I'll respect your wishes and not ask you any more questions, other than what was your last name before? And do you worry he'll try to take you back to Italy?"

"He'll never find me. That I can promise. My grandmother and uncle were geniuses. When I was born, they thought my father might one day be an asshole, so they actually put Alexa Sophia Rogers on my real birth certificate. My father was such a dumbass, he trusted them and never looked at it. He tried to dictate my name too, but my mom wanted me named something else, so my grandmother and uncle made it happen. I'm safe. There is no reason for you to worry. I promise. I can take care of myself." I lean forward and lightly kiss his lips, hoping he'll drop it and not ask any more questions.

Pulling away from our brief kiss, Grayson rests his forehead on mine and whispers, "Fine, for now. But if anything should ever change, please let me help you. This is what I do. I protect people. You will always be safe with me. I can promise you that." Then he presses his lips to mine one more time, as we hear the waiter clear his throat.

We don't talk about my past anymore, thankfully. Once we finish eating dinner, we enjoy feeding each other a monster hot fudge brownie sundae. It's so incredible. I love how natural everything feels between us.

After begging and pleading from both groups of our friends, we finally join everyone on the dance floor. I'm thrilled to see that Grayson can actually dance. We're both busting a move and laughing with our friends as they tease us.

The music changes to a slow song so most of our friends leave the dance floor to get a drink. Grayson grabs me, pulling me into his arms. We get lost in the music, looking into each other's eyes as we slow dance to 'Crazy In Love.'

"You have no idea what you do to me Lexy. Your eyes... I could get lost in them for eternity," Grayson whispers to me in his very deep, sexy as hell voice, causing goosebumps to explode all over me. We dance so close, and it's such an incredible feeling being in his arms again and moving like this.

"I feel the same way. I know we barely know each other, but on some level, I already feel like such a part of you. I've never experienced anything like this. It's both scary and peaceful all at the same time."

"I couldn't put this feeling into better words myself. I just don't want to let you go. Fuck, I have to really taste you. I can't wait another second,"

Like no one but us is in this room or on the dance floor, Grayson bends down and kisses me, instantly flaring a hungry passion like we were starved for each other. Lifting my hands and running them into his hair, we both take it deeper, our tongues battling for control.

His hands slide down to my bum, and he lifts me completely off the ground, firmly squeezing my ass, pulling me closer to him. Grayson's passion is causing my toes to curl, making me point my feet upwards like some cliché in an old romantic movie. I wind my fingers through his hair, giving a slight tug, making him moan.

"See, this is what happened the first time these two were together. I'm going to be a fucking rich man after tonight." Hearing Stevens' bragging pulls my mind out of our moment. I don't really want this to end. We were both lost in our own world of passion.

"Fuck man, I bet a hundred bucks they wouldn't fuck at least till next week. I've never seen Riggs practically attack a girl, almost fucking her in public. This is one for the books," I hear another one his friends say.

Grayson instantly pulls away, putting me back on my feet, ending the best and most passionate kiss of my life. Boy am I in trouble. Thankfully he pulls me into his arms, so I lay my head on his chest, knowing I'd be too wobbly to stand alone if he let me go. He easily speaks over my head to his rude friends.

"Shut the fuck up, Stevens and Clay. I said 'no goddamn betting on this shit'. What the hell guys!"

"Now, now Riggs, old buddy. I don't remember you trying to shut the betting down when it was Bella and me. You guys were betting on us. I think you lost money on that betting too," Drake says with his arm around Isabella, both of them laughing.

"Fitz, now that you mentioned it, we know the two of you are banging like monkeys in heat now that Isabella is already knocked up, but we are still trying to figure out when that first time was, so we can see who won that pot," Stevens says to

Fitz, as all the Brothers suddenly get quiet, nodding and agreeing with him.

"Yeah man, when was it?"

Isabella is standing beside Drake with her arm around him just giggling. "Stevens, none of you won. I already told you. The pot goes into my Foster Kids Fund," Isabella adds.

"Grayson, what is with all the betting? What are they actually betting on?" I ask, thinking they really couldn't be betting on when Fitz and Bella actually made love for the first time, could they?

"I'll tell you!" Shelly interrupts, "We had a big discussion about it while you were playing googly eyes with Grayson. They place bets on who can guess when another Brother is going to get laid. They even let me enter the betting pool for when I think you two will be doing the nasty for the first time. But I'm not allowed to cheat and encourage or discourage you, so I have to keep the date to myself. But I know you won't be easy," Shelly says while laughing.

"You didn't! Shelly, come on. You took part in their tacky betting?" I ask in shock, but I'm still giggling about it.

"Hey now, I at least didn't think you'd be nearly as easy as all the Brothers. They're betting you won't last two weeks. I'll be making out like a bandit if I win," she says with such confidence.

"Hey Shelly, that's cheating! You just told her all of us gave her less than two weeks," Stevens whines.

"That means all bets are off. This shit needs to stop. We aren't in Junior High any more boys," Grayson scolds them.

"Dude, said the man who put a hundred bucks on me banging Bella in less than six weeks," Fitz adds.

"Fitz, come on, you and Isabella have to let us know when your first time was. There's over a two grand in the pot! And with Grayson getting a woman, we have to focus on that one now," Stevens says.

"You really want to know? I'll tell you none of you won

that money because you all guessed wrong. It's all going to my fund," Isabella tells Stevens, as she looks around the room.

"Okay Isabella, when was it?" Stevens asks, pulling out an old school little flip note pad from his back pocket.

"It was the day I came home from the hospital." Several of the Brothers gasp out loud as Isabella grabs her stomach with one arm, the other still around Drake as he laughs with her. "Drake, baby, I think I'm going to throw up!" And she starts making fake throwing up noises and Fitz is laughing so hard he is wiping his eyes.

Now all the Brothers are cussing and moaning and complaining. Isabella steps away from Fitz and starts bouncing around all of them with her fists up in the air, calling them all suckers. It's like a victory scene from Rocky. Fitz is still laughing with her. "I warned you Brothers, you can't win when it comes to my little woman," Fitz grabs her and kisses her.

"Now that proves betting like that is not right, so no betting on Lexy and me. Understand? Or I'll be doing some serious ass kicking," Grayson once again informs the Brothers, who just laugh him off. These guys are so playful and close. It's nice to see such genuine friendship. It is not how I'm used to seeing men behave, that's for sure.

Grayson leans down and gives me a quick taste of his mouth. Mother Mary, that gets my heart racing. Resting his forehead on mine, which seems like something he loves to do, 'causes my heart to skip a beat. "Let's get out of here," he whispers.

"Grayson, I just walked back into your life. In reality, we barely know each other. I'm not sleeping with you tonight," I whisper back to him, making sure he is the only one to hear me.

He closes his eyes for a second, then opens them and looks deep into mine. "Okay, I won't push that. But I still want to be with you, and not with all the Brothers watching. Can I take you somewhere private? To my place or yours? It's the week-end, I want to spend it with you," Grayson pleads.

"Tomorrow is the second Saturday of the month. I always get together with my family. My grandpa has rented one of those big touring buses and they're picking my friends and me up early in the morning to go to Disneyland. Do you want to come with all of us? I'm sure my family won't mind. They'd probably love to meet you. Come with us? It'll be fun, and a great start at getting to know each other better," I ask him with a big playful smile.

"Sounds great, I'd love to. I haven't been to Disneyland in years and going with you sounds like a lot of fun. I look forward to meeting your family as well. But I insist on taking you home tonight. I promise to be a good boy. I won't even pressure you to let me stay the night," Grayson says with a wink, trying to look all innocent.

"Okay, I'd love for you to take me home. But that means taking my friends too. I promise I won't kick you out immedi-ately, that is, if you think you can be a good boy." I can't help but tease him with one eyebrow raised.

"Yes, Ma'am, I can do that. I just want to hold you in my arms and spend some time enjoying your company and give you a proper goodnight without all our friends watching. I promise I'll be back bright and early. This weekend is ours. We'll get to know each other tomorrow while spending the day with your girlfriends and family. Then Sunday, we can go over to Hawkins' place, so you can meet and get to know all the Brothers. Sunday night, it's dinner with my parents and sister. How does that sound?"

"You really want me to meet your parents on Sunday? Isn't that a bit soon? What if they don't like me?" I ask nervously, not believing he wants me to meet his freaking parents already.

"Well, I'm meeting your family in the morning! And trust

me, my mom will love you, I'm sure. Considering I've never brought a girl over, she'll flip. As for my sister, you've met her before. She was at the hot-dog place, Gray's Papaya, but she had already left for her European trip before the party at Stevens' place. She can be a little protective and a touch bitchy at times, but I'll keep her in line. We've talked about my dad before, and I don't give a rat's ass what he has to say. Please come?"

Looking into those dark blue eyes of his, I'm nervous, but how can I say no? "Okay, the weekend is ours. If you're willing to spend all day tomorrow with my friends and family, I'll spend Sunday with your family and friends."

Grayson grabs me, lifting me off the ground and spinning me around. "This is going to be the best weekend. I can't wait to get to know all about you. Your likes and dislikes. I know we'll both find out that we do have a few quirks too." Putting me back down, he kisses my forehead.

"Quirks! Me?! I can't think of any of them you wouldn't like." Rolling my eyes, I smile up at him. I just love to tease him like this.

"I can't think of anything I couldn't deal with, that's for sure. I mean, unless you're a complete slob. Or maybe you snore like a hibernating bear," he teases right back.

"Well, rest assured I don't snore, so all will be fine. Now take me home so we can ditch our friends and make out for a while," I say, adding a wink.

"Okay Anissa, Dana, and Shelly, it's time to take you home. Do I need to take you home as well, Tony? You don't live with the girls, do you?" he calls out to my friends as he throws me over his shoulder with a swat to my bum.

"Grayson, put me down! I can walk, you know," I say as I reach down, swatting at his fine bum. Dayum, my man's got back, alright. The view from here is quite nice.

Grayson gives me a playful swat on my bum, again, saying, "Be quiet, woman! I wouldn't want you to get lost in the crowd. And this way, I know your friends will follow me," he adds, chuckling as we head to the elevator.

Tony walks up and looks at me over Grayson's shoulder. "Lex, I'm going to let you have a good time with Grayson tonight. You be good, and don't do anything I wouldn't," he says with a wink, before he continues. "I'll be over at your penthouse in the morning for the family Disneyland adventure. It looks like you'll have someone else to cling to now on all the roller coasters. I'll be bringing my regular partner, like I did last month. But for now, I'm going back to the dance floor with my girl Sarah and my two new friends, Brit and Brenda." He leans around Grayson and kisses my forehead.

"And Grayson, I'll see you tomorrow too. I can't wait to get to know you better as well. I've heard all about you for so long. This is going to be really fun," Tony tells Grayson with a wink.

"I feel the same way, Tony. And a bit of information for you, Sarah's my little sister, not your 'girl'. You might want to remember that as well as the fact that Brit is Fitz and Gregory's baby sister, and Brenda is Stevens' little sister too," Grayson tells him with an odd look on his face.

"Nothing to worry about man, they both already told me that little tidbit of information, as well as a lot more," Tony replies with a taunt of his own, and yet another wink to Grayson. "But don't worry big brother, I won't do anything with the girls they don't want me to do. Oh, and as for Sarah, I already knew who she is too." Chuckling, he walks back to the dance floor where all three girls are waiting for him with big smiles on their faces. Oh, I hope he behaves himself. And what the heck is with all this winking?

My mind rushes back to Grayson. I'm just hoping and praying we aren't rushing this too fast. I know my family will never say anything they shouldn't tomorrow. Grayson won't be able to get any information out of them. It'll for sure be a blast at Disneyland with my friends and family.

It's Sunday and spending time with the Brothers that concerns me. I'll have to be careful with what I say. I'm sure my every word will be analyzed. So, it'll be game on. No way will they find anything out about me that I don't tell them myself.

My father makes sure none of our family secrets make it online. He has his own internet team searching for me, keeping everything else quiet. And with Tony always on top of it too, I have nothing to worry about. They won't be able to find out anything.

There aren't any pictures of me online. Tony and my family have always made sure of that. My eyes are too recognizable, and so was my insanely long hair, always done in some fancy updo. That's why my hair is cut, highlighted, and down in every photo now, and usually, I'm wearing glasses, or have my brown contacts in, just to make sure I keep my identity hidden and no one recognizes me.

Right now, I'm beginning to feel like Grayson and I are about to jump straight into the deep end. Let's hope we both can swim, and good.

6

FINDING OUT MORE, BUT STILL WONDERING

Grayson

I'm paying close attention to the ladies and all of their chatting as we get off of the elevator to their penthouse, and I'm finding it very interesting. They aren't even hesitant to talk in front of me. Listening to them share about the fun they had tonight, and which Brother they thought was the hottest and could dance the best is giving me more ammo I could secretly use for blackmail and information gathering. It looks like it's time to sic the preferred Brothers onto her friends, to see if they can get more info out of them. I must know the whole 'Aless to Lexy' story.

"It was nice meeting all you ladies, and I promise not to repeat a word of what I've just heard back to the Brothers," I tease them, even though I'm lying about some of this straight to their faces.

Shelly is the first to the door, and I watch her lift her hand and place it on a hidden scanner. While her hand is still on the scanner, she leans forward and scans her eye before the door unlocks. Damn, that is some major security. I wonder who installed this equipment. Whether Aless/Lexy wants to admit

56

it or not, she must believe she could potentially be in danger with this much security.

Shelly stands aside, letting us all walk in, before she looks at me and with such sarcasm and says, "Please don't tell me you are that dense in the head. We want you to report every word back to the Brothers. Do we look like we're dumbasses to you? It's called a 'feeding expedition.' We feed all this information to you and see what comes back to us.

Believe me, the conversation would have had a lot more detail if you weren't standing behind us. We're hoping you'll put out feelers for us to see what those boys thought about us as well." Shaking her head as she starts walking away, she heads upstairs and mumbles, "Duh. Men. Do we have to explain everything?"

Damn, that woman is something else. Laughing, I holler back to her "Nice to know you're cool with it Shelly, because I was planning on sharing it with them anyway. You know, 'Guy Code' and all that. When you know a chick is into one of your friends, you gotta make sure they know about it. Us men can be slow and dense, so we help each other out that way. That's how a lot of good hook-ups are made." Still laughing at her, I pull Aless into my arms and look around her place.

"Good to know you're not stupid. And FYI, I wouldn't mind hooking up with one of the Brothers at all, but I'm not looking for a relationship right now, too much shit on my plate. But hey, I wouldn't mind taking a certain one of them out for a good ride. Good night everyone, and Grayson, you mess with our girl, and I'll shoot your cock off," I can hear her laughing as a door closes upstairs. Shit, was she joking? Does she have a gun?

Feeling a hand touch the arm I've wrapped around Aless, I look to see Dana walking by as she says, "Don't mind her, we're not all so easy to bed, but we don't have standards as high as Lexy does either. So, with that thought, I do wish you luck. Good night you two." She turns and heads upstairs as well.

My head turns to her last friend as she walks up to us. "Just remember Lexy, if he starts getting out of hand, you just holler, and I'll come and zap him with my new stun gun. I'd love to see if it could take a man as big as him out," Anissa informs me as she turns and starts walking down a small hall to the left. She calls back, "Nighty night, you two. Don't do anything I wouldn't." Then we hear her door close as well.

"Thanks for all the trust ladies!" I say loud enough to make sure they all can hear me. Chuckling, I add, "Looking forward to spending quality time with all of you tomorrow!" Still laughing at her friends, I shake my head. These ladies are a riot. I'm still wondering if they actually have a real gun or a stun gun. But with this security, they more than likely do.

Aless looks up at me giggling, saying, "Really, don't pay them any attention. I hope roller coasters don't scare you because I plan on riding all of them and holding onto you for dear life." She pulls out of my arms and grabs my hand, leading me towards the couch.

"So far in my life, I can honestly say I've only been scared a few times. But with you coming back into my life, that just removed one of them. I was beginning to fear I'd never see you again." She stops and looks up at me with those clear blue eyes of hers, and smiles. She's clueless as to how much she controls my world.

Pulling her back into my arms, I kiss her with all of the pent up passion I'm feeling. I want to make damn sure she never leaves me again. Damn, I want to take this to the next level so bad but knowing I can't means I need to calm the fuck down and keep control of this.

Pulling away, Aless looks at me breathing heavily. "I'm... I'm going to go change. I'll be right back. Feel free to get a beer out of the fridge, or anything else you see in there." As she starts to walk away down the hallway opposite of where

Anissa went, she looks back over her shoulder and gives me a wink, knowing I'm watching her ass.

Fuck, I can't help myself. I always knew Aless had one hell of a body, but *damn*. I'm going to have to start thinking of her as Lexy mentally, but shit that's going to be hard. But not as hard as 'Sir' is right now, looking at those damn curves of hers. I shake my head and take a second to rearrange my obvious out of control hard-on. Oh well, she should be proud she can turn me on so fast. I hope I can calm him down a bit, or shit, I'm in trouble.

Looking around the place, it's easy to see it's a penthouse and not a regular condo. The whole top floor of this building is theirs. Two stories, and fully loaded with an incredible security system. Yeah, either these girls make a lot of money, or one or more of them is a trust fund girl because a penthouse like this with four bedrooms and all this space doesn't come cheap in Santa Monica. Something tells me it's Lexy with the money.

Walking over to the faux fireplace, I look at the pictures of the girls in New York. Some of them are candid shots, in others they are acting silly, it makes me smile. I reach out and pick up one of Lexy, with her hair blowing in the wind. Damn, her hair was long in this picture. It's way below her ass, and jet black. She looks fucking stunning, with such a serious look on her face as she is looking off into the distance, holding a pair of big dark sunglasses in her hand. You can tell she is about to put them on to cover up her gorgeous eyes. This picture wasn't taken in New York or here, it was taken in Paris. I've been to the vineyard myself. So, the girls did know her before she moved here.

She's colored her hair since then and cut an awful lot off as well, obviously wanting to change her looks. When we met almost eight years ago, her hair was up. I wonder if her father made her always wear it like that? She does have the rarest blue eyes I've ever seen. I bet that is why she's always in dark glasses. Those eyes would be easily recognized. This picture says so much.

"Looking at old pictures of me, I see. This is nowhere near the refrigerator by the way." I feel her small hand on my back as she takes the picture out of my hand and places it back on the mantel. "Dana is a great photographer, isn't she? She took that one when I wasn't even aware of it, when we were touring the vineyards in Paris. It was just days before I cut my hair and got it highlighted. They all love this picture. But as you can guess by me taking it away from you, it's not one of my favorites."

"Why is that? You look so beautiful, absolutely stunning in it. But you look a million miles away, lost in thought in that picture," I state, hoping she'd say more.

"I was. I was thinking of you, and praying I'd bump into you when we got to New York, but you had already moved to California. Now, would you like something to drink?"

Looking down at her and admiring how beautiful she looks, I realize she has changed into burgundy silk sleep shorts and a tank top. Damn, I could get lost in this woman. I would never have thought she'd just walk out here dressed like that. That bashful girl I met in New Jersey would never have walked out like this. She has definitely grown up and changed a bit as well. She's matured into a very confident, stunning woman.

Feeling Sir instantly harden to stone, I clear my throat, "No, thank you. I'd rather spend this little time we have tonight saying 'good night' to you properly." Once again, I grab her hand and pull her into my arms, not giving her a moment to think as I devour her mouth.

She's so responsive. I reach down and put both hands on her ass. Damn, she is either wearing a thong or nothing under these silk shorts. Squeezing both of her full ass cheeks, I lift her up, hoping she wraps those legs around me, which she does, without hesitation, making her moan. Oh, fuck. Leaving here tonight will be the most difficult thing I've done in my life. Walking us over to the couch, I maneuver carefully until I feel it hit the back of my legs. Sitting down, I make sure she stays straddling me. I spread my legs wide enough to make sure that her sweet pussy line up to Sir. Just when I get her right where I want her, she pulls away from our kiss, blinking those striking eyes at me. I'm breathing heavy and so fucking turned on. It feels like my world is right in front of me but hidden inside of those eyes.

Lexy whispers to me, placing her small hand on my cheek. "Do you have any idea what you do to me? I just get so consumed in you, I'm lost in the power you have over me. I know we barely know each other, but it's almost magical what you do to me and how I feel around you."

Resting my forehead on hers makes me feel like we're one when we're touching like this, so complete and whole.

"I feel the same way. You're like a dream come true, Lexy. My magical fairy that has sprinkled me with a secret potion. I'm so under your control. I know that sounds corny, but I truly mean it. Call it magic, fate, or whatever the fuck you want to. I don't give a damn, but we both feel it. It's real, and I for one have never felt it before. Nor do I ever want it to go away."

"Me either. It's like something you'd read about in a romance novel, not ever believing for a moment it could be real, but it is. I just don't know what to do. Part of me wants to slow it down so we don't burn out. The other part of me wants to hold on and run straight into the fires with you."

Pulling her closer I kiss her again, loving the feeling of her body being so close to mine. Rubbing my hard cock up into her core as she moves her hips in matching motion feels amazing. Moaning her name, I squeeze her ass again. Fuck, I don't want to leave, but I know I have too and soon.

"Grayson, don't stop," Lexy says as she starts kissing down my neck and back up again, claiming my mouth.

Damn, this woman is like no other, trying to take control of this. Fuck! Grabbing the back of her head with one hand, I turn her head to take our kiss deeper, running my fingers through her thick hair. She does the same to me, lightly scratching her fingernails on my scalp. A moan escapes my mouth as I squeeze her full round ass, pulling her tighter against my cock, grinding it upward into her.

She softly whispers, "Grayson, I'm so close."

Holy fuck, I'm about to cream my goddamn jeans. I can't stop myself. I'm dry humping her like I'm a fucking teenager. Lexy is sliding her hips up and down between my spread legs, literally rubbing her pussy up and down the full fucking length of my cock. I feel my eyes rolling back into my head. I can feel her every muscle tighten, knowing she's about to cum. Fuck, that triggers me to put both my hands on her ass and pull her as tight as I can to my cock and grind Sir right where I know she needs him.

She pulls away from our kiss, and in a soft raspy voice, cries out my name. "Grayson!" as we both explode into ecstasy. Fuck. That is the most beautiful sound I've ever fucking heard.

With both of us trying to catch our breath, we rest our foreheads together, "That was incredible. You don't know how bad I want to stay with you tonight."

"I know, but it's too soon. We can't. Not tonight. But soon. I just want to hold you all night and snuggle up to you. Do you think that's possible, without sex on the table?" she whispers to me as she starts kissing my neck.

"Yeah, it'll be tough, but I can control myself. I want that too. To be able to go to sleep with you in my arms is something I've dreamed of since the day we met," I respond, kissing her neck where it meets her shoulder, nibbling on it.

"I don't want you to leave, but I know you need to."

"I do but let me tuck you into bed. I'll lock the door as I leave. If I don't leave soon, I don't know if I'll be able to. You're too tempting. I want to get to know you, all of you, before we take this to the next level too." Cupping her full ass in both hands again, I lift her back up as I stand. I'm assuming her bedroom is down the same hall she went down to change earlier. I carry her, still wrapped around me, kissing my neck and cuddling into me.

"My bedroom is at the end of the hall," Lexy murmurs between kisses to my neck. Damn, she isn't making this any easier.

Pushing her partially closed bedroom door open with my foot, I'm faced with a huge four poster bed, with a really nice burgundy and black satin and velvet comforter. You can tell it was custom made. I walk over and lay her down on the bed.

"Lay down with me for a minute?" she whispers, sounding very tired and sleepily blinking her eyes. I lift her back up so I can pull back the covers, lay her down again and then cover her up. I sit on the corner of the bed.

"I think it would be dangerous for me to stay tonight." I brush her hair out of her face, leaning forward to take another taste of her mouth, realizing I'll not be able to live without her, or this, for long.

Pulling away, I know I should be a gentleman and leave while I still can. Lexy runs her hand down my neck and over my chest, down my stomach, stopping when she feels a wet spot. I look her in the eyes saying, "I need to use your restroom. I've made a bit of a mess of myself. See what you do to me?" Chuckling, I pull my shirt off, using it to wipe my lower stomach.

Watching her eyes blink several times as she stares at my chest, I know she's figured it out when she mumbles, "Emm, you mean to tell me that you, umm..."

"Came too? Yes, I did. We came together. But I have to admit, that was something I've never done before, blow my load like that while dry humping, not even as a teenager." Still chuckling I watch her blush. Goddamn, she still blushes so easily, and I love it.

"Emm, sorry, I guess. I didn't mean for you to, you know. I just can't control myself around you. I was so close the last time we made out like that. I just didn't want you to stop, I needed that so badly from you."

Putting my finger over her lips, I whisper, "Baby, you have nothing to apologize for. I loved and wanted every second of it too, and more. I'll be back in just a minute." Leaning down and taking another quick kiss, I get up and walk over to a partially open door that I'm assuming is her bathroom.

Walking in, I turn on the light, closing the door behind me. Looking around at all the matching towels and the over-sized claw bathtub and a massive shower, with at least eight shower heads, my imagination goes wild. Damn, the things I could do to her in here. Yeah, my Lexy girl is the one with the money. This is the master suite for sure, and she has added a lot of upgrades in here.

I take a piss and clean myself up, pausing to take a quick look around to see if I can find anything in the drawers or the hidden medicine cabinet. Not even a prescription drug, just expensive makeup and girl shit. Coming up empty-handed, I head back out with my shirt wadded up in my hand.

Lexy is sitting up in bed propped up with pillows, watching my every move as I walk back over to her bed. "Hot Damn, as Anissa would say. You are a freaking Greek God. You know that's what I nicknamed you, when we first met? I've never in all my life seen any man as beautiful and flawless as you."

Chuckling, I feel my cheeks getting a little warm. "I guess I should say thank you. But I'm glad you think so because I do want you wanting me, as much as I want you." I sit back on the side of her bed facing her. "I really do need to go. We'll be spending a lot of time together, that I can promise you."

"Good to know. I can't wait. I think the next 48 hours will

be a great start in really getting to know each other. I've got a silly question though. Was Stevens kidding when he said you call your penis 'Sir'?" Lexy asks, giggling.

Cracking up laughing myself, I shake my head. "No, but let me explain. Back when all of the Brothers were in Junior High, we were joking around and named our penises and it stuck. Come on, girls name their bits too. I've known countless girls, including my own sister, refer to her boobs as 'The Girls'. We just personalized it more."

Lexy sits there covering her mouth, and in between her laughter manages to say, "Sorry Grayson, but I've never known a girl who named her vagina. You guys are in a league of your very own."

Pulling her into my arms, she continues to giggle. The sound just warms my soul. "Just enjoy the knowledge that very few people outside of the Brothers know our penis names. I've never shared that information with anyone outside of them. It's just a running joke between all of us. When we were a lot younger, it made it easier for all of us to talk about if we scored the night before, without anyone but us knowing what we were talking about. Fitz would come up to us and brag that 'Henry' banged two girls last night, and no one but us knew he was talking about himself. Fitz was the biggest man whore of all of us. He never slept with the same girl twice."

"Oh my God, Fitz named his penis 'Henry'? You have to tell me all their names! This is hilarious."

"I'm not telling you any of their dick's names. You don't need to know that. You only need to know my dick's name." Now, this conversation sounds completely nuts, and I can't believe I'm sitting here talking about our dick's names.

Pulling her away from me as she is trying to control her laughter, I look in those gorgeous eyes again. "Okay, enough dick talk. Give me a goodnight kiss that I'll remember all night."

She instantly stops laughing and slides her small hands up

my bare chest, her eyes following them. My muscles flex on their own in response to her touch. Her hands continue to slowly slide up my neck and into my hair, pulling my head down towards her, our mouths finally colliding. A moan escapes my throat, and I try to take back control of our kiss. I slide my hand into her hair and pull it just a bit to hear her moan into my mouth. Fuck, I have to stop this before I lose control again.

Pulling away and resting my forehead on hers, I open my eyes and look deep into the heaven within hers. I slowly stand up, holding her hand, "I really need to go now. Buona notte, amore."

Her eyes go wide, "You can speak Italian?"

"A little. I spent time over there looking for you a couple of times. I came up empty handed every time, because you never gave me your last name, remember?"

"Well, I only speak English now, so no need to worry about that. And goodnight love, to you as well. Oh, and goodnight to you too, 'Sir'," she adds with a smirk on her face, her eyes lowering to my cock which instantly causes Sir to get harder than he already was. Fuck, this girl and her sass.

Snickering and shaking my head, I turn and walk to the door, turning back to look at her one more time. "I'll see you early in the morning. I'll lock up. Sleep well."

She grabs what looks like an iPad. "Don't worry love, I'll lock up from here. We do have a very high-end security system here, as I'm sure you noticed. I was bluffing about just letting you lock the door behind yourself. Come on Grayson, there are four single ladies living here. It would be quite reckless not to make sure it secure."

"Glad to hear that. You know I run Camelot security, so naturally I would notice such a high-end security system. Who installed it for you? You don't see many of these around here."

"Stark Enterprise. It's one of Tony's companies. He's a

true genius. I've known him since we were kids," Lexy informs me.

Taking one last look at her, I say, "Okay baby, I'll see you real soon. Sleep well." I blow her a kiss as I walk out of her room and head to the front door, making sure to take in as much as I can, my eyes scanning her whole place, on my way out. Once I reach for the door, I hear it unlatch. Yeah, Lexy has cameras on me, knowing just when I got to the door.

As I walk out, I instantly hear it click and lock behind me. Looking as casual as I can, I walk towards the elevator and push the down arrow, letting my eyes scan the hallway, realizing she's done a lot of remodeling out here as well. It looks like this elevator used to actually open up into the penthouse, but she closed it off, making it have its own hallway.

There are no other doors out here but hers, which means she has the whole top floor like I suspected. Looking up out of the corner of my eye, I see she has cameras out here as well. Once the elevator opens, I can tell it too has cameras, hidden behind the mirrors. Yeah, my Lexy is making sure no one can get up here to her without her knowledge. She is probably watching me right now.

All of this high-tech stuff makes me wonder, who the hell is this Tony? Stark Enterprise has been around for a few years. Has he owned it the whole time? I know I've heard of them. That is no more his real name than Lexy is Aless's. Yeah, we need to figure this shit out and fast. Tony... Stark Enterprise... It makes me chuckle. Who the hell does he think he is? Ironman? I know I've seen him around the club before. Has he been spying for Lexy? Reporting back to her who I was hooking up with, making sure I wasn't getting seriously involved with anyone? I'd bet money he was her spy.

I'm glad he's got a thing for my sister now. Looks like I'll be talking to her. I need to recruit her to help me figure out what the hell is going on. She might have to help her big brother out for the first time in her life. She can't say she doesn't owe me after all the times I've had to bail her ass out of shit when she was younger.

As the elevator doors close, I notice it only has three buttons labeled: Penthouse, Lobby and Garage. Yeah, Lexy has definitely upgraded the security, more so than I first thought. She's got money, and lots of it. She's making sure she's safe from her family. I need to talk to Hawkins, sooner rather than later.

I make sure to look as casual as possible in the elevator, knowing that Lexy is watching me from her room, or wherever these cameras lead. She could even have a feed to wherever Tony and Stark Enterprise is. Hawkins is going to have his job cut out for him with this one, that's for sure. He not only has to figure out who Lexy is, but who Tony Jarvis is too.

7

UPDATES WITH HAWKINS

Grayson

*T*wenty-five minutes later, I'm back at the Brothers of Camelot Bar & Club and headed up to our apartments where Hawkins said he'd be for the next day or two. It's hidden up here behind the main security office of the club. Giving the men watching all the security camera feeds from down in the club and at our other locations a head nod as I pass them, I briskly walk in the apartment.

The moment I close the door, I hear Hawkins voice, yelling, "YES... YES... FUCK! That's it." I quickly race to the partially open door, thinking he's found out some good information. Barging into the room, I ask, "What? Did you find out anything?"

I see Hawkins sitting in his chair surrounded by numerous computer monitors with his head thrown back, trying to catch his breath. "Hawkins, are you okay?" I ask as his head finally lowers and looks towards me with a smirk on his face.

"Yeah dude, I'm fine. Better than fine actually, with that release." Then he scoots his chair back, and Bonnie gets up

69

from under his desk with swollen lips and wiping the corner of her mouth.

"Come on Hawk, did you just get head? Dude, you ever heard of closing the fucking door when you're doing something like that?" I ask, shaking my head as Bonnie reaches up and kisses him quickly on the lips, and then walks past me waving her fingers at me.

"You never know Riggs, getting a good release with someone who enjoys deep throating could help you to think too, as well as make you a bit nicer," she says as she continues her stroll out the front door.

"Bonnie, I am nice. Geez," I yell at the closed door.

"And Hawk, fuck Brother, please tell me you were wearing a condom. You don't know where that mouth has been," I inform him.

Hawkins throws his head back, laughing. "Really?!" he pauses and looks around the room. "I didn't see you come in the apartment, Mom Riggs. Come on, Riggs. Really, that is just what your mother would say if she busted me getting head. How nice of you trying to protect me from Hoochie Cooties. Do you mean to tell me that you wore a rubber with every girl that ever gave you a blow job? Please."

"No, but they weren't paid escorts either. They were ladies. I totally vetted and knew them somewhat and returned the favor."

"Oh, so you mean to tell me, that some common girl you get to know and exchange sexual favors with is less likely going to give you a sexual disease than an escort who is physically checked out monthly to make sure she's clean?" Hawkins adds with such sarcasm.

"Whatever. I just hope you at least suit up if you fuck one of them. Or for that matter, fuck anyone."

"Naturally. I lived with you and Mom Gregory on and off growing up. Remember, we all got those sex talks, and I got even more of them because of my blackouts. There is no way in hell I ever want to answer to her if I make a sexually stupid mistake. She is still taunting Fitz over his and Isabella's little, shall we say, accident."

"Yeah, believe me, I know how my mom can be too. And I didn't come here to talk about your sex life. I want to know if you found out anything about Aless," I ask, as I walk over and sit in an oversized leather recliner beside him.

"Yeah, I found out lots of shit, but it's all lies, and very professionally done. She definitely has her connections. But just to make sure, I sent the twins down to San Diego to check out these High School and college pictures," Hawkins tells me as he touches his computer screen and shows me several pictures of a younger Aless, High School pictures, some with other girls, and college pictures as well.

"The twins? Does Carpenter know you sent his little brothers on an exploring expedition? He wasn't happy the last time because they got drunk and got into a bar fight that landed both of them in jail for the night and resulted in him losing time on the job to go bail them out."

"No, I didn't tell him, but I warned them they'd answer to you and not Carpenter if they screwed up this time. And I think they're more afraid of you firing their asses than their big brother beating the shit out of them again," Hawkins says chuckling.

"Yeah, those pictures do look real. Damn, that would mean she's been here for years, and I just can't believe that," I say, wondering what the hell is going on.

"She no more attended these schools than you did. Look how easy it is to remove her from these pictures! They were nicely done to convince people she's been here, but they're all lies. The other girls listed in the pictures are real, and the twins went to meet and chat with them to see if any of these girls really know your Aless. My bet is they're clueless about her and these pictures."

"Why would someone want to convince people she's been here longer than she has been?" I ask.

"Brother, your guess is as good as mine. But I'm thinking she's been here more like a year, possibly a year and a half. tops. Her good friend Tony Jarvis has been here for a little over two years, I believe. But I'm thinking I may have known him longer from the Dark Web. I'm trying to find that out now."

"So, you know he owns several companies, one being Stark Enterprise," I inform him.

"Yes, I'm fully aware. And I've been trying to figure out who he is for ages. Come on, he's obviously a geek and has a thing for the Avengers," Hawkins laughs. "That one's easy to figure out. But who is behind him? What's Tony Jarvis's real name? He's Italian, I'm pretty sure. But he never leaves any form of DNA behind. If he drinks, it's water out of the bottle and he'll take the bottle with him. He's good. I've seen a lot of his work around here. He's been in business in California for about two years now. No known address either, only PO Boxes. And as for her roommates, they are all Americans, went to college at NYU, and celebrated their graduation with a trip to Europe and Italy on a small budget, about eighteen months ago. I'm guessing that is where they met your Aless. But somehow, they were roommates in New York for a brief time before they all moved to California.

The Penthouse they live in is owned by a corporation called Fluff E Bear, Inc. The company is worth millions. They have assets spread out all over California. A couple are nonprofits, like women's shelters and foster care group homes. But they also bought the club that Aless works in about a year ago as well, along with a dance studio and spa. I'm pretty sure it's tied to Tony and Aless too, but their names are nowhere on anything. Did you find out anything else?" Hawkins asks.

"I know her penthouse has some very high-end security - hand and eye scanners, cameras everywhere. No one is getting anywhere near them without someone knowing. The question is, since her buddy Tony set it up, is he the one watching? Or is it Aless? Or maybe both? She told me tonight she's known Tony since they were young. And more importantly, her relationship with her father is done. He beat the shit out of her after her birthday party within days after we met. The only family she still talks to is her uncle and a bodyguard. No, she didn't tell me either one's names, but with her uncle and bodyguard turning on her own father to help her escape, she definitely comes from big money in Italy. My fear is it's a crime family. See what you can find out there, but do not mention too much intel about her. We don't want to tip anyone off to her being here if my hunch is correct. I'll be spending all day with her and her family tomorrow. She agreed to also come to your place on Sunday to meet you guys. Let's get messages out to everyone. We need to get as much info about her as possible. I'll see what I can find out tomorrow when I meet her family."

"Brother, I've already been talking to my Italian connection. I thought the same thing. How bad have you already fallen for this chick? Be honest with me. I need to know, is it just a bad case of the 'I gotta fuck this girl' chemistry? Or do you think it's something more real?" Hawkins looks me in the eyes, very serious.

"Dude, I'll be honest. I'm about to go all chick flick pussy on you, so if you give me any lip, I may have to hurt you, because I'm laying open my heart and not joking at all."

"Brother, your heart is safe with me. Give it up," Hawkins leans back in his chair, staring at me, waiting for me to pour my heart out.

Taking a deep breath, I start. "Do you believe in soulmates?"

"Are you shitting me?" Hawkins asks with one eyebrow raised. "I don't know. I've never met a girl that made that kind of an impact on me, but I'm also way more on guard and a bit fucked up in the head for that to happen."

"Brother, don't say shit like that about yourself," I sternly reply.

"Hey, if we're being honest and pouring our hearts out, I thought I'd be honest as well. I hope there are soulmates, because I could really use one. Someone that could understand my issues and look past them, and not see me as a science project." He chuckles, "Now start talking, Riggs."

"Okay. Years ago, when I was texting her goodbye, because she had to leave America sooner than she had planned, I told her when she looks up into the night skies and see the stars, to know I'm somewhere looking up at those same stars thinking of her. And I was being honest, and always have done just that. I'd also say a little prayer, hoping somehow, fate would bring her back to me. I got it bad," I chuckle and continue.

"There's been times, like when we went on our first assignment to Italy to rescue that Diplomat's daughter and her friend, I could have sworn I heard her voice call out my name. I think it was fate protecting me for her, because I turned just in time to get knocked down by that little Italian assassin ninja flying around. He shot the guy behind me, right between the eyes, saving my life. I would have never turned around if I didn't hear her voice.

"That wasn't the only time either. I've had a strange feeling someone's been watching me for the last year, and deep down inside, I felt it was Aless. I thought she was just scared to confront me again. You ever feel like that? Or have chills run down your spine when you think of someone special? I do with her. Oh, and she all but admitted she has been spying on me for some time. She had to make sure I wasn't involved with anyone before she approached me." I stop for a minute and take a deep breath.

"Hawkins, I believe she is the other part of my heart, my

soul. The corny expression is true. I feel she completes me. I've never had any of these feelings or emotions with anyone. My insides physically hurt being away from her. I know it sounds insane, and I can't believe I'm even telling you this, but it's the truth. And if you repeat a word of it, I'll kick your ass in a big way," I tell him as I reach over for good measure and punch him in the shoulder.

"Your words are safe with me. I hope to find someone like that for myself one day. I'm not holding my breath or anything. What you just described sounds nice. I don't think you're a pussy to feel like this either. I just hope it all works out for you. But I do have a couple of questions. You said you think it was fate that called your name. Which name? Riggs? Or Grayson?"

"Grayson. Why do you ask?"

"Just bouncing around some idea in my head. Did you notice how strong Aless is? She got up to those rafters in a matter of minutes. Her grace and poise, and the way she did things on those silks I had never seen attempted before."

"You can't be thinking that was her! That little assassin?" I throw my head back, laughing hard. My little petite Aless, an assassin? Ha! That assassin was swinging around the rafters like a damn monkey and had some of the best marksmanship I've ever seen. I think Hawkins is the one to be going off the deep end now.

"Come on Hawk, is that a joke? Give me a second to compose myself, will ya," I say while laughing.

Before I can say another word, Hawkins says, "All I'm saying is think about it. It might be possible. I wish you luck tomorrow with her family. I've already looked into them for you. They are who they claim to be. Lexington Rogers was transferred to Italy when their children were very little. He and his wife, Sophia, lived ten months out of the year in Italy and two months in the states for over sixteen years. He was a corporate accountant for the Lawland Company.

"His three children are Sophia, who I'm assuming was Lexy's mom, a sister, Elena, and a younger brother named Mathew. Both Sophia and Elena died in Italy, but no 'cause of their deaths is listed anywhere. Mathew and his father started their own accounting firm over twenty years ago, Lexington Accounting Corp. All legit. It's a five-star company, no connection to any illegal activities or businesses at all. Clean as can be.

"I cannot find any skeletons in their closet. Mathew is married with three kids of his own. All are as squeaky clean as the rest of them. But as I said, there is no reason listed at all for the deaths of their daughters, so there is definitely more to this story. But at least you know going into the lion's den tomorrow that these are good people. Find out what you can, and I'll keep my search going too. Be careful Brother. I don't want you coming out of this with a broken heart. This pint-size girl of yours could be trouble, and without question, there is way more to her story than just her daddy beating the shit out of her and her escaping."

Nodding, I take in every word he says, "Yeah, I'm fully aware of it too. I don't believe for a minute that she is trouble. But her Italian family, now that I'm not so sure about. I'll call you at the end of my fun filled day at Disneyland with any more information I find out. I'll work on all her friends too. Talk to Carpenter, Jackson and Clay. They were chatting up and checking out Anissa, Shelly and Dana tonight. Maybe we can encourage them to do a little more undercover work... in more ways than one," I say with a wink as I get up and head towards the door.

"I'll text you if I can dig up any intel on your pint size hottie, or her partner in crime Tony. I'm also sending out a message to everyone, cookout at my house Sunday. I'll get Isabella on it. She loves to cook, and playing detective is right up the nosy-girls' alley. We'll know everything about her in no time, I promise," Hawkins says as he gets right back into searching about her online. How that guy can pay attention to four computer monitors at one time is beyond me.

"Thanks Brother. We'll touch base tomorrow. See you Sunday, about eleven." I give a head nod as I walk out the door.

On my drive to my place, my mind is wandering. I know something happened to both Aless's mom and aunt. Neither of them returned here to America, they both died in Italy. I can't stop wondering, how? When? More questions I need answers to.

I have a strange feeling my life will never be the same now that I have Aless, rather Lexy, in it. But I will get to the bottom of all of this and protect her, whether she wants me to or not.

8

TESTING FRIENDS

Lexy

"*A*nissa, what am I doing wrong? My pancakes look nothing like yours. I did what you said. I waited till the one side was covered with bubbles and flipped it, but mine still has black edges."

Anissa walks over and looks at my pancake. "Honey, you waited too long to flip it. First, remember the heat isn't supposed to be up high." She reaches over and turns the heat down. "And the entire side doesn't need to be completely full of bubbles. Just mostly full."

"Oh God, you're kidding right? What is mostly full?" I say, getting very flustered at my second burned pancake and listening to Dana and Shelly snicker behind me. I can't believe cooking is so hard. Growing up, Chef made everything look so easy. That is the number one thing I miss about my previous life, not having a cook. I shouldn't hire one, but the temptation sure is strong. Then everyone would really think I'm rich, and I just want to be a normal girl. And a normal girl can cook. I can do this. Well, at least I hope I can.

"Sweetie, watch me again," Anissa, my best friend in all

the world at this moment, takes over and shows me step by step once again. "See? Just pour a bit of batter on the melted butter, then watch it carefully. See all those bubbles? They aren't completely covering the entire pancake, just mostly. Now take your spatula, and carefully slide it under and flip it." Then she does a spectacular job of flipping the most perfect pancake. "Now just wait about a minute, maybe a little less, and voilà! Perfect pancake. Now I'm eating this one, you make the next." She covers her pancake with butter and syrup while I try again.

Moments later, as I start my victory dance with my first perfect pancake in hand, in walks Tony. He quickly sees my victory dance and starts one of his own, dancing his way over to me. He quickly grabs my perfect pancake, before I even have a chance to take a bite of it, and shoves more than half of it into his mouth.

With my mouth hanging open in shock, I step closer, punching him in the arm. "Hey you jackass, that was mine! I ruined two other ones before I finally got one right and you stole it before I could even taste it." I grab my fork and steal the last little bite, just as I notice Sarah, Grayson's sister, standing behind Tony.

"Well, you did good with this one. Make us some more? We haven't had breakfast yet," Tony says while reaching over and grabbing my orange juice, drinking practically all of that too.

"Tony, do you have a death wish? Or do you just want to suffer a lot of pain? Steal another pancake off my plate and see what happens," I tell him as I walk back to the stove to make more pancakes, hoping they'll taste as good as the last one I made, even if I only had a little bite of it. Realizing I'm being rude, and so are my friends. I turn to Sarah. "Hello Sarah, how are you? I wasn't expecting to see you this morning."

"Good morning to you ladies. And I just lost twenty bucks

plus I have to give this jackass, as you so fondly called him," throwing her thumb towards Tony "another blow job. I was sure Grayson would be here with you. Didn't he stay the night?" Sarah asks. I watch as Tony pulls her over to the table with his arms around her.

"Nope. She kicked his ass out after they had one heavy make-out session," Anissa pipes in.

As I'm flipping some more pancakes, everyone is laughing at her comment, and I'm shocked she made it. "Anissa, why did you say that? You were in your bedroom. You have no idea what time Grayson left, or what we did."

"Oh yeah, I do. I was parched, and you know I have to have a cold bottle of water by my bed at night. I needed to get my drink, and, well, I opened my door and you two were hot and heavy dry humping on the couch. I had to wait till the ox carried you to your room for round two, before I could finally get into the kitchen for my water."

Now Dana, Shelly and Tony crack up laughing. "Well, excuse me! Did you spy on me in my bedroom too?"

"Nope, but I did hear him leave less than thirty minutes later. And you weren't banging in your room either. You left your door open and I could hear voices when I went back into my bedroom. So I knew you weren't putting out on the first date, what with you leaving the door open and all. And come on, I know you have more morals than that. It'll take him at least a couple of days before that happens."

Sarah sits down on Tony's lap, and starts playing with his blonde tipped black hair. They look awful cozy. I know they've been seeing each other for a while, but I wasn't expecting to see this level of a relationship. Sarah looks to me as I flip two pancakes onto a plate and hand them over to her, being nice and feeding our company before myself. I silently thank the pancake gods for helping me out. I wouldn't want Grayson's sister to go tell him I can't cook.

"I hope you don't mind me crashing the party. Tony asked me to come and it's been ages since I've been to Disneyland, and I loved hanging out with your family last month. Teasing my big brother and being a tagalong will be a blast. He'll shit his pants when he gets here and sees me. The dumbass has been texting all night, wanting me to spy on Tony and tell him all I can find out about the both of you. But Tony and I have known each other for a while now, and you could say we're fuck buddies. I know Grayson will just hate that. He never likes any guy I do."

Shocked, I ask, "You and Tony? I knew were friends, but how long have you been more involved, or as you call it, 'fuck buddies'?" My gaze moves over to Tony, sending him a look that he knows his ass is grass later tonight for not telling me about this one.

"Hey now, Lexy, don't be getting all pissed. I told you I made friends with several people close to the Camelot Brothers. I just didn't tell you one of them was Grayson's sister. I knew you wouldn't approve. But we hit it off great. Can't you understand? I even brought her last month to the Rogers' Family get together. Come on, did you really think we were just friends?" he says, rolling his eyes at me. Oh boy, are we having a talk later.

"Tony, I can't believe you. You're in so much shit right now, stealing my pancakes and keeping secrets. I didn't think we hid things from one another. We'll talk about it later," I inform him, not wanting to talk about this in front of Sarah, as I walk over and sit down beside them with my own plate of pancakes, finally.

"Lexy, come on. I know you've been spying on Grayson for some time. *Alexa Bellamy.* Did you actually think I didn't know? I figured that out the moment Tony took me to your family's cook-out last month. And your performance last night was great by the way," Sarah says, picking up her fork and feeding Tony some of her pancake, while he feeds her his. Oh brother, his ass is mine later. This looks to be way more than just 'fuck buddies'.

"I'm impressed you figured that out, or did Tony help you with that?" I ask, cutting my eyes at Tony again. I've been all their friends on Facebook for years. I only posted black and white pictures of myself from a distance, so you couldn't really tell who I was.

"Lexy I'm here to tell you my brother is looking into all of you. He's determined to find out every little detail of your life, and he doesn't care who he has to use to get it. I'm sure Hawkins has been researching you since before you even left the club last night. I just thought you should know. You know, 'Girl Code' and all. My brother is good at that shit, and Hawkins, well, I don't know anyone better."

"Thank you, Sarah. I was hoping he'd stop after we talked last night, but there is nothing he can find out that I haven't already told him. Isn't that right Tony?"

"Yup. He isn't going to find out shit, that I can promise. Not until you tell him yourself anyway," Tony says with a wink to me.

Getting the subject off of me as quickly as I can, I look back up to Sarah and ask, "So, Tony went home with you last night?"

"Oh yes. I had Tony at my condo within twenty minutes after you guys left last night, and we were ripping off each other's clothes off before the door was even closed." She reaches down between the two of them and cups his junk. I'm blown away by her boldness in front of all of us.

"That's one thing I'll tell you. Boy, does this man know how to use his equipment. I came four, no make that six times, if you count this morning. Yeah, Tony and I have some wonderful chemistry. He understands my kink, and I understand his." Sarah says, like it is nothing to share such intimate details.

"Well damn. If I knew you were that good Tony, I'd have

given you a ride a long time ago myself," Shelly says, cracking us all up.

"I don't mean to be so blunt. I'm just more sexually open than Grayson is. Just wait till you meet our mom. I bet the first thing she asks you is if you're on the pill. Believe me, I was so embarrassed by her as a kid. But she's nothing compared to her mom, Granny Piedmont. But I'm not spoiling that one. If you're seriously dating Grayson, you'll meet her soon enough.

"So, you're saying, Sunday night, when I have dinner at your parent's house, will be a memorable night?" I ask Sarah as I finish the last bite of my pancakes. I'm thrilled that they really taste great.

"Memorable will be an understatement, but Tony and I'll be there too. I thought since Grayson is bringing you, it's the perfect time for the folks to meet Tony as well. Mom's already met him briefly. I'm sure she will love you both. As for Dad, people don't call him Dick just because his name is Richard. He has a major tendency to be one as well."

We all start laughing again. I have an overwhelming desire to explain things to Sarah. She seems just as nice as she was on Facebook, all those years ago.

"Sarah, I'll be honest with you. At first, I felt I needed to be your friend on Facebook, so I could find out how Grayson was doing, and to make sure he made it back from his time in the military. But once I really got to know you, I admired you and all you accomplished with your modeling and fashion design. I also enjoyed reading all you shared about yours and Grayson's childhood. I envied your closeness as brother and sister.

"I loved all the pictures you'd share of the two of you and the ones with the Brothers. But the ones with your family were my favorite. I knew deep down I'd meet you one day and have the chance to explain and hope you understood. I didn't want him looking for me at that time. I have an overly protective family, and I had to wait till I could escape. I'll tell him myself that I was all you guys' friend on Facebook. I will not keep it from him. I hope you can understand." Giving her a pleading look, I place my hand over hers.

"No problem, girlfriend. A lot of girls have been my friend hoping to get to Grayson. You're just the first one to succeed. But I'll put it all behind us if you answer one question for me," she says with her head tilted and a big smile on her face. What has Tony told her?

"And what's that?" I ask cautiously.

"Is it true that you could kick Grayson's ass if you had to?"

Everyone in the room responds in unison. "Yes!" causing me to laugh while I just shake my head.

"I'd rather not answer that question. But I will tell you that I can take care of myself. You should come to the club and I'll teach you self-defense. You'd be surprised what a girl can do." I let her know, thinking once again that my ol' buddy and I have to have a much-needed talk real soon. Not realizing I'm giving him a death stare, Tony speaks up in defense of himself.

"Come on Lex, don't get your, what do they say? 'Panties in a bunch'? Sarah and I were wrestling around, and naturally, I was kicking her ass. She said it's not fair that a girl can't win when fighting with a guy, so I just had to tell her the truth that I'd put my money on you, no matter who you were fighting. It didn't matter what sex they were, man or woman, you'd kick their ass. Come on. Relax," Tony tries to explain.

"Well Tony, I wouldn't want you telling all my secrets. Nor would I want to have to kick your ass again." Letting my words drip with sarcasm, I can hear the girls all teasing Tony, just as the doorbell rings.

Knowing it's Grayson, I get up and run over to the intercom. "Good morning Grayson, come on up. We have about ten minutes before my family comes with the bus."

Turning back to everyone I plead, "Be nice. No talking about anything we were saying. Let Grayson find out about my skills on his own. I don't think he'd believe any of you anyway. Today is going to be fun. Let's make some awesome memories."

Sarah just won't let it go as she asks, "So, it's true? You were trained all your life to defend yourself from anyone? Male or female? I have to see this for myself."

Trying desperately to answer her question fast before Grayson gets here, I say "Yes Sarah, I was. My life has been nothing like yours. But I train others at the club to defend themselves too, all the time. You should come by and take some classes. Naturally, they'd be on the house. It'd be fun. You'd be surprised what I could teach you. I might even be able to teach you to throw ol' Tony here on his ass a time or two. Bring some friends with you. I'll train you personally." Looking at my old friend sternly, I wink at him, letting him know I'm not too happy with what he's shared.

"Girl, you're on. I'll be coming by Monday after work. I'll see who else I can talk into taking some classes with you. This sounds like a blast." Sarah says, before turning and kissing Tony on the mouth.

Thank Mother Mary and all that is holy, she's now more interested in sucking face with Tony. Hurrying to the front door, I quickly open it, just as the elevator door is beginning to open. I know I'm smiling like a loon, but so is Grayson the moment our eyes meet. I launch myself into his arms and kiss him passionately, wrapping my legs around his waist, as he cups my ass giving me a firm squeeze.

Within minutes, I hear someone clearing their throat very dramatically, pulling us out of our moment before we get too carried away. Ending our kiss, Grayson rests his forehead against mine, something I just love. I look into the eyes I never want to go another day without seeing. His eyes are sparkling with glee.

"Missed you. Can you tell?" I tease him.

"Missed you too, and I'll take a 'hello' like that any time," he says, slowly releasing me to slide my feet back to the floor.

Turning around and taking Grayson's hand, I look at Shelly and Anissa, "Can I help you ladies with something?"

"We were just going to let you know Pop Lexington just texted you and he'll be here in less than five minutes. We didn't think you'd want him to see Grayson nailing you against the wall, right? We wouldn't want Pops to feel the need to shoot Grayson before the elevator doors close," Shelly says, so matter of fact.

"And sweetie, you don't even have your shoes on yet," Anissa adds.

"Okay, fine. Come on in Grayson. They're right. I wouldn't want that to be Pops' first impression of you. I'll go grab my shoes and purse." We turn and follow Shelly and Anissa inside.

Grayson freezes the moment we walk into the door, causing me to pause and turn to see what he's looking at. I completely forgot that Tony and Sarah were sucking face when I went to open the door for him. Just then, I hear Grayson say, "Sarah! What the fuck are you doing? And why are you sucking face with Tony here?"

Sarah pulls away from Tony with a big smile on her face, "Oh hello to you to Grayson. Tony and I came over to have breakfast with Lexy before we all go to Disneyland. You missed Lexy's killer pancakes."

"So Tony asked you last night to be his date for today?" Grayson asks. Everyone is quiet as a mouse, waiting to hear what comes next. It's like we're watching a tennis match, looking from one to the other.

"No, not really. He asked me over a week ago, when we woke up one morning. In fact, I was shocked not to find you here when we got here. I lost 20 bucks to Tony on that bet. I was sure you'd score last night with the way you two were practically attacking each other on the dance floor. I guess you lost your touch." Sarah says with sarcasm and a chuckle as she gets off Tony's lap, pulling him up by his hand.

"Well some of us have a few morals and don't just jump into bed on the first date," Grayson says right back at her, with the same sarcasm and a wicked smile.

"Obviously you weren't listening. I said he asked me last week, when we woke up one morning. Did you really think we just met last night? Brother, I already knew Tony. We met ages ago at the club. This is far from our first hook-up. In fact, we've been together for months. But we did sleep together the day I met him, and after that, believe me, there's a good reason I keep coming back for more," she says, as she pulls Tony down for a quick kiss.

Tony winks at Grayson. "You don't remember me? I'm heartbroken. I always thought I was more memorable than that. I've met you several times. My blonde tips were navy the first time I met you, and that was without Sarah. Maybe you should go back and look at your security tapes from the club. I'm sure you have them, or at least Hawkins does."

"You sure I met you at the Club? Several times? When was that?" Grayson asks in a very questioning tone.

"Dude, the first time I met you was over a year ago. But Sarah brought me right over to you at the bar about six months ago and said, '*Grayson let me introduce you to my good friend Tony*'. The end. I can understand if you don't remember. You did have that tall blonde chick hanging all over you that you were trying to peel off. What's her name again... Bobette?" Tony says with a wink to me.

"Oh god, Bobby. I remember that. I think that was your last hook-up with her. She was getting a bit too clingy. You know I'll still wager that Grandmother Riggs is the one who keeps pushing her on you," Sarah adds.

Wrapping my arm around Grayson's waist, I inform them, "Well Bobby, or Bobette can go find another catch at the Country Club, because Grayson is officially off the market. Isn't that right?" Looking up at Grayson, I bat my eyes.

"You can definitely say that," he replies, as he bends down

and gives me a quick kiss. "Now go grab your shoes. I wouldn't want to keep your family waiting," Grayson says with a smack to my bum.

"Just remember Grayson, two can play ass-smacking games." I swat him on his nice round ass as I head to my room to get my shoes.

Grayson just smiles and chuckles. He turns back to Tony, "So, is this thing you have with my sister just fuck buddies? Or do I need to start checking you out for more information?"

Shaking my head at Grayson's curiosity, I hear Tony cough and respond. "Like you haven't been investigating me since the moment you saw me with Lexy. But feel free, search away. I wish you the best of luck. And the last name is spelled. J.A.R.V.I.S."

As I walk back into the living room, I watch as Grayson runs his tongue over his lower teeth. "Okay, smart ass. I no more believe that's your real name, than I believe mine is Easter Bunny," Grayson says with a chuckle.

"Well, that is what's on my passport, California driver's license and all of my other IDs," Tony tells him, looking to me for confirmation. "Isn't that right, Lexy?"

"Okay you two, knock it off. We're going to have fun today, not interrogate each other. Grayson, Tony's a great guy, I vouch for him myself. No need to worry about him with your sister. Now both of you relax and let's have fun," I say playfully smiling up at Grayson and putting my arm around him again.

"I can play nice. I was just a bit surprised to see my bratty sis here is all," Grayson says looking over at Sarah.

"Well, I have to put up with my dick brother. I guess we'll both live. And by the way, I told Lexy you're looking into all of them. You know, 'Girl Code' and all of that." She turns to me with a wink and starts talking to me like Grayson isn't standing in my arms.

"Lexy, do you know how many times I heard the term

'Guy Code' from my brother as well as ALL the Camelot Boys? Millions. If I had a dollar for every time, I heard that from them, I'd be one wealthy chick," Sarah finishes as she blows her brother a kiss.

"Oh, I see. That's how we're playing it is it? You are such a brat, you know that?" Grayson tells Sarah reaching over and messing her hair up.

"Okay you two, as much as I love your banter, we're playing nice, remember?" I tell them both, just as I hear the door open and see Pop Lexington walk in.

"Well, well, don't we have a lively bunch here today? I'm normally greeted when the elevator doors open, but today I made it all the way into the house." He doesn't take his eyes off Grayson as he walks over and sticks his hand out to him. "Hello there, young man. I'm assuming you're Grayson Riggs. I've read a lot about you. I'm Lexington Rogers, Lexy's Grandpa, but you can call me Pops. They all do." He says with a smile. "You're one big boy. How tall are you? 6'5 ... 6'6?"

Anissa walks over and gives him a kiss on the cheek. "Hi Pops. Sorry, we were having too much fun watching these two," Anissa nods her head towards Grayson and Sarah.

"I figured that much," he responds to Anissa, not letting go of Grayson's hand

"It's nice to meet you too, sir. Let's hope what you've been reading is positive. There is some shi..., crap online about me that just isn't true. And I'm 6'7 and close to 260lbs," Grayson responds, sounding a bit nervous.

"You know son, I am fully aware that some of it is shit, but not all of it." We all start to laugh, as he continues. "Now I have a party bus out there waiting that's full of over fifty relatives that will love to meet you. I hope you're up for the challenge. Your big stature will not intimidate any of us. We'll all have a fun time getting to know each other today. Now all of you, move your asses."

"Yes Sir!" is heard all around the room as everyone heads for the door and into the hall for the elevator. As we all board the elevator, Anissa starts to sing, "Who's the leader of the club that's made for you and me?"

Everyone joins in with, "M.I.C.K.E.Y.M.O.U.S.E."

Fourteen hours later as we're headed back to the bus, I look up at Grayson and bat my eyelashes. "I'm soo tired. Carry me?" I jump up into his arms before he can even reply. He chuckles and swings me around before shifting me to carry me like a man would carry his wife over the threshold. I instantly wrap my arms around his neck and cuddle into him.

Today was so much fun, riding all the rides and clinging to Grayson on every roller coaster while screaming my head off. We ate so much crap, my ass probably gained ten pounds. This moment is a dream come true. Today I was just a normal girl, out on a date with my guy. No bodyguards, no weird looks. I just had a blast, being normal with my man, friends and family. I can't help but sigh to myself. I love my life now. Closing my eyes, I enjoy the feeling of being completely safe in Grayson's arms. This. This here, is paradise.

Grayson carries me onto the bus and sits down with me cuddled into his lap. I might actually take a quick cat nap. Listening to everyone's conversations as they all get on the bus and take their seats is soothing. This bus is awfully plush. Pops didn't spare any money on this family trip.

Everyone was great. My family were all teasing Grayson and threatening him with bodily harm if he hurt me, which I thought was hilarious, but it made me feel good inside too. I actually have a real family. We share the same blood. They are real uncles, aunts, cousins, and grandparents. Now that I have Grayson, my life is complete.

As the bus slowly starts to move, I cuddle into him more.

With my eyes still closed, I slide my butt off his lap and into the seat beside us. The need to cuddle more into his chest and wrap my arms around him, overtakes me. Inhaling all that is Grayson, I feel him slowly caressing my back and playing with my hair. Oh, this is a wonderful feeling. I feel my eyes getting heavier.

"Grayson, I want you to take care of my girl there," I hear Pops whisper.

"I will sir. You have nothing to worry about. I'll protect her with my life."

"I'm not worried about that son. It took us a long time to finally get her back into our lives and we don't want to lose her again. She gave up a lot to come and find us, and you. She told me how you had such an impact on her life. You gave her a taste of what being normal and free would be like. I know all about how you two met when she was younger. You mean an awful lot to her, and I don't want to see her hurt any more. Her life's been hell." Pops is starting to share a little too much and I can't pretend to sleep any longer.

"Pops, I'm trying to sleep. Give a girl a break, will you?" I say half teasingly, and I feel Grayson's chest vibrate as he chuckles.

Pops pats me on the back. "Sorry, Little One. I'll shut up and let you see if you can catch a few winks. I know how tough sleep is for you." Then I hear him walk away.

Sighing with relief, I snuggle back into Grayson, thrilled that I hushed Pops up before he said more. I mumble to Grayson, "You make an awfully good bed." His chest rumbles again with his chuckle.

"I like the feel of you cuddling up to me too. Try to rest, I'll keep the monsters away," Grayson says in a soft, sexy as hell deep voice. Now my brain wanders into a fantasyland with Grayson instead of heading to sleep, so I just let my imagination take me away.

Not realizing how much time has passed, I realize I might

have even dozed off for a second. I hear mumbling again, so I pretend I'm still sleeping. This is a good time to test my friends and see what they'll say when they believe I'm asleep.

"Do you think she's really asleep? Whatever you're doing, don't move or stop it. She doesn't sleep very well - as in she rarely sleeps, and when she does, she sometimes has some major night terrors," I hear Dana whispering.

Seconds later I hear Anissa interrupting. "I'd be careful what you say Dana, she could just as easily be faking it. Then she'll kick your ass if you say too much."

"She's asleep, I can tell by her breathing. What are you talking about Dana? Lexy has night terrors? Why? What 'causes them?" Grayson whispers to her.

"I'm not saying anything Pops didn't already say a little while ago. Our girl has had a hard life, and I guess sometimes it haunts her dreams is all," Dana says, and I can tell by the sounds that she turns back around and sits down.

"Grayson, we love that girl. She means the world to us. Don't go messing with her heart or you'll have to answer to everyone on this bus. Our threats earlier weren't a joke. Camelot Brother or not, there is more than fifty people on this bus that'd make your life a living hell. We got her back," Anissa finishes before sitting back down herself.

"Anissa, this girl in my arms means the world to me too. I've been looking and praying she'd come back to me, and now that she has, you have nothing to worry about. I'll take good care of her and her heart. She's the other half of my own," Grayson whispers to her. I can feel my heart melting at his words. *I'm the other half of his heart.* I feel the same way. As corny as it sounds, *'he completes me too'.* For the first time in my life, I feel whole, complete.

"We mean it, Grayson. You hurt our girl and I don't give a fuck who you are or how powerful you may think you are, we'll find a way to hurt you. And I mean it, I'll cut that dick of yours off and keep it as a trophy." I try my hardest not to bust up laughing or show any reaction to Shelly's words. God, she can crack me up. She's all tough on the outside but a true protective sweetheart on the inside. Grayson will learn that she means every word of her threat.

"Shelly, I swear on my life. I'm not going to hurt her. Like I said, you girls have no idea what she means to me. I'll not only prove to Lexy, that she can trust me with everything, I'll prove it to all of you as well."

Yeah, I have some awesome real friends, and one hell of a new boyfriend. Now I just need to make it through tomorrow and dinner with his parents. I don't know which will be worse – brunch with the Camelot Brothers or dinner with his parents. His parents, especially what I've heard about his dad, makes me more than a wee bit nervous.

9

FRIENDSHIP DISCOVERY

Lexy

"Oh, my ever-loving God! That's… that's a real castle! Grayson, why didn't you tell me Hawkins lives in a real freaking castle? Wow! It even has a moat with a drawbridge! Look at all the construction! It's covered in wisteria. Oh, how I love wisteria. Back home, we had it everywhere. It was my mom's favorite. Is that a chapel they're building?"

Grayson just laughs at me, because I haven't shut up long enough for him to answer a single question.

"Yes, Hawkins lives in a castle. He started having this built when he was around eighteen. He moved in a year later, just as they finished it. He has construction going on constantly. And yes again, that is a chapel being built. Drake and Isabella will be getting married there in a little over a month."

"That's so romantic. Are all of you going to dress in character? Is it a Camelot wedding? I can't believe all of this. It's like going back in time. I want my own castle now." I know I look like a loon, gazing at everything and all its beauty. I can't wait to get the grand tour.

"Yup, it'll be the first Camelot wedding, but I'm sure we'll all be married up here. This way we know, it'll be private and Hawkins will be able to attend, without any problems," Grayson says with a sparkle in his eye.

"You are taking me as your date, right? I must get designers to start creating my dress. I've got to look the part too, you know. This will be so much fun. Grayson, thank you for bringing me here and sharing this part of your life with me. It's amazing. You'll have to give me a tour. Does it look as authentic inside?" I'm still in awe at how exquisite it is. I know I'm just blabbing on and on, but I'm so flabbergasted by the sight of this.

"Naturally I'm taking you as my date. Actually, I was going to ask you today when I gave you a tour of the chapel, but I guess that's not necessary anymore," Grayson teases.

"Well in that case, I'll ask you to forget about my blabbering so you can officially ask me when you give me that tour of the chapel anyway," I say with a wink.

As we pull up to the parking area, I don't wait for Grayson to open my door. I jump out of his car and take a deep breath, closing my eyes and smelling the wisteria in the air. My mom would love this place.

Feeling Grayson put his arms around my waist makes me smile as he pulls me against his chest. "I was going to open your door, but something tells me you like this place," he whispers in my ear.

"I more than like it, I love it. I want a castle of my very own now. This looks like paradise, a dream come true. No wonder Hawkins doesn't like leaving this place. I wouldn't either." Just as I finish my sentence, I see Hawkins riding down a hillside towards us on a huge Clydesdale horse, solid black except for the long white hair around its feet. He's only wearing jeans, no shirt, no shoes. Wow. I have to admit, he looks damn good.

Seeing him on horseback like that makes me wonder how the hell I'm going to get Grayson to ride a horse barefoot and shirtless. I need that visual for myself. Following behind him is Jackson, Clay and Stevens on apricot Clydesdales. It is a sight I will not soon forget. My roomies would have loved to have witnessed this. I can't wait to tell them. Next time I'll have to be rude and invite them to come with me.

Turning in Grayson's arms, I say, "Hawkins even has horses here?! You have to take me horseback riding and show me the land. It's been ages since I've been on a horse, and never on a Clydesdale. They are so huge and beautiful."

"I think I can do that. He has a really nice barn in the back. Stevens has brought him all kinds of rescue animals too - goats, sheep, cows and a few others. There are a couple of lakes here too, with some good fishing. Hawkins owns this mountain. He's always telling us he's waiting for all of us to come and build up here with him. It's very beautiful, I'll even admit it. Several of the guys stay here a lot of the time. Hawkins is not left alone that often," Grayson shares with me.

From all the intel Tony has gotten on the guys, I know all about Hawkins and why he is the way he is, but I'm not about to act like I know all he's been through, or how he suffers from severe PTSD. That story is for Hawkins to tell me himself, or Grayson when he feels I need to know. I'll just play dumb for now.

Hawkins is the first to reach us, getting off his horse with such ease and grace, holding the reins as he walks over to us. "Hey Riggs, glad you and the little lady could make it." He gives me a head bob. "Hello to you as well Lexy. I hope you're hungry. Isabella has been here cooking all morning. She kicked us out about an hour ago because we kept stealing her desserts. Fitz, the pussy, stayed with her. He wouldn't even come horseback riding with us. He said, '*since Bella can't ride, he wouldn't either.*' If you didn't know Lexy, Isabella is knocked up, and I'm guessing that being pregnant means horseback riding is a no-no in his books."

Walking over to him and his horse, I ask, "May I pet

him?" He nods, so I reach up and pet the horse on his big head. He is so gorgeous; his black hair has a blue sheen to it. "What's his name? He's just so beautiful. I've never seen a solid black Clydesdale before."

"It's Mezzanotte," Hawkins says with a wink.

"Okay Hawkins, is this your way of telling me you speak Italian or is his name really Mezzanotte?" I ask with a giggle, as Midnight nudges me with his head for me to continue petting him.

"No, I don't speak Italian, but that is his name. I bought him and two of my other horses from an Italian man years ago. Isn't that right Riggs?" Hawkins says removing the horse's lead, as Jackson, Stevens and Clay get off their horses.

"That is correct. I remember him well myself. He was an older gentleman, very proper, but very picky who he let buy his horses. He fell in love with your place and knew this would be a good safe home for them," Riggs answers.

Out of the corner of my eye, I see the biggest dog I've ever seen in my life run up to Stevens and start rubbing his enormous head against his leg. Stevens squats down and gives the dog a big hug. "Mojo, I told you I'd be coming right back. You should have followed us. A little exercise would do you some good big guy. I think you'd like it down at the lake, but you won't leave Mommy for ten minutes, just like Daddy. You gotta stay right in Isabella's sight don't ya?" He gives him a big kiss between his eyes.

"Wow! That is the biggest dog I've ever seen! I have to get one of those too. I'll have to ask Isabella where I can get a puppy." Walking over to Stevens and Mojo, I put my hand out for Mojo to sniff, and then start petting him too.

"I guess we're invisible," Jackson says from behind me.

Not even looking towards him I say, "Hello Jackson. Sorry, but this dog deserves all my attention. Don't you, Mojo?" As I continue to rub him behind the ears, I can hear Grayson laughing.

"Whatever. Yo, Riggs. I don't care about being ignored for a dog, but I'm going in for some fettucine and a little bit of everything else. I'm not waiting any longer. I'm a growing boy and need my food. I don't care if I have to bitch-slap Fitz, he better make his woman feed us. Sending us outside and out of 'her' kitchen is bullshit. We only stole one tray of Krispy treats! She has a shit-load of desserts in there," Jackson says as he swats his horse on the butt, making him take off running and the other horses follow.

"Jackson we're going in right now. You can wait a few seconds more. Where are your manners?" Grayson teases.

"Good afternoon, ma'am. I hope these rowdy boys aren't causing you any grief." Clay says, taking off his black cowboy hat and bowing to me while I'm still petting Mojo.

I know he is no more cowboy than I am, but he does pull it off quite nicely. He even has on dirty cowboy boots like a real cowboy. Standing up I look at him, "It's all good Clay, but nice of you to ask. I expect all of you to get a lot more rowdy before the day is over. Now, let's go get some... what do they call it in those cowboy movies? Let's go grab some grub, or is it vittles?" I say with a wink to Clay, and all the guys laugh. We all make our way into Hawkins' castle.

It's just as stunning inside. Leaning back and looking up this ceiling is fascinating with the huge high beams. Oh, those would be so fun to climb. I can't find words for its beauty. There's all wood and leather furniture, and what looks like fur rugs, everywhere. There are even several suits of armor on each side of the door. As the guys walk in, they pat the armor and say a greeting to Lance. I can't control my laughter at that one.

Some of the things around the house make you think you've walked back in time. There're big shields and swords hanging above the fireplace. I wonder if he keeps any of them sharp? I'd love to feel the weight of those swords in my hand and see how heavy they are and if I could work with them.

"Good afternoon Lexy. Come on into the kitchen and join the rest of us," Brenda calls to me. She's Stevens' sister and you can see the resemblance in their face and eyes, but she has dark brown hair to his light brown. She hasn't changed much, just matured into a stunning beauty. I wonder if she remembers me.

"Hi, Brenda," I say as the guys keep talking to each other about challenges after lunch. We follow her into the kitchen. The food smells so good, I hear my stomach grumble. I'm wondering if any of the girls helped Isabella cook, or did she do it all herself?

Everyone is happily talking to each other as we walk into the kitchen. Mojo is still beside me, I think I have a new friend. I can't help rubbing him behind the ear as we walk. This kitchen is massive as well, and everything looks as authentic as the rest of the house. It has the biggest kitchen counter I've ever seen. Isabella has on an apron and is cooking away.

Every Camelot Brother and sister is in here. To my relief, Tony is here with Sarah and I'm thinking the other guy is Thomas, her gay best friend that I've heard so much about on Facebook.

"She's here, Isabella. We can eat now? Come here Lexy, you have to meet my best friend, Thomas." Sarah says, waving me over to the far side of the counter.

"Sarah, do you think I can do the introductions? I would like her to meet all the Brothers first," Grayson says, shaking his head at his sister. She smirks and flips him off.

"Whatever. Welcome to the boy's club, Lexy. We're here as tokens, as you can see." Her voice is dripping with sarcasm, but she does say it with a smile.

Ignoring her, Grayson continues, "You saw all the guys at the club the other night, but I'd like to introduce you to each one personally, if that's alright."

"That's fine. Let's see if I can tell you who each of them is.

I might surprise you." Winking at Grayson, I walk over to the bar counter with him right behind me, his big hand on my hip.

"Hello Spencer, Mr. GQ of the Camelot Brothers, and the lawyer," I say with a smile, as I shake his hand.

"Hello Lexy, it's nice to meet you. And you're correct on both counts. I am the lawyer and can easily pull off the GQ part as well. I am the best dressed Brother," he says with a snicker.

Turning, I shake Clausen's hand. "And you are CEO of Camelot Enterprise and Clausen, brother to Isabella."

"You are correct again. But I may have to debate with you about Spencer being Mr. GQ. I have just as much style as he does. I look damn good in my suit," Clausen says with a wink and a firm squeeze to my hand.

"Okay Clausen, no flirting with my woman," Grayson tells him, leaning over me and punching him in the shoulder.

Ignoring him, I walk over to Liam. "Hello, Bishop. I love your chariot. You must give me a ride on that when I come to visit at Camelot Security. Rumor has it you're the sweetest of this bunch," I add with a wink to him.

"That I am, and I'll give you a ride any time," he replies, laughing as he realizes his own joke.

"Hey, I didn't expect you to be so bold Bishop. I'd really hate to have to kick your ass. No joking like that with Lexy," Grayson says, now punching Bishop in the shoulder.

"You're fine Bishop." Turning to Grayson, I give him a teasing mean look "Don't let Riggs pick on you like that, or I'll have to kick his ass for you."

Both of them start laughing as Bishop replies, "Oh, I have my evil ways of taking the Big Guy down. Riggs doesn't scare me, Lexy."

"Good to know. I'd put my money on you any day," I say, hearing Grayson laugh behind me as I walk on over to the next group of Brothers.

"Hello Hunter, manager of the clubs, and Gregory, or should I address you as Dr. Gregory?" I say teasingly with yet another wink. Both of them shake my hand and chuckle.

"Hey Riggs, you're the one that has to control your woman. She's the one that is winking at all of us with those incredible eyes and smiling. She's the flirt!" Hunter teases Grayson.

Grayson quickly pulls me into his arms. "Okay Lexy, no flirting with the Brothers. I'm surprised you do know each of them."

Turning myself in his incredible arms, I look up at Grayson with a smile. "Would you like to know how?"

"Yeah, I'd love to know," Grayson says, looking into my eyes, causing my heart to flutter. I notice Hawkins, Carpenter and Jackson are now standing behind him.

Not wanting to fall into a trance staring into his eyes, I step out of Grayson's arms. Playfully, I stick my hand out to him like I want to shake his hand.

"Let me introduce myself to you. I have another alias. Hello Grayson Riggs, I'm Alexa Bellamy, friends with all of the Brothers on Facebook."

Hearing a couple of the Brothers gasp is enough to make me giggle. Grayson smiles so bright as he shakes his head. "So, you mean to tell me Ms. Bellamy is you? And you've been friends with all of us on Facebook for years? Spying on us while we were clueless?"

"Wow Grayson, you are a genius. Yes, I'm the one and only Alexa Bellamy, aka Lexy Rogers. One and the same. Come on, I had to make sure you and Stevens made it back okay from your time in the military. It wasn't safe for me to put my real name out there, then or now, so I just became friends with Sarah, which lead to me slowly becoming friends with all of you.

"Oh, and Grayson, some of the Brothers have more than one account. But I wouldn't go throwing them under the bus, now would I? Brenden, Cameron, Asher, Gabriel, Sammy."

Now everyone is laughing, and Grayson pulls me back into his arms looking down into my eyes again. "Is that your way of telling me some of the brothers were picking up on you? Do I need to kick some asses?" Grayson teases. Before I can say anything, Jackson starts talking.

"Brother, I had no idea I was chatting with your girl. It was a couple of years ago. She was just hot and mysterious. She never sent me pictures or anything, I swear. But, umm, she may have a dick pic or two of me." Jackson slowly raises his hands in surrender and starts walking backwards to the other side of the room as he continues. "But Brother, I'm being up front and honest here. You can't go holding that against a man. You know I was just having some fun."

"What the fuck! You sent her pictures of your dick? What are you, fifteen?" Grayson calls out, sounding a bit pissed. Just as Spencer stands up and walks over to us.

Not being able to compose myself any longer, I bust out laughing. "Don't worry Gabe, I mean Jackson, I have never shown anyone your, how can I say this… unique artwork?" Shaking my head, I smile at him. Just as Carpenter speaks up and does the same thing, he starts apologizing to Grayson. Not to me for sending those crazy dick pics, but Grayson.

"Dude, Riggs old buddy, you know we'd never do that kind of shit if we had any clue you were interested in her. You know how crazy I get after a few too many beers at night alone with 'Dick-a-lick-ious.' She thought they were funny. Come on man, it wasn't like Jackson here man, just sending boner pics. My dick was fully clothed. You know what I mean Brother! You can't hold that shit against us, or try and beat the shit out of us either. That was at least two years ago, maybe longer!"

Grayson mumbles "fuck!" under his breath, leaning his head back with his eyes closed, looking up at the ceiling, trying to compose himself, taking deep breaths. I'm still laughing my head off, trying to catch my breath and wiping the corners of my eyes. I've never told anyone about those pictures of Carpenter's dick, all dressed up in different kinds of outfits. He even had backdrops for some of those pictures. I mean you could tell it was an erect dick, but it always had clothes on. I found them totally entertaining and hilarious. I know he'll be a blast for the right girl, but that girl is not me.

Sarah runs around the kitchen to me squealing with both Tony and Thomas behind her, "Girl, you cannot keep that shit a secret from me! You have pictures of their dicks? You have to show us! Please tell me, who else sent you dick pics? Do you know any more dick names? Dick-a-lick-ious is Carpenter's dick's name?! Oh my God, that's freaking hilarious. He puts clothes on it?!"

Isabella calls from behind the stove, "Lexy, please tell me you do not have any pictures of Henry? If you do, you have to send me a copy and then delete them. Drake's dick is taken," she says with a chuckle, shaking her head.

"Hey! I did not send Lexy any dick pics. I have not sent anyone any. But honey, if you want some dick pics for yourself to admire Henry, when he's not around, feel free to take as many as you want tonight, before I have my wicked way with that body of yours," Drake says as he puts his arms around Isabella's waist and starts kissing up her neck.

"Henry's all yours, Isabella. No one but Carpenter and Jackson sent me dick pics," I reply still laughing as Tony, Thomas and Sarah are still looking at me with their arms across their chests. "Sorry, I am not sharing their dick pics. I think I deleted them anyway. They were on my secret iPad."

Grayson looks down at me saying, "Make sure you fucking deleted them. And believe me, I'll beat the shit out of both of them Monday during our training session." Turning, he calls across the room to Carpenter and Jackson who are now talking to Tiffany, the head secretary for all of Camelot, and Brenda. "Hope you heard that, you 'dick Brothers'! You better be resting up this weekend cause your ass is mine at 5:30AM, Monday morning."

"That goes for me too. You boys ever heard of sexual harassment? We've talked about this before. You can be sued up the ass for childish shit like that. Come on you two, grow up. I'll be there at 5:30 too." Spencer calls out to them as well. Both Carpenter and Jackson flip him off.

I can't help but laugh at their behavior.

"Lex, you never keep things like that from me! You know better than that. We're best buds and share everything. Come on, girlfriend," Tony says, pretending to be all hurt.

"Get over it, Tony. Excuse me, but don't even bring up keeping secrets. 'Dating Sarah', ring any secret bells?" I say to him with one eyebrow raised.

"That's different. You wouldn't approve, and I really have a thing for her," Tony responds instantly.

"Lexy, sweetheart, this is my only chance to see their dicks. Come on, girlfriend. You must have a copy somewhere. I need to see this dressed up dick," Thomas says, smiling at me with such a pleading look. "Oh, by the way, nice to meet you. I've heard so many nice things about you. Can't wait to become buddies." He continues as he gives me a hug.

"Sorry Thomas, no can do. Even if I had them, which I don't, that wouldn't be right," I reply shaking my head. I can't believe we're all standing around talking about dicks.

"Don't worry Thomas, we all want to see them. I'll hack into her old iPad later tonight and see what I can find," Tony tells him, turning and laughing in my face.

"Tony, you better not hack into my iPad or computer. Some things are sacred to a girl, and my iPad is one of them." I shake my finger at him, just as Hawkins walks up behind me, looking over at Tony.

"Tony, I don't recommend hacking into any of Lexy's things. I'll help protect her from your hacking if need be,"

Hawkins tells him with a smile as he places his hand lightly on my shoulder, in a protective manner. Grayson is just watching to see where this conversation goes, I'm sure.

"Well, well, the great Hawkins finally speaks to me," Tony says, very sarcastically. "I've tried talking to you on several occasions, and not only will you not look my way, but you completely ignore me. We could really be good buddies if you give a guy a chance," Tony softens his voice and winks at Hawkins. "I must say Hawkins, you walking around all day without a shirt in those low hanging jeans, adds to the wonderful view of your place, doesn't it Sarah and Thomas?" Tony teases.

"Tony, I'm used to it. I grew up with Hawkins. And at times I've questioned if Thomas only wants to be my friend so he can admire my brother and all of his friends. You should come over unannounced sometime. You might catch Hawkins completely naked. I've done that myself a time or two. He swims in his moat regularly, butt-ass naked," Sarah says, teasing them both.

I can't help but laugh again. I know now that I'll always call before I come over here. The last thing I want carved into my memory is Hawkins' nakedness. Thomas starts whining, "Sarah, how many times have I told you I want pictures, or video?!"

Tony interrupts, getting the conversation back onto more important things "Hawkins, I'm also very aware of the blocking software you have here, making sure no one takes pictures or basically does anything using the web while up at your place. Very nice set up you got going on. Let me introduce myself a bit better to you. I'm Tony Jarvis, Lexy's IT guy. I set up all her security at her clubs, home, phones… everything. I am 'Stark Enterprise'. Heard of me?" Tony says with such confidence.

Sarah turns to Tony with her phone in her hand. "I still

have internet here. I always have. What are you talking about?"

"That's okay Sarah, he basically blocks anyone that's not directly a part of Camelot. Am I right Hawkins? Could Lexy use her phone from here?"

"She'll be able to after we eat. I'm giving her the tour and setting all those things up for her then. And yes Tony, I've heard of your company. You have even beat us with a couple of bids in business. But I also know you from somewhere else. We've shared intel before, both when you were here in America and before. I'm betting we helped each other quite a bit in Italy once," Hawkins says with a wink of his own.

"Then why so rude before, not ever talking to me?" Tony asks.

"Unlike you Tony, I only talk when I have something to say. Which protecting Lexy's secrets I also think is important, so I'll help her if she needs it."

"Well, she doesn't need your help. Lexy is my best friend and I was only teasing her because I already know all of Lexy's secrets. We go back a very long time. I've got her back, and she's always had mine. I wouldn't be alive today without her, but that story is for another day. Isn't that right, Lex?"

"Yes. You are my dearest friend, and we have each other's backs always. And that is definitely a story for another day," I say wanting this subject to change. As Tony turns the conversation back to Hawkins, I see Grayson has taken in every word we said. I so want to punch Tony myself right now.

"Just remember Hawk, if you ever need my help again somewhere else, you know how to find me," Tony winks at him again, checking him out from head to toe this time.

"Stop that, you perv. Didn't I just hear you say you have a thing for Sarah? I'd expect that from Thomas, not you," Hawkins practically scolds Tony. "Maybe things like that have also kept me from talking to you in public."

Chuckling, Tony teases Hawkins even more, "Dude, I was

just having some fun. Come on, even you would admire another dude if he had a body as sculpted as yours," Tony pulls off his own shirt and flexes his chest muscles. "See, I know I have a hot body, and am very confident in showing it to anyone. Feel free to look away, it doesn't bother me. In fact, it makes me feel good about myself, knowing that people acknowledge all my hard work in getting my body looking this damn good."

Sarah reaches over and gives his nipple ring a little pull. I hear Thomas sigh beside me. Hawkins, Grayson and I can't help but laugh. Tony pulls her in for a kiss making Grayson say, "Sarah, that's fucking gross. Do you always have to be touching him and sucking face? Gawd."

Isabella interrupts and announces loudly to everyone, "Okay everyone, lunch will be served in five minutes, and nobody will be served without a shirt on. I cooked it, and I make the rules. My mother would have a heart attack if you guys were to eat lunch at the table without a shirt. Geez, don't any of you have manners? First, you try to steal desserts before the meal, and now you're having a shirtless competition after all this dick talk. Come on, people! We're supposed to be making a good impression on Lexy."

Everyone starts laughing. Tony puts his shirt back on and Hawkins shakes his head, calling out in a little boys' voice, "Yes, Momma Isabella. I'll put a shirt on, just for you. Do I have to put shoes on too?"

"As long as your feet stay under the table, I couldn't care less. But get a shirt on," Isabella waves her arms in the air towards the bar counter. "Everyone, we're eating buffet style so get into a nice orderly line and ladies first. Grab a plate and get all you want now, because believe me, these pigs will not leave anything for you, if you think you're coming back for seconds. There won't be anything left," Isabella instructs, grabbing a plate and handing it to me. "Lexy, you are the guest of honor, so you go first. I'll follow right behind you.

Grayson can be the second man to get his food after Drake," she continues with a wink at her man. "We'll get a good seat at the table and yes, we can save a seat for our men. Just wait till you see this real authentic dining hall. It has an enormous table and big chandelier overhead with faux candle lighting. Hawkins' castle is something you don't soon forget."

Taking the plate, I smile, saying, "I can't wait, and thank you. It all looks so yummy. Are you really going to make the guys wait till after all the ladies have gotten their food? Aren't you afraid at all?"

"Nope, because if any of them give me lip, they know I'll cut them off. They all love my cooking, and the thought of me not letting them have my food, well, I could probably get any of them to do anything for me," Isabella says with an innocent smile.

"Oh, so you're the one I need to hire to teach me how to cook. I can only make eggs, french toast, pancakes as of yesterday and sandwiches. But my uncle swears he is giving me the family secret recipe for pesto when he comes for a visit in a couple of months."

"Sure honey, I'd love too. Your mom didn't teach you how to cook either? My mother didn't believe a proper woman should be in a hot kitchen. That's what the staff is for," she says with a snooty attitude. "But as you can tell, I didn't listen to my mother as a young girl, and I surely am not listening to her now. I love cooking, and Drake loves my cooking and so do all the guys. I'll give you my number, just give me a call," Isabella says as she fills her plate, impressing me with how much food she takes. She doesn't eat like a bird either. Well, maybe she's eating so much because she is feeding two. Laughing to myself I wonder what's my excuse for filling my plate to overflowing.

Feeling the need to share a bit about myself, I add, "It was my father who didn't allow it. But I'm determined to be completely independent and be able to do it all myself. So, thank you. I'll be calling you for sure very soon." This will give me yet another friend of my very own, and I'm looking forward to getting to know all these Camelot ladies.

Lunch is out of this world. Isabella can really cook. It's a mixture of American and Italian, and I can't wait to learn some of these dishes. She really did a marvelous job, and the desserts are to die for. Isabella's double chocolate fudge cake is the one I want to learn first. I actually threaten Jackson that if he takes the last piece, I'll have to stab him with my fork. They all get a laugh out of that. But Jackson lets me have the last piece, smart man, but he makes it clear it was only this once, since it's my first time at Hawkins'.

Now it's time for the grand tour I've been dying for. Hawkins shows me almost all of his exquisite home. Some areas he says are off limits to all but him, which I can understand. With his issues, he is very secretive, as he feels he needs to be. He is very close to Isabella and all the Brothers. They probably know all his secrets as well. But I do believe Hawkins is a bit closer to Isabella than the other girls in the group.

His gym is as nice as mine was back home. Oh, how I wish I could work out there, with the gorgeous view of the grounds outside. The indoor pool he told me you can dive into, and if you can hold your breath long enough, you can swim underground and out into his moat. After seeing all of this, I so want my very own castle. He tells me his dream is that one day, all of the Brothers would come up here and build homes of their own. Hawkins longs for them to all be neighbors and have their own private community. Now that would be a dream come true for me as well.

Hawkins then takes me into what looks like a massive control center. "Okay Lexy, I need to scan your hand and give you a code. This will give you the ability to get into the club, and a lot of Camelot Security and other facilities. Riggs has claimed you and wants you to have the freedom to come and go as you like. That also includes his own place."

"Are you kidding me? After only forty-eight hours, I'll be able to get into Grayson's home? The club? You guys trust me that much?" I have to ask, looking between the two of them as Hawkins takes my hand and places it on a screen. Grayson just stands there and smiles at me.

"Yes, babe. I want to prove to you I'm serious about us. I trust you completely. You can even access the internet, unlike Tony," Grayson says with a chuckle.

"I can't believe this. Thank you," I say as I continue to look between the two of them.

Hawkins chuckles, "Lexy, it's not like you can get access to any computer systems or anything. It gets you in the door. At Camelot Security, Tiffany will greet you and take you where you need to go, and yeah, this gets you into the club and up to our private bar area anytime. But it doesn't get you upstairs into the computer center just yet. I know who your best friend is, and I know he'd be hacking into our system as fast as I would be hacking into your system, given the chance. But we do trust you more than him," he tells me as he scans each of my fingers. All I'm hoping is that he can't find out any information from my fingerprints.

"Okay, all done. I'm going to let Riggs show you his room here. All the Brothers have one. Your handprint now gives you access to his room here anytime as well. That is something Riggs requested. Now I'll see you two outside in a bit. I have a few wagers I need to make before everyone starts competing. I sure hope you'll compete in some of the challenges. I'd put my money on you over any of the girls," Hawkins says as he types a few more commands into his computer, before he heads to the door.

Not being able to stop myself I ask, "Hawkins, do you mean to say I can only compete with the girls? What if I want to challenge some of the guys? It depends on what the challenges are and if I want to show any of you up," I have to tease Hawkins.

Hawkins stops and turns around to me, him and Grayson are both laughing as he says, "Okay, first off, we bet on our challenges. Starting bet is $100, so if you're wanting to lose your money, that's fine with me. I'm sure there isn't a Brother around that'd be nice enough to let a girl win with one hundred bucks on the line, but hey, give it your best shot. I wish you the best of luck."

"Hawkins, I don't lose, and I'll gladly take that bet and add to it. I'll see you at the competitions." Damn it, I can never walk away from a freaking challenge. God, now I'll have to find a mild challenge that will not give away too much about myself.

Grayson's arms go around me and I feel the tremor of his body as he tries to stop laughing. "Baby, you don't have to waste your money on a silly bet. The Brothers will bet on anything, and they will not bat an eye taking your money either. It would also give them bragging rights to tease you. You might want to think twice before you do that."

Now I will for sure be showing up one of these guys. No freaking way am I backing down now. They think a girl can't beat them? Well, they are about to be schooled by this little girl.

"Grayson, are you telling me you don't think I can beat any of the Brothers at anything? Well, I recommend you be careful where you bet. You could be the one losing money if you only bet on the Brothers. Now let's go check out your room so I can leave my bag in there. I have some money to win."

10

THE COMPETITION

Grayson

*M*y little tough, fearless woman, she doesn't know what she's getting into. I've trained these guys myself. She's going to be slaughtered no matter what challenges she takes. Oh well, looks like she needs to learn for herself. It will be fun watching her give it a try. Several of the sisters have tried and embarrassed themselves in the past, and it looks like Lexy is a bit more stubborn than them.

On our walk to my bedroom in the Brothers wing of Hawkins' house, rather castle, I look down at my little woman whose gorgeous eyes are as big as saucers as she looks around.

"You have to be kidding me! Hawkins has a whole wing of this castle just for you guys? Do you bring dates here to impress and bang them?" Lexy asks being a smartass.

"I personally have never brought a girl up here to 'bang' as you put it. This is for us to hang out, clear our heads and spend time with Hawkins. We've spent several holidays up here as well. Our parents and the girls are in a completely different wing. In our business, we're lucky we've never had to have a lockdown, but if we did, this is where all our families would come. It's the safest place.

"That's one reason when Isabella was having her troubles a couple of months ago, she stayed here with Hawkins. But those two and their friendship goes back years. If you've been watching all of us like I think you have, you probably read about it in the news or heard about it from Tony," I tease her, to see if she'll give anything away.

"Okay Grayson, I know you're testing me for info so I'll play along. Yes, I know all about Isabella's kidnapping and rescue, but I didn't know that Isabella and Hawkins' friendship went back years."

"I'll let you in on a secret most don't know. We all knew Isabella since she was about three years old. Our families were all close. Some of our parents were friends as kids or met in college and soon after. They are all still real close, even if we all grew up very differently. Any more questions I can answer? I'll always tell you whatever you'd like to know," I tell her with a wink as we reach my bedroom door.

"Here we are. Place your hand on the scanning pad and let's see if it works." I watch as Lexy lifts her small hand and places it on the large screen, hearing the click of the door open a couple of seconds later. Her perfectly plump lips break into a big smile and her clear blue eyes sparkle with excitement as I push the door open for her to walk in.

"Oh my ever-loving God! Why don't you live here? It's gorgeous. Did Hawkins decorate, or did you hire someone? This bed is enormous." She tosses her oversized purse onto my bed as she continues to look around. "I've never seen a larger bed in my life. And you mean to tell me you've never brought anyone here?" Lexy's asks as she walks towards the wine and black drapes, pulling them back.

"I told you, I've never brought a girl here. I'll give you another tidbit of information too: I've never stayed the night with a girl. I may have had sex with a lot of women in my lifetime, but I'm gone before the sun comes up." A shocked expression covers her face as that sinks in.

"So you're telling me you have sex with a girl and leave after you have your fill? Wow, that does surprise me." She's standing by the balcony window holding the drapes in her hand, not even looking out at the view yet. I can't help but smile at the shocked and questioning look on her beautiful heart shaped face.

"Why do you look so shocked? My mother preached at me all my life, to always be open and honest with the girl I'm with. If it's just sex, let them know that I'm not looking for a relationship. To me, that means you don't stay the night with a woman you aren't building a future with. Just like you don't give them flowers or jewelry unless you're getting serious."

I watch as she smiles again and replies, "Wow, I like your mom already. Those are some good rules to live by. So I'm guessing I'll be the first woman you spend the night with? And is that why you've sent me a long-stemmed red rose daily since Friday night?" Lexy asks, letting go of the curtain and wrapping her arms around my waist.

"Yes, you will be the first woman I stay the night with, and you'll keep getting those red roses as well as an occasional white rose every day of your life. It's up to you to figure out why I chose those colors. But staying the night with you, that won't happen any time soon because I want to wait till you trust me enough to share with me everything about you, like I'm willing to share everything about me. I can understand you've had a tough life, with an overbearing father. But I remember Aless, and how once upon a time, we sat on Stevens' deck and both of us were open and honest, sharing things we've never shared with anyone else. I want that and more with you. I want to know you better than Tony does. And as long as you can't be that open and honest with me, I can wait to make love to you." I watch as she blinks her eyes, looking up at me still.

"You're telling me you can wait to have sex with me until I tell you all my deep dark secrets, things I'm protecting you from, and memories I don't to relive again? And what if that takes me months, or a year? You're telling me we won't make love until then? That also means you aren't going to fuck anyone else right? Because this girl doesn't play that game."

"Neither does this guy. I can take care of myself. Or we can do as we did the other night as well. I didn't say I was keeping my hands off you, I just said we aren't making love until you can trust me. Believe me, there are a lot of things we can do to satisfy each other without sex. I didn't name my dick 'Sir Vulva-ate-her' for nothing."

Lexy throws her head back, cracking up laughing. I can't resist the temptation of her neck, so I lean down and start kissing and lightly sucking on her soft skin. Her laughter stops and a soft moan leaves her lips. She pulls away saying, "Okay 'Sir Vulva-ate-her', that is something I'll never do until I'm in a dedicated relationship with someone, and I'll possibly save that for marriage. That, to me, is the most intimate thing a man and woman can do, being all open and spread out for him to satisfy me like that. That is something I can wait for," she tells me very seriously.

"You're teasing, right? You've never had a man go down on you like that? Not ever?"

"Nope. I'm not a virgin, but that is something I've not done, and I can wait on it. So, in our messing around you can count that one off your list. You can wait for making love, we can also wait to do that. Believe me, I can take care of myself too. It's much safer."

Oh shit, this isn't going to be as easy as I first thought. Looks like a lot of dry humping and handling 'Sir' myself. But wait, she didn't say anything about touching each other. Maybe I can take care of her and she can return the favor. Thinking stuff like this has gotten 'Sir' rock hard. Hearing

Lexy gasp and pull out of my arms breaks me out of my thoughts.

"Oh Grayson, there is wisteria all over your balcony!" She opens the double doors and walks out onto the large balcony that is covered with drooping lavender wisteria. The fragrance is so fresh and sweet. "You have no idea how this takes me back home. My mother had a wisteria garden. Our entire compound had it growing everywhere, but her garden was breathtaking, full of pathways and archways of it everywhere." I can tell her mind has taken her back to that place. I see her close her eyes and just breathe it in.

Now I love the fact that my balcony is covered with this evil stuff. The thorns on these trees are sometimes three inches long and can easily rip the flesh from your body. But if Lexy loves them, I'll be planting them everywhere at our own castle. I've decided. Once Carpenter is finished with building the chapel and reception hall, it's time to break ground up here and build my woman her own castle.

"Thank you Grayson, for sharing this place. It means the world to me. I now have a wonderful fantasy to dream about, and that is making love with you here. But since you set down your guidelines, it doesn't mean I won't try every trick in the books to seduce you into making love to me sooner. I do love a good challenge, and as this is our third date, I had every intention of making love to you tonight after you took me home from dinner at your parents' house," Lexy says with half a smile. Oh shit, she is going to tease the hell out of me.

"Is that how you plan on playing this?" I say, grabbing her arm and pulling her over to me to capture a taste of that mouth. Every time our lips touch, the passion is explosive. As our tongues and mouth battle for control, I squeeze her full heart-shaped ass and lift her up to me. She wraps her legs around my waist as I walk over to rest her ass on the edge of the balcony, the same way I did the first day we made out on Stevens' deck in New Jersey.

"Oh Grayson, don't stop," Lexy moans as she runs her hands up my chest and neck and into my hair. I can't stop my own moan as she lightly pulls my hair, claiming my mouth again. I can't keep my hips still as I start rubbing my granite hard cock into her core. Reaching around the waistband on her leggings, I slide my hand into the front of her pants.

Hearing her deep moan, I continue my path to her pussy. I move her thong over to the side and slowly rub her clit in a hard-circular motion, still grinding my hips into her. I'm so close, I just have to touch her more. I slide my finger down further until I feel one finger slide into her very wet canal. Oh fuck, she is tighter than I thought. I can feel her pussy contracting tightly around my finger.

"Oh fuck, Grayson, I'm so close. Don't stop, faster, faster. I need more," she whispers as she reaches between us and starts squeezing and rubbing my cock in her small hand over my tight jeans.

That's it, I know neither of us is going to last long as I try even harder to move my hand in these tight legging of hers. I start finger fucking her faster as I feel her rotate her hips forward. As much as I want to stay on this balcony, I can't. I need to do this right. I pull away, hearing Lexy whimper as I pull my finger from her and remove my hand from her pants.

Looking into her very dilated, sexy-as-hell eyes, she watches as I lick her wetness from my fingers. Oh, now I can't wait to completely taste her folds while nibbling on them and fuck her with my tongue. Shaking my head to clear out those thoughts, that's not happening for a while.

Lifting her off the edge of the balcony, I turn us back towards my bedroom. I can't wait to get her onto my bed and out of these pants, taking care of her like I've dreamed of for years. "Babe, we're going to do this right." Her slip-on big wedge heels hit the floor with a thud and it doesn't take me more than a second to have her on my bed, my hands instantly going to the waistband of her pants. I pause, looking her in her eyes again. "Baby, if you ever want me to stop, just say so. I can always do something else. Right now, I'm going to take these pants off you and finger fuck you till you scream my name. Any objections?"

Lexy smiles and lifts her ass so I can easily peel her leggings off. Oh hell, she has on a bright red and black thong covering her nicely groomed triangle of hair. I rip off my shirt and take off my belt faster than I thought possible, as I move to lay down beside her. Lexy sits up just enough to pull her top off, showing me her massive breasts in the sexiest bright red satin bra covered in black lace I've ever seen. My face goes to her breasts, just to lightly lick her cleavage.

"Grayson I'm going to undo your pants. You didn't say I couldn't touch 'Sir' and I'm dying to touch him while you touch me," she says with a sexy-as-hell voice.

I know this isn't going to last, we're both on the edge. I watch as her small hands go to undo my pants. Fuck that, I quickly stand up and rip them off, leaving my black snug boxer briefs on. Laying back down beside her, I claim her mouth as our hands start roaming over each other's bodies.

Briefly pulling away from our kiss, I look down towards Lexy's pussy, seeing she has already spread her legs for me and her thong is still pulled to the side. I can see her wetness. I take her hand and rub her palm over herself, making sure to press it against her clit. I then put it into my boxers and she instinctively wrap's her hand around 'Sir' as far as she can and starts stroking him. I only watch for a second before I claim her mouth again, our tongues continue to battle for control.

Pushing her legs further apart, I press the palm of my hand firmly on her clit and slide my finger back into her ready and waiting tight pussy. I start sliding it in and out of her with deep strokes, making sure to keep firm pressure on her clit at the same time. She rotates her hips into the same motion. I can feel her tightening and releasing around my finger.

She pulls away from our kiss and moans, "Grayson, I need more, faster, harder."

Fuck, this woman is going to be the death of me. I thrust my own hips into Lexy's hand as she twists and squeezes my cock with her every stroke.

Realizing how small and tight she is, I take my time sliding a second finger into her tight canal, giving her what she wants. Neither of us can catch our breath we pull away from our kiss and just watch ourselves pleasure each other.

Her hand tightens around my cock as she throws her head back. "Oh God Grayson, I'm going to come. I'm going to come. Grayson... Grayson!" And with that, we both climax in perfect unison. There is nothing more satisfying then feeling that tight pussy of hers, rapidly contracting around my fingers as she rides out the tidal wave of her orgasm.

I lean over to her and kiss her slowly, with a tenderness that is new to me. Afterwards, I rest my forehead on hers saying, "Thank you, that was incredible."

"Yes, yes it was. I think this teasing and pleasing each other till I get you to break and make love to me will be quite enjoyable. But right now, we both need to get dressed again and I have to hang up my garment bag so my dress won't look like I slept in it," Lexy says as she sits up and grabs her over-sized purse, opening it and pulling out a small garment bag.

I'm still trying to catch my breath as she gets off the bed. I know I'll relive this moment over and over again in my mind. Watching her come apart and call out my name as she came... damn, that's a fantasy-turned-reality. What was that about a dress?

"Lexy, what did you just say about a dress?"

"Grayson, you're out of your mind if you think I'm meeting your parents for the first time in leggings and a top. No, I brought a dress and the things I need to freshen up. Now get a move on. Once I get out of the bathroom, we have to go down to the competitions. I have to decide which Brother's ass

I'm going to have to kick to prove to you that a girl can kick ass, you over-confident jock."

Chuckling I respond, "Wow, I need to wear you out a bit more next time, because that orgasm looks like it just gave you energy instead of knocking you on your ass."

"She walks back over to me and puts both hands on my cheeks as she says, "Grayson, sweetheart, I just needed that release so I wouldn't be thinking of you instead of concentrating on my slaughter of one of your Brothers. Don't worry, I'm not planning on embarrassing you yet, even if you do need to be taken down a few male macho notches. That can wait for another day." She gives me a quick peck on the lips and pats my cheeks as she grabs her leggings and heads for the bathroom.

I fall backwards on my bed laughing out loud, calling out to her between laughs, "Oh Lexy, this will be so much fun. I can't wait. Don't worry, I'll kick whichever Brother's ass that beats you when they tease you. Beating you is one thing, teasing you after their victory is another."

Now I can hear her laughing through the door. She calls back to me, "Grayson, I'll be the one laughing and teasing all of you that this little girl beat the shit out of one of the great Camelot Brothers," she finishes as she walks out the door with such confidence.

I don't know what she thinks she can beat one of us at, but I can't wait to see it for myself. I just don't think it's possible. She's maybe 5'3 if that, and possibly 130lbs, no way can she take one of us.

Lexy

Once we're outside, I can see that Hawkins has set up all kinds of activities, from horseshoes, to archery. He even has a knife tossing competition. I see Tony showing Sarah and Thomas how to throw a knife. I'm just laughing on the inside, knowing I could so easily blow their minds and kick their asses at several of these. Wow, they even have some sword fighting going on. I think it's Spencer and Clausen under those masks. They're doing pretty well, but I could so easily take either one of them. But not now. It's too soon to show off all my talents like that.

Tony calls over to Grayson and me, "Hey you two, wanna see who can toss a knife the best? I'll put my money on Lexy. What do you think big guy? You want to give it a try, Riggs?" Tony teases.

Grayson just shakes his head, laughing at him. "I think I'll pass for now, maybe later. But I'll gladly challenge you, Tony," Grayson counters.

"That's okay. I'm still working with your sister. She got close to actually hitting the outer ring on the target instead of missing it completely," Tony teases.

"Hey, I'm getting better. You said so yourself." Sarah insists.

I'm laughing at the two of them and their banter, when I notice Jackson and Carpenter racing up two ropes tied to the top of a massive tree. Stevens, Hawkins and Clay are cheering them on, standing off to the side. Hawkins is holding binoculars watching them very closely. As they race to the top of the tree, they tap it and start racing back down. Smiling as I walk over to them. I know I've found where I'm going to kick Hawkins' ass in his own backyard. Time to school these Camelot boys that they aren't invincible.

"I got my money on Jackson. He'll let go and drop to the ground if he thinks he's going to lose," Grayson says as he puts his arms around me, pulling my back into his chest.

"Is that the rule? You have to tap the top of the tree and then climb back down, first one to reach the ground wins?" I ask. I need to know the rules before I challenge Hawkins. I know I can make it up to the top of the tree without a problem. I've beaten several men in the Family that are Hawkins' size. I got this.

About six feet from the ground, Jackson does just as Grayson predicted. He lets go of the rope and drops to the ground, winning. All the Brothers start cheering for him and patting him on the back, giving him high fives. Once Carpenter hits the ground, he yells at Jackson, "You cheating mother fucker! That should be against the rules. I wish you'd break your damned leg. The only way you can beat me is by dropping the last six feet."

All the brothers start taunting him, calling him names and punching him.

"Loser," Clay says, punching him in the shoulder.

"You big pussy," Clausen says, walking over to join in the harassment.

"Sucker, you know how Jackson plays. How many times does he have to whoop your ass for you to learn?" Spencer says, joining the rest of the Brothers in the teasing.

"Shut up Carpenter, you whining pussy. I beat you, fucker, and that's all that matters. Hawkins made the rules. You have to tap the tree and be the first one back on the ground. The end. You lost, you big pussy. You're acting like a little bitch," Jackson says while giving Carpenter a pound on the back.

All the Brothers are being rowdy, pushing, teasing and joking around when Hawkins announces loudly over everyone, "Okay Jackson, I'm still the reigning champion of the rope race, and as the champion, I can challenge another winner at any point, so I'm challenging you, you cocky bastard."

"You evil fucker. Race someone else first. I just climbed it seconds ago, give me a minute to catch my breath, fucker," Jackson whines.

This is my chance. "Hawkins, I'll race you." Hearing the

gasps as all heads turn in my direction, I walk over to the ropes.

Grayson walks over to me, putting his hand on my shoulder. "Babe, you don't want to do that. You see how they are all picking on Carpenter because he lost? The Brothers will not be nice to you after Hawkins beats you. That's just the way the games go. I'm trying to spare you the humiliation."

That just pisses me off even more. Now I really have to kick Hawkins' ass. "So, you don't believe in me? You think Hawkins can beat me. You want to put a wager on that?"

"Lexy, you really want me to kick your little ass in front of everyone? I'm the reigning champion. None of the Brothers have beaten me. I will have no problem accepting your challenge, but you better be damn sure you can handle the aftermath," Hawkins says. He's so cocky I just want to nut-punch him.

Turning to Grayson I ask, "Do you want to take my wager or not? If I win, you have to be my slave for the rest of the night and only refer to me as 'Mistress'. And Hawkins, if I beat you, you have to let my girlfriends have a sleepover here, at your castle. Do you two except my wager? Oh ,and Hawkins, if I lose, I'll be your slave for twenty-four hours, but you better be ready to lose and deal with the fallout from my little ass." Turning around, I stick my round ass in his direction. "And if you haven't noticed, my ass is far from little."

All the Brothers start whistling and teasing. I see Tony, Sarah, Thomas and the rest of the girls come running our way when they realize something big is going on. Tony shouts, "I'm putting a hundred bucks on Lexy for the win!" I knew Tony would have my back. His antics make me want to laugh.

Holding back my laughter, I keep looking between Hawkins and Grayson, "Well Grayson, are you going to take my wager? If you think I'm going to lose, I'd have thought you'd want me to be your slave and call you 'Master', or are you actually scared I'll win?"

"You're on, babe. I'm not going to go easy on you either. You asked for it. Looks like you're more stubborn than I thought and need to learn a hard lesson for yourself," Grayson says, shaking his head as he pats Hawkins on the shoulder. "Don't humiliate her too bad. I still have to live with her," he says with a chuckle as he walks over to stand with the other Brothers still taunting us.

"Well Lexy, it looks like it's on. I hope you got a hundred bucks on you, 'cause you're about to lose it when I hand you your ass. And as for your girlie sleepover." He throws his head back and laughs before finishing, "Yeah, I'll take that bet too, because having you as my slave at the castle for twenty-four hours will piss the hell out of Riggs. Not counting the fact I'd be taping you calling me 'Master' and putting it on all his devices. Kicking your ass will be well worth it," Hawkins says, walking over and tugging on the rope.

Tony, Sarah, Thomas and the rest of the girls are gathered on my side. I'm shocked to see Isabella on my side as well. She's supporting me to win and not Hawkins. Nor is she standing by her man. I want to laugh when Fitz motions her over to him, and she just crosses her arms over her chest and shakes her head no.

Tony bends down and looks me in the eyes, whispering as he rubs my arm, "Lexy girl, you better kick his mother fucking ass. I got all my faith and trust in you. Not because I got money on you, but because I wanna see these cock-suckers, taken down a couple of notches. They don't know who they have in front of them. Time to give them a taste of your talents."

I reach up and kiss Tony on the cheek and putting both hands on each side of his face, I wink at him. "Go be my head cheerleader and get ready to party, because I'm going to hand him his ass and embarrass the shit out of him. Then I'm going to have fun humiliating Grayson when we go to his parents tonight. He'll have to call me 'Mistress' all night."

Tony bursts out laughing, throwing his arms around me and lifting me off the ground, spinning me around. "You got this, sweetheart."

Looking over at Grayson, I can see he doesn't look happy with Tony's scene. But right now, I couldn't give a rat's ass over his petty jealousy. I need to concentrate. I kick off my shoes and am thankful I have on tight leggings. I quickly tie my t-shirt in a knot behind me. I grab the rope giving it a tug and look over at Hawkins. He has such a big cocky grin on his face, I can't wait to watch it vanish.

Steven's walks over and says, "Okay, let's make this a fair match. Are you ready?" he asks looking between the two of us.

"Yeah. Let me teach this little girl a lesson she won't soon forget," Hawkins says with a wink to me.

That cocky bastard isn't going to feel so good when this is over. Looking to Stevens I say, "Let's get this over with, because I can't wait to hand Hawkins his ass and see him whine like a little bitch." I throw him a kiss just to make him mad.

"Okay, on your mark, get set, GO!"

The second the words are out of his mouth, I'm climbing the rope as fast as I can. Nothing's on my mind other than winning. As I'm hustling upward, not looking anywhere but up, I hear the cheers of the girls. Smiling to myself, I know I have this the moment I hear Hawkins' mutter of "Oh shit" seconds later.

I tap the top of the tree a split second before Hawkins. As we climb down, I notice Hawkins starts sliding down the rope. Oh, hell no. I'm not letting him win that way. So I start doing the same, but with these leggings, I can feel the burn of the rope between my thighs. Shit. Once I see I'm about ten feet away from the win, I knew the ground around this was flat and covered in soft sand. Now I know just what I need to do. I'm about to show the hell off.

With confidence, I let go of the rope, leaning backwards

and tucking my body into a back flip, hearing yells of "Holy Shit!" as I get closer to the ground, just like I'd been taught for years doing a dismount off the high beams. I stretch out and nail my landing. Raising my fists into the air in victory, I know I would've scored a '10' for that.

Feeling myself being lifted off the ground and swung around by Tony, the girls gather around, their screams deafening. As Tony put me back on the ground, I'm surrounded by every Camelot sister and friend. Looking around, I've never seen happier women in all my life. Laughing and rejoicing, all because I beat a Brother.

"I have to shake your hand. Hi, I'm Tiffany. I love, and have worked with these arrogant assholes for years, and never did I ever think this day would come. You have just knocked them all down a couple of notches. You are my hero. I take that back, you are hero to all of us," Tiffany says as she pulls me into a big hug.

I knew who Tiffany was from Tony's reports. She's the head of office staffing at Camelot Security, and she's as petite as me, which is nice. She has her own style, completely different than the other girls. She dresses in layers of long gypsy-type dresses or skirts with a long vest over it with several necklaces and thick belts. She's a bombshell hidden under all of that, I'm sure of it.

All the girls spend a good few minutes gathered around me, celebrating and giving me hugs, flipping the Brothers off. Sarah says, "You have to train us. I believe in you Lexy. You are officially the Queen of the Wenches. You did it, you took one down."

She turns her back towards the Brothers, and whispers to all the ladies gathered around. "Ladies listen up. Starting Monday, after work, Lexy has said she will start training any one of us that wants to learn self-defense. You just saw how much of a badass she is. Spread the word. Let's get our moms there too. This is just what we need. She can teach us so much. Then maybe one day we'll be the ones cheering because we've taken one of them down when they least expect it."

I can't help but smile. They're all in agreement to keeping this a secret and not tell the Brothers what we're doing. But I'm determined this won't be the last take-down of a Brother either. No way will Tony let me do this alone. He turns his back to the Brothers, whispering, "Ladies, not only will Lexy train you, but I'll volunteer to help with training and be your punching dummy. I have a black belt in jujitsu, and I'm willing to help all of you as well."

As the girls get more excited, I feel Grayson's presence behind me. Turning around, I have a big smile on my face. Noticing Hawkins wrinkled brow, as Grayson comes walking towards me, he says. "Well, I guess I owe you an apology for not believing in you Lexy. You won, fair and square, even if I do want to tan that fine ass of yours for doing that backflip. You are hell-bent, on giving me a heart attack, aren't you?"

"An apology is not all you owe me. And what did you just call me?" I ask with my hands on my hips and eyebrow raised. All the girls are standing behind me, taunting him.

Sighing, Grayson responds, "Okay, Mistress Lexy. I'm sorry. I should have bet on you. My apologies." He puts on arm over his stomach and bows to me.

"Well, I guess I'll forgive you slave. But just for the record, I'd never bet against you. Even if I knew you'd lose, I'd still stand beside you and support you. But like you said, this is our getting to know each other better period, and you just showed me something about you I don't much care for. Now I need to get ready to meet your parents."

I turn around to all the girls and say, "I'm looking forward to seeing you all real soon. Thank you for the support. We'll have to do this again. Oh, and you're all invited to my sleepover here at Hawkins' Castle." Turning back around to Hawkins, I ask, "Isn't that right, Hawk? You just need to say when. I promise we'll be on our best behavior and we will not go anywhere we aren't allowed. You don't even have to come and be a part of it. You can sulk in your own area knowing this little big assed girl just handed you your ass."

"You know you got lucky. I want a rematch during your little sleepover," Hawkins says, not looking too happy. All the Brothers are calling him all sorts of names and asking him to show them his pussy, since he let a girl beat him.

"No way Brother, you let a girl beat you. I'm the next to challenge for the title of champion of the ropes. I can show you how it's done," Jackson says, as he pounds Hawkins on the back.

"Fuck you!" Hawkins instantly replies.

"Now, now, boys. I'm the champion of the ropes and I'm the one who decides "IF" I want to accept a challenge or not. At this moment, I think I'll reign as champion for a long time and let it just eat at your souls. None of you have ever been able to beat Hawkins and I just beat him. So, until you can beat Hawkins, I'm not even considering accepting any of your challenges." Turning back to Hawkins, I say, "And as for you Hawkins, nope. I think I'll enjoy being the reigning champion for a while." I get up on my tippy toes to kiss Hawkins on the cheek as I add, "Sulking doesn't become you. Sorry. Take it like a man. I beat you. The end."

As I turn and put my arm around Grayson, he adds, "You do know none of the Brothers will rest until they beat you, right?"

"Yup, I'm aware. But I also know they got cocky and weren't giving it their all, because they thought beating a girl would be a, what do you call it? A walk in the park. Well, I showed them. And you're welcome."

"For what?" Grayson quickly asks.

"Come on, Grayson. Every one of your men will be working out that much harder and looking over their shoulder now that I took down one of them. They'll think twice before accepting my challenges because they'll never know where else I could take the winning title away from one of them. Those Brothers will be busting their asses for you in training. So, like I said, you're welcome."

Grayson laughs, "You are probably right there. Look, Jackson and Hawkins are on their way back to the rope challenge. Hawkins is going to have to make sure he can still beat all the Brothers so he can try and convince you to accept his challenge."

"But you see Grayson, that's where he is sadly mistaken. I'll never accept his challenge. I'll forever be the reigning champion of the rope race. Because as Hawkins said himself to Jackson before accepting my challenge, *it's always up to the reigning champion if 'they' want to accept,* and I never will.*"

Grayson and I both crack up laughing, all the way back to the castle. Once inside the doors, Grayson sweeps me off my feet and into his arms, saying, "You never cease to amaze me. But I'm thinking you have a lot more secrets you're keeping from me. One day I will find out all of them, and hopefully, it will be from you telling me, and not me discovering it on my own."

I don't reply to Grayson's statement, because I'm hoping my secrets can stay just that. Secret. Now my focus has to turn towards tonight and impressing his parents. I'm just hoping they don't ask too many questions I can't answer

11

DINNER

Lexy

"Grayson, we need to stop off at Divine Florist Shop. It's less than a mile from your parents' house. Judith, the manager, has the gifts I need to pick up for tonight."

"Baby, you don't need to bring gifts to my folks. You've already made me dress for dinner, Mistress, something I never do. That will be good enough for my mom and dad to love you," Grayson says with a chuckle.

"Excuse me, slave boy? If I ask something of you, slave, you must do it. So, are we stopping at Divine's?" I ask with a big teasing smile on my face

"Yes, Mistress. We're stopping at Divine's Florist, even if we don't need to," Grayson says with a sigh.

Grayson just doesn't understand how important this night is to me. I called Judith yesterday and told her I didn't care about the cost. I needed a bottle of Four Roses 2017, small batch limited edition Al Young's 50th Anniversary bourbon. Sure, it's a $400 bottle, but impressing and winning over Grayson's father I'm sure will be my hardest feat. Tonight has got to be a success. Thank God Tony and Sarah are coming as well, although they'll probably be late as usual, something Tony is known for.

"Seriously Lexy, or do I have to address you Mistress Lexy?"

"I'll be honest with you Grayson, I'm a little nervous here. I've never met someone's parents before. This is all new to me. My life was very different than yours, in a lot of ways."

Grayson puts one hand on my knee and squeezes it. "Babe, really, there is nothing to be nervous about. My mom may be a bit tough at first, but once she talks to you, she'll fall in love with you. And I don't give a fuck what my father thinks about you. He can be a dick most of the time anyway, so just ignore him like I do."

"You need to remember Grayson, until I escaped, all my friends were handpicked for me. They were children of my father's friends. There wasn't one person in my life that they didn't know. All dinners were formal, as in all men wore suits, and women were in dresses. Not until I went to university and was in charge was I able to make them casual. There was nothing in my life that you would call normal back then. So, when it comes to things like this, I'm completely out of my element."

"It couldn't have been that different. All the Brothers were the children of my parents' friends or co-workers, or some were even children of people who worked for my parents. Like the Carpenters. They now run Camelot Construction, but before that, they built my parents' house, and the Gregory's awesome tree house, after Clay's family designed it. I also have very few friends that my parents don't know their parents as well."

"Grayson, the difference is that I wasn't allowed that option. I never got to meet people outside of my family and their friends. There are so many things you take for granted that I wasn't allowed to do. A perfect example is, I was never allowed to cook, not even make a sandwich for myself, not until I escaped. I wasn't allowed to dress myself or pick out my own clothes until I was fifteen, and even then I had restrictions, if you remember. I know that's crazy to you, but it's true."

We're both quiet for a few minutes, so many memories going through my mind. Now I'm telling Grayson more about myself I wasn't really ready for him to know. I'm usually so in control, calm and level-headed. Uncle Louie and Luigi would be so shocked. They'd be teasing me if they heard me.

Grayson squeezes my knee again, "Thank you. You just shared something about yourself that I didn't know. You basically had zero freedom at all. It really means a lot to me when you share more about your past," Grayson quickly looks over to me and smiles.

"Yes Grayson, you could say that. I never wanted for anything money-wise, but all my life, all I ever dreamed of was freedom. I just wanted to be normal. Now I have freedom and the chance to be normal, well, as normal as I ever will be, and I'm never giving it up. It's just a big learning curve for me. Enough about me. I just want tonight to be perfect."

"And it will be, I promise. Don't worry. By the time Sarah, Thomas and Tony get there, all attention will be off of you. If there is one thing you can always count on, it's Sarah and her friends being the center of attention." He chuckles as we stop in front of the florist.

As we pull into the circular driveway and stop in front of the Riggs' house, my stomach does a flip. I take a deep calming breath and try to think positive thoughts. Grayson comes around the car and opens my door, taking the big vase full of three dozen tulips, offering me his other hand to assist me in getting out of the car. I hear his parent's front door open.

"Oh Grayson, those are beautiful! The colors are gorgeous. Where did you find these?" I watch Mrs. Riggs rush over to Grayson, leaning in to smell the flowers.

"Lexy ordered them for you. We just stopped at Divine's florist, I guess she ordered them yesterday when I wasn't looking. Mom, this is Lexy Rogers. Lexy this is my mom, Diana Riggs."

I hand her a big box of Godiva chocolates. "It's very nice to meet you. I've heard so many wonderful things about you," I say, trying to make my voice sound calm.

"Grayson has said nice things about me?" She leans over and kisses Grayson on the cheek. Then she waves her hand behind her. "Come on, Dick! Get out here and help Grayson with these flowers. Put them on the dining room table. Lexy, this is my husband, and naturally Grayson's dad, Richard, but when he is being a Dick, don't hesitate to call him that. He answers to both. Don't you, dear?" she teases her husband.

"Well let's go inside, no need to just gather out here." Mr. Riggs ignores her statement as he takes the flowers from Grayson, and we follow his mom into the house.

"Come with me! All the best talks happen in the kitchen in our home, so follow me. I was going to hire a cook tonight and then I decided, nope. If my son was going to bring a girl to our home for the first time in his life, I was going to cook his favorite dinner myself. We're having an old fashioned pot roast, with red potatoes, carrots and mini onions. And yes, I'll give you the recipe before you leave," she says with a wink, which really puts me at ease.

Once we're in the kitchen, Grayson pulls out a barstool for me, and we both sit at the counter. It smells delicious and I can't wait to try it. This will be my first pot roast. It sounds yummy and hopefully, it's easy to cook. Now that I know it's Grayson's favorite, I'm going to have to learn to make it. I can't believe she's already going to share her recipes. Minutes later, his father walks in through a doorway, I'm guessing leads to the dining room. His facial expression is very stern and makes me a bit nervous all over again. He's looking between me and Grayson. I realize I'm still holding the decorative bag that has his bourbon in it.

"Oh, I'm sorry Mr. Riggs. I got this for you also," I reach over and hand it to him.

He reaches into the bag and pulls out the bottle, reading the label. "Very nice. Did Grayson get this?"

"No sir, he didn't. I special ordered it yesterday. I assumed you'd be a bourbon drinker since the other day, when Grayson and I had dinner, he had a couple of glasses of nice bourbon. I'm hoping he got his love of it from you. I did my research and found that this one was in the top five best bourbons of last year. I hope you like it," I say with assurance.

"Thank you. And yes, it's always nice to have a good bourbon or whiskey after dinner. Or whenever really," he says with a head nod to me.

"Look at me, I've forgotten my manners too. It must be the shock of my son bringing home a girl. Thank you Lexy, I love the flowers and will very much enjoy the chocolates as well. Now, would you like to have a glass of wine while I finish up and you tell me all about yourself? Bearing such gifts, you obviously come from money." Mrs. Riggs says with a lift of one eyebrow.

"Mom, don't beat around the bush. Just come on out and ask the rude questions first. I thought we agreed to play nice tonight?" Grayson says to his mom, his brow wrinkled.

"Grayson, it's okay." I look between his parents, "Okay, Mr. and Mrs. Riggs, honesty is important to me, and I'm sure to both of you. I'm not interested in your son for his money. I probably have more than the three of you put together. I own several fitness clubs, spas and dance studios. I also have a couple of nonprofits." I reach into my oversized purse and pull out a file folder, laying it on the counter. "Here is a copy of my portfolio if you'd like to see it. I'm sure Grayson told you I was raised in Italy, but my mother was an American citizen. She came home to the US every summer for at least two months until she was sixteen. Naturally, that makes me an American citizen as well.

"Oh, and we haven't even had sex yet. Grayson has high morals," I hear his father cough and his mother sigh, as I continue. "So you don't have to worry. I'm not planning on getting pregnant to entrap Grayson either. But you can check with your colleague Dr. Brooks. I'm religious at getting my shots to make sure pregnancy isn't going to happen for a very long time." As I finish my long-winded spiel, Mrs. Riggs explodes in laughter. Mr. Riggs is still stone-faced.

"Grayson, this young lady is a keeper. Don't screw this up. I like her. Lexy, please call me Mom Riggs like all his friends do, or just call me Mom, for that matter. Odds are, I will be one day. No more of this Mrs. Riggs shit, excuse my French," she giggles, surprising me.

I watch as his father leans on the counter and opens up the folder I put there. His mom quickly slaps it closed and pushes it back over to me. "Put this back in your purse. I told you he could be a real dick. He can take your word. He, nor I, need to see these details. Grayson, get your lady a glass of wine and refill mine, and take your father with you. He needs to put away the bottle of bourbon Lexy got for him.

"Yes Mom," Grayson says. Getting up, he kisses the top of my head, snickering. "You're too much. I fall deeper for you every minute I'm around you," he whispers. He turns away and leaves the room with his father.

"Now that I have you alone, we can really talk, woman to woman. I know what my son sees in you. You're completely different than any girl he's ever dated. No, he hasn't ever brought one home, but I've seen them at the club and online as I'm sure you have too. You're breathtakingly beautiful and there are no words to describe how beautiful your eyes are. If this works out, I hope your children have those eyes."

With that, I laugh out loud. "You really don't, as Grayson said, beat around the bush, do you? You do know we've only been back in each other's lives for three days, right?"

"Yes, and I know how crazy my son is for you. He told me all about when he met you years ago. He even told me how he lost himself with you like no other on the Stevens's deck. Did he tell you he's even gone to Italy twice in hopes of finding you? I'm sure he'd rather I didn't share this with you, because he was hoping that what he was told wasn't true."

Now I'm starting to panic. Mom Riggs walks over to the stove and turns down the burners. Double damn. I need to know what Grayson found out in Italy.

"And what was he told? Since he didn't and still doesn't know my given name, he only knew me as Aless, he must have described my appearance."

"Very true. The only thing he could do was describe you. As we were coming out of a chapel after praying and lighting candles, I can see by your expression, you are shocked. But he was out of ideas and thought it couldn't hurt. As we were leaving, he was drawn to this elderly woman sitting outside of the chapel. He approached her and asked if she knew who the most beautiful girl in Italy was, because he met her over two years ago when she visited America. He spoke from the heart, telling her you had shiny black hair and wore it pulled up. But what stood out the most, were your clear light blue eyes, they put him in a trance and captured a part of his soul. And all he knew was that her name was Aless."

Gasping, I admit, "Yes, Mom Riggs, I am shocked. But my heart is filled with emotion just knowing that Grayson was willing to go into church and say a prayer for me, lighting a candle as well. That touches my soul deeply. Thank you for sharing that with me. But what did the elderly woman say to him?"

"Well, when Grayson described you that way, her eyes got huge when he said your name was Aless. That must have struck a bell with her. Because she responded quickly and spoke very quietly telling him, '*The only people who called the young lady I know of by that name are her closest Family friends. She has those eyes you described. But her Papa would never let her speak to you. You must leave and go back to your country and forget all about her. If it is the young lady I know of, her father will arrange a marriage for her, and it will not be you, young man. Now go, do not ask anyone else about her. If any of the Family find out an American boy is looking for her, he will have you killed. You must leave and stop looking for her. Forget you ever saw her.*' Then the woman did the sign of the cross over her body and left as quickly as she could. Could that woman have known you? Do I have any reason to believe your father or family would kill Grayson if they found out you were here with him?"

Holy shit! What the hell am I going to say to put an end to this conversation and relieve any of her worry? My mind races. I never want to lie to her, so I tell her the truth

"Mom Riggs I swear to you, Grayson has nothing to worry about. My uncle, who is my father's brother, and the one who really raised me, can vouch for me and reassure you that Grayson is completely safe. He is not in any danger, I swear it.

"My father does want me back home, but that will never happen. He was not only physically abusive when I was younger, but verbally as well. He controlled every aspect of my life. He was more a dictator than a father. He has no idea where I am. Not a clue. But that is also why I refuse to tell Grayson my family name. I do not want him trying to fix things between my father and me.

"My father has re-married and has two little children to worry about now. I'm hoping in the last year he has moved on. I still have a few contacts outside of my uncle, and if my father was even getting close to finding out where I am, I'm confident they would tell me. Please trust me. It's best this way."

Before she can say anything else, in walks Grayson. His smile is radiant as he walks over and kisses my forehead, handing me a glass of red wine. I quickly take a well needed drink. His father hands his wife a glass of wine as well, and says, "Cheers, to tonight and new friends." He and Grayson lift their glasses of bourbon as we all take a drink.

With perfect timing, in walks Thomas, wearing one of Tony's suit coats. Right behind him is Sarah with Tony beside her. He has his arm around her waist. She instantly starts her introductions.

"Dad, this wonderful man beside me is Tony Jarvis. Mom's already met him. We've been dating for a while now, and I've decided we're exclusive. No more playing the field for me. He's swept me off my feet completely." Turning to her father she adds, "And Dad, he's a successful business owner and has known Lexy since they were in their teens. Just wait till you get to know him. You'll love him as much as I do."

Watching Tony, I can tell he's very nervous. He's fidgeting with a gift bag he's holding, and he keeps putting one hand in and out of his pocket, trying to make sure he looks good. I don't think he's ever met a girl or boy's parents before. Not like this anyway. He does look good in his suit, and Thomas looks as excited as Sarah. I have to talk to Tony, soon, about this relationship, because I know the real him.

"It's nice to see you again Tony. We all had lunch last week and I was very impressed by our daughter's pick in gentlemen suitors, as your mother would say Dick," Mom Riggs says, teasing her husband.

"Well, we both know my mother wouldn't approve of that hair. What on God's earth have you done to it and why? Young man, you'd look much more professional in that suit if you chopped off all that bleached hair. That would make you more presentable for my daughter." Mr. Riggs says, proving he is a real dick.

Both Sarah and Thomas at the same time, say "No!" very loud.

"He does not have to and he will not cut off those blonde locks, Dad. He is making a fashion statement, and I love it. It's more fun to run my fingers through those long luscious locks." Sarah says while running both hands through Tony's hair as he smiles down at her. I really think he is falling for her, which scares me. I don't want her hurt, and I don't know if Sarah can handle the real him. Only time will tell.

Sarah surprises me again, by pulling Tony towards her and kissing him on the mouth. I hear Thomas sigh. "Young love. Isn't it just beautiful?"

Tony pulls away ending the kiss sooner than I think Sarah wanted him to, and he holds out a gift bag towards Mr. Riggs. "I'm sorry sir, I brought this for you both. Two bottles of the best Italian red and white wines. I just knew Lexy would bring flowers and chocolates," Tony says with a head nod to me.

"Thank you, Tony. Lexy did bring me a very nice bottle of bourbon as well. But I'll open these so they can breathe, and we'll have them with our dinner." Setting them down on the counter and opening a drawer, Dick pulls out a corkscrew. Looking back to Tony, he asks, "Now what successful business do you own? Maybe I've heard of it, if it is that successful." Mr. Riggs says sarcastically.

"I'm in the security business, similar to what the Brothers of Camelot do. My company, Stark Enterprise, provides a lot of internet security, as well as home and office security systems as well. I've even worked with Hawkins a few times, with internet research and security issues." Tony handles that question like a pro, with complete confidence in his abilities. He is so proud of his accomplishments and his company, as he should be.

Mr. Riggs looks between Grayson and Tony, I'm sure his wheels are turning. He turns to me and asks, "Lexy, you've known Tony since your teens? How did you both meet?

Tony's eyes quickly search mine. Oh, shit I've got to think quick. "Emm, our families were in similar businesses, and when we were teens, my family basically took over Tony's family business. As you can tell, we became best of friends soon after that. In fact, Tony moved here about eighteen months before me, to help get things set up. Tony was a major part in helping me get away from my own controlling father. He also set up my security system at my home and runs all of the security systems in my businesses too. He is the best at what he does," I say, smiling at Tony.

"Hmm. Grayson, have you seen Lexy's security system? Is he as good as Nicholas, I mean Hawkins?" Mr. Riggs asks.

"Yeah, Dad. Her system is excellent. Hawkins has worked with Tony online before he knew it was Tony. But that's how things are done in our world. Stark Enterprise doesn't provide the personal protection, or the 'go in and rescue people' like we do. If he ran into a client that needed that done, I'm sure he'd call on us. Wouldn't you, Tony?" Grayson smiles over at Tony, putting him on the spot. I think he's wanting this grilling to end as well.

"Yes, the Brothers would be the first ones I would call, if it was someone who wanted that physical help," Tony replies with a wink towards Grayson.

Mom Riggs clears her throat, saving us all from this conversation, "Enough with this interrogation of our children's dates. We're almost ready for dinner. Please get me a refill of my wine, Dick."

I can't help but smile at the way she takes control. Just then, Sarah practically shouts. "Mom, Mom, have you heard Grayson address Lexy yet? Come on Grayson, what's your girlfriend's name tonight?"

Hearing Grayson sigh beside me as he squeezes my shoulder, he whispers, "Mistress, you're about to humiliate me, aren't you?"

Bright eyed, I reply all innocently "Who me?!"

"Sarah, what are you talking about?" Mom Riggs looks between the three of us.

"Well Mom, Lexy is a badass. She kicked Hawkins' ass today at his famous rope climbing competition. Look, I've got it on video." Sarah pulls out her phone, bringing up the video. Tony, Thomas and I start laughing. I watch as Mr. Riggs leans over to watch the video too.

"Okay, yes Mom, I was a dumbass and put my money on Hawkins. He's always beats everyone, including me, with his rope climbing abilities. How was I to know Lexy could beat him? I realize I should never bet against the girl I'm dating, so no need to lecture me Mom."

Mom Riggs' head whips to Grayson as she asks, "Did I hear you correctly? Did you just say you bet against Lexy and she still came to dinner here? Well son, you're damned lucky, because if I were her, I wouldn't even be speaking to you, period. And Lexy, I apologize for my son being such a dick. That's why his middle name is Richard. He has his father's genes, and as you witnessed yourself today, Grayson can be a real dick himself," Mom Riggs shakes her head at him, Sarah's calling him a Dick too over his Mom's shoulder.

She continues, "Congratulations! That was an incredible feat to beat Nicholas like that. You must have incredible upper body strength. I would have never thought a girl could beat him. But be warned, he'll try everything to beat you and win back that title."

"Ma'am I'm fully aware of that, but I'm also very wise. I heard him announce the rules when Jackson challenged him for the title. I'm not about to accept his challenge for the title anytime soon. And before you ask, I've been climbing a rope like that since before I was six years old, and challenging men by the time I was twelve. Believe me, I know what I'm doing and how to take a man down a notch or two, don't I Grayson?" I can't help but smile and pat Grayson on the cheek, giving him a quick peck on the lips.

Grayson looks at me with his deep ocean blue eyes that can see into my soul as he says to me, "Yes, Mistress Lexy. You do know how to take a man down a few notches and make him eat his own words and learn from his mistakes. I'll never make that mistake again. I swear to you in front of everyone here. That I'll never bet against you again. You'll always be my number one." Then he gives me a quick passionate kiss in front of everyone. He pulls away, my heart racing and we just sit here in a trance, looking into each other's eyes.

"Richard, I think our boy is falling in love right before our eyes," Mom Riggs says with a sigh.

"I just hope he does so slowly, getting to know all there is to know first." Mr. Riggs says, pulling Grayson and me out of our trance. Yeah, he's going to be a problem, wanting to know all the details of my life. I can see it now. I'm going to have to figure this out and talk to Uncle Louie. Maybe after they all meet him, it will shut down all this investigation into my background.

"Stop being a dick Richard and be happy for our children for once. Have a bit of faith," Mom Riggs says before continuing, "Now, let's all head into the dining room and have a lovely dinner so Lexy and Tony can tell us all about their businesses."

As we all get up and make our way into the dining room, Mr. Riggs helps his wife carry covered dishes in. We all offer to help, which she instantly refuses. Looking over to Mr. Riggs I realize he will be the biggest challenge of my life, but I am determined to win him over and get his trust. I have a feeling he already has huge doubts about me and Grayson. I'm confident I can win over Mom Riggs. That's where I'll spend most of my time, winning over her trust and love. Because she's the one that can get Dick, as she so fondly calls him, in line.

After dinner, we all gather outside in the backyard to continue our conversations. It was so much fun to listen to the family dynamics, their teasing and banter and their childhood stories just made me more aware of all I missed out on growing up. This is what life is supposed to be like. With music playing softly in the background, it's such a relaxed atmosphere. Adding the cool night air just makes it perfect. I'm enjoying my glass of wine and watching the flames leap in the fire pit, leaning back in Grayson's arms. There's not another place on the planet I would rather be.

When 'Perfect' by Ed Sheeran starts playing, Grayson whispers in my ear, "May I have this dance?" Then he starts singing, "*I found a love for me. Darling just dive right in, and follow my lead.*"

Setting my drink down, I take his hands as I look into those eyes that control my world. He sweeps me into his arms and we start swaying to the beat of the music. Oh my God, not only can he dance, but he can sing too. Damn, am I lucky. I can feel my heart melting with each word. Grayson continues singing softly, just above a whisper. He is luring me into his spell. Out of the corner of my eye, I notice both Tony and Sarah as well as Grayson's parents have joined us, and are now dancing under the moon and starlit sky.

Then Grayson speaks, breaking my trance. "I'll tell you a secret. This song haunts me. I can't turn on a radio or walk into a public place where music is playing without hearing it. It's like a message from on high. It reminds me of you. It's what I want for us as well. I think I'm going to make this *our song*. What do you think?"

I can't keep from smiling like a loon. "Grayson, I love that. This is my favorite song of all time. The words are just so sweet and romantic, and I hope one day we can make every word of this song ours."

"Well Baby, I'm making it our prayer," Grayson starts singing again, his voice so deep and sexy. It's breathy and barely above a whisper, right above my head, as I'm cuddled into his chest. His thick thigh is right between my leg as we're swaying with the music. I'm getting so turned on. Damn, his singing is turning my heart into putty in his hands. He is the master of my soul, I'm lost to him. There is no taking it slow.

Right after the instrumental part of the song, he lifts his head and looks deeply into my eyes and sings loud enough for everyone to hear him, *"Now I know I have met an angel in person. And she looks perfect, I don't deserve this. You look perfect tonight."* As the song ends, he leans down and kisses me, and I know without question, this is what real love feels like. I don't even care that everyone, including his parents, are watching us. I don't think I can survive without him in my life again. This chemistry is real. I never want to be apart from him.

Once Grayson pulls away, he leaves one arm around me, looking towards his mother who is smiling so big. "Mom, thank you for the pot roast. It was wonderful. But it's time to take my girl home." He walks over and kisses his mom on the cheek.

Once he releases his mother, she comes over and throws both arms around me, whispering, "Lexy, you make my son happier than I've ever seen him. I've always known he had a beautiful voice, but I never thought I'd ever see him sing a love song to a woman. Thank you. Tonight was wonderful. We must do lunch very soon, without Grayson," she says with a wink.

"Okay. Come to my club tomorrow night with Sarah, and we will plan a date. Thank you. Dinner was wonderful."

Grayson and I finish our goodbyes and head out. My heart is so full of love, I feel like I am floating on a cloud. I never imagined I'd truly feel like this. It's magnificent. I'm free and falling in love, and I think Grayson feels the same way. Life can't get any better.

NOT WANTING TO ACCEPT THE FACTS

Grayson

*S*tanding in Lexy's elevator on our way up to her penthouse, I'm unable to keep my hands off her, wrapping my arms around her and pulling her to my chest. She's such a short little thing, even with six-inch heels on. I never thought I'd like such a petite woman, but damn, it gets me hard just thinking about all the things I can do with her. She probably doesn't even weigh a hundred and thirty pounds, and most of that is tits and ass. Saying goodnight and having to leave is going to be incredibly difficult, but I have to stick to my word. She has to trust me, and right now, she doesn't.

Every minute we spend apart, the harder it gets. If someone was to tell me I'd be this serious so quickly with any woman, I'd have called them nuts. But just the sight of her sends my blood rushing, my heart pounding and brings my cock to life in an instant. No one has ever affected me like this. How can I make her trust me and tell me about her life as Aless? My mind is racing as I bend down and start kissing my way up her neck.

"Are you really leaving me tonight?" Lexy asks turning in my arms, stopping my pursuit of her ear. Looking up at me, she runs her small hands up my chest.

Gazing into those eyes that hold a part of my soul, I answer, "Babe, leaving tonight or any night for that matter will be very difficult for me. You have no idea of the internal battle between my body and my heart. My soul wants to wrap you in my arms and stay forever, but we need to wait until you can trust me. I want you to be *my one love*. There can't be anything or anyone between us. I need and want to be your best friend as well as your lover. We can wait until you feel the same way," I say as the elevator dings and the door opens.

"I do feel the same way. The chemistry we have and the internal pull that is constantly tugging at my heart is undeniable. I want you so bad."

"Damn, Lexy. There is nothing I want more, but you aren't ready. Tony knows you and all your secrets. I'm not saying that in a jealous way. I can deal with you and his friendship. I just need to be the one who knows you and your secrets more than he does. And right now, I'm not. I can't allow myself to go that deep into this relationship until I believe you trust me, enough to give me all of yourself. I'm ready to give myself over to you whole heartedly. There is no going back once I have you completely," I say, unwinding my arms from her.

"I feel so empty and at such a loss when we're apart."

"Believe me, babe, I feel it too. I wish I didn't have to say goodnight. I'd love to take you home with me right now and keep you there. But like you said yesterday, we both need to get to know each other's quirks."

Lexy walks over to the door and places her hand on the scanner, leans in and scans her eye. Turning back around to me as the door opens, she asks, "Are you going to come in for a while or literally be that old fashioned and play hard-to-get and just kiss me goodnight at the door?" She looks down, trying to look pitiful. It really makes me want to laugh, but I refrain.

"I'll come in. I told you how much I love fooling around with you. But you've told me where you're unwilling to go, and I've told you sex is not an option because I want more from you than a quick hook-up. I want to make passionate love to you all night, and when exhaustion sets in, you'll be the first woman I stay the night with and hold in my arms till the next day turns back into night. We both have to wait for that, but until then, we can make out like teenagers," I lean down and kiss her on top of her head.

She takes my hand and pulls me into her penthouse, down the hallway to her room, unzipping her dress with the other hand. "So, if I were to slowly strip in front of you, you think you can so easily walk away?"

"I didn't say any of this would be easy, but I also didn't say I wouldn't touch you." Once we walk into her room, I close the door behind me with my foot and slide my hand into the back of her dress. Leaning down, I start kissing her neck as I slowly push her dress off her shoulders. I freeze as I see what looks like an exit scar from an old bullet wound. I kiss it and slowly turn her around as I continue to push her dress the rest of the way off her shoulders. Looking, I see what is, without question, the entrance wound of a bullet. Aless has some serious secrets I need to know about. Kissing back up her neck to her ear, I ask, "When did this happen?"

"When did what happen?" Lexy mumbles as she does a little shimmy that makes her dress fall to the floor. Grabbing my shirt, she starts to unbutton it, kissing her way up my chest.

Damn does she look hot in burgundy lingerie and those 'fuck me' six-inch heels. Her body is so toned and curvaceous, it's a major turn on for me. I'm used to dating tall, thin women with fake tits. But fuck, Lexy is the polar opposite and I love it. But I have to get my mind back on her scar and see if

I can pry any information out of her while I try and seduce her.

Bending down, I start kissing the bullet wound scar on the front of her shoulder. I look into her eyes and ask again, "This bullet wound. It went straight through your shoulder. I know what it is, so don't try and deny it. I have a couple of bullet wounds of my own. When did it happen?"

Hearing her gasp, I'm sure she would much rather I hadn't noticed it. Let's see how she explains this one. I wish I had turned on the light switch by the door, but right now, the only light is coming from the lamp she left on beside her bed. I need to check out every inch of her to see if there's more scars like this one.

"Umm, a very long time ago. I'm fine. Nothing to worry you about."

"I can see you're fine. I just asked when you got shot straight through your shoulder," I say as I run my tongue from the scar up her neck, making sure to exhale so my warm breath tickles her skin making her moan.

"Grayson, you aren't playing fair. You're not supposed to interrogate me. I thought we were going to have a little fun."

"Babe, how can I not ask what happened when I see an obvious bullet wound marring your beautiful body? Just tell me about this one, and I won't ask any more questions tonight. I swear," I ask pleadingly as I nibble on her earlobe.

She sighs as I push her onto her bed.

"Fine, just this one. I was shot as I was leaving my sixth birthday party. I'm sure you've heard there are some parts of Italy where there is crime Family violence. Well, you could say I got caught up in the crossfire. The end. Now shut up and kiss me."

As I kiss her passionately, the only thought through my mind is that I need to head over to talk to Hawkins. That will have to wait. I'm going to show Lexy how good I can make her feel, so maybe it'll soften her stubborn heart into trusting me. But the moment I leave her, I'm going straight over to Hawkins to give him this intel. He needs to search and see if we can figure who the hell Aless, rather Lexy, really is.

Lexy wraps her legs around my waist, rubbing herself back and forth against Sir. I need to teach her who's in charge in the bedroom. Reaching around, I unwrap her legs, bending them at the knees as I push them apart. Damn. I watch as they both fall completely flat on the bed, spreading her wide open for me. Holy Shit. Not only is my woman hot, she's also very flexible. I've never seen anyone spread like this with such ease.

Looking down at her, I ask, "You want me to tell you what I'm really thinking? It's dirty."

"Yes! Talk dirty to me."

"Looks like that hungry pussy of yours is eager to get that release." I grind my granite hard cock right into her clit. Hearing her let out a deep moan, I can't help but smile.

"Oh God Grayson, yes. You got me so wound up at your parents' house, I wanted you right there."

"Baby, all you need to do is tell me. I know just how to give you a fast orgasm. Does that pussy want me to make you come now? Or do you want me to tell you what I'm going to do to it once you trust me?"

"Tell me. I want to know," Lexy says, trying to catch her breath. She is so close and so turned on right now this is going to be easy. She looks up at me with those sexy eyes and grabs the back of my head, pulling me down for another kiss. I keep grinding my cock right into her clit, knowing how close she's getting.

Pulling away from the kiss, I start kissing my way to her breast, using my teeth to pull the cup of her bra down, revealing her perfect nipple that I immediately latch on to, sucking it deep into my mouth. I listen to her moan as she grabs my head, holding it in place.

"When you learn to trust me," I murmur, "I'm going to spend the first twenty-four hours making hard, passionate love to you. That tight little pussy of yours will be so good and sore, it will need a bit of a break afterwards to recover from the multiple orgasms I'm going to pound out of it. Then I plan on giving that sore little slit of yours a full good licking like this." I flatten my tongue and lick her hard nipple with the full pressure of my tongue as I continue to grind and circle my hard cock around her clit.

"Then I'm going to tug and bite on your clit like this." I wiggle my tongue back and forth across her very erect hard nipple, right before I suck it back into my mouth. Releasing it again, I instantly start lightly tugging on just her very protruding nipple, with the suction of just my lips. I can't resist as I start to bite down just a touch as Lexy arches her back and lets out a deep moan. Oh yeah, I got my woman just where I want her.

As she moans again, in such a breathy and sexy as fuck whisper, she asks "And then what? What will you do to my pussy?"

My woman likes dirty talk, that makes this even better. Fuck, now I'm determined to make her aware of the control I have. I just want to blow her mind with the knowledge of what awaits her little pussy after she trusts me.

"Then while I'm tugging and sucking on your clit, I'm going to finger-fuck you fast and hard." I attack her nipple again doing just what I said I'd do to her clit, as I slide my hand over to her well-groomed pussy and instantly slide two fingers deep into her, pumping them in perfect rhythm.

Lexy closes her eyes and starts thrusting her hips up to ride my fingers as I torture her nipple.

"Grayson... Grayson... I... I... I'm going to come!" Lexy cries out.

Looking down between us briefly, I've never seen anything more beautiful than seeing my woman open and spread for me so I can see her pussy contracting around my fingers, trying to reach her release. "Come on, baby. Let go and fly," I say as I go back to her nipple, loving how big and beautiful her breasts are. Damn, one day I am going to hold these babies together and fuck them. They're so firm and real, a true rarity these days. I thrust my fingers in and out faster, making sure to rub in just the right place to hit her 'G' spot.

"That's it… That's it… Grayson… Grayson… I'm… I'm flying…" I release her breast and just watch as she goes limp on the bed, her pussy squeezing my fingers. I slow the movement of my fingers to help her ride out her orgasm.

Slowly, I start kissing my way up her neck until I reach her mouth, then I claim it in a passionate kiss, full of emotion. Her arms wrap around me and one hand threads through my hair. This kiss seems to go on forever. Without question, I'm falling in love with her, if I haven't already fallen. Lexy pulls away from our kiss, her eyes glazed and sexy as hell. I can tell I've worn her out. I smile down at her, unable to resist teasing her. "Who would have thought that blushing young girl I first laid eyes on at a hotdog place in New York would like for me to talk dirty to her?"

Blushing to the roots of her hair, she giggles and says, "I would never have thought I would like it either, but damn, it is a major turn on. Now it's my turn to show you what I can do to 'Sir' with my hand so you can get your release." She reaches down between us trying to grab my cock.

I quickly sit up, stopping her pursuit. "No Lexy. Tonight was all for you. I'll be fine. I needed to show you what kind of control I have. I can go without for now. Seeing you like that and hearing you cry out my name again was all I needed. We both have early mornings tomorrow, so I guess it is goodnight, my love." I lean in and claim another quick taste of her mouth.

"Grayson, you don't have to leave like this. I believe you have undeniable will power, but that" she points to my very hard cock, "has to be uncomfortable. Let me give you just as much pleasure as you gave me."

"That's okay. 'Sir' will be just fine. All it'll take is for me to just think of Grandmother Riggs and all the girls she's introduced to me over the years hoping I'd fall for one of them. That gets me soft every time."

"Your dad's mom is trying to find you a wife?"

"Yup. She has been since my high school years, but she swung into high-gear when I returned from the military. There is nothing more that woman wants than for me to marry some high society girl with a good family pedigree. Oh, and she wants me to start popping out great grandchildren immediately too. Don't worry, I have no problem telling her I'm not interested."

"Really? A high society girl? Isn't that what you normally date?"

"No. I don't really date. I have hook-ups. Only occasionally is there a full meal involved. Usually, it's just a few drinks, chit-chat and a complete understanding that this is not the start of a relationship. It is just two adults helping each other fulfill a need, with a good fuck and a release. Period."

"Wow, that doesn't even sound romantic," Lexy teases, "I think if you made me that offer, I'd turn you down. I would for sure pass up on the banging adventure."

"Well babe, as I said before, that is not even an offer for you. Sex is off the table. I told you what I want from you after we have gained each other's trust. The days of random hook-ups are over for me. I found something a hell of a lot better with you. And for your information, what we do have has been more fulfilling than any random fucks have ever been."

"Aww, you're such the romantic," she teases as she pulls me down for a kiss.

Sitting back up, I re-button my shirt. "I said we both have early mornings tomorrow. I need to go, but I do plan on seeing you every day, even if it is just for coffee. I think I owe you several of those anyway, 'Mystery Woman'," I tease her with a wink, knowing she's the one who was randomly buying me coffee.

"I don't know what you're talking about," Lexy says with a giggle and a blush.

Standing up, I cover her with her comforter. "I love that you still blush." I kiss her on the tip of her nose. "But it's *buona notte amore*. Now lock up, like I know you can from here."

"Now you're trying to turn me on again, talking Italian. *Bunoa notte mio dio greco*."

"Shit, you sound a hell of a lot better speaking Italian than I do. What did you say? Did you just call me a Greek god?"

"Well, isn't your Italian better than I thought it was? And yes, you'll always be my Greek God."

Chuckling, I walk to the door. "See you tomorrow love," I say, throwing her a kiss and taking one more quick glance at her. Damn, she is so fucking beautiful. I rub the center of my chest. It feels like an open wound, the pressure and discomfort is just building. Being separated from her now actually 'causes me physical pain. She has to open up to me. I'm going to have to figure this out, and fast.

Twenty minutes later, I'm in my car speeding out of town towards Hawkins' place. I've got hundreds of things racing through my head, trying to figure Aless, rather Lexy out. I've got to talk to Hawkins. This can't wait. I push the hands-free button on my steering wheel, "Call Hawkins."

"Yes Sir. Dialing now."

That bastard has turned into a real prankster. He's put that same submissive woman's voice I have on my home monitoring system on my car's navigation system now too. I snicker. That little fucker. Stevens nailed it, it makes me sound like a freaking Dom.

Hawkins answers his phone on the second ring. "Like your new navigation system? Please tell me Lexy heard it," Hawkins greets.

"Hawk, you little fucker! I'm alone, thankfully. I'm on my way to your place and I have new intel you need to start researching before I get there."

"What did you find out Brother?" Hawkins fires back.

"Lexy has a scar from a bullet wound on her left shoulder. The bullet went through the front of her shoulder and exited out the back, leaving a nice size scar. She wasn't sewn back up by any plastic surgeon either. It's obvious what it is. When I asked her about it, she told me she was shot leaving her sixth birthday party. She actually asked if I've heard there are some parts of Italy where there is 'crime Family violence'. She claimed she got caught up in the crossfire. The end. Between us, I call bullshit."

"Yeah, I'm thinking her Family was one of the crime Families. I'll see what I can find out on my end and on the Dark Web. Riggs, how far away are you?"

"I'd say at this speed, maybe fifteen, twenty minutes tops. I'm making good time. I just hope there aren't any cops out tonight because I'm kind of breaking every traffic law going this speed," I reply, just getting off the freeway and taking the turns too fast, making me realize I need to slow down a bit before I start heading up into the hills.

"Well, since I own and created most of this mountain, it's usually a police-free zone. The local officers also know I have my issues. They know there are times I go out car-dancing."

"You still do that? Dude, be careful. I'd much rather you do that shit in an empty parking lot. We can have Carpenter flatten out a section of the land up there and you can do that shit up there."

"Come on Riggs, it's not the same and you know it. Driving around just gives me a feeling of normalcy. You know what I mean. When I'm hitting the road, blasting my music and just driving to the beat, I like to randomly hit a parking lot or an empty road and do multiple donut turns. It takes me back to being sixteen, when my life was normal. Putting a parking lot up here wouldn't be the same."

"I get it, I do Hawk, but come on Brother, if you must do that, do it in town, not up here on these roads. It's too dangerous. If something happened and you went off the road, you could get seriously hurt or killed."

"Man, I know what I'm doing. I don't do donuts in the middle of these narrow roads. I wait till there is a turn out and it's safe. But usually, it is more in town, around four a.m. when all the parking lots are empty. You gotta trust me."

"Fuck, Hawkins. I'll be honest and say that sometimes you scare the shit out of me. How's everything else? You know we're all here for you, right?"

"Yeah, yeah, I know. You guys keep me busy. I have my good days and my bad ones, like I always do. Recently there have been more good days than bad ones which is good, so don't worry about me. We need to stay focused on that pint-sized little shit of yours. She stole my title you know. I'm thinking she cheated with that ten-foot back flip. I think I need a rematch," Hawkins changes the subject, something he is a pro at doing when he starts getting uncomfortable talking about himself.

"Hey Brother, we all saw it. It was a fair win. She did the same thing Jackson did moments before and you personally said his dropping to the ground was fair. I think you'll be waiting a long time before she'll give you that chance for a rematch. Lexy is very proud of her win."

"Shit. She's going to rub this in my face for ages, isn't she?"

"Yup, but I think anyone who beat you would make you suffer a while before a rematch. I'll be there shortly. Is there any of that chicken parm of Isabella's left? That sure is sounding awful good right now."

Hawkins starts laughing, "Stevens, Jackson and Carpenter are staying the night up here so you can fend for yourself in the kitchen. But if you're nice to me, I'll share some of my secret stash with you. I'm not stupid. I hide the good stuff up in my wing of the castle."

"*What*?! You have the good shit hidden in your wing? Hey Hawk...Hawk..." That asshole hung up on me.

Seventeen minutes later, I'm walking into Hawkins' kitchen, seeing the guys teasing each other and fighting over French bread. I hope we never lose this banter. Stevens and Jackson are playing tug of war with a whole loaf and it rips in two.

"I got the bigger bit! Just like my cock, you dickless wonder," Jackson says, holding up his longer piece of French bread.

"I'll have you know my cock is just as big as yours. You wanna see, you dick lover?" Stevens jokes, standing up and making like he's going to undo his pants.

"Okay, enough. Keep your dick in your pants Stevens. Now where's my chicken parm?"

"Don't worry you, pussy-whipped boy. We saved you some after Hawkins said you were headed this way," Jackson replies, shoving a massive fork full of spaghetti into his mouth.

"You hungry Jackson?" I tease as I walk over to the table and grab a seat across from Stevens.

Stevens smiles at me while shoving a huge meatball in his mouth. He turns and pushes over a metal bowl that he had sitting beside him upside down. Looking at him oddly, I lift the bowl to reveal my big plate full of chicken parm, covered in a shit-load of extra cheese over spaghetti squash. My best friend knows me well.

"Thanks man, you know just how I like it. I owe you one." Grabbing my fork, I start to eat this wonderful second dinner before me. Yeah, after all I've eaten today I will for sure be getting up for a run in the morning, before we head to headquarters for our normal workout.

"You want some of my bread?" Stevens offers, ripping a hunk off the bread he was fighting Jackson for when I got here.

"No thanks. I don't need the extra carbs this late at night. This is my second dinner. Mom made my favorite pot roast tonight, in honor of me bringing my lady over."

"And you didn't save me any of that? I should take the chicken parm away from you, you selfish jackass," Stevens disputes.

"What did Mom Riggs make for dessert, you asshole?" Carpenter questions.

"I don't know what it was called, but it was damn good and Lexy loved it. It was some kind of Italian dessert with like soft cookies soaked in I think Amaretto, covered in some kind of light chocolate whipped cream stuff. It was mouthwateringly good," I can't help but tease.

"You are a jackass. Give me back that chicken parm! You know I'm a dude with a chocolate addiction, and I gave your woman that last piece of chocolate fudge cake," Jackson returns, reaching over with his fork, trying to steal some of the chicken off my plate. I reach over and block his attack.

"Fucker! Stop trying to steal my chicken parm Jackson, or it'll be me and you boxing in the morning, when you're slow from eating all that pasta and bread this late at night. Not to mention God knows how many crispy treats before I got here."

"Yeah, you missed out on those. Isabella was a true sweetheart. She made each of us a tray and we finished those off about an hour ago," Carpenter adds.

"I seriously doubt Isabella made you each a tray. She probably made three trays to share with everyone, and you pigs just ate them all."

"Oh no, she left six trays. Clausen and Spencer took one home with them, and I know Hawkins didn't eat all of his. I think he hid his in his wing, so he didn't have to share with you," Jackson states.

"Hey, why am I the one that is supposed to share with Riggs? And for your information, Isabella made me a couple of desserts that I don't have to share because she loves me more than all you jackasses," Hawkins finally speaks up from the head of the table, a laptop open beside him.

"What other desserts? Did she leave you some fudge cake? If she did you better share that shit," Jackson, the chocolate junkie speaks up, and we all laugh at him.

Hawkins ignores him and looks up from his laptop asking me, "How old do you think Lexy is, Riggs?"

"I've never really asked, but I'm thinking she's the same age as Sarah and Brenda because we met at their High School graduation party. That would make her close to twenty-five maybe twenty-six."

"Nope, not even close. According to her driver's license, she will turn twenty-three in a couple of days. Her birthday is literally two days before you turn twenty-eight."

Stevens starts coughing, choking on his food, as he starts banging on the table with his other hand.

"Dude, take a drink of water before one of us decides if we're going to do the Heimlich maneuver on you," I inform my friend, as the rest of the Brothers start laughing.

"No...No..." Stevens manages to get out as he finally catches his breath and takes a quick drink of water. "You, Grayson Riggs, are a pervert. You were dry humping a fifteen-year-old girl on my deck eight years ago."

Everyone turns to me, pointing and laughing hard with this new information. Wait a minute, I quickly do the math in my head. Fuck, Stevens is right. I had just turned twenty. That can't be right. "Hawkins, are you sure about that? Maybe she lied on her licenses too."

"Nope, sorry Brother. I hate to tell you that if you were making out with Aless or Lexy or whatever you want to call her eight years ago, you are a secret perv, 'cause she will be turning twenty-three in a matter of days, and then you, 'Sir' will be an old fart at twenty-eight," Hawkins teases with a big smile on his face, leaning back in his chair.

"Fuck it. Well, she didn't look fifteen, and I don't regret one minute of it. Did you find out any more information?" I ask, wanting to get them off of Lexy's age. I need answers about who she really is.

"Yeah, I think the FBI or CIA is helping her build her cover story online. Carpenter's brothers called earlier from San Diego and said none of the girls in the picture knew who she was. They even showed them their real yearbook. Your girl, Alexa Rogers, only shows up in the online version. The same goes for her college degree. Fake. But you can't get those with just a simple hacking job. It was possibly done by Tony, but I'm thinking more likely the FBI or CIA. I'm talking to some of the guys we know there, trying to get them to talk."

"Shit, do you think she works for them? Or maybe she's in the Witness Protection Program?"

"No, I don't think she is in Witness Protection, because her appearance hasn't changed enough. She what, cut her hair and highlighted it? They would have her wearing contacts, covering up those very distinctive eyes, and they would have made her cut much more of her hair off and completely change the color to blonde or red, something more common for blue eyes. She has too big of a footprint, you know, too many things people could find her easier with. Lexy must have given one or both agencies something huge for them to be helping her create such a detailed cover story. What she gave them, I have no idea," Hawkins says as he starts typing on his laptop again.

"There's just something about her...she's different. Hawk, you sure she couldn't be an agent? Maybe they helped train her. No average girl can climb a rope like she can," Jackson adds.

"As of right now, I don't know. I do know that she owns a multi-million dollar corporation called Fluff E. Bear, but so far, that's about it. Starting tomorrow, I've got Carpenter's brothers tailing her. I want to know what she does every minute she is out of her penthouse. I'd love to get a bug in her place, but I know Tony is too good and would find it. It'd be sweet if we could get one of our girls to spy on her, but after today, I think they'd be more likely to spy on us and tell her," Hawkins says, shaking his head.

"Did you find out anything about a six-year-old girl getting shot at a birthday party in Italy?" I have to know. As much as I don't want it to be true, my gut is telling me that Lexy is a mafia daughter. The money, the scar, the insanely controlled life... Next time we're together, I'm going to inspect that magnificent body of hers to see if there are any more scars.

"You have to realize that those crime Families keep everything wiped off the web. They have cops in their pockets. I found nothing about a little girl getting shot. I'm asking around on the Dark Web to see if anyone is willing to talk, but I think Tony has Italy in his back pocket and they'll protect her. That's why I'm talking to our other connections in the FBI and CIA. Maybe I can get some information out of them, or make a trade for it."

"That's a good idea, Hawk. Let me know if you need help. I'd have no problem going to our connection directly and talking face to face, to see if I can get a feel for if they're lying. Or maybe they're protecting her too?" I suggest.

"I'll let you know. How well do you guys remember your trip to Italy, when you rescued that diplomat's daughter? Jackson, Carpenter and Stevens, what do you remember?" Hawkins asks them.

"I remember it like it was yesterday," Stevens says as he reaches down and raises his pant leg, pulling out that metal pipe he still carries around everywhere, tapping it on the table like it's a drumstick.

"You still carry that thing with you everywhere? Not only did you get shot, or should I say, nicked in the arm, you got hit over the head with that thing too," Carpenter teases.

"Hey, your fat ass was safe in the van babysitting all the kidnapped girls we helped rescue. I went back in to fight," Stevens comes back at him.

"Yeah, yeah. Those little girls were a mess. Absolutely scared shitless. Those fuckers really did a number on them. Someone had to stay with them," Carpenter professes.

"Knock it off you two and get serious for a minute. I want to bounce something off of you. Riggs just laughed at me when I suggested it the other day, but after we all saw how well Lexy can climb that rope today, what do you think about the idea that the little flying Italian mob assassin could be our little Lexy?"

"No way. That boy was a sharp-shooter. He was one of the best I've ever seen. I mean he was flying around on ropes and was able to release and hang on with one arm and have perfect aim. That takes a hell of a lot of upper body strength. No way is that dude Lexy. He was a short stocky guy," I immediately reply.

"Yeah, I have to agree with Riggs. No way. I heard his voice. Carpenter and I saw him and his sidekick working together. That little guy was a boss for sure though. He spoke with authority and all the men jumped and did just what he said. Did that mob boss have a son?" Stevens says.

"No, Al Canzano's only son is three. He does have an adult daughter, but you can't find anything out about her online. The internet is wiped clean. No pictures or anything. I would expect that if she was still a child, but with her being an adult now, I would think you could find something, but she's a ghost. He also has an infant daughter now too. It must be a second wife with a big age difference. No info on what happened to the first wife. He is an evil son of a bitch from what I've read and what you guys told me about him."

"I have to agree with Stevens and Riggs. That ninja assassin was definitely a dude. No way would those Italian asshole men listen to a woman boss them around like that guy was. We all know how chauvinistic and arrogant that Canzano bastard was. The Mob boss or 'Capo' was so full of himself. Fuck, he talked down to us the whole damn time and constantly referred to us as 'boy'. I wanted to kick his ass myself.

And that short assassin was a dude. There's no way it could've been a chick. He was just as arrogant as the Capo. He saved me and Fitz's asses when we were cornered and surrounded. He took out two men flying over our heads, yelling to warn us. We asked him his name and tried to thank him, but he wouldn't even respond to us. No. That dude was an asshole, just like their Capo," Jackson remarks.

"Okay. It's just an idea, but keep it in mind as we watch Lexy. I'll keep searching. Oh, just to let you all know, little Lexy has all your mothers and sisters and even Tiffany starting a special self-defense class at her studio two nights a week. They all added it to their calendars tonight. The moms could be taking it for shits and giggles to get to know your girl Riggs, or this could be serious, and after her little performance today on the rope, Sarah and the girls are convinced she can teach them a few things," Hawkins informs us with a smirk on his face.

"Let them. It'd be good for all of them to learn a few self-defense skills," I add, thinking it would be cute to watch Lexy teaching my Mom how to defend herself from an attacker. Mom is probably a good six to seven inches taller than Lexy.

"Hey, wait a minute," Jackson interrupts my thoughts, sitting up straighter and looking towards me. "Your woman is the same Sexy-Lexy that owns 'A Better You' Health Club and Spa, right?"

"Don't call her 'Sexy Lexy' or I'll have to kick your ass. But yeah, she owns it and works there. I've heard talk about her club for over a year, but I never went there. Right now, thinking back I sure as fuck wish I had. I would've realized it was her ages ago. Have you ever been there?" I ask, wondering where this is going.

"Nah, not me, but that's where all the 'old-ladies' go from my dad's bikers club. She trains them in a private class. They call her 'Sexy Lexy' too. The club whores say she teaches a real badass class called, 'No Holds Barred' where she trains them to fight dirty and defend themselves when the men get drunk and out of hand. She's a real badass. Believe me, I've seen how the women do after finishing her classes. You know the club whores don't have the money for security like we provide for the escorts, but after taking Lexy's classes, they can damn near take care of themselves or at least get away. Shit, I can't believe it just dawned on me it's the same chick."

"Are you serious? Those women are like the common street-walking-hooker types, right?"

"Yeah, sort of. I mean they are a few steps up from that, they get a medical check-up monthly and they're under club protection, and Big Cuddle Bear is not someone you wanna mess with. I just told Fitz we need to advise the women we provide protection to, to take her classes. She's very well known for her skills. I'll be goddamned. We live in a small mother fucking world, to think this is your Lexy." Jackson leans back in his chair rubbing his chin.

"Is my mom taking lessons from Lexy?" Carpenter asks.

"Yeah, even Jackson's mom is taking them. Like I said, *every* one of the females are taking her classes twice a week. Lexy is a busy owner. She does all the private training herself. When she bought the place, every single person was re-trained, by her. I also think her buddy Tony works there with her at times. That is what some of the chat rooms are saying," Hawkins adds, not even looking up from his laptop.

"Well I think it'd be good for our moms and sisters to learn a little self-defense. It sure won't hurt anything. Now I'm wondering if my mom will tell me anything about these classes. I know I won't get jack-shit out of Sarah. The traitor," I say thinking out loud.

"My mom can pretty much fend for herself, you know, having to put up with my dad and me and the twins. Maybe she can teach sissy some of that shit. She's growing up too damn quick in my books," Carpenter adds shaking his head. His little sister Rachel is a young teenager now, and Carpenter is already getting scared. Man, the next few years are going to be fun.

"Carpenter, your little sister is in the classes too. Right now, even Grandma Piedmont has signed up."

"My grandmother? How the hell do you know that?" Knowing that freaks me out a bit. I don't know if I'm ready for Lexy to meet her so soon.

"Like I said before, I have access to all of their calendars, and everything on their phones. If the ladies track their cycles on the calendar, have a date or a doctor's appointment, I know about it - if I want too. But there is no reason to tell them I have complete access to their phones. I just need to know these things. I have to know where all of you are, you know that. I have issues like that. Sorry dude." Hawkins goes back to typing. I'm sure he's regretting telling us so much. I've always known he has to keep a close watch on all of us. That's one reason all the girls have tracker earrings. I didn't know he was spying on our phones as well, but it isn't like we have secrets.

"Well, I'm calling it a night. We have a lot of shit to do this week with these crime families moving into town. I don't want to see a turf war between the Russians and Italians, nor do I want them messing with our club either. I'll see you all no later than eight a.m. sharp in the gym. Then we'll hit our regular rounds and see if we can find any intel on the streets. Jackson, hit up your dad and see if he's heard anything about what's going on with them too. With Cuddle Bear having the 'club whores' as you call them, he has a stake in this too."

"I'll head over there and take Carpenter with me right after our work out in the morning. Ride your bike to head-quarters in the morning," Jackson replies, with a head nod to Carpenter.

"I'll check in with the twins and let them know they answer to you, Riggs. They won't push their luck with you. They still have a dream of becoming one of us one day," Carpenter throws his head back laughing, before adding, "Hell no! Those boys can work for us, but they are not 'Brother' material."

"They can keep the dream, but I agree with you. They hit the time clock. They work for a paycheck as employees. I don't see a vote ever happening where all twelve of us would agree to them becoming full Brothers." Making my opinion known, I stand up to leave. "Okay Brothers, goodnight."

Hawkins gets up and follows me to the door, not saying anything until we are almost to my car. I know he's got some-thing on his mind and is building up the nerve to say it, because walking me to my car is not his norm.

"I emm, I think you really need to search your heart and see how you'll deal with the fact that Lexy could easily be a mob boss' daughter. She could even be Al Canzano's daughter since I can find nothing online about her," Hawkins says, looking at his feet.

"I'll deal with whoever she is. I'm not scared of Al Canzano or any Italian father who thinks he can take Lexy from me. She's not leaving. She is here to stay, and I swear, the day she trusts me with her whole story is the day I may marry her. I know that sounds completely insane, but like I told you yesterday, being separated from her… it hurts man. She's the other part of my heart," I say looking him straight in the eyes.

"Okay, Brother," Hawkins says, nodding. "Well, we'll know

everything she does and anybody she talks to the moment she leaves her house. Oh, there was a male employee who was crushing on her, named James. One of the male club chat rooms kicked him out after he got fired. I guess one night he tried to kiss Lexy and she turned him down, but he started to imagine they had a chance so she had to fire him. She told the men at the club to leave him alone, that she'd handle it, and they all believe she can easily take him out if he ever tries anything. Just wanted you to know. I'm looking into him as well."

"Thanks man. Let me know if this jackass is stalking her. I'll have a little chat with him if he is and nip that in the butt real fast."

"Okay, but Grayson..." Hawkins pauses again, looking down and picking at his fingernails. "I... I ... just don't want to see you heartbroken. There is a lot we don't know about her, and it looks like you did more than just jump into the deep end of the love pool. I don't want you drowning."

I pat him on the back, "Sorry dude. It may be too late for me but you're the best swimmer I know and you'll help me figure this out. Everything will work out."

"Okay Brother. Okay. We'll figure this shit out, I promise," Hawkins says, nodding his head again before turning around and heading back into his castle.

Pausing for a second, I just watch him. I think I'm going to give Mom Gregory a call tomorrow to check on him. Hawkins seems a bit off, and she has always been his miracle worker. Then it dawns on me, yeah, the anniversary is rapidly approaching. Time to make sure we're around constantly for the next month. Thank God we have Fitz and Isabella's wedding in a little over two months. With all this Lexy shit going on we'll be able to keep him busy and make damn sure this month goes by smoothly.

13

TIME TO MAKE A STAND

Lexy

*C*lutching the card to my chest, I lean back in my office chair and close my eyes, inhaling the sweet smell of fresh roses. Grayson has sent me at least one long-stemmed rose every day since I came back into his life. Opening my eyes, I look around my office. I'm completely surrounded by these red and white beauties.

It started with one long-stemmed red rose a day for the first twelve days. On day thirteen, I got a white rose. Since then, I don't know what to expect, but it will be either a white or red rose for sure. He wasn't teasing when he told me he'd be sending me a rose every day for the rest of my life, and to think I'm the only woman he's ever sent flowers to is even more thrilling.

I never know how many it'll be, or where I will receive them. Like today, Steer and Roid bring me two stunning bouquets with twelve red roses and one white rose dead center in each. Those two beef-cake protein powder junkies love teasing me about becoming a softy with Grayson and all these roses. They may be my assistant managers, but they are also dear friends, and I couldn't care less what they say or think about them. I love it. Keeping my cool while they are in here is difficult, but the moment they leave my office, I spring up from my chair and grab it:

"To My One Love,
    These roses do not compare to your beauty or the passion I feel for you. One arrangement should stay in your office as a reminder of my love. The other one should be placed beside your bed so they're the last thing you see before you fall asleep and dream of me.
    Yours for always,
    Grayson"

My heart just melts. He's never actually looked me in the eye and flat out said '*I love you*', but he writes it and implies it all the time. Without question, I know this is love. This feeling I have for him is beyond overwhelming. He is the other part of my soul and I know it. I haven't said those words to him either, and I won't until he says it first.

It's hard to believe it's only been two months. I can't help but smile as I touch the heart shaped ruby earrings Grayson gave me on my birthday. At least he was honest when he told me he had them designed just for me, and that these earrings also gave him peace of mind because Hawkins had added a tracking chip in them, just like the ones all the females within their Camelot world wear. I've tried to reassure him he has nothing to worry about and I've let him know over and over again that I'm very capable of protecting myself. He knows I teach self-defense classes and am very confident in my abilities. Grayson knows that if I ever did need help or back up, he'd be the first person I'd call.

Over the last month and a half, we've celebrated our birthdays and our eight years of longing for each other. I've tried everything to seduce him, but he never allows it to go past heavy making-out, and as he calls it, 'petting'. That's the strangest term to me. There are some expressions and sayings I just haven't caught onto yet. I can't really complain, he does always leave me very satisfied. I just need to figure out a way to convince him I do trust him, without telling him I am a mafia princess.

God, why does he have to make it so difficult? There is no way I will open up and bare my soul like he wants. I'm not going to lose him. I don't know if he can deal with my past. I worry that no one can really handle the full truth about me. Everyone has welcomed me into their little world, and it feels like I've been a part of them for years. They've even welcomed my dearest friends.

The self-defense classes I'm teaching the ladies are such fun. I'm getting to know all the moms, sisters and their friends really well. They haven't shown even a hint of hesitation towards me or my friends. Tony and Thomas are our attack dummies and have taken beatings quite a few times. They volunteered for it, so they can't complain. They're impressed with how great the ladies are doing. I was surprised to learn that Thomas is a Black Belt in karate. He's pretty good at kick-boxing too. Thomas is so flamboyant that you'd never believe he's such a badass.

Grayson's Granny Piedmont is such a riot. She walked right up to me and hugged me the first time I met her, and told me she is the kinky one in the bunch. She didn't even blush or whisper when she told me she was into BDSM and lived the lifestyle way before Fifty Shades was even a thought. Mom Riggs came running over so fast to make sure her Mom didn't go into a lot of details. I laugh just remembering it.

Granny Piedmont literally has her boy-toy, Jeffery, be her partner in the class. The guy is in his late twenties. She told me she does a lot of training in the club she belongs to, to make sure the guys really want to learn the lifestyle and are not doing it just for shits and giggles. I just stood there, trying not to look too shocked.

I told the ladies that this coming Thursday, I'd have Steer and Roid come in for the training to see if any of them could actually get the upper hand on a guy their size. Both of them are almost six foot four and well over two-hundred-thirty-five pounds. They wouldn't really hurt anyone, but they would give them a great work out. Both of those guys are true sweethearts and complete health food nuts. They drink so much protein shit and male enhancing crap that they always have that pumped-up look. They swear they don't do steroids though. I think it'll be good for everyone to have them in class for a change.

Tonight is Drake and Isabella's wedding rehearsal at the castle. I'm probably as excited as she is. I can't wait for Grayson to see me in my formal 'wench dress' as Sarah referred to it. Both her and Tony helped design it and then had their crew make it. It's nice to have personal designers to work with. Sarah probably knows more about my past life than anyone. I don't know how much Tony has told her. He really needs to talk to her about himself, soon. I don't want to see both of them get hurt. I can see how the three of them are so close, and I think Thomas is crushing on Tony as well. This could be such a huge cluster-fuck if he doesn't handle this the right way.

Maybe I'll be a nice boss and go get my staff some coffee. A quick trip to Starbucks should clear my head so I can get some work done. Placing the card back in its envelope, I add it to the pile of notes that Grayson has written to me, which I keep in a Camelot-era looking treasure chest. Taking one last smell of my freshest arrangement of roses, I head to the door.

"Hey Steer and Roid, I'm headed to Starbucks to grab us a coffee. I'll see you two in about thirty minutes. Do you two want your usual? Coffee with coconut milk and that's it?"

"Do you think you'll ever call us by our real names?

Christopher isn't that bad of a name. I'd even be happy if you called me Chris." Steer says, shaking his head at me.

"Now why would I do that? I think Steer fits you so much better. Believe me, I don't want to look like one of those young girls that follow you around all mesmerized. You know what I think if all that mail-order male enhancing shit you drink every day. You don't know if it has hidden drugs in it. And I can't promise I'll actually ever stop calling you by your given name of 'Steer'."

"Come on Lexy, you don't want your clients to think we take that shit, do you? "Roid says firmly, before he continues. "But yes, since you're buying, I'll take a venti, but I'm going to splurge today. Get them to add three Equal sweeteners. Make sure it's the blue one, I hate that pink shit."

"Hey Matt, why don't you get a skinny mocha if you're going to be a girl and sweeten it?" Steer teases his friend.

"Just because I'm adding a hint of sweetener doesn't make me a girl, 'Steer'," Roid teases Chris, refusing to say his real name.

I watch as Steer flips off Roid. Calling an end to this nonsense, I say "Okay you two, you're supposed to be working. Knock it off and go flex. Give the women in the club an endorphin rush. See you in a few." Putting on my big sunglasses, I head to the door.

Taking a deep breath as soon as I step outside, I smell the ocean in the air. I love it here in Santa Monica. The weather is perfect and always has a light breeze. I walk towards the closest Starbucks, looking in the windows as I go. Fuck! In the reflection, I see that not only do I have James following behind me, but one of Carpenters' little brothers is tailing me too. I'm thinking it's Ethan. He's always a bit closer and more nervous than Benny. These boys better not still be following me after I get my coffee, or I may have to make my stand and put them in their places.

This shit has to stop. James has been following me for over

six months now. I've already spoken to him twice about it. I think he's getting a bit obsessed with me, bordering on stalking. I had to fire him months ago, because he tried to kiss me after work one day and I instantly set him straight. He was a friend, nothing more. The End. But he didn't stop making advances. Since then, he's started following me several times a week, and what pisses me off the most is that I'm pretty sure he's taping my ass with his phone as he walks behind me. Fuck. Time to limber up a bit more, just in case I need to put on a little show. This is California, and sometimes someone will just act a little crazy for no good reason.

I grab ahold of the next street sign I pass and swing around it a few times before I let go, landing back on my feet. Seeing a bench up ahead, I grab the back of it and quickly flip myself into a handstand before dropping my feet to the seat of the bench before gracefully stepping down to the ground and continuing my stroll like I didn't just pull off a cool acrobatic maneuver. Glancing in the window reflection again, I see both idiots are still following me.

As I reach for the handle of the door to open it, I check out the reflection one last time. Shit, they are both still on my tail. Lucky for me, there is only two other people in line. Glancing out the window, I see both James and Ethan have stopped about ten feet outside the door.

James is flipping through his phone, probably checking out his new videos of my ass. Ethan looks like he is FaceTiming someone, because he's looking into his phone and talking. It's probably Grayson or Hawkins. Whoever he is talking to, he's turning and showing them James with his phone. Fuck. I have to put a stop to this, right now. It's sad to think both dumbasses don't even realize I am completely aware of the both of them. Grayson really needs to train his men better. I would never stand for this type of stupidity with my men. Geesh.

"Lexy, let me guess. You'd like a venti coffee with coconut milk, and a skinny mocha with three Equal this morning? Oh, and your usual Venti Mocha Frappuccino with three extra hits of mocha." Shawna, my favorite barista calls out.

"Yes please, and could I get a carrier? And would you please stuff extra napkins around the drinks so I won't spill them?"

"Okay Lexy, you got it." Within a couple of minutes, the drinks are ready and I watch Shawna start tucking several napkins all around them so they don't move in the carrier. I shove a twenty into her tip jar as I grab my carrier and head for the door. It's time to make my stand so that they all get the message this time.

As I stroll down the sidewalk back towards my club, I check out the reflection again to catch James still taping my ass, and Ethan holding his phone out in front of him like he is talking to someone and showing them that James is taping my ass on his phone. There is a bench about six feet in front of me with no one sitting on it, a perfect place to hand James his ass, and stop this tailing me shit, now!

I casually place the drink carrier on the bench, then I grab the seat of the bench, and before James realizes what is happening, I do a quick handstand, kicking my legs straight out, making sure to knock James's phone out of his hand and send it flying into the air. Like magic, I hit the ground and reach out and grab his phone before it hits the ground. Within a split second, I do a spin kick, making sure my foot hits the side of James's face, taking him to the ground. I quickly land on top of him, placing my right hand on top of his Adam's apple pushing it with just enough force to still him.

Dropping his cell phone beside me, I lift my sunglasses and lean down, looking into his eyes, only inches from his face I say, "This ends today James. I never want to look behind me and see you. No more stalking me or taping me. You remember Tony? I'll have him hack into your computer and destroy your life. And if he finds any videos of me on there, I'll make sure the police get copies and I'll play the innocent damsel in distress and you'll go to jail. Do you want that?"

James' eyes look like they're about to pop out of his head as I loosen my grip on his neck. "I asked you a question. Are you finished with your little stalking game?"

Nodding his head he mumbles, "Yes, Lexy. I'll never follow you again, I swear."

I pick up his phone that is resting beside my leg and slam it as hard as I can into the sidewalk, hearing the screen shatter.

"Ma'am, are you okay? Did this man try anything with you?" I notice a man's dress shoes beside me.

Still looking at James, I slide my sunglasses back over my eyes. I accidentally-on-purpose knee him in the good ol' family jewels as I move to get to my feet. I whisper, "You know what I'm capable of James. This is over. You're pissing off my boyfriend." As I get up, I look at the man in the business suit. "I'm fine sir. Thank you. I've taken many years of self-defense and when this asshole kept stalking me and taping my ass with his phone, I just got to my breaking point and put an end to it. He won't be bothering me again." Looking down at him I ask, "Will you, James?"

James is curled into a ball, both hands between his legs, coughing and shaking his head as he mumbles. "No." Cough. "I'm sorry, Lexy." Cough. "You'll never see me again." Cough.

Looking back to the good Samaritan, I say, "Thank you again, sir."

"Ma'am, there is an officer coming this way if you'd like to inform him of what happened. Stalking is a crime and can put this guy behind bars. I'm sure he can make sure this man doesn't bother you again."

"That won't be necessary. He's an ex-employee, and I'm sure he understands me now, don't you James?"

"Yes, I understand. I'm done, I swear it," James whispers, loud enough for both of us to hear through his grunts of pain.

Then I turn and wave at the cell phone Ethan has pointed at me. Looking into the camera, I lift my glasses and say. "Grayson! Get your ass and whoever else is watching the show to my office. You have one hour before I come to you." Then I look at Carpenter's little brother and continue. "Let me see if I can guess which twin you are. You are Ethan, am I right?"

He is still holding his phone on me as the good Samaritan comes over to me again and places his hand on my back. "Is this boy bothering you too? Maybe you should take a minute and talk to the officer. You are a little thing and I wouldn't want you to suffer continual harassment from these boys."

"Sir, I can assure you, this will stop today. This boy is actually a lousy bodyguard my boyfriend has tailing me everywhere I go." I reach into my belt and pull out two business cards, handing him one. "See Sir, I own and run the 'Better You'. I spend my days training women. I can handle myself. I just allowed these two idiots to get away with this far too long. Now I'm making my stand and just showing my over-protective boyfriend that I can handle myself."

The good Samaritan looks at my card, and I can tell by his reaction he must have recognized me. "Oh, I've heard about you. You're Lexy Rogers, the little badass the ladies in my office talk about. You're the one teaching those 'No Holds Barred' classes that teach them how to fight dirty and stay alive and safe. By the way they talk, I was expecting you to be a lot bigger. I guess with some people, size doesn't matter," he says with a wink and a big smile. "You do have a very good reputation. You can definitely handle yourself. If your boyfriend continues to doubt your abilities or you get tired of his over-protective nature, I'd love to take you to dinner and get to know you better. I'm not a Neanderthal like your boyfriend seems to be." He reaches into the pocket of his suit jacket and hands me his business card. Then with the cutest smirk on his face, he leans in and winks at Ethan's phone. I'm sure he's pissing Grayson off with his flirting. "I'll see you around Miss Lexy Rogers."

Giggling, I take his card, "Thank you. It's nice to hear that some men actually aren't living in the Stone Ages."

The man winks at me one last time before he turns and walks away, just as our regular neighborhood officer comes walking over to me. "Ms. Rogers, is everything okay?"

"Yes Officer, I'm fine. James White, who is still on the ground, will not be bothering me anymore. But if I do see him anywhere around me again, you'll be my first call, because at that point I'll be pressing charges for stalking. But I think he got the message loud and clear, didn't you?"

James is still cupping his balls as he sits up, slowly nodding his head.

"Well, since no one is willing to go on record for anything there isn't much I can do." The officer's head snaps to Ethan. "Aren't you a Camelot Brother?"

"Emm yes sir. I work for them." Ethan is getting more nervous. I want to laugh so bad.

"What is your involvement in this?" The officer walks closer to Ethan who is still video chatting this. I have to intercede.

"Officer Baker, it's okay. I have this handled as well. He was just about to walk me to my club and get some information on my self-defense classes for himself. Since his mother and little sister take classes from me, I wouldn't want them kicking his butt." Turning to Ethan, I add, "Aren't you, Ethan?"

"Emm, yeah, I guess I am. I... I... was very impressed with all the ninja shit, I mean stuff I just saw, you used to take this guy out."

"Okay. Are you sure you don't want to press charges on this man on the sidewalk?" Officer Baker turns and asks one more time.

"No sir, but you can remove him from in front of my club. I would appreciate it."

"You got it, Ms. Rogers. I'll just take him down to the station and have one of the men talk to him about what could happen to him if you should decide to ever press charges. He looks close to pissing himself anyway. And thank you, my wife loves your classes too, by the way." Officer Baker gives me a head nod as he helps James off the sidewalk and leads him to his squad car.

I loop my arm into Ethan's, pulling him towards the club door, making a quick stop by the bench to grab the coffees. Once inside the door, Steer notices me and comes walking over.

"Picking up more Camelot Boys, are you? Lexy, I got a feeling Riggs will not be too happy to find out you are looping arms with Carpenters' little brother. That borderlines on flirting." Steer says teasingly.

Ethan is such a nervous dork, right now it actually looks a little cute. Letting go of Ethan's arm, I see he's still holding his phone up at all of us. Surely he's not still video chatting? I reach over and easily take away his phone to see Grayson rubbing his face and Hawkins laughing beside him.

"Well, well, just as I thought. Hello Grayson and Hawkins. Anyone else there with you to see this?"

"Yeah. Stevens, Carpenter and Jackson were here until I kicked their asses out about two minutes ago because I couldn't hear over their laughing," Grayson says.

"We need to talk. I'm tired of this pathetic tail. I do not need to be followed, and I want it to stop. Now. So get your ass down here or I come to you."

"Fine, no more tail. But we'll have to talk about it tonight after the rehearsal dinner. I'm already at Hawkins' and so is Mom. We have a shit-load of crap to finish before the actual rehearsal. Okay? My Mom, Mom Gregory and Ivy are barking orders at everyone and I think Isabella or Fitz may kill someone if they don't calm down. They've been sending everyone on errands all over town. Sorry baby, but I gotta help with all this shit."

"Okay, I understand. With you having the first Brothers of Camelot wedding in the chapel, I'm sure they want it perfect. Grayson, we are going to talk about this tonight. I thought you were better than this. But if Ethan and Benny are the examples of how you've trained your men, maybe I'm the one that needs to worry about your safety. I offered to work with Ethan. I know I can help him. I can probably help all of you if this is how you work."

"Shit! I didn't train them, but I will after what I just witnessed. I trusted Carpenter to handle it and he'll be hearing about it as well. He obviously doesn't know shit about tailing someone. He should have taken James out long before he got anywhere near you," Grayson replies, trying to save face.

"Hey, I knew they were tailing me since day one. It stops now because I don't care which Brother you have following me, I'll kick his ass, and that includes you. Do I make myself clear? And don't make me prove it to you, because I can and will."

Now Grayson's chuckling. "Babe, I'll agree you're a badass, but actually kicking one of the Brother's asses, and not a little flunky? I don't think so. But I'll cancel the tail for now."

My temper starts to seethe as I look over to Hawkins. "Hawk, listen to me. Tell the other Brothers to be ready for an embarrassing ass-whooping if they think for a minute of tailing me. I swear I will hand any of you your asses. I'm tired of this shit. Do not try me. *Do I make myself clear?!*"

I disconnect the phone before anyone can say another word, not caring if Grayson gets pissed. I'm done. Handing Ethan back his phone I take off my sunglasses, knowing the power behind my eyes. "I mean it, Ethan. I was playing nice with James. I've been trained by the best. I know several different martial arts and can hold my own in hand-to-hand combat with any man. If I ever need back-up, I'll let you know. You might want to warn the Brothers I have ripped more than one man's balls almost off, to the point they had to have surgery to correct what I did to them. I do not play well with others. I fight dirty and I fight to win. Consider yourselves warned."

"Shit, I'm not going to mess with you. They can follow you themselves. My balls are too important to me to risk them. But I have a question: you said you train my mom, what do you mean?"

"Just like I said," I hand Steer and Roid their coffees and take a big drink of mine, before I continue. "Your Mom is one tough lady. I recommend you watch yourself when teasing your little sister too. She's quite a powerful little thing. She might kick your ass just for shits and giggles. Lucky for you, she likes you best. But you might want to warn Benny that if he messes up her hair before he drops her off at school, she might take him down in front of her friends just to put him in his place."

"Are you shitting me? I'm not telling him jack shit. I'll enjoy hearing about her taking him down a few pegs. He's a cocky bastard and it would serve him right. Thanks for the heads up. Were you serious, you train guys?"

"Yeah, you should come next Tuesday and watch the moms and sisters. We can always use another guy to beat the shit out of. But I promise we'll all work with you and so can Tony and Thomas. And next Tuesday's a full house because both Steer and Roid will be there too."

"Cool, I'd love to come. Thanks for the invite. I'll be there." Ethan finally relaxes a little bit as he puts his phone in his back pocket.

"Hey, little shit. I've seen and trained with Lexy myself. You might want to warn the Brothers she can take them out because they all follow the rules, and our girl Lexy doesn't know what a rule is," Steer informs him.

"I'm not telling those overly confident fucks anything. I hope she does hand them their asses. Seeing them taken down a couple pegs would be even better than see it happen to Benny." Ethan says as he heads towards the door.

"Yo Ethan, come down any night and I'll personally work with you. You looked a bit nervous when you got here. I'm the youngest boy in my family too. I'll teach you a few of your own tricks," Roid says to him. He knows that sometimes siblings, even if they are playing around, can take it a bit far, not even realizing they're crushing the self-esteem of their brother.

"Really? That would be so cool. Thanks dude. I'll see you later in the week." Ethan says, finally giving us a genuine smile as he walks out the door.

"Thanks, Roid. That was awful sweet of you."

"Damn Lexy, I could tell the boy was scared shitless. I think he's doing all this tailing and shit trying to fit in. I think he wants to do anything to make his brother's think he's tough. He just wants to be one of the guys but I don't think he really likes all this stuff. Maybe I can help the kid out. They're what, nineteen or twenty? Maybe he'd rather be doing something else but is too chicken-shit to speak up."

Walking over, I give him a hug. "See, I knew you were a true sweetheart under all those massive muscles. You have a soft heart."

Roid laughs and hugs me awkwardly. Steer just can't let the tender moment go.

"I'd watch it if I were you 'Roid'. Grayson might get pissed that you're trying to move in on his woman."

"Fuck you. I'm not trying to move in on Lexy. It was you who was originally crushing on her anyway. You better hope no one online ever talks or it'll be your ass that gets kicked."

"Okay, you two, enjoy your coffee. I have a ton of paperwork to do and I need to get a fast workout in before the rehearsals tonight. It'll be a weekend wedding, so I'll see you guys back here on Monday. Have a great weekend. Remember to take more condoms than you think you need," I tease, as I head to my office, completely ignoring Roid's teasing of Steer. I was fully aware that he originally had a crush on me, but he always knew my heart belonged to another. Tony had to have a talk with him and I just acted like I didn't know.

Once I'm in my office, I smile to myself and enjoy the sweet smell of the roses. Tonight will be so much fun, but tomorrow will even be better. The first Camelot wedding. I know where my mind will be: imagining my own wedding to Grayson. It could really happen. Not this year, but one day. I need to introduce him to Uncle Louie. That is what I'll do after the wedding. I'm going to call him and let them speak over the phone. It's time.

14

THE REHEARSAL AND LAST-MINUTE CHANGES

Grayson

*T*his has been the longest day of my life. I was ready to shoot Ivy, Isabella's mom, myself. I even told my mom I'd volunteer for the job if she needed me to do it, and I'd do it with a smile. We could even get rid of the body, never to be seen again. She knew I was teasing, but it did lighten her and Mom Gregory's spirits. Until about two hours ago, she was being a bigger bitch than I've ever seen her be.

Fitz finally had enough after she berated everyone and everything. When she went after the florist because the flowers were too open and wouldn't look as fresh for tomorrow in her opinion, the final straw broke and we all heard Fitz yell, "*Ivy shut the fuck up before I have you removed. I will not allow you to ruin Bella's big day.*" When Fitz was finished, there wasn't one person here that wasn't thrilled and ready to rejoice. We couldn't help but smile ear to ear.

Then Isabella let loose. '*Mom, I agree with Drake. Shut The Freak Up or I'll have Drake call the police and have you removed and locked up until after the wedding. I do have a couple of officers that are my friends and would gladly help me out. I'll tell them the truth, that you're harassing everyone here. I don't want to do it but I will. This is my wedding and it'll be perfect as long as my friends are here. You and Stanley can either shut up and stop barking orders or leave."*

I was so proud of her for finally standing up to her mom. Ivy just stood there for a second looking around at all of us. We were trying so hard to hide our smiles of pride that Isabella put her in her place. Ivy realized not one person was on her side. So she shut up and said, *"Okay, Isabella. You're right, it's your wedding. I just wanted it to be perfect for you. But it's obvious that your perfect and mine are different. I'll not say another word."*

And with that she finally shut up, moping quietly. But luckily, she is doing whatever Mom Gregory is telling her to do. It's hard to believe sometimes that my Mom along with Stevens', Gregory and Isabella's moms, have been friends since they were all little kids. They are all so different, and yet still very close to this day. More like sisters than friends, with the way they can fight sometimes and still be friends afterwards.

I walk out to the front of the chapel where I can see the driveway better. I know Lexy is going to love it, the wind is blowing all the wisteria and you can probably smell it from the castle gates. I can't wait to see my girl. I can only hope she is not still pissed at me for having Carpenter's brothers tailing her. I was only doing it to make sure her family wasn't planning on kidnapping her. She did impress me and the Brothers with the way she took out that idiot James. He totally deserved to have his balls handed to him, and she did a great job of doing just that. My girl has more skill than I first thought.

She should be here any minute. She's coming with Tony and Sarah and I wouldn't be surprised at all if Thomas is with them too. They have been like three peas in a pod for the last few months. This is the longest relationship I've ever seen Sarah in. I think she really is falling for Tony and it makes me a bit nervous. No one knows anything about him other than him being Lexy's childhood friend.

But as Mom and Granny keep telling me, *I need to worry about my own relationship and not Sarah's. She's a big girl and has to make her own bed. It's not my place to decide who she shares it with.* I don't know what it is, but something just isn't right. Maybe when Lexy starts sharing with me, I'll be able to figure more out about Tony.

The gravel crunches and I turn to see Tony coming up the driveway in a red Alfa Romeo, Gilia Quadrifoglio. Nice car. Might have known he'd be like Lexy and have an Italian car as well. Lexy's sitting in the back with Thomas, looking around with a huge smile on her face. I know how much she loves it up here. I can't wait till next year when I show her our future castle being built on the other side of this mountain. Hawkins is enjoying helping with the creation and planning. He's so overjoyed that one of us is finally taking him up on his offer and moving up here closer to him. Everyone just has to keep it a secret for now. Mom doesn't even know.

The car's engine hasn't even stopped before Lexy is opening the door to get out. "Oh my God, this is just so beautiful." She runs over to me, grabbing my hand, pulling me through the rows and rows of wisteria arches. "Grayson, you have no idea how this takes me back to my childhood." She stops us in the middle of one of the arches and closes her eyes, just breathing in the sweet smell. "Nothing brings more peace to my soul than the sight of all this wisteria. Who's idea was this? Did you help build all of them?" she fires off so many questions all at once, I can't get one word out. I love to see this kind of excitement in her.

Pulling her into my arms, I look into those eyes of hers that have awakened my heart and soul like nothing else ever has. "I don't even get a 'hello' or a 'kiss my ass' for earlier?"

"Well hello, Grayson. As long as you've called off your boys, and if you trust me enough not to follow me every step of every day, I have nothing to be mad at you for now."

"Then shut up and kiss me because I trust you, my little

184

badass." I can't wait a second longer. I lean down and capture her mouth in a passionate kiss, wrapping my arms even tighter around her. I reach down and cup that scrumptious ass, lifting her up. She wraps her legs around my waist automatically as her hands dive into my hair, nails lightly scraping my scalp, sending shivers down my spine. Damn, I have reached paradise. Every second I am with her is heaven.

"Okay, put the woman down Grayson. Now is not the time to jump her bones. We all need to get to the chapel. Can't you hear Mom calling everyone?" Hearing Sarah's voice pulls me back to earth and I slowly pull away from Lexy, resting our foreheads together for a second before lowering her back to the ground.

"Grayson! Sarah! It's time to get all the Camelot Brothers in the chapel, and the girls, rather Wenches, up here too. Isabella wants to see how it'll all look or if we'll have to change anything up. The priest is here and we need to get started with the rehearsal. The caterer will have dinner ready within the hour." We hear mom's voice bellowing from the front door of the chapel.

Wrapping an arm around Lexy's small waist I sigh, "Well, you can hear who's in charge at this minute. The boss has been changing all day. Let's go see what all the fuss is about."

Lexy just giggles before saying, "I can't wait. I'm probably as excited as Isabella about tomorrow." She looks up at me, blinking those beautiful eyes of hers, "You'll finally get to see me dressed as your wench," she says as she cuddles into me, making Sir even harder than he already was. Shit. I am so hoping no one notices I'm sporting a boner in a church.

"I already know that to me, you'll be the most beautiful woman there. I think tomorrow will be spectacular."

Coming out of the wisteria arches, we see the rest of the Brothers are already headed into the chapel. It feels good to get smiles and head nods from the Brothers as they see me and

Lexy together. I know I have their approval, they just want to know her past as much as I do.

My heart flutters deep in my chest when I look down at Lexy. I think we'll probably be the next couple to walk down this aisle. I know the moment she starts opening up and telling me about her past, I'm marrying her. Without question, I know she is the one who holds my heart completely. I never thought I could love someone the way I love her.

As we walk through the massive arched wooden doorway, I watch as Lexy slows down and looks up at the ten-foot-tall double doors. Each door has the Brothers of Camelot shield on it.

"Wow, you guys have done a lot to finish this. I love the shields and it all looks so authentic. I feel like I am stepping back in time."

"Clay and Carpenter's families are really great at all of this. They can create whatever we request. I love it up here too. Mom has already announced we're having Christmas Mass up here, and it is mandatory for everyone," I inform her with a little laugh, at my mother dictating orders.

Entering the chapel, we see Isabella talking on her cell phone, Fitz's arms wrapped tight around her. She looks so stressed, which isn't a good sign for someone getting married in less than twenty-four hours. It's completely quiet, as everyone stops what they're doing and listens to Isabella.

"Is everything okay, Tory? I hope you aren't stuck in traffic or lost."
Pause:

"Oh honey, I promise it's okay. You're a wonderful mom, and Little JayJay always comes first."
Pause:

"Sweetie, really, there was no way any of us could have planned for him to get so sick."
Pause:

"I understand. I do. We'll be okay."
Pause:

"You need to stay with him in the hospital. I'll check with you after the rehearsal dinner. I do not want you to worry about any of this. I'll have it figured out. You stay with your baby."

Pause:

"I love you too, Tory. Give JayJay a kiss from me. You take all the time you need."

Pause:

"Honey, I would expect you to act like this. Tell your mom and dad we send our love. JayJay is getting the best of care. He'll be just fine very soon, I promise. He won't be in the hospital that long. He'll be better before you know it. I'm sure he'll be his playful self in a matter of days. I'll talk to you in a few hours."

Once she disconnects the phone, she turns and throws her arms around Fitz and starts crying. Both my mom and Mom Gregory run over to her and join in the hug, trying to comfort her, telling her everything will be okay.

Ivy comes walking over to me, looking Lexy up and down. "Grayson, have you seen your girlfriend's dress for the wedding? I hope it looks genuine."

Chuckling at her, I say "Ms. Anderson, don't be so rude. Let me introduce you to Lexy Rogers, my girlfriend. Lexy this is Ivy Anderson, Isabella's mom."

Lexy smiles, sticking her hand out to shake Ivy's as she says, "Nice to meet you, Mrs. Anderson. Isabella is a real sweetie. You must be so proud of her."

"Hmm, you haven't lost your manners, Grayson. I'm surprised. As for you," She quickly shakes Lexy's hand. "It is Ms. not Mrs. I am not married to anyone, nor do I plan to be. Now let's get down to business. How does the dress look that you're wearing to the wedding?"

"It's gorgeous. I should know, I helped to design it." Sarah walks up adding her two cents.

Then within seconds, a very red-eyed Isabella walks over with tissues in hand, pushing her way closer to Lexy. Poor girl is still drying her eyes. Fitz is right behind her.

"Hey, you guys. I know I probably look a mess, but I'm okay. These baby hormones are making me an emotional blob," she says while rubbing her baby bump. "I even cry over cat food commercials. My apologies for crying, and I'm hoping my Mom wasn't being rude," she says, hugging Lexy and then me.

"Oh Isabella, there is nothing to apologize for. I hope everything is okay with your friend?" Lexy quickly responds sweetly.

"Thank you. I just found out my best friend Tory's baby boy has pneumonia and a very bad ear infection. She's my assistant manager at Rainbows and Unicorn Day Care Center, and when she got home from work today, she discovered his high fever and listlessness. She took him straight to the hospital. They are admitting him. Her parents feel horrible. They hadn't even noticed his high fever because he was sleeping, or they would've called her and taken him in themselves. Little JayJay is like family to me. I hate that he is so sick.

"Mom Gregory has reassured me she will make sure he gets the best of care. So naturally, Tory won't be able to make the wedding, which means Britney will now become my Maid of Honor, leaving me short a bridesmaid." Isabella looks over at Lexy with hope and pleading in her eyes, trying so hard to control her tears, but they continue to fall.

Lexy throws her arms around her, "Oh Isabella, I'd be so honored to help you out. I'll gladly stand in and be a bridesmaid."

"Thank you so much. I'll move everyone around to make sure Grayson and you are paired up. Mom Riggs will be thrilled I'm sure for those, shall I say, 'practice pictures' of the two of you walking down the aisle." She smiles, looking between us and winks.

Damn, I'm sorry little JayJay is sick, he's such a cute kid. But on the plus side, this wedding is getting better for me all the time. Now I get to walk Lexy down the aisle. I wonder if she'll be thinking like me - that this will be a practice run for us. I couldn't have planned this better if I tried. Now I just have to make it through the night. Damn, I can't wait.

After sneaking out the side door when the Brothers are going on and on about Bishops legs, I sit in a lounge chair outside by the pool at Fitz's house, needing a minute to myself. Today feels like it's never-ending. Shit. After having a big scare at the wedding rehearsal with Isabella, and then Stevens and all his antics... I need a break. I'm supposed to be inside taking part in Fitz's bachelor party, although there's not really anything party-ish about it. It's just another night hanging out with the Brothers, with a bit of extra ripping on Fitz that I somehow keep getting dragged into.

Leaning back and looking up to the starlit sky, I remember all the years I spent wondering if Lexy was looking at the same stars and thinking about me. I'm pulled out of my thoughts as Hawkins starts blowing up my phone. What the hell?! It's a video of Lexy swinging around on ropes from the arched high ceilings at his castle. Damn, that some scary shit. I can't believe he allowed that.

I know what Hawk is trying to do. He still thinks Lexy is that Italian ninja assassin. She can't be! Just because she can swing around the rafters with ease, doesn't mean she can do that and shoot someone dead. It makes me want to laugh at the thought of Lexy killing someone. Shit, no way.

My phone goes off again, this time it's Sarah. Fuck! It's Lexy dirty dancing with Tony. What the hell is this? Why is Sarah even sending this to me? Enough of this shit. I write a text to Sarah:

Me: What the fuck, Sarah! Why is Tony dancing with Lexy? I thought he was your boyfriend! You're okay with this? Because I am not!

Sarah: LOL! I just wanted to show you how well they dance together.

And yes, Tony is my boyfriend. But I'm also confident in my relationship, and know they are just friends. You on the other hand...

My phone beeps again, this time from Hawkins. I click over to him.

Hawkins: I thought you might enjoy watching Lexy and her boy dancing. I wonder if they've ever fucked? Have you asked her? Could you handle it if they have? Because damn, from this video it looks like they might have...

Me: Fuck you! And Sarah is already sending me these videos. It looks like you guys are having more fun than we are over here. And why is Tony over there anyway? He isn't a chick! It's supposed to be a girl's bachelorette party. Did you invite him just to piss me off and spy on him?

Hawkins: No, I did not. They – meaning him and Thomas - just showed up with Sarah. I blame you guys. You should have invited them over there, you dicks. But nooooo, now I'm stuck with them. The girls weren't about to not involve them in the wedding celebration. See what I have to put up with?

Me: LOL, What can I say? It couldn't have happened to a nicer guy.

Hawkins: You didn't answer my question!!! Do you think they were fuck buddies at some point? They are practically doing it in front of everyone as they cheer.

Me: NO! They were not fuck buddies. They are friends. You're telling me you've never danced like that with one of your female friends?"

Hawkins: Yeah, that's what I'm telling you. I have never dry-humped someone on the dance floor I wasn't going to REALLY hump them later. Maybe that's what they have planned. You did say you were keeping 'Sir' in your pants till she tells you about herself. LOL LOL LOL

Me: FUCK YOU!!!

Hawkins: You sound a little worried. Oh shit! Three cops just showed up... Oh no, wait...

What the hell is going on?! Hawkins just stops the text right there. I'm running my hand through my hair, trying to calm down and think. Do I go in and tell the Brothers and get Spencer to go over there? Or do I give him a minute to give me more info?

Me: Hawk! Hawk! Want us to come over there and bring Spencer? What is going on?

Hawkins: Relax dude. Tiff or one of the other girls invited three of the club male dancers, or rather, strippers. They aren't wearing their police uniforms anymore. Wait... they're chasing Isabella. Drake is going to shit himself. She's running from them! LOL! Lexy to the rescue. Damn... she intercepted them and is now dancing with them. Oh hell, your lady can move! I can see why all the strippers go to her for lessons. Has she stripped for you yet, you lucky son of a bitch? Damn! She is hot, dancing with the male stripper. I think his name is Dan.

Me: Stop watching my woman, you asshole. And fire Dan if he doesn't get the hell away from Lexy! Are the girls drunk? Is Lexy the only one dancing with them? What the fuck, man!

Hawkins: Watch the video. And no I'm not making her stop. What am I supposed to do? Grab her and tell her that 'Riggs says you can't dance with these guys'? Not happening Brother.

I click on the video and, shit! Lexy can move better than any stripper I've ever seen. She is standing by some guy in fucking speedo-type underwear with what looks like a police badge on the front. What the hell, man. I wonder what she'd think if I was dancing with some stripper in pasties. Not cool. I'm getting more pissed by the second. My phone buzzes in my hand again. Shit, it's Sarah. I'm sure this is another video of Lexy dancing with the stripper.

Fuck! Now she's dancing with two male strippers and they are doing the butt shimmy. Damn! She looks good, but I hate her doing that with men in speedos on each side of her. Shit. What the fuck am I supposed to do now?

Fitz calls me from the other side of the pool, pulling me out of my angry thoughts. "Riggs! I'm talking to Bella. You do know there's nothing for you to be worried about, right? Hawk is just yanking your dick to mess with you. Lexy and Tony are dancing with your mom right beside them."

"What? My Mom is there? Shit!" I look up from my phone and ask.

"Yeah, all the moms are there. Bella just told me Hawk and Sarah are just screwing with you. The girls and moms are all a bit drunk and having fun."

"Did she tell you strippers are there?"

"Yup she did. But nothing will happen, not with all our moms there. Relax Brother."

"I guess you're right. I'm just pissed. They're all drunk and have strippers. Who would have thought they'd be the ones to pull this shit, and we're the ones being all good like church boys?" I yell across the pool to Fitz.

"Yeah, I know. I just didn't want you to freak out about Tony. We should have invited both him and Thomas over here with us."

"You're probably right there. But there is no fucking way they'd come over here now. Those fuckers are the center of attention over there with the Wenches and our moms. You know they're eating it up." Shit. Even if I called now and asked them to join us, they wouldn't.

Fitz calls out again, "Probably, but there is nothing to stress over. Let them have their fun. Give me about five minutes and we'll go in and join the Brothers at poker. I'm feeling lucky."

"Okay, I'll meet you in there. Tell Isabella thanks and good night for me," I call back, beginning to relax a bit, just as my phone rings. I give Fitz a head nod as a crooked smile spreads across my face. I walk a little further away before I answer it. Finally, Lexy is calling me.

"Hey you. I have a strange feeling Hawkins is taping me and will possibly be sending you some bad videos of me dancing with some of the club's male strippers. We're showing the moms and some of the other girls new dance moves," Lexy says sounding a little out of breath.

"Yeah, the dick and my sister have been sending me videos. In their videos, it looks like you're the only one dancing with them. I don't see anyone else from the angles they recorded." Hearing others were dancing with her makes me feel better, and really makes me want to kick Hawkins' ass. Freaking me out like that is not cool.

Lexy calls out to someone away from her phone. *"Tiffany, could you please send Grayson the full video? It seems some people are trying to cause some trouble between us by not being totally honest here. Hawkins! Sarah! Grayson told me what you did, you lying dogs! This girl isn't stupid and your little joke just crashed and burned, as you guys would say."* I can't help but laugh out loud as the stupid weight I had on my chest lifts.

"I'm having Tiffany send you the whole tape. You'll see for yourself that I'm trying to teach all the drunken moms new moves, which in itself is quite funny. But your mom is really good. She wants me to give her private lessons so she can surprise your dad with a striptease pole dance."

"Eww, I really don't want to know anything about my parent's sex life. I heard and witnessed enough of that as a kid. Thanks all the same." Just the idea of my mom stripping for my dad at her age is enough to turn my stomach.

"Come on Grayson, your mom is the coolest. She's got some real talent. Are you saying you don't ever want me to dance for you?"

"Fuck no! I would love to watch you dance for me. Well, and strip for me too. What man in his right mind wouldn't want to see that from his woman? But I'd rather not have the visual of my mom doing it."

Lexy laughs as she finally catches her breath. "I think it's great your mom and dad are still hot for each other at their age. A lot of couples nowadays are trading in their partners and getting divorced for younger models. It gives me hope that they keep things going."

"Well since you put it that way, yeah. But please, no sharing any more of that with me. Sarah and I are already scarred for life from what we heard and saw as kids. Don't get me started."

"Oh, really? My parents slept in different wings of the house with their own master suites. You're lucky. I know they'd occasionally visit each other's bedroom, but not that often," Lexy says, sadness filling her voice.

"Okay, enough about talking about our parents. I want to know when you will dance or strip for me. I'd love to see what you can do on a pole."

Over Lexy's giggling, she fires right back at me, "Well Mr. Riggs, I could ask you the same thing considering I've heard you have danced at the club on Ladies Night a time or two."

"Oh shit. Let me guess, my sister has a big mouth. Believe me, it was rare and I never wore those fucking speedo looking things. I had on long boxer briefs and stayed on stage the whole time. I lost a bet and that was my wager."

"Well if you don't want everyone to see me strip down to my underwear, I do not recommend you make that bet again with the Brothers. Do you understand me Big Guy?" Lexy says teasingly.

"Nope, I'll never do it again, I swear to you. And for your information, the few times I did it, Hawkins did something at the club with the computer system making it impossible for anyone to tape it. But I'm sure he probably has a copy somewhere so he can blackmail me with it later," I say chuckling, knowing damn well Hawkins has a copy.

"He does, does he? Well now, I'm going to have to see how I can get him to show it to me."

"Hey, I'd rather dance for you live. It was the whole security team that lost the bet, so it's not only me, but Stevens, Fitz, Carpenter and Jackson dancing as well."

"Now I really want to see it!"

"Lexy!"

"What?! Remember, I've already seen Carpenter's and Jackson's junk. Watching them dance in their underwear is nothing."

"First, I'd rather forget my perverted Brothers were

sending dick pics. And second, I said 'I' stripped down to my long boxers, I didn't say what they stripped down to. But I can damn well promise their dicks were covered – barely - or Spencer would have their asses."

"Come on Grayson, now you really have me wondering," she keeps teasing. Oh, so she wants to play this way? Okay then. I've got the best comeback.

"Okay baby. You wanna play this way? I'll see what I can wager with your little buddy Tony. I bet he might have some embarrassing videos of you. See how you like them apples! Let's level the playing field, huh?"

"Okay, you win. I will not ask to see your video, but I will take you up on you dancing for my entertainment one day. And you, sir, can also look forward to the performance of a lifetime very soon. I just have to pick the perfect song and surprise you with it."

"Hot Damn, I cannot wait. It'll be the best gift ever. Have you ever danced for another man before?" I regret asking that the moment the words are out of my mouth.

"Emm well, I may have danced once, but I was completely clothed. I didn't take one thing off, and I even had on shorts under my dress, so you couldn't even see my underwear, unlike you. Now I'm closing this conversation down while I'm ahead. And I don't want to be rude but I've got to get back to the party. Bye, my love. I can't wait to see you tomorrow. Have fun at Fitz's party, I hear it's a real bummer," Lexy giggles and hangs up.

Oh, this conversation is not over. Just the thought of her dancing for some men makes my blood boil. Thank God she kept her clothes on… But when and for whom? I bet anything that good ol' pal Tony has a copy of said dance. I wonder if it was on a pole. Hmm. No, it couldn't be. Her father would have had her ass for sure. Looks like I'm going to try and get some information out of Tony, soon. If there is a tape of her dancing out there, I have to see it.

15

MY LIFE FOREVER CHANGES

Lexy

*M*y mind wanders back to the wedding. It was so very different from what I'm used to. Coming from my Family, I had to be a part of every activity: wedding, christening… you name it, I was there as the Canzano Family Princess, properly dressed with tiara and all. Growing up, attendance wasn't an option for me or anyone in the Family for that matter. I could not even begin to tell you how many weddings I've been to in my life. After I took over as the Capo Donna of the Northern part of Italy for the Family, I allowed people to make their own choices. I hated dictating everything. Most people still came, but it was because they wanted to and not because they feared retribution if they didn't show.

You could easily say I've attended hundreds of weddings, but never have I been to one like this. Drake and Isabella's wedding was one for the history books. It wasn't all the typical prayers, scripture readings, kneeling and more that went on for over an hour. No, it was brief. Drake took over and it was personal between him and Isabella, and I loved every minute of it.

Oh, and the chapel was exquisite, beyond anything I could have imagined. The music, it was so beautiful, the way the guitar echoed all around the chapel, showing off how wonderful the acoustics are. I'm going to have to sneak back in there when no one is around and play the piano. Not that I'm really any good, but the sound quality in there would make anyone sound like a pro.

My mind didn't wander to my own wedding when Grayson escorted me to the front of the chapel, as much as I loved walking beside him. Nope, it wasn't until I watched Clausen walk Isabella down the aisle that I choked up. It made me stop and wonder how excited I'd be having Uncle Louie walk me down the aisle of this chapel. I've already decided I want to be married here too. I wonder if I'll cry, or if he will, because without question, he'll be the one to give me away at my wedding to Grayson. I know it sounds crazy, but I can't imagine marrying anyone else.

Uncle Louie's the one who's been my real dad. Nonna wanted him to walk me down the aisle as well. Those were some of her last words. I can't wait for him to meet Grayson and all the Brothers, well, everyone for that matter. I told him over the phone last night after I spoke with Grayson that I'm ready to introduce them to each other. I'm going to tell Grayson tonight that at some point in the near future, he's talking to my uncle. I've stressed to Uncle Louie to 'play nice' when they do, but all he did was chuckle at my pleading. My two favorite men have to get along. They are so much alike, I think they'll hit it off just fine.

Thinking back to the service as we make our way to the reception hall, nothing went as we practiced at rehearsal, other than walking into and out of the chapel with our part-ners. It was so romantic and spontaneous, making it even more wonderful. They seem to be perfect for each other, a complete balance. My father would have never stood for anyone doing something so non-traditional. I loved it. I hate that I'm always thinking of what my papa would do or say about something. I can't wait until I'm able to completely block him out of my thoughts.

My family is great right now, just the way it is. I have a big extended family. The Rogers' are real blood relatives. I've got cousins, another uncle and an aunt. We've gotten so close since I've been in America. They'll be the ones to help me plan my own wedding one day. They are the ones that matter to me, not the people back in Italy. Yes, I do still love some of them back there, but this is my home and that is all a part of my hidden life. I just don't know how all my new friends would respond if they knew everything about my Italian family's criminal life. What would they think of me if they knew I was a murderer? I have to keep it hidden. I can't lose them.

It's time to get my mind off my past life and go enjoy the reception. This period dress is beautiful but it's so damned hot. Who would have thought this much velvet would not only weigh a ton, but 'cause you to glow - and not from beauty, but from sweat. Sheesh. I need to talk to Britney and make sure she announces when we can finally shed these and just wear our bloomers and corsets. We all agreed that after the wedding when we're ready to hit the dance floor, we'd act like the Wenches they enjoy calling us and shed these dresses. The Brothers are in for a little shock of their own. They're about to see what a Camelot Wench really looks like. Grayson's going to learn how much of a free spirit I am tonight, and I can't wait.

Gosh, my feet hurt. I can't wait to get out of these lace-up booted heels we had to wear with our dresses. Isabella wanted a true Camelot wedding, and boy did she get it. Everyone's dresses are stunning and complete replicas of the different styles of the era.

Oh, and the way the Brothers looked... Every one of them was hot as hell, or as Isabella would correct me, 'Hot as Hades', but I much preferred Sarah's expression, what was it again... 'Hot Dayuumm!'. That's it. I'm going to have to steal that one and use it myself. Just thinking of how massive Grayson's chest looked in that breastplate gets my blood going. He was breathtaking, and the way his fitted black pants looked tucked into his leather knee boots... Dayuumm. He actually wore a real sword to his side. Boy was I tempted to take that sword from him and show him how well I can handle one myself. But I didn't. That too will wait.

He looks just as scrumptious now at the reception. He's taken off his breastplate and is wearing that off-white blousy lace up shirt that was underneath it. Yum. I'm going to have to figure out a way to seduce that hot alpha man of mine. That planning can wait till after I get out of these boots.

Strolling in the night air and smelling the wisteria in the breeze is paradise. I love it up here at Hawkins' castle. As much as I love my penthouse, there is no place I'd rather be than up here with Grayson. I would love to live up here one day.

At this moment, I'm a bit thrilled to have a couple of minutes out here by myself while he is talking to Hawkins, Carpenter and Jackson about some Camelot Security business they have going on later in the week. It gives me a couple of minutes to see if I can go into the chapel and play the piano to hear those acoustics myself.

But first I have to get out of these clothes. I hate to even admit it to myself, but the one thing I do miss about being Capo Donna is having someone else take care of things like this for me. It took some getting used to, taking care of my clothes myself. God, I lose so much shit not having someone else to make sure it's all together and where it belongs. The days of me being the pampered princess are long over. I've got this.

Opening the door to the Brides chamber, I see my garment bag stuffed in the corner. I quickly grab it and hang my dress up on the rack with everyone else's dresses, so it can be sent out to be cleaned. I can still hear Mom Gregory instructing us, *'No need to wear those dresses home ladies, I have to get everything cleaned anyway so I might as well get all you girl's dresses cleaned as a thank you. Just leave them here and I'll get them back to you.'* She is such a sweetheart, and believe me, I was thrilled she volunteered for that. Now to get out of these boots. I sit and quickly unlace them, stuffing them into the bottom of the garment bag, taking a second to rub my aching feet. Today has been one of the best days ever.

Getting up, I glance at myself in the mirror before I walk out of here, and I must say, I kind of like this look of only being in my bloomers and corset. It makes me feel like a true Wench, and it's not like you can really see anything. Chuckling to myself, I head for the door thinking that Grayson will really enjoy this look.

I take a peek around the back foyer and luckily, I find that I am still the only one in the chapel. I walk out of the Brides' chambers and over to the chapel doors, opening one up very slowly, sneaking inside and closing it just as reverently behind me. I love the beautiful circular faux-candle centerpiece that hangs from the vaulted ceiling and dimly lights up the chapel.

Hawkins told us last night that he likes to leave them on all night long because of the way they make the angels look so badass in the stained glass windows he can see from his side of the castle. I have to agree with him. The designers did an incredible job with them. The ones in the back of the chapel are my favorite. I think they look like the angels Michael and Gabriel, guarding and protecting all of us. They have their swords held in a stance ready to attack, with their massive wings spread behind them. It gives you chills looking at them at night.

Looking around the chapel one last time to make sure I'm

alone, I quietly walk over to the piano. God, it's been a long time since I've played. As I sit down on the bench, I just let my fingers glide over the keys, enjoying how beautiful the music sounds in the chapel. I start playing 'Praying' by Kesha. I close my eyes as all of the horrible things my papa has done to me over the years come rushing back to me. This song is my life put to music. I can't stop myself from bellowing out every word, feeling the power it gives me.

Well, you almost had me fooled
  Told me I was nothing without you.
  Oh, but after everything you've done
  I can thank you for how strong I've become.

'Cause you brought the flames and you put me through hell
  I had to learn how to fight for myself
  And we both know all the truth I could tell
  I'll just say this is, "I wish you Farewell."

From the moment I heard this song for the first time, it became my personal anthem, because of the hell my papa put me through all my life. I'm thankful for who I've become. I am no longer that evil assassin he created. I'm good. I only wear a white hat now. I'm no longer the monster he created. I can breathe for the first time in my life. I'm free, I'm happy, and it feels wonderful.

I tune everything else out other than the words to this song. It's a release of horrible built up frustration. Singing out loud gives me a feeling of peace, joy and relief. I don't need him, or anyone. I'm my own person. I'm strong, successful, and I'm *me*. I continue to sing, each word of this song coming straight from my soul. It's like my personal prayer.

I'm no longer ashamed of who I am or what I've become. I surely hope he is somewhere praying for peace for what he did to me. He'll never have me in his life again, and it feels spectacular. I can make it on my own, and I did. As the song builds, I'm overcome with emotions, throwing my head back and singing as loud as I can,

Whoa oh oh oh, some say, in life, you're gonna get what you give
But some things only God can forgive

YEAH!

Swaying back and forth with my eyes closed, I finish the song. I hadn't even realized my eyes were filled with tears, when suddenly I hear Grayson's voice from behind me.

"Okay, whose ass do I have to kick, because that song was full of pain and meaning for you, not just a song you were singing. Someone hurt you and I want to know who. Was it an old boyfriend? What was his name?" Grayson says very seriously and I know he is not going to leave this alone without a truthful answer. Shit. Taking a deep breath, I look at him as he walks over to the piano bench and sits down beside me.

"No, it's not an old boyfriend. It's just my papa, I mean father. This song is like an anthem to me. He can't control anything about me anymore. I can only hope he is dealing with the fact he has lost me forever."

"Do you really mean that? You'd never forgive him?"

"Well, it's like the song says, 'sometimes only God can forgive'. He'll never change. If he walked into my life today, after all the time I've been gone, he'd start trying to control me and demand things of me. I'm just done. He has never been a real father. He never loved me like a father should love his daughter. I was a pawn that he could and did control. But don't feel bad for me. I have my Uncle Louie, and because of him, I know what it feels like to be loved, cherished and treated like a daughter. Uncle Louie is my father, in every way but DNA. I'm going to introduce the two of you over the phone very soon."

I'm wondering how much of my performance he actually saw, and I'm hoping I can get him talking about something else. Quickly. He lifts his big warm hand and cups the side of my face. "I'm so sorry your life was so hard on you while you were growing up. I can only imagine. I'm so glad you escaped. I swear I'll never try to reunite you with your father, especially not after what I just witnessed in your performance. I saw a part of your hurting soul. It was so powerful and moving. I didn't know you could play the piano and sing like a rock star. You were truly breathtaking. I learned something new about you and your many hidden talents today. And as for your uncle, I'd be honored to talk to him and I look forward to meeting him in person." He leans forward, kissing me inno-cently on the lips.

"Okay, how much did you see of my performance?" I need to know.

"I walked into the foyer the moment you started singing. You were so lost in the song you didn't even hear me open the chapel doors. I was speechless and I didn't want you to stop."

"Thank you, I guess. I hope no one minds me coming back in here. I just couldn't pass up the chance after hearing the guitar in here for the wedding earlier. The acoustics in here are unbelievable. You guys did a great job."

"Lexy I know what you're doing. You're trying to change the subject and I get it. I really do understand. I just hope one day you'll trust me enough to share your pain with me, so I can help you carry the load."

As Grayson pulls me into his arms, I just breathe him in. It is such a peaceful feeling being wrapped in his arms. I never want him to let me go. I know he means every word he says. I feel like I need to share something with him, to let him know I'm really okay. As tough as it is, he needs to know something. Closing my eyes and taking in a deep breath I tell him, "My father had a mistress for years before my mom died. She was much younger than my mom. She's a nice lady and I actually like her. A couple of years after Mom died, he married her and they started a new family together. He has another son and daughter. Well, I guess you could say I've been replaced with a half-sister and half-brother. I've never met my sister. She was born after my escape. My Uncle Louie has shown me pictures of her. She looks like the both of them, nothing like me. My little brother is adorable and he's probably the only one I miss.

"I feel sorry for my father's wife because she really doesn't know him or what he is capable of. But the good thing is, he is actually being a real parent to their children, something he never was to me. He looks genuinely happy. That makes it even better that I'm gone. My father and I always butted heads, and before I left, the power struggle between the two of us made everyone around us nervous. People were beginning to believe one of us was going to kill the other. It got really bad and I think my father even thought at times I might take him out." I let out a sigh of relief that I told Grayson some of my past.

Pulling away from Grayson's hold, I look him in the eyes, placing my hands on his cheeks and pulling him down to rest my forehead to his, the position we both love so much. "Grayson, I really am okay. I'll probably always have the emotional scars, but that life is behind me now. I'm a very strong, capable woman. No man will ever control me again. I've made it on my own, just like the song said. It truly is my anthem, and I'm okay with it. Do you believe me?"

"Yes, I believe you. You are the strongest woman I know. Just like the words to our theme song," Grayson says with a wink, like I'd ever forget that night over at his parents' house. 'Perfect' by Ed Sheeran is the most powerful love song of all time, just because of that one verse. It's the only song where a man sings about a woman being the strongest person he knows, and how much he loves her. She's perfect to him, just the way she is. What's not to love about that? God, I pray Grayson can really see me like that one day.

"Thank you. Grayson, you're my everything, and I mean it." I lean in and kiss his lips lightly, and within seconds, Grayson runs his fingers into my hair pulling me closer to deepen the kiss.

Grayson suddenly pulls away breathlessly, resting our foreheads together again as he says, "Let's get out of here before we do something in the house of God we'll both feel guilty about for ages."

I can't help but giggle as I respond to him, "Yeah, I was thinking the same thing. I've done a lot of bad things in my life, some really bad things, and I don't want to add doing naughty things in a chapel to my list. That's a bit too disrespectful, even for me."

Grayson stands up and takes my hand. "I find it hard to believe you've really done bad things, but I'll wait for you to tell me about that later. Right now, let me take you home so we can fool around there and not feel guilty at all. And have I told you how hot you look in that outfit? I also love the fact you don't mind being called my Wench."

"Well if I'm your Wench, where is my 'Wenches of Camelot' t-shirt like Isabella has? You better get one pretty quick because the moms told us we could all be called Wenches officially. We're also thinking of designing our own shield and making our own all-girls club."

Grayson grabs me by the waist, letting out a deep belly laugh as he throws me over his shoulder, giving a swat to my bum. He loves carrying me around on his shoulder like I weigh nothing at all.

"Oh, is that right my little Wench? Well, us Camelot Brothers thought you ladies might do that, so Hawkins and I just asked your boy Tony and my sister to work on your own Wenches logo."

"Really? You guys are okay with it?"

"Well in reality, Mom Gregory told us, and I mean 'told' us tonight, that is how it's going to be. She even had the gall to tell us 'she' created The Brothers of Camelot, and 'she' makes the rules, which in a small way, she did. But hey, she also told us the day any of you Wenches marry, you become a 'Princess of Camelot'." He swats me on the bum again as he continues, "So that makes Isabella and all the moms Princesses. Mom Gregory actually made herself the 'Queen of Camelot'." We both chuckle.

"You know I can walk right?"

"Yup, I know. But I love to tote you around like this, and right now you're barefoot and I wouldn't want you stepping on anything. Also, this way I know I won't lose you because you can't get away," Grayson says with another deep chuckle as we walk out of the chapel and back into the dining hall, I'm sure to say our goodbyes.

"Okay if you insist. The view from here of your bum is quite nice I must say."

"Is that your way of saying you're checking out my ass?"

"Definitely. Yours is a nice asset, that's for sure." I can't help but giggle as I reach down and smack his backside.

Grayson swats me on the bum again. "You do know that for everyone time you hit my ass, it's three times I get to swat yours. It's kind of a guy code thing."

"I've never heard of anything like that."

"Naturally, you wouldn't. You're a girl. Duh…"

I swat his bum again as I inform him, "I'm just letting you know I totally disagree with that 'guy code'. I'm a firm believer we're equals here. You swat my bum and I'll swat yours just as many times. But really, I'm not keeping count.

And for your information, I agree with Mom Gregory. There can only be one Queen, and from all the stories I've heard, it was her that started telling you guys about Camelot and the Knights of the Round Table. So she does deserve the title and honor of being the 'Queen of Camelot'. That makes her the boss, not you guys."

Grayson continues to chuckle as everyone watches him walk around the dining hall with me over his shoulder, like it is nothing out of the norm. Gosh, it's awful hard not to love my Neanderthal man.

"Hey Riggs, I see you have control of your Wench, and she's barefoot... Does that mean you've knocked her up too? You know barefoot and pregnant is just the way you like your woman," Jackson teases Grayson, throwing his head back and laughing at his own stupid joke.

"I'd watch what I say if I were you, Jackson. She was just informing me we're equals here. So I might have to put her down and see if my little Wench can kick your ass, cause those were probably fighting words for her."

"You're damn right they were. Jackson! Barefoot and pregnant, huh? Would you like to challenge me and see who's the one with bigger balls? I am quite confident I could kick your ass at a few things." I push up on Grayson's back, making sure Jackson can see I'm not too happy with his comment.

He lifts his hands in the air in surrender. "Okay Lexy. Sorry little 'spit-fire'. But yeah, I'll accept a challenge from you, just name it. But I don't play fair or by the rules either, so you probably won't win as easily as you did with Hawkins," Jackson says as he walks around Grayson to look at me in the eye.

"Well then, next weekend I'll think of the challenge and you're on. But remember this: if I beat you, I'm going to dress you in drag like a pregnant woman because of your smartass comments. You still want to challenge me?"

I watch as he stares at me with his brows drawn together,

thinking hard about the conditions of my challenge. "I'm not giving you an answer now. I'll wait till the weekend to find out what the challenge is. But if I win, you will be my slave for eight long hours." Then he leans in almost nose-to-nose as he whispers, "And you'll be calling me Master Jackson and you'll have to do whatever I tell you to, starting with cleaning my condo, and I'll make sure to miss the toilet all week to make your job even more fun because I never play nice," he says with a deep chuckle.

"Good to know, 'cause neither do I, and I'm sure the Brothers and your dad and all the members of Hell's Fury, your dads bikers club, would just love to see you dressed in drag. Oh yeah, I know all about them," I inform him with a wink of my own. He doesn't look too happy.

"Okay you two, knock it off. We have to finish saying our goodbyes. I'll see you tomorrow morning Jackson at our meeting. My money is on Lexy by the way, and I'll enjoy taking pictures of you dressed up as a pregnant chick," Grayson teases Jackson, who flips us off with both hands as we continue on to say our goodbyes to everyone.

After about twenty minutes and some awkward hugs, because Grayson refuses to put me down, we finally get in Grayson's car and head out towards the freeway. Grayson takes my hand in his and caresses the top of my hand with his thumb. I love the little things he does like this. We just fit.

I've got a bad feeling deep down that at some point we're going to butt heads, and it won't be pretty because we're both strong people, leaders, and that is where it's going to be tough to figure out. You really can't have two leaders in one relationship, it doesn't work. So, what will we do? Grayson just has to see me as an equal that stands beside him, not someone he needs to stand in front of. I'm not looking forward to our first real fight, but I'm not going to dwell on that now.

I'm going to hate for today to end. Saying goodnight to Grayson is getting harder each day. He has more willpower than any man I've ever known. No guy in the Family would have turned down a sure- thing with me. But Grayson walks away every night, some nights without a release. But he never leaves me without at least one mind blowing, soul-ripping, explosive orgasm. I just don't understand this man. God, I love him, but nothing I've done has been able to break his resolve in waiting until I open up and share my secrets. What am I going to do?

"You're awful quiet over there, are you falling asleep on me?"

"No. I'm just thinking of ways to seduce you."

"Well that's nice, but you know whatever is rushing through that mind of yours is not going to work. Sexual control is something I have a lot of. I've told you on numerous occasions, I can wait. I don't want to just have sex with you, Lex. I want to look you in the eyes and see the complete openness and honesty two people in love share, as I ravage your body and passionately make love to you over and over again. I believe it'll be worth the wait," Grayson says as he releases my hand and runs his big warm hand up my thigh, stretching his fingers onto my inner thigh and giving me a firm squeeze.

"Grayson, you don't play fair."

"I never said I did. But honesty and trust are the most important things to me. I've told you before and I'll tell you again, I've fucked a lot of women in my life, I know that, and it was all meaningless releases. I'm at the point in life that I want more. I don't want to settle. I want it all and I believe we can have it. I just have to prove to you that you can trust me with your secrets. There is nothing you could ever say that would change the way I feel about you. Nothing."

Sighing, I mumble, "I don't know about that."

"Try me. I mean it. Nothing you could say or do could ever make me walk away from you. In fact, if you try to ever leave me, I'll dedicate my life and every dime I have to searching the entire planet for you, until I find you and bring you back again. I'm never letting you go Lexy, and that isn't just a promise. That, my lady, is a solemn vow."

"Grayson I'll never leave you. Like you told me before, you are the other part of my heart. Mine can't beat without you by me. I just wish you didn't have to leave at night. I feel actual pain in my chest every night when you walk away."

"So do I. It's too difficult to explain and put into words. Just saying you complete me isn't enough, what we have is even more than that. It's a bonding of heart, soul and mind, and one day soon, I'm sure we'll be adding body to the completion we feel."

Minutes later we stop in front of my building and unfasten our seat belts, just sitting there looking out the windows at the night sky. I turn in my seat as Grayson turns in his and looks at me. Without saying a word, I place both hands on his cheeks and lean over and kiss him briefly.

"As tough as it is, I don't think you should come up tonight. I want more. It's too difficult to enjoy the sexual satisfaction you give me every night and then have you walk away without allowing me to do the same for you."

"Baby, it's okay. I love exploring your body and finding out what you like and how to please you."

Placing my finger over his lips, I say, "No, it's not okay with me tonight. Today was just so special to me, and all I want to do is love you and hold you all night. But like you said, we can wait until we're both ready. I need to think, and I can't think with you playing my body as you do."

Grayson kisses my fingers over his lips before he removes them, then leans forward resting his forehead to mine. He slowly opens his deep ocean blue eyes, looking into mine as he whispers, "Alexa Sophia Rogers, I'm in love with you and I probably always have been. You are the reason for my heart to continue to beat. There is nothing and no one I have ever loved more than I love you. I'll wait as long as you want me to, but I'll never let you go. You're my one love, my true love, and as I said moments ago, there is not one thing you could ever say that would change my love for you. Absolutely nothing!"

My eyes fill with tears and my heart races. Grayson just told me he loves me, and so much more. Oh, God! What am I going to do? This just got beyond real. I believe him. But how... how can I tell him about what I was before? As we sit still resting our foreheads together, just looking into each other's eyes, I know I need to tell him how I feel too. Then I have to think. I've got to figure this out, but my mind keeps racing. What do I tell him? He makes me believe that if I tell him about my past, things won't change. But he'll want to know it all, and I'm just not ready for that.

"I feel the same way you do. There has never been anyone in my life I love more than you. I left my family and everything I knew, in search of you, in hopes that what you ignited in me all those years ago was real, and it is. We both know it. I love you too, Grayson Richard Riggs." Before I can finish my sentence, Grayson puts his hand behind my head and pulls me into an earth-shattering kiss. My mind can't stop racing so fast, I can't do this now. I have to think... to figure a way... a plan to tell Grayson who I really am.

Pulling away from the kiss, we're both breathing like we have just completed a marathon. Catching my breath, I place my hand on the side of his face. "Tonight we say our good-night right here. No walking me up to my place. I need to think. Please trust me and allow me this without questions."

"Okay baby, if that's what you want. But starting tonight, I'll never allow you to leave me without you hearing me remind you that you are my one love, now and always." Then he pulls me back for a tender and gentle kiss goodnight.

Damn, I have a lot to think about tonight. Geesh, and I'm having lunch with the moms tomorrow. What am I going to do? My life will never be the same after this moment. I'm going to have to figure out a way to tell him the truth. Soon, very soon.

16

ADMITTING, PLANNING AND WORRY

Grayson

*W*alking into headquarters at Camelot Security, I'm already on my second cup of black coffee and it's not even 8 a.m. Shit, with barely any sleep last night, today is going to be a long ass day. After I finally told Lexy I love her, my world has kind of stood still, while my heart hasn't fallen into a perfect beat since. I'm full of semi-panic. Did I tell her too soon? What's going through her mind? She wanted time to herself. Is she trying to figure out how to tell me about her past? She admitted she loved me too. Oh God, I almost want to put a tail on her to make sure she doesn't run. But deep down, I don't think she will.

My vision of what I thought would happen after I told her I loved her was totally different than what actually happened. I thought we'd go up into her room where she'd tell me all her secrets, and the rest of the night we'd spend making love. Instead, she basically kissed me goodnight and ran into her penthouse without looking back. What in the actual hell?!

Something inside me believes she just needs time to figure

212

out how to open up and tell me the whole truth about her life. I'm ready for whatever it is. I just have to make sure I don't react in any bad way, no matter what she tells me. I'm starting to think that Hawkins is probably correct; she's the missing daughter of Al Canzano, the dick Capo from Italy. I don't even know what I'll do if that's true.

I'm supposed to see Lexy tonight for a real late dinner, after my meeting with the Russians. They think they can boss me around in my own town? Well, they have another thing coming. This is going to be a crazy Saturday, I can already feel it.

"Are you just going to stand there in the doorway, or are you coming in?" Tiffany asks. "Hawkins is already here. He's down in the security office. He's been there for hours. I got here at seven thirty and he was already pounding away on several computers. I think he came here after the wedding last night for some reason. He didn't feel like sharing with me, so I didn't push it. I did take him breakfast and demand he eats, but my only response was a mumble. I'm not a dumbass, I know when he mumbles like that, that's my cue to exit," Tiffany continues as I listen, giving a nod of thanks before I walk through the half partition wall that separates the visitor's area from the actual headquarters.

"Well, we do have a meeting scheduled in less than an hour. We had some stuff come up with the mob conflict we've been working on, which is still on the down-low and not to be spoken about in front of anyone."

"Riggs, as always, I know nothing and I see nothing. Have you eaten? Would you like me to bring you down some breakfast too? What time are the rest of the Brothers due to arrive? If everyone is coming, I just need to know if you all want breakfast or lunch."

"Thanks, Tiff. I've already had my morning workout. I'll just grab a second protein drink from downstairs. I ate enough junk yesterday so I'll pass on breakfast. Lunch for everyone would be great, because I know we have a lot to go over."

"You got it boss. I'll bring down some quick breakfast foods and disappear. Just buzz me about an hour before you want lunch and I'll do the same."

"You're the best. Thanks again, Tiff."

"No problem. I'll hold all calls for you guys too. Let me know if you need anything else."

"Will do."

As I head to the elevator, I can't help but think that Tiffany really is the best employee we could ever ask for. She's a great friend and completely gets all of us, even with our little quirks. Tiffany is a true gem. At times she can be a bit of a handful with her overly honest mouth, but for the most part, none of us could imagine how this place would run without her. A lot of the time she knows what we need before we ever realize it.

Plus, she can cook like there is no tomorrow. She not only has a business degree, she also finished culinary school, so there is literally nothing she can't cook. She'll make someone damn lucky one day. She's like everyone's baby sister. We've known her since she was in her early teens. We basically watched her grow up and helped her when she lost her grand-father. She's one strong cookie, that's for sure, being on her own and handling everything like she did. That girl has some balls of her own I am sure of it.

Within minutes, I'm walking into our underground security headquarters. Hawkins doesn't even look up, but somehow he knows it's me. "Riggs, you're here early. Does that mean you came to talk about Lexy? Or to get intel about the Russians and Italian crime families before everyone else so you'll look smarter?" Hawkins says with a chuckle, still typing away.

"Probably a little of both. Did you find out anything more about either?"

Looking up at me with a crooked grin, he says, "What do you think big guy?"

"Are you going to tell me or do I have to beat it out of you?" I tease.

"Well, if you beat it out of me you'd be up shit creak for sure because everyone knows I'm the mind of this business, so I really doubt that is even a real threat. But first, you tell me what you found out, cause with a quick glance at the time and the look on your face I'm thinking you've got a lot on your mind. Did Lexy finally talk?"

"I didn't get much sleep last night and it wasn't because I was having a lot of fun, if you know what I mean. I told Lexy I loved her for the first time last night, and you can guess with me being here so early, it didn't go as planned."

"What? She didn't jump your bones and shout her undying love for you?" Hawkins asks, snickering.

"Fuck you! Yes, she told me she loves me but she said she needed time. She kissed me goodnight and sent me on my way. To say I was shocked is the understatement of the day."

"So you haven't found out anything new about her since the last time we talked?"

"I didn't say that. I think your guess about her being Al Canzano's missing adult daughter is right. Last night I found her in the chapel after the wedding. She was singing, and damn it was good, but it was also gut-wrenching. There was so much of her soul open and exposed as she sang. She actually said Prayer by Kesha is her own personal anthem about her father. She told me he married his much younger mistress after her mom died and they have two children together: a baby sister she hasn't met because she was born after her escape, and a little brother she admits to missing. It matches what you told me about Al Canzano. You said he had two small children, one being an infant daughter."

"I'm going to have to research the song and see if there is

any hidden message in it. Did she slip and say anyone's names?" Hawkins asks curiously.

"No. She's good at leaving out anything she knows I can use to put things together on my own. I think she's trying to figure a way to tell me who she really is. As I watched her walk into her penthouse elevator last night, the struggle was written all over her face."

"You are probably very correct there. It won't be easy for her to tell you. Look at your family compared to what we think hers is. You come from good, clean money. Yeah, you have Granny Piedmont, but she is just a rebel. She's afraid you'll dump her because of her family's criminal life – if we're correct about her," Hawkins says, leaning back in his office chair and swaying back and forth.

"You're probably right, but I keep telling her and trying to reassure her that there is nothing she can tell me that would make me change my mind about her. Nothing. I really love her, like no other. She is a part of my soul, Hawk."

"I believe you. Let's take another look at this. Do you realize how deep this shit goes? We need to find out how far the connection between the Canzano and Benassi families really goes. Is it possible Lexy is just a cover, and she and Tony are still working for the Canzano Family? By all rights, she is the Family Princess."

"No way in hell is she working for them. She probably doesn't know anything about what is going on. That much I can promise you. The last person she'd help would be her father." I straighten him out on that idea. No fucking way is she helping them.

"Well between the two of us, I know for sure ol' Tony Jarvis has been helping me online with my intel. He's trying to camouflage himself by bouncing me all over the place, but I'm as smart as he is in this area. I remember some of his answers when we joined forces to bust the Russians the last time. Be careful. The boy knows his shit, and he is tight with your old lady."

"Now Tony, hmm… he does know her from way back and he is from Italy too. He might be working with the Family. He does have Lexy very protected. I mean you should see her house and business security systems. It's all top notch. How close is our connection with the Benassi Family? Do you think they'd tell us anything?"

Hawkins throws his head back, laughing. "Yeah, they'd help us about as much as Tony would sit down right here and now and tell us who he and Lexy really are. I've dealt with them a couple of times, both online and in person. They're about as cocky as you said the Canzano Family was, and they've got egos to match. They wouldn't tell us jack shit about Lexy, or Tony for that matter. That is if they even know anything. The Benassi Family took over the largest crime Family in New York, just days after you went into the military, and they've been the controlling Family in the US ever since. They do have less criminal activities than they used to, but believe me, there are lots of skeletons in their closets."

"Well, hopefully Lexy will tell me the truth soon so we can be prepared for whatever is headed our way. Changing the subject now, what did you find out about the Russians?" I ask.

"You're not going to like it. They have a hit on you. They believe you are the head of security and taking you out would make a statement."

"Shit! Today just keeps getting better and better."

"I'm glad Fitz is on his honeymoon. I'd hate to have to explain to Isabella why I think Drake should wear a bullet-proof vest everywhere he goes for his own protection. We have two weeks to figure this shit out and shut it down because it's tough for me to lie to Isabella. As for you, Jackson, Carpenter and Stevens - you'll all be wearing a vest from the moment you leave here today until further notice. Figure out whatever you want to tell Lexy, but I don't want to take any chances.

Personally, I'd rather none of you go anywhere by yourselves. That's one of the Russians favorite calling cards: ambush when you're alone."

"Hawk, you have nothing to worry about. We got this. I'm still planning on meeting with them tonight. Both Stevens and Jackson are going with me. I want to talk to them face to face. I think we can remind them of how it didn't end very nicely for them in Italy."

"Remember, that's why they have a hit out for you. They know you were helping the Canzano Family and they consider you our leader. Taking you out would be their vengeance. One of the head Russian crime Bosses sons died in that raid. The Russians aren't too happy, and want revenge. Oh Shit! I just remembered," Hawkins says, stopping himself mid-sentence and running both hands through his hair, "They also have a one million dollar bounty on Al Canzano's daughter, dead or alive."

"Fuck! Are you kidding me?"

"Nope. If Alessandra Canzano is Lexy, we better hope they don't realize she is dating you or we're in the midst of a major shit storm."

"Fuck! Maybe it isn't just her father Lexy is on the run from. Maybe Tony knows? That would explain the high end security and her wearing contacts and glasses everywhere she goes. It's not just her Family she's hiding from, but the Russians. She's Al's oldest heir and they want to hurt him, that's what they do. We need to get her boy Tony in here and interrogate him."

"Wait right there, there's more I need to tell you." Shit! This day is getting drastically worse by the minute. Hawkins runs his hands down his face and takes a deep breath, before he turns in the chair and looks at me.

"I've been to her health club on two different occasions, wanting to see her in action. Well, the first time I watched her and Tony train. He's one bad mother fucker. Tony has a black belt in jiujutsu and some other training as well. But when him and Lexy spar, it's real. She is not the delicate little lady you take out on dates. He can throw her, flip her and punch her and she pops right back to her feet and attacks him again. Sorry Brother, don't get pissed, but I've sparred with her too. She's damn good, better than I thought she ever would be. She can definitely handle her own. If someone was to seriously attack her, she'd catch them by surprise for sure and could easily kick their ass long enough to get away. I don't care if she's only five foot nothing. She's a little badass herself."

My mind is fucking blown. "What the fuck! When did this take place? And why didn't you tell me immediately after it?"

"Because look at you! You're ready to kick my ass right now. You need to shut that down until you see her yourself," Hawkins says, just as we hear Jackson, Carpenter, Stevens and Clay horsing around as they come barreling in.

"Shit, you're already here. I won ten bucks on that one. See, I told you dipshits there was no way Riggs would let us beat him here. No, pussy for him last night. You still hanging on to your virtue and handling 'Sir' yourself? Or are you at least letting Lexy help you out with him?" Stevens, my old buddy, calls out as they all head to the bar counter where Tiffany set up some breakfast goodies for them when I wasn't looking.

"First of all, what Lexy and I do is none of your fucking business. And second, unlike the four of you, I've already been up for hours and had my morning run on the beach to wake myself up, followed by a full workout. How many of you are hung over?"

"None-ya-business," Carpenter smarts off, pouring himself a cup of coffee and drinking it before he even puts the pot down.

"Well that answers that question. You better sober your asses up and fast. We have some important business to discuss," I inform the hung over idiots who are piling food on their plates like they haven't eaten in days. I shake my head at them and Hawkins just laughs.

"*Look!*" Carpenter yells in excitement as he grabs a couple of homemade biscuits and starts pouring gravy all over them. "I loooove Tiffany. I'm marrying that woman," he tells us for like the hundredth time. He's always claiming he's going to marry any woman who can cook. It'll be hilarious if he falls for a chick that can't cook shit.

"Fuck that. You can't have her all to yourself. Look, she got me dark Karo syrup and real butter. Damn, this is one of my favorite breakfast snacks. It goes to prove she loves me best," Jackson says, elbowing Carpenter.

"I gotta ask, what the hell do you do with Karo syrup and butter? I don't see any pecans or eggs to make a pie, and that's what my mom does with those items." Clay says looking over to see what Jackson is doing.

Jackson walks over beside me and pours a huge glob of syrup on his plate, probably at least a cup full. Then he slops a big hunk of butter in the middle, mashing and mixing them up until it's all blended. Picking up one of Tiffany's famous cinnamon biscuits, he swirls it around in the syrup concoction then looks around at us, "Now this... this is Goddamn mother fucking good. It's by far the best." Then he eats it.

"Jesus. Are you aware of all the carbs and sugar that shit you just shoved in your mouth has in it?" I ask him.

Clay starts laughing and adds his input, "Let's hope you don't have any diabetes in your family, because that shit could put you in a sugar coma."

Mumbling around yet another bight of the sugar filled carb fest he says, "I don't give a fuck. It's damn good. I'll never marry a woman if she cannot make me mother fucking cinnamon biscuits like this. Not fucking cinnamon rolls, I want the damn biscuits," Jackson informs us.

"I give you about five years old buddy before that six pack

of yours becomes an out and out beer and carb pooch," I can't help but tease Jackson.

"That'll never happen. I get plenty of exercise, both in the bedroom and out, unlike you," Jackson stands up and thrusts his hips forward as he shoves another syrup covered biscuit into his mouth.

I just shake my head at his nonsense and tell him, "We'll see. But believe me, when it happens, I will not show you any mercy."

As the door opens up again, Bishop comes in riding his chariot with Hunter, Clausen, Brenden and Spencer right behind him.

"Looks like the gang is all here. The last thing I expected was to have to be here before noon the day after Fitz's wedding." Brenden says and the other Brothers mumble in agreement as he heads over to grab some food with Bishop and Hunter.

Clausen and Spencer are still standing by the door bickering like two chicks holding their Starbucks foofoo shit. "Look at what you did to my t-shirt! You ruined it with that shit. I told you, I run at least twice a day. I could easily beat you in a run around the building." Spencer waves his hand over his damaged shirt.

"Dude, it was an accident. Do you want me to buy you another pussy Harvard t-shirt?" Clausen chuckles at him.

"No, I'll get my own fucking t-shirt. And it's Harvard Law! Didn't they teach you pretty boys how to read at Princeton?" Spencer fires right back at him as Tiffany walks in.

"Spence, I'll just set your egg white, mixed diced peppers, mushrooms with white cheddar cheese omelet with a side of sourdough toast and one pat of butter and crushed strawberries on the table." I watch as Tiffany carries a black plate and silverware in a napkin and sets it down on the table. Reaching into her pocket, she puts a couple of salt and pepper packets down beside it with a mini bottle of hot sauce.

"Thanks Tiff, you're a doll, always ordering my special breakfast," Spencer says as I watch him pull his coffee-stained t-shirt off and toss it to Tiffany, who catches it. I'm a bit shocked to see her eyes casually check out his body as she hugs Spencer's t-shirt to her chest. "Can you order me another athletic gray Harvard Law t-shirt? Clausen, the asshole, accidentally-on-purpose spilled his coffee on me when I kicked his ass in a challenge run around the compound. You know I can't wear it with a coffee stain on it."

"You got it, Chief. I'll order it once I get to my desk." I watch as she innocuously sniffs his t-shirt and turns to me. I can tell by her wide eyes that she's hoping I didn't notice. I play it cool, realizing our Tiffany is crushing on 'Spence' as she calls him. "Don't forget to buzz me an hour before you guys are ready for lunch," she says, before she turns towards the door.

"Okay Tiffany, I will." And before I can say anything else, she hurries out the door. I look over at Stevens to see he is shaking his head with his brows drawn together. Yeah, he picked up on that too, and doesn't look too happy about it. Stevens is the closest to Tiffany because her grandfather, as well as her father, served in the military with Stevens' dad. Those two go back practically as far as Stevens and I do.

Hearing Hawkins snickering draws my attention to him. I'm sure he picked up on the vibe as well, since he is sitting there with a big crooked grin on his face. "Hey Spencer, when did you start getting the special treatment? 'Egg white omelet'? You're kidding right? Orders out?" Everyone starts laughing at Spencer, who looks around seemingly confused. He can't really be that much of a dumbass, can he? Doesn't he know Tiffany cooks all this shit herself? I never would have pegged Spencer to be this naïve. This is really funny now that I think about it.

"I never would have pegged you for such a dumbass, but whatever dude. You'll learn, and this should be very entertaining. Besides, you're lucky Isabella isn't here. She wouldn't let you eat shit without a shirt on," Hawkins says

"It isn't any special treatment. Tiff sends out from somewhere for my breakfast when I'm in the office. She's always known how I like it and what to order. She knows I don't eat the shit the other Brothers do," he says waving his arm towards the counter full of biscuits, croissants, and pastries. "It takes a lot to keep my body so defined. I look amazing and I know it." He just blows off our laughter while he flex's his stomach to show off his slim eight pack abs. The dude really is well defined for a little guy.

"Aw... look he's got a little six pack," Jackson teases. "Did you get them tattooed on? Or are they actually real? Can I touch them?" Jackson leans towards him like he's about to caress his stomach with his sticky syrup fingers.

"Don't touch me with that sticky paw of yours. I'm already a touch sweaty from beating Clausen with our run around the compound. Just because you're an inch taller and like forty pounds heavier doesn't make you more fit than I am. In twenty years my trim body will still look a hell of a lot better than your bulky one. You ever seen a bodybuilder in his fifties? They have bigger tits than most of the girls I date," Spencer says with a chuckle of his own, walking over to the bar and grabbing a Camelot Security t-shirt and pulling it on. "And no, they are not tattooed on you jackass. I work hard at keeping my body in perfect form. You never know when GQ will want me for another photo shoot. You know, for one of the most available bachelors in Santa Monica... again."

Everyone chuckles at their banter as Jackson flips him off.

"I'm not going to have old man tits. What's this shit with you and Riggs picking on my body today?" Jackson whines.

Carpenter calls out, "Don't listen to those jackasses who would rather suck down that green protein shit they fill their blender with than eat real food. We know how to use a blender the right way. 'Margaritas'!" he shouts out, giving

Jackson a high-five. "We like our food like we like our women - anyway we can eat them." Then both of them crack up laughing. That wasn't even that funny. I'm thinking they both might still be a bit drunk from last night.

"Okay, everyone listen up. We've got a major problem. so pay complete attention while you feed your faces," Hawkins spends the next twenty minutes informing everyone about the Russian and Italian Mob families, thankfully leaving Lexy out of it for now. He goes all the way back to when we worked with the Canzano family in Italy, and the death of one of the Russian mob sons. He goes into detail telling them how they're most likely still into the sex trade, wanting to open up strip clubs and probably have prostitutes working the area and their battle with the Italian mob family. He doesn't miss a beat.

"So, no one travels alone. We're too easy a target. Right now they're only talking about getting Riggs. But if they can't eliminate him, they want to take out one of our men that fought in Italy. Which means Stevens, Carpenter, Jackson and Riggs are targets. I don't want to see any of you without bulletproof vests on at all times while you're outside this building. I'm keeping an eye on the Dark Web as well. If I get any clue they are moving towards our families, we're bringing everyone to my castle or here. Do I make myself clear? That means everyone: parents, sisters… everyone that the public knows you're related to. They'll either be here or at the castle. I'm not messing around if the threat gets any closer."

"Okay, Hawkins. I'm going to check the inventory and supplies for our surgery center here. I'm hoping I don't need it, but I'd rather be safe than sorry. Last time the Russians and Italians were involved with us, both Riggs and Stevens got new scars to add to their collections. I'll give Tiffany the heads-up as well. I'm glad Fitz and Isabella are out of town for the next two weeks on their honeymoon. I would not want to tell Isabella she's being sequestered because Fitz is in danger."

"I told Riggs the same thing before you all got here. You all know I have incredible instincts and I do not have a good feeling about this."

"Hawk, I know you're worried about our meeting tonight, but there will be three of us. We're going to wear our vests. I'm not going to look like a scared pussy to them. They said they wanted to talk and we're going to talk. It'll be okay, I swear it. The three of us are much better shots than any of the Russians we battled with in Italy, and they aren't going to pull out Uzis in the middle of Santa Monica. That I can promise."

"I trust your abilities, we just don't know if this is a set up or not."

"Well if it makes you feel better, I'll call them and switch the location at the last minute so they won't be able to plan a surprise attack. I'll give you plenty of time to prepare the location so you can keep an eye on us."

"That sounds even better. I want all of you hitting the range, and if you have any suspicion or feeling you're being tailed or anything like that, call me ASAP. And please, keep a gun with you at all times. We all know how to use them, and right now, you just never know."

Everyone mumbles okay, and conversations rumble throughout the room. I know without question that I'm getting Lexy to talk to me tonight. If I have to outright ask her if she is Alessandra Canzano, I will. I need to make sure she is safe.

Maybe I'll talk to Tony tonight as well and point-blank ask him what he knows about the Russians. All I know is that the next twenty four hours is going to be hell. I have to keep my shit together because I need a calm level mind going into this meeting with the Russian Crime Boss.

Maksim Osokina is not someone you can take lightly. He's a heartless son of a bitch, one who is wanted in several countries for some evil shit. He loves to capture very young virgins and pick one out for himself and break her by using her as his own personal sex slave. Then once he's done with her, if he doesn't kill her, he continues his torment by putting her into a brothel somewhere or selling her. I'd love to put a bullet between his eyes, but not tonight. Tonight we just talk.

We've already had several secret meetings with both the CIA and the FBI, along with a couple of international organizations. They all want to know what the Russians are up to here, and warned us of the dangers. But I'm confident we can handle it. I know we can call on them for backup if we need it. There are a lot of secret agencies like our own out there willing to help.

Our local detectives, Jerkins and Franks, were even hitting us up at the wedding yesterday. I'm sure they were just putting out feelers to see if we knew anything. We played dumber than dirt. They don't know shit, and I hope to keep it that way.

"Let's go hit the shooting range downstairs. I got two hundred on no one being able to beat me today," Stevens challenges.

"You're on, you big pussy. Plan on handing over that dough when I kick your cocky ass," Jackson says, accepting his challenge.

"Count me in on it too. I'm going to love taking all your money," I let them know.

"Well, I'm not even going to wager you guys. I need my two hundred dollars for bills," Carpenter says, softer than his normally loud roar as we all head out of the office.

"Try not to break any laws if you can. I'd rather not have to worry about bailing anyone's ass out of jail. I need to brush up on my international law since this is going down," Spencer calls out as he and Clausen head upstairs to their offices.

"Hawk, Clay, Bishop and I'll keep an eye out at the club and touch base with you later tonight," Hunter calls to him

"Okay, Brothers. I'm staying here at the compound until

this settles down. Feel free to take any of your family up to the castle if you're even the slightest bit nervous. No one could find that place and you know they'd all be safe there." Hawk says as he turns his back to everyone and starts typing away, watching monitors again.

I cannot wait to see and talk to Lexy tonight. I've got a strange feeling this is going to be the longest day of my life.

17
CONFRONTATION

Lexy

Thankfully, I had Anissa drop me off at the hospital to meet the moms for lunch. I had forgotten about my car being in the shop for its yearly tune-up. Mom Riggs said she'd gladly drop me off at my club afterwards because she wants to see if she can get in another training session with Steer or Roid, if they aren't too busy. It's really fun to watch them work with her. They're afraid that if she gets a bruise, she'll accidentally tell Grayson how it happened and neither of them want to deal with that. The thought makes me laugh. I just love those guys. They work really well with the moms and I'm so glad they stayed with the club when I bought it and took over.

Walking into the Emergency Room entrance and handing the security guy my ID, I say, "I'm meeting up with Dr. Riggs in the Doctor's Lounge."

I watch as the guards' eyes slowly work their way up my body before reaching my face. I've got on my dark sunglasses, so I quickly lift them with a smile, which he returns, with an overly bleached white smile.

"Well Miss Rogers, you have such beautiful and unique eyes. I'm sure you hear that all the time. You truly are a rare beauty." As he extends his hand to give me back my ID, he lightly touches my hand and adds, "Here you go Miss Rogers. Do you know where the Doctor's Lounge is? Or would you prefer I give you a map and highlight the route?" he says with another big smile, adding a wink this time. He's getting a bit too flirty for me and I'm going to shut this down.

"No, thank you sir. I have met up with the Mothers of Camelot here several times. I'm Grayson Riggs' girlfriend. I know just where I am going," I say with a smile.

His eyes widen and he turns away, getting his focus back on his monitor. "Oh, excuse me, Ma'am. I didn't mean anything by that… you know."

"That's okay. Have a nice day." I say as I turn and start my walk down the long hallway, knowing that after my little announcement, he will not be checking out my ass. That just makes me smile to myself.

A very strange feeling I haven't had in a long time overcomes me as I turn the corner. Instantly, I become alert and take more notice of my surroundings. As I get closer, I see two orderlies pressed up against the wall, opposite the Doctor's Lounge door, which is oddly propped open. Oh, shit! Something is seriously wrong here.

"Lexy, get down and come over here." I hear Detective Jerkins call out from his huddled position on the ground beside the door. I quickly hurry over to him.

"What's going on?"

"It looks like a psych patient escaped and somehow got a surgical knife and is holding Barbara Stevens by the throat in there. Mom Riggs and Mom Gregory are trying to talk some sense into the guy."

"*What?!* Do you have your gun? How accurate are you?"

"No, I don't have my gun. I was here for a follow up

appointment with my mom and she hates me taking it everywhere with me."

"Shit."

"And why the hell are you asking me how accurate I am
with it? Have some of the Brothers been talking shit
about me?"

"No! Get over yourself. I was just wondering because if
you had had a gun on you, I'd want to borrow it."

His head jerks around to look at me. "You're kidding,
right? Now is not the time to be joking around. I took a quick
look in there and that bastard has the blade on her jugular.
He's already nicked her skin to show the ladies he means business. I have already called headquarters and made them
aware of the situation."

"What about the hospital? Have you notified them? There
are lots of officers here. Maybe one of them has a gun. If you
don't think you can take him out, I know I can."

"You have to be shitting me! The last thing I would do is
give you a fucking gun. And the guards here are rent-a-cop.
Yeah, some may have guns, but I doubt if any have ever used
them on a human."

"Pssst! You! Orderly! Go and tell the hospital what's going
on, but tell them not to announce it on the loudspeakers.
Make sure no one else comes down this hallway. I wouldn't
want to startle him." One of the orderlies nods and takes off
running.

"Lexy, stop giving orders. I'm in charge. You need to go
back down the hallway yourself. I think the doctors in there
can keep him calm until backup gets here. I don't want to
cause a panic in the hospital. We're talking one guy with a
knife."

"Forget that! You said he had Mom Stevens. I'm not
waiting for shit. I know what I'm doing."

"You own a health club and teach self-defense. This is real,
and you don't know shit! You're going to be a good girl and

run like hell back down that hall and wait there till this is over."

Then I notice the remaining orderly fiddling with a syringe in his pocket. "What's in the syringe?"

He looks over to me, lifting it completely out of his pocket now. "It's a cocktail of Haloperidol and Promethazine. It will calm and knock him out within moments. We just told the officer, right before you got here, that we've been looking for him for less than five minutes, and were just about to call for a hospital lockdown when we heard one of the ladies scream from within the lounge. We knew it must be him so we came running over here. Once I opened up the door, I saw him holding Nurse Stevens with the knife to her neck, so we quickly propped the door open and stepped back into the hallway. That was when the officer came running towards us. Now we're trying to figure out what to do next. We don't want to get Nurse Stevens hurt. She's a really nice lady and that guy is completely whacked."

"Slide the needle over to me. I've got an idea. I'm going in there."

Both the orderly and detective say a bit too loudly, "No!"

"I'm very serious. I can handle this. You don't know me like you think you do."

Detective Jerkins grabs my forearm firmly. "You aren't going anywhere. I'm not answering to Riggs if he finds out I let you go in there, or God forbid, you get hurt."

I jerk my arm out of his grasp, lift my glasses and look him square in the eyes like I would one of my own men. "Listen up, asshole. No one tells me what the fuck to do. And since both of you lost your balls the moment you heard one of the moms scream, I'm handling this. The moment you hear an obvious commotion, come running in the room. We'll probably need your strength to help control him. If he is psycho, he'll have the strength of a wild animal and I'm not stupid."

Watching the shocked look spread on his face is comical. Then

I turn to the orderly, "And you better run your ass in there and inject him with that shit since you refuse to give it to me. And if Mom Stevens gets seriously hurt, both your asses answer to me."

I quickly get up and hurry into the Doctor's Lounge, pretending nothing is wrong. With a quick glance around the room, I see Mom Riggs and Mom Gregory are about seven feet away from the psycho, talking to him in a very quiet tone. The room looks like a massive living room, with a large entertainment center, a TV, as well as a nice stereo system. There's a table and chair set along with couches and recliners. It even has some nice size vases in here with some large decorations in them. Why couldn't they be closer to some of this shit? I could easily use it to distract him. But no, they are standing in the far corner of the room a few feet away from the wall.

Then I notice that Mom Riggs and Mom Gregory are standing about five feet in front of an exit door to the parking lot. The clicking of my six inch stiletto heels gets everyone's attention, as all heads turn my way.

"Lexy, sweetie, you need to go back out into the hallway," Mom Riggs tells me.

I look into her eyes hoping she can read my expression through my sunglasses. Giving her just the slightest head shake. I watch as her eyes widen. She knows I'm trying to tell her something.

"No Mom, what's going on? Why is he holding Aunt Barbara by the throat? Mom! She's bleeding!" I hurry over to Mom Riggs and cling to her.

"Honey, it's okay. I'm fine. This gentleman isn't going to hurt me. Now you listen to your Mom Lexy. Leave, please," Mom Stevens says, pleading evident in her soft, shaky voice.

"I'm not going anywhere, Auntie." Then I wrap my arms around Mom Riggs and pretend like I'm about to break down and cry as I say. "Mom, that man can't hurt Auntie. He can't!" Then I quickly whisper, "Remember your training, be ready to attack. I'm taking this man out." I pull away and bend over and grab a tissue from a box on the end table. Pretending to sniffle, I wipe my nose turning back around. I'm hoping me putting my ass up on display like that would have caught his attention… which it did.

We both just stand there and look at each other. I notice the man is probably in his late forties, medium build and is about six foot tall. I'm confident I can take him out. He's definitely mental. His hair is going in all different directions, like he's been running his fingers through it for hours, and pulling it at the same time.

The hand holding the surgical blade to Mom Stevens' neck is very shaky. He may not have purposely cut her neck, it could easily have been from his shaking. He takes notice of me in my retro 50's fitted black and red dress. I look like a 50's pin-up calendar girl.

He slowly lets his eyes roam my body. He isn't even trying to hide the way he is looking at me: like a hungry tiger and I'm the fresh live meat his trainers just threw into his cage.

"Sweetie, I think you should listen to your Mom and go back into the hallway, okay?" This time it's Mom Gregory warning me. I'm sure she's watching the way psycho-guy is looking at me and it's making her nervous. I can tell by the quiver in her voice.

"She's not going anywhere." The man says. "Take off your glasses. I want to see your eyes. You're the most beautiful girl I've ever seen."

"Will you put your knife down? My Auntie's neck is already bleeding and I don't want her hurt. I'll do whatever you want, just, please, don't hurt my Auntie." I'm hoping I can get him fixated on me so I can get that knife out of his hands. I step away from where the moms are standing, moving a bit closer to him. I'm sure the four of us can handle him until that orderly gets in here.

"How about I hold it away from her neck? Then will you

take off your glasses?" I watch as he wraps his other arm more securely around her waist, pulling Mom Stevens very tightly to the front of his body.

"I guess I can do that. But don't let my eyes scare you. A lot of people think I have witch's eyes; that's why I always wear sunglasses."

"Witch's eyes? Are you a real witch? Cause you've put a spell on me and pulled me into your web," he says, looking at my boobs and licking his lips before his eyes slowly go back up to look at my eyes. He slowly lifts the blade about six inches away from Mom Stevens' neck. God, I try not to let his disgusting pickup line affect me. I want him to see me as a vulnerable girl so I can get closer to him.

"No, I'm not a witch, but a lot of people think I am," I say as I slowly lift my sunglasses, batting my eyes at him as I slowly take a step closer to him.

"Goddamn! Your eyes! They are beautiful, seductive. You could get me to do anything with one look," he says as I lock eyes with him and take another slow step in his direction. He takes a step closer to me with Mom Stevens still clutched to his chest.

"Do you have a car here?"

Trying to sound very young, I reply, "No, my girlfriend dropped me off so I could have lunch with my Mom and Aunties."

I watch as he looks me up and down again, the hand holding the blade is more relaxed than before, the blade now about eight inches away from Mom Stevens' neck, almost resting on her shoulder. This is it. I lock eyes with Mom Stevens and motion for her to throw her head back into his face as I yell, *"Attack!"* At that moment, my switch flips and I don't hesitate to quickly spin and kick the surgical blade across the room at the exact second Mom Stevens throws her head back, crashing into his face, causing him to release her as he stumbles back.

Instantly, I give him an upper cut to his chin, taking him to the ground. Jumping on top of him, I continue my assault, punching him in his face and nose. He tries unsuccessfully to punch me, but I dodge him each time. Then he tries grabbing for my hands but fails, so he covers his face as he starts screaming "You are a Witch!"

He starts bucking and arching his back, trying to throw me off of him, screaming "Witch…. Witch…!"

Mom Riggs gets closer and says, "You sick bastard, looking at my future daughter in law like that." Then she kicks him in the crotch. For a few brief seconds, it pauses his bucking, then he starts coughing.

I hear Detective Jerkins yelling at the orderly, "Give him the fucking shot you jackass, before he hurts Lexy."

Detective Jerkins is now on top of psycho-guy's legs, trying to help hold him still. Both Mom Stevens and Mom Riggs are on their knees on each side of us, trying to capture his flailing arms. Once they finally have them, it takes all four of us to pin him to the floor as he continues trying to twist and arch his body like a bucking bronco.

We hear Mom Gregory's angry voice say, "I've had enough of this shit!" The clicking of her heels gets louder as she grabs the syringe from the useless orderly and leans in, harpooning the psycho in the shoulder. Within a few seconds, we feel him slowing down in his writhing. Everyone is breathing heavily, and I look around to find I'm practically covered in this man's blood. Jesus. I can only pray this man doesn't have some kind of contagious disease. His whole face is covered, and there's a pool forming around his head. Either Mom Stevens or I must have broken his nose but good, because he is still bleeding.

"I've got him now Lexy, you can get up. Nice job. I'll admit you shocked the shit out of me. But you're lucky this time. Don't do stuff like that again. You could have gotten yourself and the other women killed."

"No Detective Jerkins, that never would have happened. Not on my watch. And if I wanted that man dead, he would be. Now this conversation is over. I do not have to answer any of your questions so do not even ask."

"Where the fuck were you anyway?" Mom Riggs leans down and gets into his face. "I saw you peeking around the corner, and you just left us in here? Then you allowed my future daughter in law to come in here and rescue us! I would shut the fuck up while I was ahead if I were you or we'll all throw your ass under the bus when your so-called backup gets here. Do you understand me?"

"That's right. The man is captured and no one is seriously hurt is all you need to be reporting. Do we make ourselves clear?" That coming from Mom Gregory, standing there with her hands on her hips surprises me. She is usually the calm and sweet one.

"Yes Ma'am. I'll just tell them what I know. You ladies attacked him when you saw a vulnerable moment, and once we heard a scuffle going on, we rushed into the room to assist and apprehend your attacker."

"Good," Mom Stevens says, "Now come on ladies. Let's go get me checked out and get Lexy cleaned up. This officer looks like he can handle it now."

Mom Riggs puts her arm around my waist as I glance at the man on the floor. He is still awake even if his body cannot move. His eyes are racing back and forth looking at me.

"Mom Riggs, will the man remember any of this?"

"I really don't think so. He is having a manic schizophrenic episode. He obviously hasn't been taking his meds. They'll have to watch him more carefully. I'm just glad you're okay."

The four of us head for the door, leaving Detective Jerkins and the orderly to handle the psycho on the floor. "Barbara, how does your neck feel? Let me take a quick look at it," Mom Gregory says.

"No, I can wait till we get to Diana's office. I would rather not be in here when the rest of the police get here. The last thing I want to do is be asked fifty questions that will not help anyone," Mom Stevens says as we walk down the hall.

Once in the elevator, I notice both my hands are covered in psycho-guy's blood. Thank God we're in this elevator alone. Damn, not only is my dress ruined, but I need a shower, badly, and I have to depend on Mom Riggs to get me home.

Taking my hand, Mom Riggs pulls a tissue out of her pocket and wipes off my knuckles. "You didn't break the skin thankfully. I'll pull his chart the second we get to my office. I feel like I should give you a good shot of antibiotics and make you take some for the next ten days just to be safe, but I don't really think it will be needed." Then she pulls me into her arms and hugs me tightly. "God Lexy, you scared the ever loving shit out of me, but you saved Barbara. We'll forever be in debt to you."

"That isn't necessary, really. I just did what comes naturally to me. I just hope that cut on Mom Stevens' neck won't leave a scar."

"I think he just peeled a thin layer of skin up, causing me to bleed. But he knew right where my jugular was and flat out told me he wouldn't have any trouble slitting my throat and watching me bleed out. That was the scariest thing anyone has ever said to me. I've never been more afraid of dying in my life," Mom Stevens says.

"You and me both. Look, I'm still shaking," Mom Gregory says as she removes the tissue Mom Stevens has covering her neck. "Yeah, I think after we clean this up, you'll just need a little skin glue and you'll be as good as new."

Just then, the elevator door dings and opens and we hear three people gasp. I'm sure it's because they see all the blood on me and Mom Stevens.

"Don't worry people, we're just leaving a training exercise. We've all seen Gray's Anatomy before. Just think of this as a scene from that show. No real injuries," Mom Riggs announces as we exit the elevator, hearing their sighs of relief. We keep our heads down and walk as quickly as we can to Mom Riggs' office. Once inside, we all kind of giggle with relief.

"Okay Lexy, I'll check his records. You get into my shower and scrub all that blood off you. Feel free to put on whatever you like. There are scrubs as well as some exercise clothes in there. But I want you to make damn sure you get every drop of the blood off of you. Put all your things in one of those plastic bags and I'll take care of getting them cleaned myself. I promise." Then she leans in and kisses me on the forehead whispering, "Thank you again. Love you, my sweet girl. Now scoot," she says as she turns me towards her bathroom door with a light swat to my bum.

My heart melts. That felt like something a real mom would say and do. I walk into her personal shower and strip, making sure not to let any of the clothes I take off touch anything other than the bag. I am going to have to plead with the moms not to share this with anyone. The last thing I want to happen is for Grayson to hear I went all assassin on some guy before I tell him about myself. God, I'm going to have to tell him. Sooner rather than later.

I got about two hours of sleep last night. I thought the odd familiar feeling I was having was because I know it's time to tell Grayson about myself. And then this happened. But I still have that feeling I've always gotten right before something horrible happens. Closing my eyes and looking up to the heavens, I whisper, "Mom, if you can hear me, whatever's about to happen, please guide me and protect all those that I love."

Maybe when I get to my office, I should call Uncle Louie, just to make sure all is okay and that Papa isn't hunting for me here. I pause and think, wouldn't Uncle Louie call me if there was trouble headed my way? Yeah, he would. Luigi would also warn me, and I haven't heard from anyone. I'm just being paranoid. Finishing up my shower and stepping out to dry myself, I listen to see if I can hear what the moms are talking about.

"God, Barbara, I thought that man was going to kill you right in front of me," Mom Gregory says.

"Believe me, I was beginning to wonder myself. Noah and Brenda would have been destroyed."

"Well, thank God everything is okay. Thanks to Lexy. I'm still blown away by how her whole appearance changed when she called out, 'Attack'. Did you see how she jumped up and spun around kicking that thin surgical blade out of his hand? The accuracy of that! She is truly amazing. Grayson will shit himself when I tell him," Mom Riggs says, and that is my cue to walk out of the bathroom.

"I'm sorry, and I hate to ask all of you this, but please don't tell anyone about this just yet. You see, there are things I need to tell Grayson about myself before he goes and hears this story. Right now, I don't think he'd believe any of you. He sees me as a weak damsel in distress, but that's about to change."

"Lexy, what are you talking about? Is something going on between you and Grayson? Do I need to kick my son's ass?"

Chuckling, I can't help but love how quickly Mom Riggs is ready to defend and protect me. "No ma'am. I just realized yesterday that it's time to tell Grayson the whole truth about myself. I promise after I tell him, we'll talk. I just hope when I come clean, all of you will feel the same way about me as you do today."

All three moms get up and come over to me, hugging me. "Sweetie, there is nothing you can say or do that would ever change our love for you. You're one of our kids now. You're a 'Camelot Cutie'," Mom Gregory says.

Now that's a first. I've heard them refer to the girls as Wenches, but I do kind of like the 'Camelot Cuties' too. It makes me feel special.

"Lexy, Grayson and you are head over heels in love. We

have all watched it bloom over the last couple of months. So don't you worry for one second. Nothing you say can change that with him or any of us. You're one of our girls now," Mom Stevens hugs me and whispers, "Thank you again for rescuing me. You're my hero, now and always."

I return her hug and look closely at her neck. The cut is covered up with a bandage. As they notice me looking at it, Mom Riggs speaks up.

"Barbara's neck will be just fine. Monica called it correctly. Just a little glue to close it and some special cream, and I don't think it'll be noticeable in the months to come.

"As for the man that attacked us, you have nothing to worry about. He is free of disease. We guessed correctly, he is a manic schizophrenic and has been hearing voices for decades. He ended up in the psych ward here because he comes from money and his family put him in a home with a hired nurse who wasn't supervising his medication as she should have been, obviously, because he had stopped taking it and ended up here just a couple of days ago.

How he escaped the psychiatric ward, I have no idea. But after his attack, he'll be arrested for attempted murder and kidnapping. I've already spoken to Detective Jerkins, and the three of us have to go down to the station and fill out reports. The patient will now be locked up in a more secure facility, and probably receiving his meds via injection instead of orally."

"Umm, the three of you? Do I have to go down as well?" Fuck! Going to the police station is the last thing on the planet that I want to do. I watch as Mom Riggs looks to the other moms and they all give her a head nod. Oh shit, something else is going on.

She walks around to me and lightly places her hands on my shoulders, looks me in the eyes and says, "Lexy, Sweetie, we've talked about this amongst ourselves, and with you not wanting to talk about your family and you escaping Italy, and let's just say all these secret talents we've discovered... we think you probably escaped what we'd call a real Mafia family, and there is no way in hell we'd allow you to go downtown and be questioned. Us moms are going to protect you with our dying breath. We mean it. You're one of our girls now."

I can barely compose myself as I throw my arms around her. "Lexy, sweetie, really, it's okay. We already told Detective Jerkins to keep you out of everything or we won't talk. He agreed."

Stepping back away from her, I feel one lone tear roll from my eye and I wipe it away quickly. "Thank you. I really have nothing to hide from the local police. Even if they took my fingerprints, I really am American. But I wouldn't want pictures of me out in public." I look around at each of them, "Having family and friends like this is very different for me. I swear, after I tell Grayson, I'll tell you all the truth as well. I still hope you feel the same way after you know about my past."

Mom Gregory walks up to me and looks me square in the eyes as she taps her finger over my heart. "Young lady, we mean this, we know your heart, and we love who you are, no matter what your past is. Now, when you're ready to tell us, we're all ears. I'm sure some of the stuff we've imagined is way worse than anything you could have done. But even if it isn't, that's alright too, because we know who you are and we love you." Then she pulls me into a big hug. Mom Stevens and Mom Riggs join her in our second group hug today.

"Okay, I'm starved and we're off for the rest of the day, so let's go grab some nasty, unhealthy hamburger, fries and shakes. We'll work them off tomorrow night at the club. Then we can drop off Lexy and have Spencer meet us at police headquarters for safety's sake," Mom Stevens says.

"Sounds like a great plan. I just want to say that I love each of you from the bottom of my heart. Thank you. Now let's go." We walk out the door with our arms looped around each other. I can only think how incredibly lucky I am, and for the first time, I really believe Grayson will be okay after I tell him the truth.

Standing up from my office chair where I've been sitting the last three hours, I take a break from going over the planning and scheduling for the new 'Rainbows and Unicorn Daycare Center' here. Isabella's proposal is awesome and there is no way I'll pass up on a sure-thing that I know will be a success. We're going to do it. It's going to be a wonderful added feature to have trained daycare workers here for people to leave their child with while their parents work out or get a spa treatment.

Jesus, I feel so stiff from sitting for so long, so I stretch up as high as I can and bounce for a second before bending over at the waist with my legs spread, reaching my hands downward. Then I do some leg lunges. Yeah, there is nothing like a good stretch before I jog home for the night. I texted Grayson about thirty minutes ago and haven't heard back. I asked if we could just do dinner in, at either his place or mine. I really don't want to tell him the truth about my life out in public, and for the first time, I'm anxious to share my past with him.

Roid walks into my office and sees me stretching. "What are you doing? You've already taught two classes today and worked out with me, and now you're in here stretching?"

"Not that it is any of your bees wax, but my car isn't ready, so I'm stretching before jogging home. Do you have a problem with that?"

"No, not really. I could leave Steer here and drive you home. I've heard there's been a bit of trouble brewing around town so it might be safer."

Standing up from my deep leg lunges, I look at him very seriously. "Really? You think I can't jog a little over two miles home? Are you kidding me?" I say as I pull my oversized zippered black hoodie sweatshirt on, then grab a pair of lose sweatpants and pull them on over my leggings.

Roid just blinks his eyes and looks at me, "I know you'll be fine. Just feed my protective ego and don't listen to music on your jog home. Pay attention to your surroundings."

I smile at him and reach up, patting him on the cheek, "Okay Daddy. I'll text you when I get home too. If I don't call within the hour, make sure to call my big brother Tony to come hunt me down. Does that make you feel better?"

"Well yeah, it kind of does."

"Fine. I'll text you, I promise. See you in the morning." I pull my hood up over my head and wave my goodbyes as I head out the door.

Men! They all know I can handle myself. Jesus, it's not like I'm jogging in East LA. I'm in Santa Monica. Yeah on this jog I do have to run past a couple of old abandoned buildings, but I rarely ever see anyone around them besides a homeless person or two. Maybe once or twice I've run by a drug deal going down in one of the dark alleys, but they don't even notice me, not with this oversized hoodie and sweatpants. I just look like a short chunky person out for a run.

Letting my mind run free as I pick up speed, I know that tonight's the night I'm telling Grayson all about me, and hopefully soon after that, I'm going to jump his bones and *finally* make wild, passionate love to him. God, I can't wait.

Suddenly I get chill bumps all over me. I freeze for a second mid-stride. Was that gunfire? That overwhelming feeling sweeps over me and my head whips from one side to another as I hear another gunshot from the alley about ten feet in front of me. Without even thinking, I run over there and drop low, getting behind the back end of a big black SUV that is sticking out of the alley.

"What the fuck, man? We said we were going to talk! If you fire one more shot, I swear one of you is going to die!"

Fuck! That's Grayson's voice. Just then, I hear another couple of shots.

I crouch down as low as I can, pulling my hood further over my face, carefully pulling down the zipper in case I need to grab a throwing star from my bra. I slowly move my way to the side of the SUV, and I see Jackson laying on the ground beside a dumpster, with his Glock a few inches away from his hand. I've got to get over there and get his weapon. As quickly as I can, I run over beside him.

"Mother fucker. Shit!" I hear Grayson cry out. Looking down the alleyway, I can see the back of a black town car. There looks to be someone sitting in the back seat. Standing beside it are three fucking Russians. I recognize their familiar look.

"Aw, you American pussy-boy. Did you really think we came to talk? And what, ask each other questions we'll both answer with lies? You've proved you aren't a smart man. You're just a big boy playing with guns. But you'll fall dead just like any boy with a bullet. I think it'll be fun to torture and kill a few Camelot Brothers. Leave our mark, and prove you're nothing special." They say in a very heavy accent, proving I'd guessed correctly. They're definitely Russian.

"Look, everyone knows where I am. Backup is coming. You think my people don't have this alley wired? Why do you think we changed our meeting place at the last minute?" Grayson calls out.

Looking over at him, I can see he's been shot in the right hand and his gun is on the ground. Mother fuckers! I have to put a stop to this. I can only hope Grayson is telling the truth and Hawkins is watching and sending the other Brothers, or even the cops, for backup.

Leaning over Jackson's body, I pray they don't notice me. I can feel he has on a bulletproof vest, and can see he is breathing. Thank God and all that is holy, he isn't dead. I grab his gun and make sure the safety is off and that it's loaded. I hear

Jackson moan, and I quickly glance at him, hoping he isn't waking up just yet. I notice his forehead has a nice size gash in it and he's bleeding like a stuck pig. Typical of a head wound.

Just as I hear three more bullets fire, I look towards Grayson and see him go down with a loud moan that roars into my head over and over again. I can only pray he has on a vest like Jackson.

Without a second thought, I tuck the gun into my chest at the same time I roll towards the middle of the alley. I instantly jump up into a kneeling position and fire off three shots. Standing up, I know all three Russians are dead. I keep my gun at the ready as I dash over to the back door of the car and open it, ready to fire, when I hear a voice I recognize.

"Fuck, Princess. Is that you?" Orlando asks. He's bent over in the back seat with his hands zip-tied together, staring me straight in my eyes.

"What the hell, Orlando! Why the fuck did the Russians capture you? And what are they doing here?" I quickly stick the gun in the back of my pants and reach into my belt, pulling out the blade I always have on me. I cut the zip ties and hold the blade to his neck. I get into his face, giving him the most threatening look I can manage, "If you tell a goddamn soul in my Family you've seen me, I'll hunt you down and make Gigi a widow. Do I make myself clear?"

Orlando looks completely horrified. He bows his head to me and whispers, "I give you a solemn oath. I will not utter a word."

Looking down at the three dead Russians, I'm hit with the realization that I just killed the last son of the Osokina Family. Jesus. On the pinky finger of the man in the middle of the alley is Lilith's Family ring. I step over to him and bend down, and quickly cut his finger off and hand it to Orlando with the ring still on it. "Give this to Dante to give to Lilith. It's the Family ring they stole from her when she was kidnapped."

He shoves it in his pocket and looks at me. "You work with the Brothers of Camelot?"

Getting in his face again I say, "They are forever under my protection. Get the word out. We'll talk later. Now get the fuck out of here." He nods and takes off running in the opposite direction.

I stash my knife back into the hidden compartment of my belt and run over to Grayson.

Dropping to my knees beside him, I see his left leg has a bullet hole in it and it is bleeding pretty bad. I can hear him breathing and moaning. Thank God he is alive. Feeling around, I find his other leg has a rip in the side of his pants. I take a closer look to discover he was hit again, but this one is just a flesh wound and will only need stitches. Those goddamn Russians were just toying with him.

"Grayson, baby can you hear me? I'm going to get you help. You're going to be okay. I rub my hands up his chest and feel his bulletproof vest. Briefly, I close my eyes and thank the heavens and my Mom for watching out for him. Just then, my finger feels something odd. Opening my eyes and looking over his chest more closely, I realize he was hit in the side of the chest, and his bulletproof vest saved him.

"Who the fuck are you? I saw every goddamn thing you just did. Was that Orlando Benassi you let go? Are you working with him?" Jackson asks, squatting down beside Grayson while holding his hand over his still bleeding forehead cut.

"Not now, Jackson. We have to get Grayson up and to the hospital. He's been shot at least three times. Possibly more. I don't want to be sitting ducks if the Russians have other men coming," I bark at him like he was one of my own men.

Grayson mumbles, "No hospital. Take to Head-quarters."

Thank God, Grayson's waking up. "Grayson, I'm here," I say as I push his hair out of his face, watching his eyes blink, trying to focus on me. "You've been shot in both legs, but we're going to have to stand you up and get you into the SUV, or I can call an ambulance." Fuck. I'd rather not have to explain why there are three dead Russians in the alley, but I have to get Grayson help.

"No hospital. I can help," Grayson mumbles, trying to sit up.

"Lexy, fuck, your hands are covered in that Russian's blood. I wasn't seeing things, you did cut his goddamn finger off! What the fuck, girl! Who the hell are you? No better yet, what the hell are you?" Jackson bellows.

Okay, I've had enough of Jackson's mouth. I get up and grab his chin with my fingers, pulling his face down to mine.

"Listen here, you mother fucker, I don't want to hear another goddamn word about what you think you saw, or I might just put a bullet in you myself to shut you up until we get Grayson to your compound. Do I make myself clear?" I squeeze his chin hard for added effect, letting him know I mean every word of it.

He wrinkles his brow and stares deeply into my eyes for a second before he nods and says, "Fine, but tonight we talk. Understood?"

"Fine." Just then I hear a motorcycle approaching, so I reach down and grab Grayson's gun and get the Glock from the back of my pants, aiming towards the far end of the alley, where I can see the motorcycle coming towards us.

"Fuck, don't shoot! That's Stevens," Jackson says, putting his arm over my chest, halting me.

"Shit! What the hell is he doing, coming from the opposite end of the alley where the Russians are?"

Stevens quickly stops in front of us, pulling off his helmet as he rushes over to Grayson. "Oh shit!" He lifts his arm to his mouth and shouts, "Grayson's been shot! Get Gregory ready, we're bringing him in." Then he leans over Grayson, lifting his upper body into a sitting position. "Can you hear me, Brother?" Grayson's eyes flutter as he tries to open them.

"Stevens, protect Lexy," Grayson mumbles.

"Dude, Lexy's fine. You guys already took out all three Russians. Damn, right between the eyes. You must have known they had on vests too. We've gotta get you in the SUV and to headquarters ASAP."

"Stevens, he's been shot in both legs. His left leg still has a bullet in it, and it's bleeding pretty bad. His right leg as a pretty good size flesh wound. The shot to the side of his chest is what knocked him out. Thank God the vest protected him. I haven't finished examining him for other wounds."

"You doing okay other than the head gash, Jackson? It looks like you just got grazed, 'cause I don't see brains or bone, just a lot of blood. At least you took the Russians out first. Let's get Grayson up." Stevens takes Grayson's arm and wraps it around his shoulder before starting to lift Grayson up. I run around to the other side, wanting to assist.

"Fuck, Brother, it wasn't us. It was Lara Croft over here," Jackson says, throwing his thumb over his shoulder in my direction. Then he moves me out of the way and helps get Grayson to the back of the SUV. "Goddamn those mother fuckers. They got me in the chest, knocking me out cold for a minute. I must have hit my head on something going down, because my head feels like it's exploding and my vision is a bit blurry. Now I feel like I'm going to throw up."

Stevens chuckles, "No throwing up until we get Grayson's fat ass in the SUV. And you definitely hit your head if you don't remember taking out the Russians." Then he mumbles "Lara Croft" in disbelief and starts chuckling again. He must think Jackson is messing with him.

"Man, I swear it was..."

"Jackson! I still have both guns," I warn him as I smack him on the back of the head, not giving a rats ass about his headache. I just want him to shut his mouth.

"Fuck! Goddamn Lexy! Fine!" Jackson shakes his head a bit, and thankfully shuts up.

"Lexy's just carrying them to the SUV. I'll put the safeties on once we get Grayson inside," Jackson says, I'm sure trying to appease me.

"I've already done that. I kind of know my way around a firearm."

Stevens gives me a head nod, "Good to know."

Jackson puts one hand on top of his pants pocket and I hear all the doors to the SUV unlock and the lights inside come on. Once they get Grayson onto the back seat, I can see he has another flesh wound on his shoulder. Fuck... There isn't going to be a Goddamn member of this Russian family left when I get through with them. I've got to get ahold of Tony and let him know what's going down. I slide my hand onto my belt, pushing the middle red stone three times quickly. That is my signal to Tony that I'm in trouble and he needs to find me.

"*Fuck!* This hurts like a mother fucker," Grayson calls out, ripping my heart into a million pieces. His eyes are still unfocused, but he is waking up more with each second.

Once they have Grayson in the back of the SUV, Stevens runs around to the back and opens it, grabbing what looks like a large duffle bag. Opening it, he throws some gauze pads and a roll of athletic tape at Jackson. "Wrap your head up until we get to headquarters where I can take a better look at it."

"Does Hawkins have eyes on this alley like Grayson said? We need to get out of here. Give me the keys!" I start barking orders.

"Yeah, I'm sure he does. Do you hear the roar of bikes coming? That'll be Clay, Carpenter and Clausen. They'll escort you to the underground entrance where I'm sure Brenden, Bishop and Tiffany will meet us," Stevens shouts at me as he grabs some kind of big gauze dressing and puts them on Grayson's leg wounds, wrapping them tightly. Once he hops out and tosses the duffle bag back into the trunk, I'm jumping in the back, practically straddling Grayson. I lean over him, resting our foreheads together. His eyes instantly open up and he looks at me with a small crooked grin fills his face. "I'm going to be okay baby, don't worry. I love you," he mumbles.

"I love you too, and I know you're going to be okay. I'm not going to leave your side." I lightly kiss his lips, and he gently responds.

"Okay, Lexy! No jumping the man when he's down." I hear Stevens call from the front seat, as he leans in and starts the engine. I look down at Grayson's leg see the gauze is already covered in blood.

"Jackson! get in here and apply pressure to Grayson's leg. It is still bleeding like a mother fucker." I grab Jackson's hand and press it to Grayson's wound.

"Shit!" Grayson's shouts.

"Sorry baby. We have to stop the bleeding," I say with one last kiss to his lips, before leaping up front into the driver's seat, quickly moving the seat up as far as I can so I can reach the peddles.

"Alright, let's move it. Keep your eyes open for the cops. Carpenter, you and Clausen lead the way, Clay and I'll follow," Stevens calls out. I see Carpenter in my rearview mirror as I throw the SUV into reverse, getting the hell out of the alley.

"Lexy, are you okay?" I hear Hawkins's voice over the speakers in the car.

"Yeah, I'm fine. Is Brenden already there? Grayson's left leg is pretty fucked up. It still has the bullet in it."

"Yes, he's here and they are ready to take him into surgery. Were you hit? The Russians got off a couple of shots."

"If I was, I don't feel a damn thing. My mind is on Grayson. How far is your compound?"

"You'll be here in fifteen, maybe twenty minutes at most. We need to talk."

"Hawkins, right now everyone wants to talk to me, but I'm not saying jack shit until I've talked to Grayson."

"Lexy, this is Brenden. Grayson's leg wound - was the blood coming out in a pulsating motion?"

"No. I don't think it hit the femoral artery, but it's close. It's above the knee but towards the inner thigh."

"Shit. What are his other injuries?"

"He's got about a four inch gash to the side of his right leg that ripped right through his pants and flesh. It will need stitches. Glue won't cut it. He still has his vest on, and there's a bullet is lodged in it. It is on his left side, lower than his heart. It probably bruised his lung real good. I'm sure that's what knocked him out. His shoulder also has a graze wound. I didn't see any other injuries."

"What about Jackson?"

"He was hit in the center of the chest. His vest protected him but the hit took him out. He fell to the side and probably hit his head on the edge of the dumpster on his way down. From the way he describes how he's feeling, I'd say he's dealing with a nice concussion."

"Jackson! Jackson! Are you awake back there? No sleeping with a concussion!" Brenden calls out.

"I hear you, but fuck, I can barely keep my eyes open and if I move, I feel like I'm gonna barf."

"Yeah, sounds like a concussion. I'll have Stevens check you out and keep an eye on you until I get Grayson put back together. No sleeping for a bit, and when you do, we're going to be waking you up to check on your ass, so get used to that idea."

"Then you better keep me fucking entertained. As for Grayson, he's lost a lot of blood, he might need some. He's in and out of it. He hasn't been awake for more than three minutes before he passes out again," Jackson informs Brenden.

"Fuck you. I'm just closing my eyes, trying to will the pain away," Grayson mumbles from behind me.

"Well, good to hear you mumbling Grayson. We'll make all the pain go away once you get here."

I'm not even aware of how long I have been driving for when we finally pull into a very nice building. The sign reads "Camelot Inc." Under that, it has a list of all the businesses including Camelot Security, Camelot Law Firm, Camelot Construction, Camelot Architectural Design and Camelot Training. Now it is obvious why they refer to it as 'headquarters'. I guess this is where all the offices are at. I follow the motorcycles as they drive around the building to where two very large, solid steel gates are slowly sliding open. I drive through, and wow, this building seems to go on forever. Once we reach the back, I watch as two more doors attached to the building slide open, revealing what looks like a huge garage.

Carpenter gets off of his bike and waves me to drive in slowly. Once I am inside, I hear the doors close behind me, and that's when I feel us lowering. This is some kind of massive freight elevator.

"You can turn the engine off. You aren't going anywhere. In fact, I'm going to send Clausen and Clay to go pick up your roommates and bring them here. We've got apartments down here as well. I'd like to talk to them," Jackson says from behind me.

I push the button turning off the motor and just enjoy the brief ride down to their lower security department. I wonder if Tony's system will pick me up down here. Well, we're giving our signal a good test right now. I want to laugh at Jackson, thinking that talking to my friends will make me nervous. They will never tell him anything.

"You're wasting your time, Jackson. My friends don't know shit."

"Oh well. I've been wanting to get to know Anissa better

for a while anyway. Now's just as good of a time as any. Maybe she can keep me entertained and awake."

All the elevator doors open and I quickly jump out and push past Carpenter to watch as they lift Grayson out of the SUV and put him on a gurney. "Lexy!" Grayson calls out.

Within a second, I'm right beside him. "I'm right here baby," I say as I run my hand down the side of his face. "I'm not leaving you."

"Lexy!" Grayson calls out again, and before anyone can stop me, I leap up and onto the gurney to straddle him, leaning forward to rest my forehead against his. His eyes open and he whispers, "Who are you?"

My heart is pounding like a runaway freight train unable to stop. "I swear, once you are out of surgery, I'll tell you everything," I whisper.

"I need to know now. Who are you?" Grayson asks again, and I know no one can hear him but me.

I take a deep breath and lightly kiss his lips, whispering for his ears only, "I 'was' Alessandra Sophia Canzano, the Capo Donna of Northern Italy, and daughter to Al Canzano." I'm sure Grayson cannot only hear my heart pounding, but feel it where our chests are touching.

Grayson lifts his hand and puts it on the side of my cheek and looks me in the eyes. "I love you with all my heart, mind and soul. You are my one love, my only love, Alessandra Sophia Canzano and nothing will ever change that Aless. Lexy."

"Okay, enough of that. We have to put your man back together again." Hawkins says as he puts his hands around my waist and lifts me off of Grayson.

"No! I want to go with him. I can assist. Blood doesn't scare me. I don't want to leave him." I struggle to get to Grayson, but Hawkins keeps both arms wrapped around my waist as Brenden, Liam and Tiffany take off, pushing Grayson down a hallway that I assume leads to the O.R. I try to pull away from Hawkins, but he refuses to let me go.

"Not happening. You aren't going anywhere. I am personally not letting you out of my sight until you start talking." Hawkins says as he moves his arms from my waist to my shoulders, leading me in the opposite direction of the double doors they just took Grayson through.

"If anything happens to him and I'm not there, you'll regret the day you were born."

"I'm not worried about that. He's in good hands, that much I am sure of." Hawkins reassures me.

God, I sure hope Tony gets here fast. I need to find out what he knows and start planning.

18

SHARING TRUTHS

Grayson

I hear voices and try to open my eyes. Then I feel lips lightly kissing mine. That's Lexy. Then reality hits me. Shit! I'm being kissed and awakened by a real Princess. My own Mafia Princess, but she's no longer theirs, she's mine.

God, I can't wait to completely erase the Mafia memories out of her mind and make her a Camelot Princess, for life. My life feels like a fucking fairytale in my mind at this second. Well, except for these dumbasses talking in my room. Then I feel Lexy cuddle into my side. Fuck them. I'm in paradise. I'm in my bed with Lexy, finally.

"I'm giving him another thirty minutes and if he doesn't start waking up then, I'll call an ambulance myself. Fuck my medical license. He shouldn't still be out of it right now. All his stats are fine; he's just not waking up like he should. His head could have been hit harder than I first thought," I hear Gregory sounding overly stressed.

But that doesn't matter to me. All I can feel is Lexy's warm body cuddled into my side, her head resting on my chest and I feel her hand on my heart. Her unique sweet smell wakes me even more. My eyes flutter open to the dim lights in my room at headquarters. Looking down, I see the top of Lexy's head.

Slowly turning my head just slightly to the right, I do a double-take. What the fuck?! I see Stevens sitting in the chair beside my bed, in full makeup and dressed like a fucking drag queen. What the hell kind of drugs did they give me? Damn, I feel like I've been put through the ringer. Goddamn lying Russian mafia and all their bullshit. They shot me! I try to clear my throat and manage to croak out, "Stevens, why the fuck are you dressed like a drag queen? What did I miss?" I sound like I swallowed nails. Damn.

"Brenden, did you hear that? Grayson just spoke. He's awake," Lexy says, moving to sit up in bed beside me, leaning down to look into my eyes as she pushes my hair out of my face. Damn, those eyes of hers are sexy as hell and I can't stop the smile from spreading across my face.

"I could have sworn I was just woken up by a real princess kissing me on the lips. Then I saw Stevens in drag." My eyelids feel like they weigh five pounds each but I still manage to give Lexy a wink as I say, "Hey baby. I love you, Princess, come here and kiss me again."

She gets closer to my face and I reach up the hand not attached to an I.V. and pull her into another kiss. This time, I am more than capable of responding.

"Okay, knock it off. You two can do that later. I need to know how you're doing Riggs. Fuck, you should have woken up over an hour ago," Gregory blurts out.

Letting go of Lexy as she pulls away from our kiss, I answer him, "Well, I can't help that. I'm awake now. Why the hell is Stevens dressed up like a drag queen?" I ask again. Lexy just sits back on her heels beside me in the bed watching me as Gregory starts checking all the shit I am connected to. No one is answering me about Stevens, who is opening and closing his mouth like he's about to explain, but ends up just rolling his eyes instead. Lexy is just sitting there, shaking her finger at him.

"They'll explain all about Stevens' appearance and him losing a bet with Lexy after you answer some questions for me. What's the last thing you remember? Do you know where you are now? How are you feeling? Does anything hurt?" Gregory fires off too many questions for me to answer right now.

"I'm fine. My head hurts a little, but it hurts like a mother fucker to take a deep breath. I'm sore as fuck all over."

"Do you remember what happened to you?" Gregory asks again.

"Yeah, yeah. The fucking Russians didn't come to talk, they came to torture and kill me. I remember getting my gun shot out of my hand, then a couple of them shot at the same time. I felt my leg burn and something hit me in the chest and I guess that knocked me out. Next thing I remember is somehow Lexy being there, and I felt the need to protect her. But someone, I think it was Stevens, said the Russians were already dead."

"So, you were out cold when ol' Lexy there took out all three of the Russians herself. No, I'm not fucking lying to you. She came running over to me out of nowhere, grabbed my gun and did a fucking forward roll over to the middle of the alley, jumped up on one knee and bang, bang, bang, shot all three of the fuckers between the eyes," Jackson says, standing at the foot of my bed all excited, holding his fingers out like they're guns.

"Jackson, I have no problem kicking your ass. Shut the fuck up and let Grayson wake up," Lexy barks at him. Jackson just shuts his mouth, shakes his head and goes back to the chair at the foot of my bed.

"What the hell is going on?" I ask.

Gregory is now waving a little light in my eyes. "There is plenty of time to tell you about all you missed while you were passed out or in surgery, but right now I need to know how you are."

"I'm fine. How many bullets did I take? Like I said, I feel like I've been put through the ringer. It even hurts to take a deep breath."

"Well that would be from the severe bruised ribs. Thank God you listened to Hawkins and had a bulletproof vest on, or you might not be here with us right now. You did get three flesh wounds: left leg, right shoulder and right hand. Your hand only needed glue. The other two needed just a few stitches. The bullet you took to your right leg was the bad one. If that bullet entered your leg just a hair over, it would have taken out your femoral artery, meaning you would have more than likely bled out before we could have done anything.

"I want you off that leg for at least a week, and it's going to hurt like a bitch after the stitches come out in about ten days, and you start using it again. It was pretty deep, tore right through your muscles too but it's all put back together. No leg workouts for at least three to four weeks, and if it hurts when you try something, listen to your fucking body. Don't push it."

"Shit. It must still be numb from surgery because I can't feel a thing from it. I'm just sore all over, like I was hit by a truck or something."

"That would be from the bullet to the ribs. That probably knocked you on your ass. The force of a bullet is pretty fucking powerful," Gregory says as he starts removing little sticky things from my chest.

"Yeah, you're right there. It probably knocked me up in the air a bit too before I landed on my ass on the pavement. That's what happened when the Russians shot Jackson. He literally went flying back and into the side of the dumpster. I thought for a minute he was a goner, and then I saw his chest moving and realized the vest had protected him too. They didn't shoot him in the head like I first thought. He must have hit his head on his way down."

"That is what happened man. My chest hurts like a mother fucker too, but my head feels like it's going to explode at any minute. I must have hit that dumpster hard. I just hope I don't get any dumpster disease. You know how many people piss on dumpsters?"

The room busts out laughing, and some of the Brothers tease Jackson.

"I'm going to look at your head again and give you something for the pain too. A round of antibiotics might not be a bad idea," Gregory says with a chuckle.

"Okay, now what were you saying about Lexy and the Russians Jackson?"

"I'm telling you, she is the one that killed all three of the fuckers. I came to just in time to catch the show myself," Jackson says, coming to stand at the foot of my bed again. I slowly sit up a bit more and shove another pillow behind me, needing the extra support.

"Jackson, I mean it. Now is not the time," Lexy says as she moves back beside me, shoving even more pillows behind me. "Can I get you anything, honey?" I can't help but smile at her, trying to look all innocent.

"Yeah, let Jackson tell me his story, that is, unless you want to tell me yourself." She cuts her eyes to Jackson, obviously not too happy with him at all as he raises his hands in surrender.

"Okay, let's just say I have this switch in me that I cannot control, and when it is flipped, I just respond with instincts. I was jogging home from my club when I heard gunfire. That kind of flipped the switch in me. I ran over and saw what was going on, and before I could really stop myself, not that I would have anyway, three Russians were dead. The end. Now I'm sure you need to rest, doesn't he, Brenden?" she asks pleadingly, looking to Gregory for help.

"Well in reality, since he got hit in the head pretty hard and he's been out for so long, it's probably good for him to be up and talking, just to make sure everything is okay. His leg will probably be numb for a few more hours which is good," Gregory says as he removes my I.V.

The moment my hand is free I put it around Lexy and pull her into me. "Are you trying to change the subject?"

"Well, maybe. You and I need to talk, and I didn't think you wanted it to be in front of everyone."

"Baby, I think they probably know more than you think they do. We've all been trying to figure things out for months now."

"Let me be the first to say thank you, for saving our asses for the second time. I'm pretty confident after seeing your little performance tonight that you were that little Italian assassin flying around the rafters in Italy. You saved mine and Fitz's asses when we were being attacked and were cornered. Am I correct? Or should I ask your side kick and partner in crime, Tony?"

I cannot help but chuckle until I see Lexy looking down and starting to bite her lower lip. No fucking way. She couldn't have been that assassin, could she? Looking around the room, I see Tony sitting in the corner staring up at the ceiling, making damn sure not to make eye contact with anyone. Fuck!

Looking over to Hawkins, I see he has an overconfident, shit-eating grin on his face. I subconsciously shake my head, no. I feel a knot developing in my stomach as I look down at Lexy in my arms. She honest to God looks nervous, and no one is saying anything.

Looking between Stevens and Jackson, I will one of them to tell me they're joking, but Jackson keeps looking between Lexy and Tony, like he wants one of them to say something. I change the subject for a second.

"Stevens, explain to me why you are dressed in drag. And what bet did you lose with Lexy? Answer me this time. Don't look at her, answer me." I pull Lexy tighter into my chest.

"Well, for the next twenty two hours, she's the boss of me. So, if she says I can't talk, I can't say jack shit. And I'm guessing by the way she's giving me a death-look with her scary blue eyes that I'm not supposed to say anything," Stevens says, crossing his arms over his skin-tight glitter t-shirt that I can see a black push-up bra under. Jesus. What the fuck is going on? Looking back to Hawkins, I raise an eyebrow, hoping he'll tell me something.

"Okay, I'm not sworn to secrecy. I didn't bet against her. I'm not a dumbass like you were Stevens, and because I have to agree with Jackson. I think your little half-pint hottie is everything I told you I thought she was. But she refuses to tell us anything until she talks to you," Hawkins informs me.

Hearing Lexy sigh in my arms, I turn her head up so I can rest my forehead on hers, as I whisper, "Do you want me to clear my room so we can talk alone? Or would it be easier for you just to tell us all a brief story of who you are? I remember before I went into surgery, you told me you were Alessandra Sophia Canzano, rather that is who you used to be. But you also said something about being the Capo Donna? Which is easier for you? I'll kick these assholes out of here in two seconds flat if that's what you want, but you know they aren't going to let it die until you tell them something."

Hearing Lexy sigh, she relaxes in my arms as she shakes her head, before she speaks up quite loudly, "Okay, listen up you nosy assholes. I'm going to tell you this once, then all of you are getting your goddamn asses out of here so I can talk to Grayson alone. He deserves that much." Then she whips her head towards Jackson, "You're welcome, and I didn't do anything you wouldn't have done for me. I'm sure. And yes, that was me and Tony working with you in Italy. If you want any more information about that, Tony is allowed to fill all you nosy fuckers in on the whole story. I give him permission. Now, will you all leave us alone?" Lexy barks. My girl has balls alright. My men nod and all get up and head towards the door.

"Thanks Brothers. We'll talk in the morning. No one come

in that door until after ten a.m., is that understood? If I need anything, Lexy will come and find you," I bark out at them.

"Okay, hope you feel better. You have your phone on the nightstand in close reach. Feel free to text me if you need anything or a good strong mind to bounce things off of," Hawkins says with a head nod towards me. "Same goes for you too Lexy. I'm staying here, at least until Riggs is able to leave. And thanks for letting Tony fill us in. It'll make things easier. And Lexy, I promise no matter what Riggs or Tony says, I will not keep secrets from you. I know the importance of knowing the full truth."

"Thank you, Hawkins. That means the world to me. I hope you mean it because I think we can easily help each other out. I do have a lot of information you might be interested in hearing as well. We'll meet up over the next couple of days and go over everything," Lexy says, making my mind wonder what in the hell they are talking about.

"Tony, you know I'm pissed at you, so tread lightly. You know what I mean," Lexy practically growls at Tony.

"Yes, boss. I made an oath and I never go against my word after that." I watch as he practically bows to Lexy before walking out of the room, with Jackson right behind him. Luckily, Gregory had finished tending to his head.

"Is anyone going to explain to me why Stevens is in drag?" All the Brothers chuckle as Lexy just sighs again.

Spencer walks by my bed and pauses as he announces, "Well, I'm not sworn to secrecy either. Your boy Stevens lost his title in firearms to, as Hawkins called her, 'your little half-pint hottie'. That girl humiliated him and handed Stevens his balls, literally. When you're up to it, you'll have to see the auto-graphed target in the office. I've got Tiff getting it framed so we all can remember your girl is one badass with a gun. I've never seen anything like it." Then he looks over to Lexy, "Sorry, I had to tell him. But please, don't shoot me. I'll be the first to admit

I'll be hitting the range very soon, cause you girl could take me out with one eye closed, I'm sure of it," he teases her with a wink as he walks out of my room, just as she calls out to him.

"You don't have to worry about me shooting you, but you might want to protect your balls. I've been known to cause great pain to men that piss me off. Why don't you ask Tony about that one."

"Shit, I'll definitely be talking to Tony," Spencer says. He's the last to leave my room, covering his balls with one hand while he closes the door.

"So, you challenged and made a bet with Stevens for his title in firearms. How? He and I both battle each other regularly for that title. Tell me, how did you distract him and cause him to lose?"

"What makes you think I did anything to distract him? I'll have you know I don't miss. It's like a gift."

"So, you really killed those three Russians tonight?"

"Yes. I meant it when I said I've been training my whole life. I've been this way since before I was sixteen. I call it my instinct. It's like I get suddenly overcome with a feeling, and an internal switch in me is flipped, and I just handle things."

"Okay. How many shots did it take to beat Stevens? Was it accuracy or speed?"

"Both. I asked for seven bullets."

"Seven? And you still beat him. He could get off a kill in less than three. Usually one. You must have distracted him."

"No, I didn't. I put one bullet between the eyes, one to the center of the heart and five bullets into a smiley face cupping his balls - rather the target's balls. But you get the gist of it. That is kind of my trademark when I want to show a man up on the range."

I cannot help but throw my head back and laugh, which causes my head to hurt like a mother. But damn, what I would have done to have seen that! I bet Hawk has it on tape. I'll have to ask to see that in the morning. Damn, my half pint hottie is a marksman... an assassin.

"Will you tell me about yourself now?"

"Damn." Lexy gets up and starts to pace back and forth in my room. She pulls off an oversized Camelot Security sweatshirt she had on. I instantly notice her shoulder has a bandage on it.

"What happened to your shoulder?"

"Fuck! Nothing. I was just grazed. One of the Russians must have gotten off a shot before I killed them all. Just a few stitches. Stevens sewed me back up and I'm as good as new."

"You were shot? Does it hurt? Jesus Lexy, how many times in your life have you been shot? You act like it was nothing."

"Because it wasn't anything, and do you really want to know how many times I've been shot?" she says pausing for a second with her hand on her hip, like obviously it's been more than once. Shit!

"Okay. With your pacing, it doesn't look like this is going to be easy for you to talk about. So, let me tell you this, first and foremost. I love you, now and always. I don't care if you've killed three or thirty three people."

"Sorry, it's probably been a bit more than that. But really, I'd rather not count," Lexy says, looking at the ground as she starts pacing again.

"Fuck! Are you serious? Forget it. It's not like you went out shooting people for shits and giggles. Your life has been completely different from mine, and odds are it was someone in your Family whose life was in danger and that is why you did it."

"Well, I did start to torture someone once because I wanted to watch him suffer and die like one of his men did my mom, but I ended up killing him quickly to shut him up. But that was a rival Family's Capo, and he's the one who ordered the attack on my Family and put a hit on my mother and me on my sixteenth birthday. Yeah. Happy fucking birthday to me. One of his men shot my mom in the gut, right in front of me. After I killed that mother fucker, I held my mom until she died in my arms. I was determined to eliminate his damn reign over his Family after that. The war he caused between our Families ended that night. And I did just that, with his own wife and children's blessing. So yeah, you can say my life was a hell of a lot different than yours was growing up," she continues to pace back and forth across my room.

Jesus, I just want to hold her and tell her everything will be okay, but I can tell she doesn't need or want that right now. This is how she needs to tell me. God, I hate this for her.

"Lexy, as much as I want to hear this, I can wait. I know it brings back so much pain for you. I just want to hold you and love you. You'll never have to go through all that again."

"You're damn right I'll never have to go through all of that again, because I'm the one in charge. This is what my father wanted of me. He started grooming me for this when I was six years old. I knew how to shoot any weapon put in front of me. I could break it down and clean it in record time. I was taught to be on alert at all times, constantly aware of everyone and everything around me. I had to be able to turn anything into a weapon. My goal was never to maim, it was always to kill. And I am good at it. But since my escape, tonight was the first time that switch was flipped again."

"Lexy, I'm serious. If this is too much…"

"Grayson, look. Since the day I walked back into your life, you've wanted to know everything about me. Well, now I'm going to give you a brief synopsis. Yeah, it's hard to tell you. Some of it I've never spoken about out loud, or told anyone outside of the Family in fear of what they would think of me. I'm also afraid you won't love me or feel the same way about me after you know the real me. But you need to know, and I understand that, so let me just tell you and get it over with."

"Baby, come here let me hold you. I love you, Lexy. You

mean more to me than the air I breathe. Nothing you can say or do will ever change that."

"I can't let you hold me right now. I need to pace, to get it out."

"Okay baby. Tell me. I won't ask any questions until you're finished."

I watch as she takes a deep cleansing breath and begins her pacing again, not really looking at anything, just walking back and forth before she starts talking again. "Like I said before, I never had any control of my life, not until about a year after my mother's murder. At seventeen, my father not only sent me off to university, he informed me I'd be getting a business degree, which did come in handy. He also had me running the whole Northern side of the Family businesses. He put me in charge of over two hundred men. I oversaw and ran everything from the strip clubs to the restaurants, the legal, legit Family businesses, and the ones that weren't so legal. I learned the ropes and ran everything myself. I kept meticulous notes of all the other criminals my Family was involved with, and used it to help with my escape.

"Like I said, I was the Capo Donna, what you would call the Mob Boss. The first female to have so much power within our Family, ever. I slowly made a lot more of the businesses legal too. I earned the respect of all my men, because I never asked them to do something I wasn't willing to do myself. I fought beside them and gave the orders. I didn't hide at some secure location like so many other Capo's do while the men are in danger.

Oh, I should probably warn you, I'm sure once my Family gets wind of what went down tonight, you'll be meeting several of them personally. I would not be surprised in the slightest if Uncle Louie and Luigi aren't here by the weekend to check on me, and to see if you Camelot Brothers have what it takes to work with me," she says with a big smile and a laugh.

"You're telling me some of your Family are coming here? Are they going to try and take you back? Do I need to call the Brothers now and warn them? Put everyone on lock down?" I ask grabbing my phone, ready to call Hawkins.

"No, put your phone down silly. You aren't listening. I said they'd want to check out all of your skill levels, to see if you have what it takes to battle with me and be my equal."

Now I can't help but laugh at that. "Yeah, I think we got your back, babe. You just took out the three Russians. I'm sure the others tucked tail and ran back to Russia. I think this little war they were planning is officially over."

"No. I know more about these Russians than you do. Tonight, I killed Maksim Osokina, who was the last of the Russian Mob Capo's sons." I watch as she looks up to the ceiling for a second before she rubs her hand over her face like I do when I'm majorly stressed. Oh, shit I'm not going to like what she's about to tell me, I can feel it in my bones.

"Well, I kind of already killed his other two sons. You see, his baby boy Boris tried to kidnap me, and let's just say, he took a knife to the stomach and I left him for dead. That was the night our girls were kidnapped. Then a few nights later, the second son, Nikolai, the one who was overseeing the kidnapped girls, I took him out when he was coming out of his office the night when we rescued the girls from the warehouse. Tonight was son number three. So, I'm sure the Capo himself will be coming, thinking he can take me out, but that won't happen."

"Your goddamn right that won't happen. Your ass is going up to Hawkins' castle first thing in the morning until we get this all worked out," I inform her. She freezes mid-step, then slowly turns around, glaring at me.

"What the fuck did you just say?" she demands.

Struggling to sit up in bed a bit more so I don't look as worn out as I feel, I say firmly, "You heard mem Lexy. I'm not playing around."

"And neither am I. *I do not hide!* You can deal with that any way you like, but I am not some fucking weak-ass woman that needs your fucking protection. I do believe I have proven to you myself by protecting your ass not once, but twice."

"That was different," I argue.

"Oh, really? Enlighten me, oh great one. How was that different?" she says with a smirk on her face and her hands on her hips, knowing goddamn well she has me on this one. But fuck! Those were flukes. I am not going to let her get hurt, or even worse, killed. Nope, that is not going to happen. I have to get her off this subject for now so I can talk to Hawkins and figure out a plan.

"Let's not worry about that now. We don't even know if they found the bodies yet or not. Maybe the cops have them and the Russians are clueless. Let's wait until we get some intel to figure out how we'll handle this. Now, what were you saying about your Family coming to check us out?"

"Grayson I'm not an airhead. I know full well you are trying to change the subject because you need time to try and figure out a way to twist this. But I'm telling you now, that will never happen so don't push me. I'll play along for now. As for my Family, there is a good chance that possibly four of them will be showing up, checking all of you out and giving you pointers."

"Four? Who are the other two? And what is or was your relationship with Luigi?" I need to know what to expect so I'm prepared.

"Well Uncle Louie is like my dad, so expect him to treat you like a girlfriend's father would." She finally seems to relax a bit and her smile looks more natural and happy as she finally walks over and sits on the corner of the bed.

"I think I can handle that, even if this is the first time I'll actually be meeting a real girlfriend's father." I grab her and pull her over to me, needing her close to me.

She completely relaxes now and cuddles into my good side

as she continues to share. "Luigi was one of my bodyguards and we trained together for years. If there was ever someone within the Family I thought Uncle Louie wanted me to fall in love with, it was Luigi. But it never happened. He is married to a wonderful woman, Sandy, and they are expecting their first child so you have nothing to worry about. He is like a big brother, and has been treating me like that for many a year."

"Hey, but were you and him ever... you know.... involved?"

She giggles like an innocent girl. "No, we weren't, not really. Yeah, we spent a lot of time together and flirted around, but as I told Luigi several years ago, we were more each other's fantasy than anything else. He was older and always around me. We saw each other every day and trained together. All my friends were crushing on him because he was so hot, but it was never anything real. For many a year, he was my best friend and we shared everything."

"Oh okay. But he is definitely married now, right?"

"Yes, very happily married and I consider his wife a good friend. There aren't any feelings between us other than sibling affection. Does that make you feel better? Geez, I think you were getting jealous."

"Well, I just wanted to make sure he was married so I have nothing to worry about. I mean, you said your uncle wanted you to marry him, what was I supposed to think?"

She laughs before saying, "Well if you must know, he was on my father's list of possible husbands for me. But seriously, hand over my heart, there was nothing between us, no undying love or anything."

"Good to know. Now, who are the other two?"

"That would be Rocco and Lucca. They are also older and were originally my mother's bodyguards. They became more like very close uncles to me. They oversaw the men at my compound. They're great guys as well.

"They'll just want to see how all of the Brothers act and if you can handle your own, which you can, so no need to worry. They'll go back to Italy after that, unless they are needed here should the Russians not go back to where they came from. Then they might stick around to help out."

"Well, I think it'll be great to meet your real family. Do they call you Lexy now too? Or do they still call you Aless?"

"Well in all honesty, Uncle Louie calls me 'Little One', like my Grandpa Rogers does. I think I told you that before. But at times they all call me that or Princess. I've been working on the 'Lexy' thing with them too. They're getting a lot better."

"I know you're going to hate this, but I kind of like calling you Princess."

She rolls her eyes and flops down on the bed beside me, "Oh brother. No. I'm Lexy now. If you must call me something else, call me Little One. I always like that name."

Leaning over her and looking at that beautiful porcelain face of hers, her stunning crystal blue eyes immediately drawing my attention as her black hair spreads across the pillow. "Do you know how much I love you?"

"Not as much as I love you. That much I am sure of."

"And why would you say that? I would give up my life for you tomorrow if I had to. I don't think I could or would be able to continue to live without you being a part of it."

"Well, that feeling is mutual then because I never want to go a day without you in it."

And with that being said, I cannot stop myself and capture her mouth in a kiss. Her hands instantly dive into my hair, pulling me closer to her. Oh shit, the pain and discomfort in my leg and my bruised chest make themselves known, but damn if I'll pull away or stop this kiss. Lexy is the one who finally pulls away. She slowly pushes me back till I am laying on my back, and she kisses my lips very quickly before saying,

"As much as I'd love to take this to another level, you, young man, and 'Sir', need to control yourselves. You just had surgery on your leg, have stitches in the side of your other leg and shoulder, and I for one need a shower, badly. So, you are going to stay right here and rest while I go and steal a clean shirt of yours and take a shower. Tonight I'm spending all night in bed cuddled up with you, and if you're better tomorrow night, we'll see about taking this a bit further. I don't think the good doctor would want you doing something like that tonight," she says as she kisses the tip of my nose and gets up out of bed.

"Emm how about you putting on a little show for me and leaving the bathroom door open while you take that shower?"

She giggles as she sways her ass a bit more than usual as she walks to the bathroom. "I'll think about that. But you mister, need your rest, and watching me take a shower isn't going to help you with that."

"You're right about that, but come on, you can't blame a man for trying."

She comes back over and flops down on the bed, resting her chin on my chest as she whispers, "How about I make you a little promise? Once I think that leg is all better, I'll do one better than letting you watch me take a shower. I'll give you a private performance, one I can promise you'll never forget." Then just as quickly, she kisses the tip of my nose again and heads for the bathroom.

"A private performance? What might that entail exactly? I can feel a miraculous healing coming on," I say with a deep chuckle, as I watch her make it to the bathroom and close the door.

Damn, I'm so in love with her. We have got to figure all this shit out. I have to protect her, and possibly even from her overly confident self. Fuck! My leg better heal up and fast. I can't wait to make love to my woman. And now with all her secrets out on the table, there is nothing keeping us apart.

This will be making love for the very first time, without any protection or anything between us. I think it's about time

'Sir' gets a little up close and personal with Lexy himself. I just have to remember to take it slow. I can do this.

Shit. My cock is rock hard right now and it's causing my leg to hurt like hell. I need to calm myself for today. Soon I say, as I try to stroke 'Sir' a bit, hoping to relieve this aching hard-on before Lexy gets out of the shower.

My dreams are coming true. I've got Aless back and she's being honest with me. The question is, how am I going to handle all of this and keep her safe? She is a powerful woman and not used to following directions. She's used to leading. How is that going to work between us? We have a lot of shit to figure out.

Closing my eyes and thinking of Lexy in the shower makes me wonder… is she touching herself like I am? Fuck, my leg is beginning to hurt like a son of a bitch, but I need this release, fast. As I lean back spreading my legs a bit more, I reach over and open the nightstand drawer and grab some lube and tissues. I have to make this fast. Shit, I squeeze some lube onto my hand as I grab the base of my granite hard cock, and start to stroke upward, closing my eyes and imagining the water cascading down Lexy's magnificent body and then imagining the things I'm going to be doing to her over the next couple of weeks.

Fuck, my leg is beginning to throb. Who would have thought your thigh muscles tighten up so much when you get closer to reaching your climax? Trying to keep myself quiet as I continue to visualize the things I'll do to Lexy, I finally reach my release which almost brings me to tears from the throbbing in my thigh. Jesus. I look down and see I have bled through my bandage. Shit. I clean myself up with the tissues and wad them up, tossing them into the garbage can beside the bed. I can't help but chuckle.

The last thing I want Lexy to know is that I was whacking off while she was in the shower, but worse than that, how am I going to explain this to Gregory? I hope I didn't rip any stitches out while I was whacking off and climaxing. After pulling my boxer briefs back up, I throw my arm over my eyes, chuckling and pleading with the Gods that my coming didn't break the rules of 'taking it easy for a few days'."

"Grayson! Your leg is bleeding again. I'm calling Brenden. Did you try to get up and walk? What were you thinking? He said to stay off that leg. That means not trying to surprise me in the shower you big dummy."

Saving me from worse embarrassment, I'll take her reasoning. I don't have to agree or deny it, I'll just let them assume. "Yeah, we might want to call Gregory, my leg is hurting like a mofo."

"Duh. Do I have to duct tape you to the bed when I leave the room? You know I will if you try a stunt like that again," Lexy says as she marches that cute round ass over to the phone. I can't wait to nibble on that baby. Fuck, I better stop thinking like that or I'll be in the same rock-hard shape again, and I don't think my thigh can take another release right now.

"Brenden? Yeah, it's Lexy. This big idiot you left in my care tried to come and surprise me in the shower." (Pause) No, he didn't fall, well, maybe back into bed in pain, but his leg is bleeding again. Can you come back up here and yell at him and check on it for me?" (Pause) "Okay, see you in five."

"You just told him to yell at me," I tease, trying to act all hurt. But secretly, I'm very thankful she doesn't know how I really hurt my leg.

"Yes, I did. And I hope he does yell at you. You deserve it. But I will admit that shower did a world of good for me. Those five heads and jets coming at you in all direction is a great stress reliever. I feel a lot better myself."

"I can tell. You're more relaxed and not ready to bark orders at everyone. And you aren't swearing at me like one of the men."

"Sorry. As Isabella would say, when that internal switch gets flipped and I go all Boss Lady, I'm used to dealing with all men, so I get a bit of a potty mouth too. But hey, Uncle Louie never liked it either. Sorry."

Reaching over, I pull her onto the bed beside me. "Come here my little 'Half-Pint Hottie' and let's make out until Gregory gets here," I say and Lexy just giggles, all carefree sounding, just the way I love her.

19

LAYING DOWN THE LAW

Lexy

I've reached the doorstep to paradise, after sleeping and cuddling in Grayson's big strong arms all night. I don't think I've ever slept better. Getting out of bed was the most difficult thing I could do this morning. But after a heavy make out session, and being interrupted by Tiffany and Hawkins bringing in breakfast for us at ten a.m. on the nose, it was probably for the best. The last thing I want is for Grayson's leg to start bleeding again like it did last night. Luckily he didn't rip any stitches, but Brenden told him to give that thigh muscle a couple of days healing before he tries to flex it too much. Grayson does have some killer massive thighs.

In making my departure, I told Grayson that Tony and I had an important business meeting this morning that I forgot about, so it was too late to cancel. I do have a hint of guilt at not being completely honest, but now is not the time to tell him I'm going to crash a Family meeting.

As I walk into what looks like a giant living room/game room combo in the compound, I see Jackson and Tony playing against Liam and Carpenter at air-hockey. Geez, looking around this massive room, I can see it looks like a teenage boy's wet-dream. It has every kind of video game, pinball machines, foosball and a full wall TV with a collection of gaming systems connected to it. I cannot believe my eyes. Popcorn, soda and beer on tap along with a hot dog machine on the counter. You have to be kidding me. Wait, is that a freaking Whack-a-Mole and bowling game in the corner? I can't help but wonder, how much time do they all spend here when they could be training or doing something more productive? Oh gawd, do men ever grow up?

I'm pulled out of my thoughts when I hear Jackson's loud voice, "I would have never thought you, Mr. Goodie-Goodie Bishop, were a cheater," Jackson yells at Liam.

"I'm not a cheater. I'm just here at the compound more than you and have more practice with the air hockey table. Admit it - you can't handle being beat by a gimp."

"Hey, don't go pulling that gimp shit. That doesn't fly with me. I've seen the way you beat up on Stevens at basketball, which is why we challenged you here at the table," Jackson fires back.

"Well, I hate to interrupt your game, but I have to steal Tony. You'll have to have a rematch which will give you time to practice. As pissed at Tony as I am, we have a business meeting we can't get out of. Hawkins said you'd buzz me in once I return in a few hours. Jackson, keep an eye on my man and kick his ass if he tries to put any pressure on that leg of his."

"You got it, Boss. Do you need any help at your meeting? I do clean up quite nicely and can be very persuasive when I need to be," Jackson says, blowing on the tips of his fingers and acting like he is buffing them on his shirt.

"I'm sure you can be, but believe me, Tony and I have this. Thanks for offering. Can take my girls back home if you still have them held hostage here? They do have jobs they probably need to get to."

"Well, about that. They kind of thought it was cool being sort of kidnapped by us, so they called in and took today off work so they could get the full experience of being inside our sacred sanctuary," Jackson says with a grin.

"Okay then. Tell them I'll be back in a bit and to behave. And Jackson, you be nice to Anissa. She's my girl. You mess with her, I mess with you. Get me?"

"I get you. Believe me. Let's just say I'm checking out the landscape to see if we're on the same playing field. I need to see if she's just a dabbling or if she's the real McCoy," Jackson says like he is trying to figure out if I understand his code or not. I am pretty sure I do. That just lets me know I need to talk to my girl, Anissa real soon. I need to make sure she knows what she's getting into because I don't think he's a dabbler. I think he's totally into a lifestyle of kink.

"Jackson, we'll talk about sticking your toe in her pond very soon. Walk with care. I wouldn't want to have to hurt you for messing with her."

"She's safe with me Lexy, that I can promise. I don't dabble, and I think she does. I can wait and watch and see. We'll talk," he says with a wink as Tony falls in behind me.

"I'll see you guys in a few hours, but I need to ask, is it okay if I bring Sarah back with me? I'll make sure she doesn't tell Mom Riggs anything. She listens to me," Tony calls back and asks.

"I'll check with Riggs first and text you later," Jackson calls back to us, before turning back to the Brothers. "Bishop, escort the two of them out. You can play me after I hand Carpenter his ass for the title," Jackson taunts.

"Eat shit Jackson. You gotta beat me first, and just remember, I grew up with one of these in the garage at my house and you did not," Carpenter fires right back at him, as the two of them start playing.

"Either of you want a soda?" Liam calls over to us.

Tony and I both respond in unison. "No, thank you."

Hearing the banter between Jackson and Carpenter is funny. Gees, everything between these guys has to be a competition. That would drive me nuts after a while, even if I could really show them up at a lot of things.

"Okay Tony, you're taking me to my place to get ready for our meeting," I say as we leave the room. He just nods his head. Liam pops back over and leads us through a maze of long hallways, all keeping with the decoration of Camelot, with faux torches as hallway lighting. I have to say I love it. Even the lowest level of elevators has wooden bars that close in front of it.

It takes us almost ten minutes before we're in Tony's car and on the road. I know now that no one can hear us, so it is safe to talk. I need to inform him of what my plans are. "You need to mentally prepare yourself for this Tony. Don't for a minute think we're all good because we are not. I don't know how much I can trust you, so let's just say this is a test."

"Princess, I am so very sorry. Really. I meant it last night when I said I enjoyed seeing you happy for the first time in your life. You deserved those moments of being normal. I knew at some point I'd have to inform you. I never thought the Russians would attack like they did or I swear, I would have come clean and told you everything earlier."

"We aren't rehashing now. You know where I stand, and it'll never happen again. Correct?"

"You have my word."

"Okay. I need you to drop me off at my place so I can get ready to step back into my role as Capo Donna of the Canzano Family. We can't do anything with your two-tone hair, but I want you in the basic Family uniform. I'm sure you kept that suit. As nice as it looks on you, it would have been foolish to have gotten rid of it."

"Naturally I have the suit, and I can make my hair pass

inspection as well. You ever heard of spray dye? It washes right out. But why are we doing this?"

"Because the two of us are headed over to the Benassi Family Headquarters. I am confident you know where it's at."

"Oh shit. Princess, they all know you escaped, and I can't promise that they will not inform your papa or someone in the Canzano Family."

"And they also owe me. Big time!"

"That is true, but don't you think Grayson will be pissed?"

"Grayson knows we have a meeting, but I didn't tell him with whom. He doesn't need to know yet, and turnabout's fair play as every one of you have been keeping secrets from me. I'm just getting the word out and being prepared if I need to call in some owed favors."

"Okay, Princess. You're the boss. I'll drop you off and be back in less than an hour, looking just as much a part of the Canzano Family as I was the day I left."

"Sounds perfect." I don't say anything else. It's time to get in the right frame of mind. I need to show no signs of weakness at all. I need every damn one of the Benassi Family scared shitless of me, as they should be. Smiling to myself, this could be really fun.

Boy was I surprised when Tony pulled up at my penthouse fifty minutes after he dropped me off. I bet Sarah would love to see him looking like this. He is in his custom-made, fitted black Family issued suit and shirt with a burgundy tie, a perfect match to my clothes. He knows me so well. It's like he read my mind. We've always clicked like this.

That tie complements my burgundy peplum jacket with fitted black skirt perfectly. I kept a lot of the clothes Laura made for just these types of Family business meetings. You never know when one would be needed. Papa would shit himself because the skirt compliments my every curve and hugs my ass. It goes down about three inches past my knees, but then the slit over my right knee goes up about two inches above it, which instantly draws attention to my very toned legs and very high heels. Just what I need to distract a man. Chuckling to myself, I can't help but think that men are so easy to distract. I know full well that this fitted jacket and three inch thick black patent leather belt, with the high low skirt around the bottom of the jacket, is just what I need to accent all of my assets. A true power suit for a woman with curves who's ready to use them.

I have to admit, Tony does clean up quite nicely. He's all freshly shaven with perfectly combed back black-as-night hair with his standard issue Family sunglasses. We're perfect. We'll pull off the Family Power Team just like I knew we would. They'll be putty in my hands. I have it to admit to myself, this is getting quite exciting.

"Has Grayson ever seen you dressed like this?" Tony asks, pulling my mind from my thoughts. I fire back at him,

"Has Sarah ever seen you dressed like that?

"Touché."

"I hate to say this Tony, but I think Sarah would like that look on you for a change."

"Well if we're being honest, Grayson would be on you in a matter of seconds if he saw you dressed like that. First, he'd have his hand on the back of your head, pulling that large clip out of your hair and letting it fall down like I know he likes it. Then I'm sure he'd enjoy the view of taking that suit off piece by piece, cause Boss, you look hella fine in that. Hot damn!" Tony says with a smile while shaking his head and rubbing his chin. Even when I am mad at him, he can still make me laugh.

It isn't long before we're driving outside of Santa Monica, coming up to Culver City. "How much further do we have to go? And how many men are usually at their headquarters?"

"Well, Renzo and Nero are there every day, since they both have estates behind those gated walls. Several other members have smaller, more traditional homes there as well. But considering everything that went down last night, I would not be surprised at all to see Orlando and Dante, if that's who you're thinking about. I'm sure there will probably be about a dozen or so other men there. Jackson told me about you cutting off Maksim's finger," Tony adds with a chuckle. "Did that have anything to do with my sister?"

"Well, I was pissed when I saw he was wearing Lilith's Family ring on his pinkie finger. You would have done the same thing. And believe me, I had no clue Jackson was alert enough to know what I was doing. He wasn't even completely awake when I killed the Russians."

"You're probably right there. I would have wanted to leave that statement as well," Tony laughs out loud before he adds, "But you did totally scare the shit out of Jackson. I think he might be having a bit of hero worship going on. He flat out told me he's never seen a woman who's such a powerful badass." He laughs again.

"Nice to know. I think he'll be easy to have on my side when it comes to the Brothers."

"Yeah. Grayson's going to have to figure a way to think of you as an equal and not his 'pint-sized hottie' as they all like to call you, because as long as he only sees you as a sexual being, he will always feel the need to protect you. You might have to take him down in order for him to realize your strength."

"I know, I was thinking the same thing. Last night he actually suggested I go and hide out at the castle until 'they' got this handled. You and I both know that shit isn't going to fly."

"Yeah, and I hate to say this, but I think you and Grayson are going to butt heads in a big way at some point."

"I agree. I've told him several times that *no man* will *ever* dictate my life to me again. And as much as I love him, he has to figure out a way to meet me halfway. I need him to be my partner, not my dictator. But let's not worry about that now."

"Okay. Just remember I've *always* got your back. No more secrets. You can count on me. You'll be the first person I share my intel with, and if you want it shared with the Brothers, just let me know."

"I'm going to talk to Hawkins myself later today and see if they are going to be as open and honest with me as he implied last night. Now, what kind of security are we going into?"

"Well, I set it up, if that answers your question," he says with a confident chuckle.

Laughing to myself, I should have guessed. Tony is the best. "Do you think they will search us?"

"They'll probably ask that we leave our guns with the guards. The Benassi Family has always liked you, but the Capo hasn't seen you in action. Renzo is just like your Papa. He's a cocky son of a bitch who's allowed himself to get out of shape. He doesn't fight with his men in battle. Both him and Nero will be locked up in a safe house somewhere. They have cleaned up a lot of their Family businesses, making them legit, but believe me, they have a lot of underground shit still going down."

"I didn't expect them to be clean. Hopefully, they aren't into the sicko shit. Please tell me they aren't in to selling minors as sex slaves or drugs to little kids. I'll have a problem if they're doing that shit."

"They're not. They are running an Italian Family style strip club, and want to open a few more. But you and I both know that the girls are at least eighteen and they are doing a hell of a lot more in those private rooms than a lap dance. The Family gets a big cut."

"That's to be expected with the Family. I'm just thankful that the Brothers of Camelot don't do that shit."

"Well Lex, you do know about the protection they provide the high class escorts, right?"

"Yeah, but they aren't their pimps, and they don't take a cut. They just make sure the ladies and their kids are safe, and they are paid for that service. I was surprised when Isabella told me that she provides a daycare center within Camelot Headquarters where the escorts can leave their kids and feel safe. It's also cool they can get some very good male role models there from the Brothers and the other men they have working there. I actually thought that was pretty nice."

"I agree. But they are still prostitutes. They just make a lot more money. And I've been to Gentlemen's Nights too. Their women have strict rules, and there are no private dances. If you get a lap dance, it's in front of everyone and no touchy-touchy either. Nothing extra going on there for sure. Believe me, I pushed my luck just to see."

"Remember, I helped Bonnie and Ginger get the gig there," I remind Tony. I had to make sure it was all above-board personally.

"That's right," Tony says with a head nod, driving us into a more suburban area of town.

"I'm fully aware of their standards. It was also my way of checking out to make sure they were legit with it. I would have had issues if the Brothers were taking a cut, that would have made them just as much their pimps as any common whore on the streets. What they do for the escorts is a completely separate thing. They provide background checks and security when needed. That's it, and I'm fine with that."

Tony changes the subject and cracks a joke, trying to make sure I'm relaxed before we get there. He wants me to keep my mind clear and not stress about all the 'what ifs'. I've got a good feeling. I'm going into this meeting completely confident, knowing it'll all work out. I might have to flex my muscles a bit and put a few men in their place, but I can handle that, no problem.

As we pull up a pine tree lined hill, you can tell this is definitely not the typical Culver City community. We take a left into a long driveway with spotlights at the base of each pine tree. We've definitely reached the Benassi Compound. The front gate has a nicely sculpted brick video speaker box. Once Tony stops the car and rolls down the window, a voice asks, "What business do you have here?"

"Princess Alessandra Canzano would like to speak with the Capo, as well as other Benassi Family members."

There was a long pause before a different man's voice asks, "Did you say Princess Canzano? As in Capo Donna Canzano?"

"Yes, the one and only."

I want to chuckle. I'm sure the guard about pissed himself when he heard my name. Tony looks in his rearview mirror at me, with that cocky grin on his face as he shakes his head. "Well at least we know either Orlando didn't tell the Family you saved his ass last night, or they are keeping it only with the upper brass."

"I did tell Orlando not to tell anyone he saw me. Maybe he did keep it a secret."

Just then, we see the gates slowly start to open as the guard says, "You are Pietro Caza, her personal guard?"

"I go by Tony Jarvis now, but I am her personal guard."

"Okay. Please drive up to the main house and you will be greeted there."

"Thank you," Tony says rolling up his window before continuing. "Let the fun begin. I think they're going to try and taunt me, but we'll be ready for them."

"I will not allow them to do so or I'll hand them their balls, literally."

"Let's hope it doesn't come to that. Do you have a plan you would like to share?"

"Tony, where is your trust? I'm just laying out the rules and making sure they know their boundaries, and for them to be prepared in case you and I decide to handle this Russian

conflict and eliminate their Capo ourselves. I just need to stall
to allow Grayson some time to heal."

"He does need time to heal. But if the Russians do attack
again before he's a hundred percent, I'm sure with the Brothers' and Benassi Family helping, we'll take them out. We just
need to work with the Benassi Family some. They are not up
to your standards, as you can see by just looking around the
grounds."

As I examine our surroundings, I see several men with AR-
15s and AK-47s hanging off their shoulders like a woman's
purse, or hanging over their back. Not one man has even
looked at the car to see who is inside. Not good. I'd never stand
for that. They are in groups of three or four, chatting and
laughing like teenage girls while smoking. Shit! This is crazy.

"Are they always this lax? Is it that safe here that they don't
even have to worry about a threat? Orlando was kidnapped
just yesterday by the Russians. What the hell?"

"Yup, I thought you'd find that entertaining. Their Capo
would instantly grab his wife and other important members
and head to their saferooms inside each home. They'd for sure
be safe there until they got backup, but they would take a
major hit and loss of life beforehand."

"I have to agree. Not one of them have looked over to see
who's coming up to their main house. That is insane."

"Agreed, but it wasn't my place to tell them that. I just
installed the equipment."

"Well from one Capo to the next, I will inform, if not
outright show Renzo, how unprepared his men are for an
attack."

"Now this I can't wait to see."

We pass several traditional looking nice sized homes. I can
see at the top of the hill is where Renzo must live. It's a
massive estate with huge pillars and balconies covered in
wisteria. It has a typical fountain in the middle of the circular

driveway. As we pull up, I see one young guard walk out the front door of the estate to greet us. And like the other men, he also has an AR-15 over his shoulder.

Once Tony parks the car, he immediately gets out and opens my door, offering me his hand to get out. Wanting to make this look good for the young guard who is probably only a year or two older than me, I take Tony's hand, making sure my skirt shows just enough of my leg. I catch the guard checking me out. Yeah, this will be so easy. I saunter over to the guard, Tony falling in step right behind me.

"So, you are the escaped Princess Alessandra Canzano that everyone talks about. Have you come to ask for our protection?" The guard says, still checking me out.

"No, I do not need your protection. I'm here to speak with your Capo. And for your information, when I escaped, I was the Capo Donna, so you can say this is a meeting between two Capos."

The kid chuckles, "Emm, you are no longer the Capo Donna. Luigi is the Dom of Northern Italy. Yeah, one of your bodyguards took over."

"And you think I didn't arrange that? I would hush if I were you before you find yourself in trouble. You obviously know nothing."

His expression turns more serious, I'm sure he's trying to figure me out. He says, "Pietro if you have a weapon, you need to leave it with me."

Before Tony responds, I walk past the guard and into the foyer of the estate. I turn around and look at his shocked face. "Well, are you going to ask if I have any weapons?"

As the guard starts to walk over to me, he doesn't even try to hide the way he brazenly checks me out. His eyes roam from my feet all the way up to my chest, where he pauses and stays focused for a second, before licking his lips and looking up and into my eyes. "Do I need to pat you down and see for myself?"

"I don't recommend that if you'd like to live past today."

He throws his head back and laughs as another guard walks into the room. "Vinny, is that really Princess Alessandra Canzano? Let's see her eyes."

I slowly lift my sunglasses and smile to the older guard, who's probably thirty, and doesn't look like he is even carrying a gun.

"Fuck, it is her."

"And you are?"

"I'm Roberto, Capo Renzo's second in command."

"So, you are the one who trains and is in charge of the men on the grounds?"

"I am. Why do you ask?"

"Just a bit surprised how lax it is here," I say, as I watch him look over at Tony, who has moved and is back to standing about a foot behind me. He seems to have completely ignored my comment.

"You're Pietro Caza. Are you her guard?" he asks Tony with his head tilted to the side, just waiting for a reply.

"Yeah, I was a bit surprised too. I had heard he was a fag and got kicked out of the Family." Vinny says, from besides me where he's still focused on my chest.

Now I've had enough of this. I quickly reach over and grab Vinny's balls, giving them a tight squeeze and a bit of a twist. He lifts his hands to cup his balls as I release them. I instantly slide in beside him and remove the AR-15 from his shoulder, and within seconds, I remove the oversized magazine. Knowing there is a bullet still in the chamber, I put the gun under his chin and look him in the eyes.

"Now Vinny, this goes to prove there is no need to check me for a gun, because it took me less than fifteen seconds to disarm you, and if I wanted you all dead, you would be. Now, if you don't want me to decorate Renzo's foyer with your brains, you are going to apologize to Tony, and if I ever hear you calling him a fag again, that will be the day you meet the Lord. Do I make myself clear?"

"Yes, Princess. My apologies. I'm sorry Pietro, I mean Tony," he barely speaks above a whisper before he coughs.

"Bravo, Princess. I've always wanted to see you in action. Very nice. You had my man disarmed in seconds," Renzo says, as he, Nero and Orlando walk out of a door just off the foyer.

I remove the gun I have shoved under Vinny's neck and quickly release the bullet from the chamber as Tony reaches up and catches it. I hand the gun and magazine back over to him. "Never carry your gun loosely off your shoulder like a woman carries her purse. You saw how quickly I could have killed you and everyone else. Never assume a shapely woman is a weak, useless creature. I've trained lots of women here in this country who could do the same thing I just did to you. You have one of the most important jobs of guarding the Capo. You should never be checking out a woman like you were doing to me when you are on duty." I instantly turn and walk away from him as Tony hands him the bullet he caught, staying just a step behind me.

"Roberto, do you even have a gun on you? If Tony and the Princess had come in here to kill me today, they probably would have succeeded." Renzo turns to his guard, who is standing there dumbfounded by what he just witnessed.

"Sorry Boss. I... I... it won't happen again," he says as he lowers his head, ashamed.

"You are correct. It will *never* happen again, or Dante might be replacing you as my personal guard."

"Yes sir. I understand," Roberto replies stepping away from us backward, never turning around. At least he has been taught never to show the Capo your back.

"Princess, I am sorry. As you can tell, my men have gotten a bit too relaxed in their positions. Come, join me in my office. We have a lot to talk about," Renzo says with his arm extended towards his office where both Nero and Orlando step aside for me to enter.

"Yes, we do. And if all goes as I hope, I might even be willing to help train your men. They are not doing an adequate job of protecting you," I reply, dropping the hint.

"Now that strikes my curiosity. Please come in and have a seat."

Casually walking into his very large office, I see that it looks typical Italian Capo with its all mahogany wood, from the desk to the accents. It even has the standard deep burgundy leather chairs and sofa off to one side. Sitting down in one of the winged back chairs in front of Renzo's desk, Tony follows and stands at attention behind me. Nero comes over and nods as he sits beside me, I'm sure wanting to make sure he has my permission to sit that close to me. I respond with a small head nod as well. Orlando and Roberto go and stand behind Renzo.

Well, well. It looks like Orlando has climbed quite nicely within the Family as he is standing in the first guard position, also letting me know that Roberto wasn't being honest in his introduction earlier. I would have never guessed. I guess he is blood, being Renzo's oldest nephew. I give Orlando a small smile and head nod, and he returns it.

"There is no need for small talk. I'm sure you are here either for protection or to inform us you're working with the Camelot boys," Renzo spews the moment he sits behind his oversized desk, leaning forward and placing both elbows on it.

"As I told your guards, I do not need, nor do I want your protection. As for the Brothers of Camelot, they are *not* boys, and they are *under my protection*. If you get near any of them in a negative way, you or your Family member just signed their own death certificate. Do I make myself clear?" I inform him firmly.

"So, it is true. You're fucking one of them. Is it Riggs? He does have a lot of similarities to Lou, your uncle, not only in size, but fables say a daughter always chooses a man like her father," Renzo says with a wink to me.

Shaking my head with a smile, I can see he wants to tone this meeting down a notch or two. "Grayson Riggs is my boyfriend, if that is what you'd like to know. As for similarities with Uncle Louie, they both like to boss me around and they have both found that to be a very difficult thing to do. I am a leader, not a follower. But that isn't the business I'd like to talk to you about. How much did Orlando tell you about last night? And how much intel do you have on the Russians?"

"Alright, straight to the point. As I informed your papa just last month, this Osokina Family has a way of getting other Capos to come around to their way. First, they like to kidnap your personal guard to prove how close they are to you. Then they torture them until they die, sending you bits and pieces along the way. If that doesn't work, they go after your oldest child or wife. You rescued Orlando before they had the opportunity to get him to their warehouse to start their torment, and for that, I thank you."

I nod to him without saying a word, knowing now I had guessed correctly about Orlando's position within the Family. Thank God I was able to save him before they started cutting off fingers or hands. Gigi couldn't handle that. It just makes me more determined to rid the world of this evil Russian Family.

"How did you discover this?" I need to know where this intel came from.

"The Boron Family in Northern France had a conflict with Ivan Osokina. They wanted to take over all the brothels there. They started with kidnapping his right hand man, and in a matter of a day they sent him his fingers, and when they didn't give over the property, they continued with his hand, his dick, then finally, his head. And when that didn't get them to shut down their brothels or hand them over to the Russian's control, they captured his daughter. The sick bastards sent videos of them taking turns raping her. Needless to say, that caused Boron to put his wife and remaining family into hiding and that turned into an all-out war. Many on both sides lost lives. But the Boron Capo couldn't let his daughter's horrible death go unpunished, so he has a two million bounty on Ivan Osokina's head, and he wants to return the visual favor by recording a group of his men raping Ivan's new wife or daughter."

"That is pretty fucked up," I reply.

"True. But you know this business isn't one for the faint or wary. I do have a video of my own that will put a smile on his face, and I'm sure will get me a nice reward from the Boron Family. I should consider splitting it with you, that is, once I have your permission."

Looking over to him, I wrinkle my brow, wondering what the hell he's up to and why the hell he needs my permission. I interrupt him and ask, "And why would you need my permission?"

"Well you see, after you rescued Orlando, we did you a favor. We rushed back to the alley, knowing you had to get the hell out of there, and knowing that the Camelot boys keep their fingers clean for the most part, they wouldn't go back and clean up your mess. They'd just leave the bodies for the cops to find and try to put the pieces together. I couldn't allow that to happen either," Renzo says with a smile on his face, leaning back in his office chair and resting his hands behind his head.

"Are you telling me you got rid of the bodies for me? What did you do to them?"

"You see I have a very nice butcher's shop, and I donate a lot of overstock meat to the food kitchens in town," he says, just waiting for me to put the pieces together. Oh shit, he didn't!

"Come on, Renzo. You're dying to tell me. Go ahead and explain what you did."

"Well once Orlando got back with Lilith's Family ring still attached to a Russian finger, and told us what went down, I sent Orlando back with some of our best men to gather up the Russian's bodies and take their rental car to a chop shop. After they got it all bleached and cleaned up, they drove and dropped off the bodies at our farm in Bakersfield and fed them to a special group of pigs we have up there, just for this type of disposal. Let's just say we have cameras on those pigs at all times, in case we need some very special videos."

I just nod and listen to the men chuckling, knowing full well he fed all three Russian's bodies to his pigs. I just hope he doesn't make sausage out of them to sell in his many butcher's shops or restaurants.

"Would you consider informing the Boron Family about the disposal of Ivan Osokina's oldest son Maksim in about a week or two? Explain to him we'll get rid of Ivan Osokina ourselves, we just need time to train and prepare our men. Letting Ivan stew and worry about what happened to his last son is well deserved."

Leaning back in his chair again, Renzo sways back and forth. "So I can tell him about the tape, but you don't want me to sell it to him yet? Do you want money from it?"

"No. Not a dime. You may keep all of it. You can even give him the tape if he can keep it to himself. I've watched and battled with this Russian family on two different occasions and they are not that good with any weapon. They are over-confident and think the bigger the gun, the more killing they can do. They have bad aim and have difficulty shooting a moving target. I'm confident if I have time to properly train your men as well as the Brothers, we'll be able to end this battle quickly, with very few injuries and possibly no loss of life on our side."

"And you are willing to train my men as well?"

"As long as you don't mind me handing a few of them their cocks."

The room erupts in laughter and coughing.

"You don't mince words for a woman, do you?"

"Look, I know when to be a proper lady, but I am used to working, training and battling with men, and I didn't get their respect by batting my eyes at them or spreading my legs. I demand it. I don't take their shit. Any man that starts swinging his dick around and acting superior over me will be brought to his knees, possibly without his dick. I've been training for this before I even had these tits. I know how to handle a man."

I hear the men trying to hold in their laughter, while Renzo seems to be studying me very seriously before a smile spreads on his face. "Orlando, grab us a bottle of grappa and some glasses. We're toasting our new agreement with the Princess."

"Yes, sir," Orlando responds instantly, rushing over to a bar on the other side of the room before giving me a smile and a head nod.

"I must ask, how are you planning to train my men? This I have to hear, and I will also be coming to watch. As you can see, I, like your papa, have gotten a bit out of shape and will not be joining you in battle," Renzo says, patting his portly stomach.

"I've been informed you were old school and didn't fight with your men, which is your prerogative. But I am completely different as I am sure you have heard. First, I'd like to meet eight to ten of your best men at one of your training facilities. I'm sure you have at least one."

"That can easily be arranged. But you are what? Five foot tall? My men are men. They are not like Tony."

I instantly hold up my hand towards Renzo, stopping this subject and warning him. "I highly recommend you do not bring my dear friend and guard into this conversation like that. You saw what I did to your man in the foyer. I would have no problem doing the same, or worse, to you."

He smiles widely, "Oh but Princess, you don't have any

293

weapons and you are sitting by my brother with two of my guards in this room."

In a flash, I'm standing and placing my hand at my waist, releasing one of the many blades I've hidden in this wide leather belt that Tony designed for me. It's great at concealing my weapons, should I need them. Instantly, I flick it into the center of the desk between his hands, watching it wobble back and forth. Watching Renzo jump and hearing them all gasp gives me great satisfaction.

"That could have easily been your neck. Now, what were you going to say about Tony? Maybe I should inform you, Tony and I have trained for years together. We're both known as the Italian assassins." Out of the corner of my eye, I can see Tony has already come to my side, fully alert with knives in both hands, making sure everyone stands down.

"Very impressive Princess. I've got a feeling even if my men did search you or Tony, they wouldn't find all your concealed weapons considering you just pulled out one to throw and Tony is putting away another two. But I got your point, in more ways than one." He taps the top of the blade stuck in the center of his desk, causing it to wobble even more. He looks up to me and continues. "You have larger balls than any man that has ever sat in that chair. Successfully pulling out a knife like that, I do believe you could have killed me. Thankfully we're both here as friends. I will not insult your man. I understand and respect your protection of him."

I sit back down as I smile at Renzo. "I would also like you to allow Tony and myself to work privately with your two personal guards. You are the Capo, and this I will do because you need better protection. I guess here in America you aren't confronted often, but I'd like you to live to a ripe old age and see many a grandchild. And right now, you aren't protected as you should be. You should add Dante to this training as well. In your position, having a third guard fully trained is a very good thing. I know we'll all work well together, and you'll be protected as you should be."

"Yes, I would like that," Renzo says with a little chuckle. "Thank you, Princess. I'll be forever in debt to you. But you are right. It is safer here in America, and I rarely meet face to face with clients. I usually have my men send my messages, but I'd feel better if I had the protection you've pointed out to me that I lack."

Orlando pours us all a nice glass of grappa, handing one to Tony as he says, "I'd be honored to train with you, Princess. Would you like us to come to one of your clubs after hours?"

"Yes, that would be perfect. I have two men I've also trained on my staff that would be great for sparring with you in hand to hand combat. But they are clueless as to who I am, so no calling me 'Princess'. If you didn't know, I am really an American citizen, and very close to my maternal grandparents. My name is legally Lexy Rogers, and when in front of anyone outside of your compound, I would prefer you to call me Lexy."

"I need to express my sorrow on the loss of your mother and Nonna. You've had such a tragic life. I knew Sophia very well growing up. We all knew she was American. As well as almost all of the Family, we were just sworn to secrecy. Your papa should have told you many years ago. You should know, he is still looking for you, but we have not told him anything," Nero says as he pats the top of my hand.

"Thank you for your condolences, and for not telling him. I've always been a possession to him, never his daughter. I know one day I'll have to deal with my papa again, but I'd rather not have to deal with it at this point in my life. Let's get these Russians handled first."

Renzo stands up with his glass in hand, "Let's stand and make a toast. I feel like we have a lot to celebrate. To new friendships!"

"Salud!" we all respond in unison, and down our shot of Grappa.

"I will hand pick ten men, and inform them that they are to respect you as they would me. Nero and I'll be there the first day to watch your training ourselves. I'm actually hoping you'll have to sacrifice one of the men by handing him his balls, as you so eloquently put it." Renzo says with a chuckle, as he pours us all another glass of grappa.

I instantly down the second glass, before he has a chance to make another toast. "Tony and I have a busy schedule so we need to depart." Turning to look at Orlando, I say, "I assume you have Tony's contact information. Text him where you'd like to start your men's first training session tomorrow. And please do not tell Gigi or Lilith you have seen me. I'd rather handle this Russian problem before I have a reunion with old friends."

"I wasn't planning on it. I've thought you might be in the area since we hired Jarvis Inc. to install our security system and discovered it was Pietro. Lilith and Gigi are normal Family wives and know nothing about the business or who we are working with. Dante did tell Lilith this morning when he returned her Family ring that it was a gift from you. She naturally was overjoyed and wanted all the details, but we told her now was not the time. She would love to personally thank you herself. Both the girls see you as more of a fictional female superhero."

I can't help but chuckle at my friends. "Thank you. One day I will come back into their lives, but now is not the time." I walk over to him and surprise him by pulling him into a big hug. He hesitantly returns my hug before kissing me on top of my head.

"I look forward to working with you. I will also inform all the men that should they disrespect you, they'll answer to me," Orlando says with a wink.

We say our goodbyes to Nero and Renzo, who just smile like loons and walk us all the way out to the car.

"You might call yourself Lexy, but you will always be Family royalty and Princess to us. I've always liked you, and wish you much happiness with this Camelot boy. But just remember, if he cannot accept you for who you are and all the power and ability you have, there are good Italian men within this Family that would."

"Thank you, but I'm sure we'll be fine. Grayson Riggs is my soulmate and my one love." And with that said, I get into the back seat before Tony closes my door.

20

AM I READY FOR THIS?

Grayson

his morning sucked in a big way. I was going insane just lying in bed wondering where the hell Lexy was and what business her and Tony had this morning. I just have a knot in my stomach that she is up to something. Possibly something risky, or dangerous. It took me a couple hours of fighting with both Gregory and Jackson before they finally agreed to allow me to come out here in this wheelchair and hang out with everyone in the Family room of the compound. This way I can at least chat and get my mind off wondering what she's up to. It gives me the chance to try and get intel out of Lexy's roommates. I mean, since they are all here hanging out and playing games with the Brothers, maybe they'll slip.

I've eaten more crappy junk food today then I have in years, and fuck, I can't even work it off. The only injury that really is a pain is the bullet I took to my thigh. The others will be fine by tomorrow. I don't even feel them. They're just more of a nuisance having to have bandages all over. Those Russians are lousy shots. I don't think they were trying to just graze me, I think they thought they actually caused more damage than they did.

And that bullet that hit me in the chest makes taking a deep breath hurt like a mother fucker. But even that shot wouldn't have killed me. It would have probably punctured a lung, but if they were intending it to be a kill shot, they were way off. Next time we'll know they're lying pieces of shit and there will not be any negotiating.

That is *if* there is a next time. Hawkins said there was still no talk of finding the bodies. When Stevens drove by there on his bike this morning, he said there wasn't a trace of anything, just a strong smell of bleach. So either someone is cleaning up after us or the Russians found their men and are planning their own attack on us. I need to get better, fast, because we have some major training to do to prepare. Maybe we should move everyone up to the castle for safety's sake.

"Well, well, guess who's back?" I hear Hawkins call out. Turning my head in his direction, I hear him bark orders out. "Bishop, go meet Tiffany and bring them back here."

"Is it Lexy?" I have to know. It can't be anyone else because everyone else is already down here.

"Naturally. Tony has Sarah with him. You ready for your sister's attack?" Hawkins says, looking up from his computer over at the bar counter.

Reaching down, I start to wheel myself over to him.

"Hey, I don't think so, buddy. You were told to sit there and be a good boy, which means no rolling around," Anissa says as she leaps to her feet, dashing over and pushing my wheelchair. "Okay, where do you want to go? Back to your room?"

"No, and I'm not a boy," I say with a chuckle, "I was just going to wheel over there to Hawk. I got this. You can go back and watch Jackson and Carpenter kill each other at pinball."

"No sir. Jackson said you were not allowed to push your-self anywhere," Anissa says as she continues to push me over to Hawk. Fuck, this girl follows Jackson's instructions to the tee. Watching these two earlier, it became quite obvious to me that they are checking each other out. But Anissa seems like too nice a girl for Jackson, not what I'm used to seeing him with at all. I just hope he isn't planning on playing games with her. Lexy may kick his ass if he messes with one of her girls, which means I'll have to also. I wonder if I shouldn't talk to him now, before any shit goes down.

"Can I get you anything Grayson? A hot dog, soda, popcorn? This place down here does have everything. It's been fun, even though it was supposed to be a kidnapping."

"No thanks, Anissa. I've eaten enough shit for one day. And no one will let me have a beer, because of the meds they have me on, so I'm fine, thank you. And my apologies, my asshole friend should have stepped in and pushed me."

"It's fine. Everyone else is busy playing a game or competing in a challenge. It was no problem."

"Well thank you, and umm, I would like to ask you something personal, if that's okay?"

"Okay, but if it has anything to do with Lexy, I don't know any more than all of you already know. And even if I did, I would take it to my grave. I'd never share secrets she entrusted to me. Wenches Code of Honor and all, you know."

"I figured that much out already. I wanted to ask you if you had a thing for Jackson. You're a very nice, sweet woman, and well, I hate to say this about my Brother, but he's more… how should I put it… rough around the edges. Let's just say, I've never seen him with a woman more than a couple of times before he moves on to the next one. And you're one of Lexy's girls and I think she's a wee bit protective. I'd hate to see her kick his ass."

Anissa blushes and giggles, "Oh Grayson, neither of you have anything to worry about. Jackson has been the perfect gentleman. He hasn't made any sort of a move on me. He's just… nice, and… and… well, Jackson."

I'm completely lost by that answer. What the hell? Women talk in code, all stutter and stuff. I think I'm better off talking to Jackson. Well, I tried to warn her.

"Okay Anissa. I'll just hang out and wait for Lexy. Thanks for the help."

"You're very welcome, Grayson. Just holler if you need anything," she says with a beautiful smile.

"Nissa! Get me a fresh frozen mug from the freezer behind the bar and pour me a beer. I need a refresher so I'll be ready to kick ol' Tony's ass when the pussy gets back in here. Thanks, sweets," Jackson calls out from across the room.

Hawkins turns his head to me and mumbles under his breath. "'Sweets'? When have you heard Jackson refer to anyone as 'Sweets'?"

"I haven't. I think it's time I have a talk with him. Fucking around with one of Lexy's friends may not be such a smart idea."

"I couldn't agree with you more. Anissa is way too sweet for Jackson. Fuck. Lexy could rip off his dick and hand it to him."

We both laugh as we watch Anissa scurry over behind the bar, grabbing Jackson a fresh frozen mug and pouring him a beer from the tap. Jesus, she didn't even have to ask which one he wanted, she already knows which brand he drinks. Yeah, I'm talking to Jackson the moment the girls leave. I gotta nip this in the butt, at least for now. He can keep his dick in his pants until Lexy and I have our own shit figured out. I don't need him on a pussy hunt rocking my boat.

"Lexy should be in here in a matter of minutes," Hawks says, as he continues to type away.

"Good. I can't wait to see if she tells me where this supposed meeting was, and to see if she has any idea where the Russian's bodies disappeared to."

"I've got a couple of guesses and you will not like either

301

one of them, so let's see what she says," Hawkins says as he looks up from his laptop and towards the elevator.

Seconds later, the doors open and I see Tony and Sarah walk out with their arms around each other. Shit. Tony actually dyed his hair back to black. Then I see Lexy step out right behind them. Damn. She looks as hot as hell. Where the fuck has she been, dressed up like that? What kind of business meeting was this? As she strolls across the room, a big smile spreads across her face. She reaches up and takes a giant clip thing out of her hair, and I watch as it all cascades down and around her face and past her shoulders. Goddamn, she is so beautiful. I get a little stiff every time I see her.

"What are you doing out of bed? Last I heard, Brenden demanded you rest and put no pressure at all on that leg," Lexy says as she walks right over to me.

"First of all, my fucking leg is sticking out in the air, not touching the ground and I'm in a damn wheelchair. Second, I was going stir crazy and it took me over two hours to persuade your guard dogs to let me out of my cage."

She turns her head towards Jackson. "Yo! Thanks Jackson, for making him be a good boy and behave while I was gone."

"Anytime," Jackson calls out, lifting his beer in a cheer to Lexy before yelling, "Hey Pussy Tony, get your ass over here. We need to see how good you are at pinball. Well, well, look at you all cleaned up, and you dyed your hair. Damn… what meeting were you at?"

"Oh you missed me, did you Jackson? You ready for me to hand you your ass? Oh and this is just spray color, I'll be back to my normal hot self by morning," Tony calls right back to him. Sarah releases him from her hold and Tony gives her a quick kiss before he walks over to Jackson. Sarah's eyes stay focused on me as she starts walking my way.

Catching me off guard, Lexy leans down and her mouth captures mine in one hell of a kiss. I pull her practically into my lap to deepen it. She quickly pulls away. "I'm not supposed to be in your lap, you have a hurt leg. I'll sit over here," Lexy says sliding out of my lap and standing beside me.

"I'll have you know I had to swear myself to secrecy, not only to Tony, but Jackson, Hawkins and Brenden before they would allow me over here. I guess I can't tell Mom you got shot or how, but can I ask how are you doing?" Sarah says, leaning down and giving me a hug.

"I'll be perfectly fine by next week. This leg just needs a bit of rest time before I walk on it is all. Everything else was nothing. Really."

She just stands there, looking at me questioningly. "Is it true what they said, Lexy saved your life?"

Oh shit. I wish the Brothers hadn't told my sister this stuff. I'm never going to live this one down now. I grudgingly reply, "You could say that."

"Well damn Grayson. It's nice you have a woman that's your equal. Now don't go fucking it up waving your dick around," Sarah says, leaning down and giving me a much tighter hug this time. "I love you bro and I'd hate to ever lose you. I'm damn thankful Lexy was there." Then she turns to Lexy and hugs her. "I knew you were a badass. You know you'll forever be my hero for saving my brother's life, and for taking two Brothers' titles. I can't wait till you claim more. 'Wenches Code'," Sarah says, pulling away from her embrace and giving Lexy a high five before she heads back over to Tony.

"Nothing to thank me for Sarah," Lexy says as she turns back to me and starts taking off her very wide belt before removing her suit jacket and placing it over the chair. For some odd reason, she puts that belt back on. Fuck, she has a tiny waist and with that belt on, it really shows off the ass I can't resist reaching over and grabbing as I pull her closer to me.

"Are you going to share with me who your meeting was with, and why you're dressed up so fine in that suit?"

She looks at me for a second before looking over to Hawkins and saying, "How much do you think you know about my meeting?"

"Nothing as fact, but I could possibly make a good guess. The Russian's bodies have been removed, there is a strong odor of bleach in the alley and no intel anywhere about any police or FBI or anyone finding them. Can you tell us what happened to them?"

Lexy looks around the room to make sure everyone is far enough away so as not to hear our conversation. She pulls out a barstool between me and Hawkins and sits in it. Damn, she is sitting higher than I am and giving me a damn good view of her perfectly toned legs that I can't wait to get between.

"Yes, I know where the bodies went. Are you sure you want details or will the knowledge of them having been disposed of be enough?"

Hawkins' head turns quickly to Lexy as he lifts an eyebrow, "Their bodies were disposed of... Like... is it possible parts of them will reappear from the ocean in the months to come after their bodies have decomposed from the cement boots they were put in?"

Lexy chuckles before she smiles and responds, "You watch too many American crime TV shows. No, their bodies will never reappear, that I can promise you. But it buys us at least two, maybe three weeks before the Russian Capo figures out his oldest son isn't ever coming home."

"So you know who disposed of their bodies? And what they did with them?" I have to ask.

"Yes, I do. I'll tell you if you must know, but I'd rather not," Lexy responds, this time looking at me. Oh, shit. I'm a bit scared to ask, but I must know.

"Well, we'd really like to know all the facts, because we wouldn't want to be blindsided," I say, just as Hawkins interrupts.

"Let me guess and see how close I am. Last night when

everything was going on here, all our cameras in the alley were disabled, but not stolen. I'm leaning towards some of your old Family friends."

"You could say that."

"Lexy, I want details. Enough of this talking in code with Hawkins," I demand, her head whips to me.

"Says the man that has been keeping many secrets about everything that is going on. Honesty. You want honesty? Are you sure you can handle the truth coming from me?"

"Yes, I'm damn sure I can handle the truth."

"Fine. Tony and I went to meet with the Benassi Family Capo. I went as Alessandra Canzano, that is why I am dressed like this. You can say this is my Capo Donna uniform. When I freed Orlando last night and told him the Brothers of Camelot were under my protection, he took that as, you could say, an order, to help protect you."

"That is what I was thinking," Hawkins says, giving Lexy his complete attention.

"I'll be honest and open with you Hawk, but I demand the same kind of respect. *No secrets*. If you find out anything, you tell me too, and I'll do the same for you."

Hawkins says 'Okay', at the same time I say 'No'. Both of them turn to me, Lexy's temper flaring.

"What? No? What the fuck Grayson?"

Yeah, this isn't going to be easy. Lexy's swearing has let me know she is still in her Capo Donna mindset. "Look Lex, I didn't mean we'd keep things from you, just give me a bit of time to adjust to this, okay? I'm not used to working with women. I'm used to protecting them."

I can hear her sigh as she shakes her head. We need to get off the subject of us sharing our information with her. "Okay Lexy, would you mind telling us what they did with their bodies? Did they bury them in the woods or something? Since you laughed at the cement boots remark, I'm guessing they're nowhere near water."

Without batting an eye and as serious as can be, she turns and looks me straight in the eyes as she says, "No. They're old school Italian. Their bodies, or shall I say, remains, will never be found because there aren't any. The Benassi Family have a large farm in Bakersfield, and let me put it to you like this, they have a special collection of talented, hungry pigs, that have cameras on them while they're eating, just in case the Benassi's need video proof that their special treat has been disposed of properly."

"You are shitting me!" Hawkins says a bit louder than he meant to, as the room gets quiet for a second and several heads look our way. I just shake my head, and on cue, the Brothers get everyone back into their game playing.

Hawkins lowers his voice to almost a whisper, "You're saying they fed the Russians to some pigs? Shit!"

"You asked and wanted the truth. Yes, they did just that. Maksim has a bounty on his head too, from a French crime Family, so the Benassi Family will let them know he's been eliminated, and will prolong releasing the tape to them as long as they can. I bought us two weeks before they hand over the tape to collect the bounty. But once they do, I'm sure they'll show it to Ivan Osokina. He will not be happy to find out that his oldest son has officially been killed and fed to the pigs. Now, in reality, that gives us at least three weeks to train and prepare to be ready for them."

"Fuck. Three weeks isn't that long. I don't know what condition my leg will be in."

"Grayson, we got this. We'll talk to Brenden about your leg. We'll also try other ways to end this with the Russians without going to war with them. But if it does come down to a battle, we need to be ready. They do not have really good aim. Last night they used handguns, and not one shot could actually be classified as a kill shot in my books. Usually, when they go to battle, they depend on automatic weapons like altered AR-15s and AK-47s. They prefer to just pull the trigger and blanket enemies with bullets. We need to outsmart them, disarm them and keep moving. It's harder to hit a moving target, and body armor is crucial."

"I know that. I was thinking the same thing. Most of my injuries are nothing more than flesh wounds. But Lexy, I honestly wish you'd let us handle this," I plead with her.

She looks at me, sternly. "Grayson, if a battle comes, I am in it. I do not hide. Get that through that testosterone filled bullhead of yours. This is not open for discussion or debate. I can easily make a few calls and handle this without endangering any of you."

"Lexy that is not necessary. Give Hawkins and Tony time to do what they do best, and we'll figure this out together. Give me some time to heal first. Okay? Don't make any calls yet. Maybe Ivan Osokina will throw the towel in and realize he is fighting a fight he can't win."

Lexy gives me a small smile as she leans over and pats my cheek. "Sweetheart, you do not understand how Mob Families work. You want a war to end, you need to take out the Capo. I've killed all three of his sons. He's not going to tuck his tail and run back to Russia. He's going to figure out who his strongest men are and send them here, and with what I've heard about him, he might even come himself. But if he does, don't worry. I'll take him out too."

Closing my eyes and leaning my head back, I wish I didn't have to deal with this right now. I've got at least three weeks to figure this out and make a plan. If I need to get the FBI or CIA involved, I will. I will do what I have to do to protect Lexy and end this war.

Turning my face into her hand that is covering my cheek, I kiss it. Opening my eyes, I take her hand in mine. "Okay, my little badass. We have a few weeks to figure this out, like I said before. Let Tony and Hawkins work on it and see what they can come up with. Maybe we can delay them longer, giving me time to get back to a hundred percent function."

"As long as you understand that I will not stand down."

"Understood." Looking over to Hawk I say, "If you hear anything online or discover anything on the Dark Web, let me know. I'm going to have Lexy take me back to my room."

"Oh, okay. Going to try and persuade her in other ways to stay out of this? I wish you luck, Brother. You're going to need it," Hawkins says with a chuckle, as he sits there and shakes his head.

"You know me too well, Hawkins. That will not happen," Lexy says as she hops off her barstool and gets behind my wheelchair. "Come on Sweetheart, let's get you to bed. I need to steal another shirt of yours anyway. I've had on this suit long enough," she says as she starts pushing me towards the bedrooms.

"It'd be awful nice to watch you take off that lovely suit. Can you do that slowly, and to music?" I tease.

"Grayson, are you asking me to strip for you again?"

"I guess you could say that."

"Well, the answer is no. Not tonight. But I promise you, once your leg is better, I'll give you a show you won't soon forget."

"Is that a promise?"

"Yes, it is. But I will, at some point, want you to return the favor."

I cannot help but laugh as we reach my room. "Are you asking me to strip for you?"

"Yes. I think we've discussed this before. I want an equal relationship. If I can perform for you, you can return the favor, and I'm thinking the perfect song would be 'Save a Horse, Ride a Cowboy'."

I throw my head back, laughing hard. This could be really fun. "I think that can easily be arranged. I think I'd like for you to ride this cowboy in the very near future."

"I'll be counting down the days. Believe me, you perform to that song and I'll jump right on and ride you hard," Lexy says as she pushes my wheelchair into my room, stopping for a second to reach between my legs and give my cock a good squeeze. Oh shit. I start repeating to myself, 'take this slow, we need to take this slow' I continue to repeat this over and over again in my mind.

"How about you go put on one of my shirts? Not a t-shirt, though. Find a dress shirt. I want easy access."

"Do you need help getting to bed?" Lexy asks, letting her eyes roam up my body as she starts to unbutton her blouse.

"No, I got this." I hop out of the wheelchair and sit on the corner of the bed, carefully pulling off my gym shorts and watching her look right at my rapidly hardening cock. I slide backwards up the bed, making damn sure she sees 'Sir' standing completely erect in my boxer briefs.

She licks her lips, staring right at my cock, before she pulls her blouse completely off, revealing a sexy as fuck burgundy satin bra. She slowly turns around and unzips her skirt that clings to her ass like a glove. Damn. My baby got back. I love that heart shaped round ass of hers. I just want to swat it and watch it jiggle and then nibble on it. Oh shit… she slowly wiggles her hips and lets the skirt drop to the floor, showing me even more of her ass in matching burgundy booty-short underwear. Holy fuck, they are riding up her ass and exposing those full cheeks.

She looks over her shoulder saying, "I'll be right back to help you handle that." She licks her lips again, and with a wink, walks into my closet.

Reaching between my legs, I take 'Sir' in my hand and give him a firm squeeze and a couple of strokes over my boxers, giving myself another pep talk. 'We're taking this slow. Very slow.' Reaching over to my nightstand I grab a bit of lube out of the draw. I don't think I'll really need this, but the slipperier I can make this, the easier it'll work. Lexy is a little thing, and I'm not stupid. I know I have a very large cock. Having a mother and grandmother who love nothing more

NECIE NAVONE

than to explain everything sexual to me and how the female body works, is actually coming in handy. For the first time in my life, I am so glad they were like that.

Getting under the covers and sliding out of my boxers, I put a bit of lube on the top half of my dick and just stroke myself a couple more times, thinking of that fine ass of hers.

"Hey, that's my job." I'm busted as Lexy walks back into the room with a smile on her face. She scurries over to the foot of the bed and climbs up it like a cat.

"Come here, woman. Tonight we're taking this slow. I'm not completely making love to you while my leg is this fucked up, but we can start to get to know each other's bodies a bit more intimately."

"Sounds nice. I could take the lead, so you don't have to strain yourself," Lexy says as she reaches me and instantly starts kissing me as her hand dives right for 'Sir', taking over the stroking of my cock.

I slightly pull her hair, deepening the kiss and listen to her moan. Damn. I need to make this last and no fucking way am I letting her take charge. My hand glides down the front of the shirt, and luckily, she didn't button most of the buttons. She isn't wearing a bra either, making this so much better.

Fuck, her tits are big, even bigger than my hands. Pushing her onto her back, I stop her from stroking my cock. I lay on my good side and push her shirt apart so I can start kissing and sucking on one nipple while rolling and gently tugging on the other.

Lexy moans and arches her back, running both her hands into my hair and pulling it slightly, like I did with her, making me moan as well. Fuck, my right leg is throbbing, but no fucking way am I stopping this.

Releasing her nipple from my mouth with a pop, I make sure my warm breath hits her nipple as I say, "As for you taking charge, hell no. This is one area I won't budge. I'm the

310

boss in the bedroom," I say as I start to tug on her nipple again.

"Grayson, you keep that up and you're going to make me cum. I never realized you had such a dominant side, but I will say, it makes me even hotter with that challenge."

"It's not a challenge. It's a promise. And as for your climax, I'm in control of that too, and you don't get to come yet. I forbid it." I allow my hand to leave her breast and slide down her stomach until I reach her neatly groomed pussy. Fuck, she had the same plans I did, because she removed those cute booty shorts. I part her legs and slide my fingers between her folds. Oh yeah, she is so ready for me, my finger sliding inside her easily.

"I won't put up a fight right now, because damn, I like that. Don't stop," Lexy says as she widens her legs more and starts lifting her hips to the pumping of my finger. I quickly slide in a second and speed up my pumping. She's so tight, but I can tell she loves it, as she reaches up and starts firmly squeezing the breast I released.

"Grayson, I want more... I need more..."

Fuck it. I roll her to her side and pull her ass towards me as I slide my granite hard cock between her folds from behind. She instantly arches her back and tightens her thighs, contracting her pussy over my cock as I begin to slide in and out of her folds, rubbing against her clit with every hard thrust in.

"I want to feel you bare. Please tell me you're on birth control."

"I get my shot every three months. I'm good," she says, filling me with such relief that I don't have to suit up. She slightly parts her legs and arches more, allowing 'Sir' to align himself with the entrance of her tight pussy. I slowly slide in inch, then back out. Fuck, I can feel myself tremble. This feels fucking awesome. I've found my rhythm. Every third thrust I go deeper by another inch until I'm about halfway in. I hear

311

Lexy gasp and I pull out a bit. "Don't! I want him. It's a good burn," she says as she pushes back into me.

My eyes roll upward and I bite my lip. I've never felt anything so exquisite. I continue to rock my hips into her and then slowly pull out until the head almost pops out, then I push right back in a little faster, but never going deeper than half way. Oh God, I am not going to last much longer. With one hand I tease and tug on her nipple, and I slide my other hand to her clit and push hard and in a circular motion.

"Oh God Grayson, Grayson! I want more. I'm close... so close." She tries to push back and get Sir deeper, but I pull back and continue my assault on her clit.

"Babe, this is one area you will rarely boss me in. I got you," I inform her, picking up speed. I can feel her tighten around me. I know she is getting close. My pumping increases in speed, and I'm beginning to see stars. Nothing has ever felt this good.

"That's it... don't stop... don't stop. Grayson...I love you!" And just like that, I feel her tight little pussy clamp down hard on my cock and then it starts contracting, making me explode with my own climax. I push in a bit more than halfway as I feel my cock pulsating, emptying inside of her. This is a first for me, and I love it. Slowly rocking my hips back and forth, sliding into her much easier, I draw out our orgasm. I feel her go limp in my arms. I start lightly kissing and sucking up her neck till I reach her ear.

"I love you, more than anything. You'll forever be my one love." Just then, I feel the pain in my thigh burning like hell, making itself known. I'm just praying it didn't start bleeding again. You use your thighs a hell of a lot while having sex, but damn, it's worth it. I slowly pull out and roll Lexy onto her back, kissing her with everything in me.

Pulling away, I rest my forehead on hers. "Grayson, you're my one love too. There has never been, nor will there ever be, anyone but you. That was incredible, but how's your leg? I don't want to have to explain to Brenden what happened if it's bleeding again."

"It's fine. Hurts like hell, but it's time for pain meds again anyway. That was worth the wait and any extra pain. That was phenomenal, and a first for 'Sir'. I love you, Lexy."

She slowly pushes me back away from her, and I practically collapse backwards on the bed. She quickly looks at my bandaged thigh. "Thank God. No new blood." Then she climbs up my body and cuddles into me, laying her head on my chest asking, "Where are your meds? I'll get them for you."

"I can't think. My brain isn't functioning yet. It's still recouping from the best climax of my life."

I hear Lexy snickering, "Well that's good to know. I won't have to worry about you going back to any of those Amazonian women you used to date."

"You definitely don't have to worry about that. None of them ever meant anything to me. You're it for me," I say as I slowly open up my eyes. The pain in my leg is really hurting like hell now, so I reach over to my nightstand and grab a pill bottle.

Lexy sits up and takes it from me. "Mister, I said I'd get these for you." She reads the instructions on the bottle then opens it and hands me one before reaching behind me and getting a bottle of water. "Take this and I'll be right back."

Opening my eyes just a bit, I watch Lexy saunter across the room to my bathroom. Damn, that's a nice view. I flip the lid to my water and take my meds. Fuck. My leg has to heal. Fast. I cannot wait to completely make love to my woman for the first time. There is no better feeling on this planet than falling asleep with Lexy in my arms and waking up with her still there. I think I'm going to make this permanent. I think it's time she moves in with me, and I'm going to tell her just that. Yeah, I'm so ready for this. *We're* so ready for this.

21

A MOMENT WE WON'T SOON FORGET

Lexy

*I*t's been two weeks since Grayson was shot, and Brenden is finally letting him come home. Mom Riggs thinks he's been traveling for business. I have not enjoyed lying to her during our weekly training, but we all had to keep up a normal life so the parents wouldn't find out. You'd never know by our behavior that anything has happened. I lie to her regularly about FaceTiming Grayson several times a day, and how badly I miss him, when in reality there hasn't been a night where I haven't fallen asleep in his arms since he was shot.

The last two weeks have been insanely busy. Thank God I have a great staff at the club so I can be away and not worry. I've spent three days a week training with the Benassi Family, and it takes me back to my days at the Villa, training with all my men. I hate to admit it, but it feels good.

In addition, Orlando and Dante have had their men working out five days a week, with a minimum of three hours a day. I think when the battle hits, they'll be ready. They're good, they had just gotten lax in the training and the comfort of being in America. They are now aware it's not as safe as they thought it was. I think the Benassi Family are strong once again.

As for the Brothers... that's another story. I've had more of a blast training with them, because they were clueless as to what I know. I'm not stupid. I realized quickly they were taking it easy on me until I'd gut punch them or bust their lip, then they'd fight like a man instead of a pussy.

The first couple of days, Grayson would just sit on the sidelines watching closely, but not saying a word to me. It felt like he was studying my every move. Every now and again he'd call a Brother over to him and give them some kind of instruction, but he never spoke loud enough for me to hear, nor did he ever call me over for instructions or comment on my combat skills.

I'll admit the Brothers did impress me, which is hard to do. I'd be confident going to battle with any of them. Grayson still refuses to talk to me about any plans for when the Russians show their faces again, or what he's thinking about when it comes to Ivan Osokina and his Family. I think I've won over most of the Brothers and proven my skills are worthy.

It was loads of fun watching them fall on their asses as they tried to shoot dummies with paintball guns while swinging from grappling hooks. I'd have to say Jackson and Stevens were the best at it.

One big plus about hanging out with all the Brothers at their compound is the enjoyment I get from watching Grayson work out. Watching him take off his tank top when he gets hot from his upper body workout which includes weights and pushups... just...damn. I couldn't concentrate on anything but his arms and chest flexing. The man is just too yummy.

Then when he added slow squats to his workout... that was my favorite. He knows he needs to start working his legs out to build up their strength, which will also help them to heal. My eyes and mind were focused on his fine defined ass. I so want to bite it. I think he'd have a heart attack, but I am sure at some point I'm going to do just that. Grayson is such a turn on and a major distraction, and that's the only time anyone has ever gotten the upper hand on me.

Wait! Is that what they've been doing, those assholes?! They've been playing me! They wait until I'm watching Grayson. I think they've planned that. Is that what Grayson was talking to them about days ago? He was planning on getting off his ass from just watching me to purposely distracting me with his body. Those cheating assholes! No need to bet on that one, Grayson was in on it all along. Well boys, I got your number now. I am damn good at controlling myself too, you just wait...

Still, the sad thing is that even after watching me take on the Brothers in hand to hand combat, proving I can make my size work to my advantage during a fight, I can tell by the expression on Grayson's face that he still doesn't buy it. Looks like next week if his leg is better, I may have to take him down to show him up-close that I can handle myself. I didn't spend my whole life fighting with men and being taught every dirty trick in the books to lose.

Grayson

Tonight I'm finally going to Grayson's penthouse for the first time. He's asked me countless times before, but I refused until he was willing to trust me. He reaffirms his love and trust all the time now. I've got plans for tonight that Grayson isn't aware of. This only making-love-halfway shit we've been doing has lasted long enough. I've got several surprises in store for him tonight.

Pulling into Grayson's driveway, I see Stevens' 1990

Silverado truck. Grayson told me it belonged to Stevens' dad. He bought it the day Stevens' mom went into labor to have him. They both grew up loving that truck. It's a part of Stevens' dad that he still clings too. That was the first brand new vehicle his parents bought. When Stevens turned sixteen, his mom gave it to him which meant the world to him. Stevens swears he'll drive it till the day he dies. He works on it himself and keeps it in tip top shape, and it looks it.

Well, well, Stevens being here works out even better for me. I can have him help me get one of my gifts up to Grayson's bedroom without any problems. I can't help but to smile to myself as I get out of my SUV. Tonight is going to be incredible, once I get rid of Stevens. I'm not in the least bit nervous either.

Walking up to the massive double black wooden doors of Grayson's white brick, two story condo, I take a good look around. This is very nice. Gated neighborhood, nice views, pretty properties. I wonder, would Grayson's place be called a condo, or would it be classified a penthouse? I mean, it is on the top of the hill, above all the other condos. It's the King Condo. Geesh, my mind goes wandering to the silliest things sometimes.

I see the Brothers of Camelot shield scanning pad that they have at all the doors of their homes and buildings. I wonder if my palm print will open his door. I have to try it out. I lift my hand and place it on the screen, watching the red light scan my hand, the door latch clicking open a couple of seconds later. A very sultry woman's voice says, "Madam Lexy Rogers has arrived. Welcome." I quickly look around as I walk in. What the hell? Does Grayson have servants he neglected to tell me about? Who is that? Grayson's voice pulls me from my thoughts.

"Oh shit!" I hear Grayson say, followed by a couple of other guys laughing. I slowly walk into his immaculate white marble entryway looking around at the high ceilings, heading in the direction of the voices.

"Hello!" I call out, "I just wanted to see if your scanner would recognize my handprint and it did. I guess I don't need to ask for a key," I reply, half joking.

I watch as not only Grayson, but Stevens and Hawkins walk around the corner to greet me. "Hi Lexy, do me a favor and say, 'Hello Madame. I'm Lexy Rogers, Grayson's girlfriend,'" Hawkins says as he approaches me. Grayson is walking without his crutch, and he only has a slight hesitation using his right leg.

Feeling pretty confused, I look between the three of them. "Say what?" I ask Hawkins.

"You heard correctly. Say 'Hello Madame, I'm Lexy Rogers, Grayson's girlfriend.'"

"Why? Does Grayson have a staff here? Is that why it's so immaculate?"

"No, it's because your boyfriend is an insane clean freak and borderline O.C.D. Take your shoes off and leave them in different rooms of the house and watch him freak out," Stevens says with a chuckle, pounding Grayson on the back.

"I do not have O.C.D. I just don't see a need to trash my house, since it is only me here most of the time. I think I can manage to throw away my pizza boxes and beer bottles, unlike you who collects all your takeout food containers and shit to build trash towns with."

"Haha. Those structures are badass, I'll have you know. I could have been an architect," Stevens fires back.

"Come on, Lexy. Say it!" Hawkins says again.

"Babe, don't listen to him. Come on in."

Grayson puts his arm around me as we walk into a huge living room with thick white throw rugs over dark wood floors and black leather overstuffed furniture. These guys must shop at the same place. Every single one of them has the same overstuffed couch, loveseat and recliners in their living rooms. The only thing different is the colors.

Wow, Grayson has a black grand piano by his balcony window. The view behind it is stunning. Damn, it must be amazing to open the window up and hear the ocean as you play. I think I might have to come over here and play some-time when Grayson isn't around.

Looking back to Hawkins pleading look I say, 'Hello Madame, I'm Lexy Rogers, Grayson's girlfriend."

"Yes!" Hawkins says giving Stevens a high five. What the hell are these two up to? Grayson sighs, shaking his head when I hear that sultry voice again.

"It is very nice to meet you, Ms. Rogers. I am Madame, Sir's personal assistant. Is there anything I can do for you?"

Grayson closes his eyes once again and shakes his head, as both Hawkins and Stevens bust out laughing. Then I realize the voice came from speakers overhead. Is there some woman watching us from another room? Wait, she said she was 'Sir's' personal assistant! My head whips to Grayson.

"Who the hell is that?! Is there something you forgot to tell me Grayson?" I ask, wondering what the hell is going on.

"Emm, Madame is my home's personal assistant. Hawkins here thought it'd be funny to have her address me as Sir, and she only responds when you call her name, and you just programmed her to recognize your voice," Grayson says, as he reaches over and smacks a laughing Hawkins on the side of the head.

"You're kidding! What can she do?" Oh, this could be awesome. I'm thinking I need to talk to Tony and get some-thing like this for myself. Screw asking Siri everything, this would work out even better.

"Lights, TV, order food, Google searches. She's like an updated version of Alexa. You know that Amazon thing everyone has?"

I cannot resist giving this thing a try. "Madame, can you order us food from Benassi Pizzeria?"

"Yes, Ms. Rogers. Would you like to order Sir's usual order?"

"Your home's personal assistant addresses your dick? Or are you a secret Dom and just waiting for the right time to tell me? Or do you just like her addressing you like that?" I cannot help but tease. Geesh, I'm going to have so much fun with this.

"No, I just have a jackass for a tech guy who refuses to change it. Maybe I can talk to Tony and he'll fix it for me," Grayson teases Hawkins.

Both Hawkins and I say "No!" at the same time, before I interrupt and inform him. "Sorry honey, that is not going to happen. I like Madame. I will not allow Tony to change a thing." Now I'm laughing along with Stevens and Hawkins. Grayson can't help but join in our laughter, giving us double handed birdies as he does.

"Okay assholes, now that you've turned Lexy to your side, you can get your asses out of here. Bye Bye." He waves like a little boy at them as he looks up and says, "Madame, please deny access to my home to both Stevens and Hawkins. Remove them from the approved list of welcome guests."

"As you wish Sir. Their access has been removed, effective immediately."

Then Grayson actually sticks his tongue out at them, reaching over and grabbing me and pulling me into his arms.

"And you think I can't go home and bypass your orders? Please." Hawkins fires back, shaking his head in pity.

"Yeah, but you'll have to at least go back to either the club or home to access the main computer system to do that, and that'll get your asses out of here for now."

"Wait! Before you kick them out, can I send them to my SUV to bring something in for me? I got you a gift and it'd be awful nice if they could help me out with moving it."

"Sure Lexy, what do we need to bring in for you?" Stevens, the forever gentleman, is the first to ask. I reach into my purse and grab my key fob, tossing it to him.

"I have a big box in the back. If you could bring it in and put it in Grayson's bedroom, I would greatly appreciate it," I ask of them.

"No problem. We'll do it right now before we leave and give you two some time to yourselves. I'm sure that's why my good ol' buddy is being such an asshole right now. We've always teased him about Madame," Stevens responds as he shoves Grayson.

"This is the first time I've been to his house, so you're probably correct on that one."

"What? He hasn't invited you to his house before? Now that's just being a dick," Hawkins quickly adds.

"Hey, it's not like that! Believe me, I've invited her, but she refused and held it against me. But I'm not telling you our personal shit. Just go get her stuff," Grayson barks at them.

I'm sure he did that because he didn't want them to know he was withholding sex from me until he trusted me, knowing full well they have money riding on when Grayson and I finally have sex. They've been trying to figure that out for months.

"We're going asshole!" Stevens pauses for a second as a big smile spreads across his face. He looks between us. "Hey, is tonight the night? You two finally going to bump uglies?" He bumps shoulders with Grayson before turning his assault onto me. "Lexy, you finally gonna jump on Grayson's beaver-basher? You tired of just tasting his custard-launcher? I'm sure you're ready to take a ride on his weenie wagon," Stevens asks with a deep chuckle, as he dodges Grayson's swat and heads to the door.

Pulling me back into his arms while he's still laughing at Stevens' parting comments, he apologizes, "Sorry baby.

Stevens can really be quite childish at times. Sometimes I think the man will never grow up."

"Says the man that moments ago was sticking his tongue out at his friends and waving bye-bye. I think he's really funny. Where in the hell does he come up with these names? Weenie wagon? Custard-launcher? Eww, that is just gross." I can't control my own laughter. Besides, if anyone needs to know, there is nothing 'weenie' about Grayson's junk.

"Don't get him started or he'll never shut up. He has hundreds of names for both male and female anatomy. Now tell me, what's in the box? You didn't have to get me a gift. I feel bad I didn't get you anything. But what's the occasion? Did I miss an anniversary or something?"

"No, you didn't miss anything, I just know you'll like this. But you don't get to see what's inside of it until your Brothers leave."

"Okay, now you've really struck my curiosity."

We watch as Hawkins and Stevens carry in a big wrapped box, complete with a big red burgundy bow on top.

"You said you want this in the bedroom? What the hell is it?" Hawkins asks as they continue their slow walk towards the staircase.

"Do you not see that it is wrapped? That means it's a surprise, not for you, but for Grayson. And no, he is not opening it till later tonight," I tell them, before I pull out of Grayson's arms. "I'm going to run to my SUV and grab my suitcase, so they don't have to make an extra trip."

"I can go get it, Lex. I'm really okay. I haven't even used my crutch today."

"No, I got it. You go make sure they don't try and open it. It'll only confuse them," I say as I reach up on my tippy toes and kiss him on the cheek, before making a mad dash to my SUV.

"Confuse them? You've already confused me and got me

wondering," Grayson says, shaking his head as he follows them up the stairs.

Minutes later, I'm standing in Grayson's bedroom all excited and giddy, as Hawkins and Stevens finally leave. Grayson is just standing beside his massive perfectly made bed. Well, I have to admit Grayson and my taste in décor is different. Surprisingly, his penthouse is very bright and spacious, with zero clutter anywhere, not even on the night-stands. All the walls are white with wood floors throughout. At least his furniture is black and burgundy. That looks to be the only thing we have in common - our color choices.

"Hey, are you going to stand over there and daydream or can I open my present?" Grayson asks, pulling me out of my thoughts.

"No, you may not open it." I gaze upward as I call out, "What is it you say in America? Oh yeah. 'Madame, lock the house up like Fort Knox," I say with a wink to Grayson. "I wouldn't want your friends to come back on our first evening in your home."

"Sir, do you give the authority to Ms. Rogers to give me orders?" Grayson's house assistant asks.

"Yes, Madame. Reprogram yourself to follow Lexy's commands as you do my own."

"Yes, Sir. Program updated. Ms. Rogers, the house is offi-cially locked and secured as you requested."

"Madame, please call me Lexy."

"Yes, Ms. Lexy. Is there anything else I can do for you?"

"No, Madame. You are finished for the night."

"Goodnight Ms. Lexy and Sir."

Reaching into my pocket, I pull out two sets of handcuffs, and twirl them around my fingers. Grayson notices what I have in my hands and his eyes pop open with surprise.

"What, may I ask, are those for? Because they sure the hell aren't for me."

"Well, they are for you, if you cannot control yourself," I

say as I slowly walk over to him, dropping the handcuffs on the floor beside his feet. I grab the waist of his sweatpants and quickly yank them to the floor. Before Grayson has time to respond, I stand back up and push him onto the bed.

He quickly sits up, resting on his elbows. "What the hell Lexy?" he says with a chuckle.

"Well, I promised you a show, but there are a few rules you must follow."

"A show?" Grayson replies looking me up and down. "I should have offered to take your coat when you got here, but when I saw the seam in the back of your stockings, the idea that you might not have anything on under that jacket crossed my mind. Am I about to live out one hell of a fantasy?"

"For the next fifteen minutes, I'm in charge. You'll find out what's under this coat in a matter of minutes, but first I want you to get comfortable on the bed."

Grayson reaches one hand behind his head, grabbing the back of his t-shirt and removing it before he scoots back up to the headboard, sitting halfway propped up on the pillows, looking at me like a kid on Christmas morning, wearing nothing but very tight boxer briefs.

"Rule number one, no touching me. You touch me, I put the cuffs on you. You may enjoy the show, but no satisfying yourself. I will allow you to briefly tease yourself, but if I see you getting anywhere near an orgasm, the cuffs go on," I say as I walk over to the box and slowly remove a thin layer of clear plastic protecting my surprise wrapping, before walking back to the side of the bed.

"Oh, fuck. Are you really going to strip for me?" Grayson asks smiling, all bright eyed and showing off both dimples. He looks like a little boy who is about to get the new toy he's waited a lifetime for.

"I said nothing about stripping Grayson. I'm going to perform a special number just for you, to celebrate both of us being able to be here together for the first time. You need to pay attention to each word of this song because it has real meaning. I'm about to give you a treat we won't soon forget."

"Oh shit, okay. You won't need those handcuffs for me, but don't be surprised if they wind up on you before the night is over," Grayson teases, with an evil smile and a wink, "And besides, I don't think you could get them on me in the first place. I will follow the rules," he says as he reaches his arms back, placing his hands across the back of his mahogany headboard. Damn, he looks good. I can't help but stare at his spectacular chest and arms as they flex. Yum.

Shaking my head to clear my mind, I can feel my core contracting in eagerness, knowing what is ahead. I casually walk back over to the large box and stop, looking back over my shoulder. I know without question that Grayson's eyes will be glued on me, and I am correct. Grayson is sitting there licking his lips, looking me up and down.

"Do you remember the rules?"

"Yes, Ma'am."

I slowly unfasten the belt from around my coat and let the sleeves drop until I catch the collar with my right hand and toss my wrap coat over to a chair.

"Holy. Fucking. Shit."

I'm standing with my back to Grayson, and all he can see is the back of my matching bright red and black bra and thong set that I wore the first time we fooled around. But this time for his viewing pleasure, I have on thigh high black stockings with the old-fashioned seam straight up the back of my legs and my six inch Louis Vuitton black leather, red soled shoes, knowing how much he likes this look. I slowly bend over at the waist, knowing full well my thong just went up my ass cheeks even more, putting on a nice display for him. I can hear his breathing get heavier from here.

I reach over and pull the corner of the ribbon from the top of the box to trigger its opening. As I do, all four sides of the box fall open. I leap on top of what looks like a square table, which just happens to have the Brothers' and Wenches of Camelot shields on opposite sides. So if anyone sees this after my little performance, they will think it's just a table. I love that I can tell Tony something I want and he can have it made and delivered to me in a matter of two weeks. You just gotta love that guy.

As I stand on the table with my back still towards Grayson, I lift my hands up and remove the clip from my hair, gently shaking my head side to side, allowing it to cascade down past my shoulders to my mid back. I slip my left foot over and push one of the black accent metal nobs on my box. Taylor Swift starts to play 'Ready For It'. I push the opposite corner black knob and my pole starts to rise from the center of the table. I grab on to it as it continues to rise, and I spread my legs and swing around the top of it, flipping back down as I continue my routine.

I hear Grayson mumble. "Goddamn." I look over to see he has already removed his boxers and is stroking himself, biting his bottom lip. Shaking my finger at him for touching himself so soon, I start to sing every word to him. He stops stroking and spreads his arms out on the pillows. He keeps his eyes locked on me as he licks his lips. I'll occasionally see an involuntary muscle flex, and 'Sir' is standing straight up, thick and hard against his stomach, touching his navel.

Damn, my man has one hell of a beautiful cock. I straddle the pole, dropping my hips down to the ground, before thrusting back up. I'm so fucking turned on right now. I continue singing the song, hoping I don't sound too out of breath.

I leap to the floor, between my pole and the bed as I sing,
"I-I-I see how this is going to go"
Looking Grayson in the eyes, I reach between my legs and touch myself as I sing,
"Touch me and you'll never be alone."
In a single motion, I remove my thong and take my time

sliding my hands up my body, as I continue my singing. I squeeze both of my breasts as I kick off my stilettos, at the same time whispering,

"No one has to know."

And just as the chorus begins, I make eye contact with him as I get on the bed. I start crawling up his body, never breaking contact, or missing a word. Once I'm straddling his legs, I make sure I allow my lips and breath to touch the full head of his cock as I hum. Mmm. *"I know I'm gonna be with you. So I take my time."* Hearing Grayson's gasp brings me such pleasure, knowing my plan is working. I have him in a sexual trance.

Suddenly I rise up on my knees, lining myself up with 'Sir' as I ask, *"Are You Ready For It?"* Then with quick movements, I slide Sir into me halfway while rotating my hips and using my thigh muscles. I spread my legs further apart, allowing him to go just a bit deeper. Grayson lets out a deep moan. I know he is enjoying this as much as I am.

As I continue my torment on Grayson, I repeatedly contract my core muscles around his massive erection. I can feel a hint of a burn as it stretches me. I rise up slowly before I drop back down, allowing 'Sir' to pop in and out of me to the beat of the music. This feels marvelous.

Looking at Grayson, I can see his eyes rolling up and partially closing, his hands squeezing the pillows beside him. I know he's trying so hard not to grab me and take control.

Once the next verse begins, I slide up and off of him, doing a backbend getting up to my feet at the foot of the bed where I continue with my routine. I love doing this for his complete entertainment. How much he loves it is written all over his face. I cannot wait for the end of this song. This is going better than I thought.

By the time the next chorus starts, I am back to hovering right over him asking, *"Are you ready for it? Oh, are you ready for it? Baby let the games begin."* And right on cue with that, I rotate my hips and use all my thigh strength to allow 'Sir' to slide halfway into me again, knowing how much he liked this moments ago. Then I quickly lift myself back up, riding half of him hard while contracting my core, never stopping the rotation of my hips.

Grayson looks down to where we are joined, and oh God that turns me on even more. Oh, how I'd like to watch Grayson entering me like this. While I am still singing and performing, I reach behind me and remove my bra. Grayson focuses on my chest, just watching me fondle my breasts. He's breathing so heavy.

As the song reaches the final chorus, I take his hands and put them on my breasts and he takes over squeezing and tugging on my nipples. As the music builds and keeps on going, we are both grinding with it, not missing a beat with our thrusting. With each thrust, we go a little further than half-way. At this point, I am barely singing with Taylor Swift. I'm experiencing such pleasure with just a hint of a burn of discomfort. This is taking me to another level of pleasure and I don't want to stop.

Just as the final few lines of the song begins, I make eye contact with Grayson again and sing,

"Baby, let the games begin
Let the games begin
Let the games begin
Are you ready for it?"

And on that final question and before he can stop me, I slide all the way down, taking Sir completely into me. Gasping in surprise at the full stretch of him inside of me, there's a bit more discomfort than I was expecting. Grayson instantly wraps his arms around me, flipping us over until he is on top of me as he starts kissing me like his life depends on it.

We battle for control over the kiss and I'm relieved he doesn't pull out, even though the sting is a bit intense. Grayson just stays still inside of me. Our kiss begins to slow, becoming more tender and loving. My heart and soul melt and become one with his. We are officially one body and one soul. Nothing and no one will ever be able to separate us again. We are one.

GRAYSON

We're one. Pulling away from our tender, but passionate kiss, I rest my forehead on hers and very slowly rotate my hips a bit, watching her facial expressions. I only pull out about an inch before pushing all the way back into her. Hearing her gasp again, I ask in a whisper,

"Are you okay baby? I love you more than mere words can say."

"I love you too, Grayson. Don't stop. This is our beginning. We'll never part now. I give myself to you completely, to stand beside you and share all of my life with you," Lexy says like a vow, straight from her soul.

"Right now we're one. You are the other part of my soul, my air, my life. My heart doesn't beat without yours. We are bonded together, never to part," I say as I lean down and kiss her tenderly again, letting our tongues caress and taste each other completely. I never dreamed love could be this life altering. Lexy is my world.

She wraps her arms around me and starts caressing my back, lightly dragging her nails down my spine and squeezing my ass, encouraging me to move. With slow and gentle strokes, we begin to really make love, passionately and with more feeling than I ever knew was possible.

This is by far the best moment in my life. I'm making love to the woman I've longed for, for years. She's mine, now and always. I've claimed the other half of my soul.

Lexy's knees are bent up beside me and she arches her back, allowing both knees to fall apart completely as she continues her incredible hip rotation and thrusting. Damn, my woman can move. She is trying to speed things up. This woman is going to battle me every day of my life for control, and at this moment, I am so ready and can't wait for the challenge. Lifting myself up a bit, I bring myself halfway out and quickly thrust back in, with Lexy rotating her hips in unison. Nothing has ever felt this good. This is truly paradise.

Looking down into Lexy's beautiful face, I see a single tear run out of the side of her eye, freezing me in place. "Baby, are you okay?" I ask as I bend down and kiss away the tear.

"Yes, I'm fine. I just love you so much, my heart feels like it's exploding with emotion I've never felt before."

"Baby, I know what you mean," I say as I tenderly start kissing her lips over and over again.

"Grayson… Grayson… I'm getting so close. I need more. I want more. Let's reach this together."

"Always, babe. I don't want to hurt you. If I'm going too fast or hard, just say something. We can finish this slow and steady instead."

"No, Grayson, I want more. I want to explode into paradise with you."

"Baby I'll always give you what you want. This is one area where I want you to know I'll always take care of you first. I love you. You're my life."

And with that, we start kissing passionately, thrusting our hips faster. I can feel her core tighten around me and I know we're seconds away from our biggest release ever.

"Grayson…Grayson… I…I…I… Love you!" Lexy digs her nails into my shoulders as she cries out with her release, taking me with her into passionate bliss. I see stars flashing behind my eyelids, as every muscle in my body contracts and explodes in joy. Our bond is official and real, and even more importantly, it is forever.

Rolling our bodies until Lexy is on top of me, we both try to catch our breath. I slowly run my fingertips up and down

Lexy's spine, inhaling the scent of her hair. I lightly kiss up her neck as I listen to her breathing slow and a low moan escapes her throat. My hands have a mind of their own, touching whatever part of her I can reach. Lexy's legs are on each side of my hips, and I'm still completely inside of her.

"I'm never letting you go. You are mine, now and always. No one will ever take you away from me. I love you. Seriously Lex, you are my everything. My heart couldn't beat right without you," I whisper.

"The same goes for you. You are mine Grayson. No marriage license is needed. I am never letting you go. We belong together."

"Yes, we do. No other man will ever touch you like this again."

"No other man has ever touched me like this and reached into my heart and touched my soul the way you have. I cannot imagine life without you in it."

"And you'll never have to imagine, because we are one, now and always. Enough talking. You're not leaving here all weekend. This is the moment I've waited for, forever. We're spending the whole weekend in bed, ordering food, and *really* getting to know each other. No working for either of us. We're both sending messages to all our friends stating we've escaped for quality time and aren't to be disturbed unless someone dies."

"Agreed. I was hoping you felt the same way I do. I don't want to leave your bed till Monday."

"You do know that I'd love for you to move in and stay forever, right?"

"Grayson, you can't be serious!" The thought of moving in so soon in our relationship makes me giggle. "Geesh, you just love to just jump into the deep end. Have you ever considered getting in the shallow end first to allow your body and mind time to adjust?" she teases me, still giggling.

I slowly push deeper as 'Sir' thickens inside of her.

"Madame, play the Lexy Playlist, starting with 'Thinking Out Loud' by Ed Sheeran."

"Your wish is my command, Sir," Madame replies, and music quietly fills the room.

"I'm not going to give up on you moving in with me Lexy. Looks like I've got the weekend to convince you."

"Come on, babe, I think my uncle would have a heart attack. It's a bit too soon. But please, try and convince me while I just lay here and melt in your arms over the fact you have a 'Lexy Playlist'."

I touch our foreheads together, looking deep into her eyes. I'm sure she's seeing my soul. "Okay, let the persuading begin."

"God, how I love you."

As I start kissing her, we start exploring each other's bodies, just enjoying each other's closeness. All my dreams have come true and I could not be happier. I've finally got her back, and this time it's forever.

22

ALL OF ME

Lexy

*M*onday morning came too quickly. This is the first time since I arrived at Grayson's on Friday night that I've been able to sneak out of bed without him waking up and following me. I was even able to take a fast shower and get ready for work, without him waking up to join me. Standing here now and looking at his hotness lying across the bed, it begins to turn me on all over again. That ass of his... and those thick thighs... they are enough to start a fire burning within me, causing my core to flutter back to life. Geez, I'm turning into a nymphomaniac.

Thinking back to just a little over an hour ago when he woke me up to make love to me again, I have to admit, it's one hell of a way to wake up. I'd prefer that any day over my damn phone alarm. One minute I was dreaming of making love to Grayson, on the verge of reaching my orgasm, when I was suddenly woken up by him swatting me on the side of my ass, realizing it wasn't a dream.

He whispered in my ear from behind, "I love this ass, now

stick it up in the air and spread those legs so I can have my wicked way with you." Dayuuum, it was good.

I have to get out of here and go start breakfast before I wind up attacking him again. Taking a deep cleansing breath, I turn to leave the bedroom.

I feel a smile spread across my face as I make my way to the kitchen. I can relieve this weekend over and over again in my mind whenever I want to. It was so good this morning that he's still passed out in a climactic state of unconsciousness. I shake my head at the discovery of how different we are once again. After I reach climactic bliss, I'm wide awake and totally refreshed, so unlike him who is ready to pass out cold.

Walking into the kitchen, I go straight to the coffee machine and make myself a cup. I walk over to the fridge and grab the bacon, eggs, butter and cheese. It's time to impress my man with a simple but yummy breakfast.

Letting my mind roam over all the things we've done and shared this weekend as I start to fry some bacon, I can't help but sigh. I couldn't have dreamed up a more perfect weekend. I don't know what I enjoyed more, making love on his private beach as the sun rose yesterday morning or when I rode him hard and fast as he lay reclined in his double-wide chaise longue while we held hands and just stared into each other's eyes as the sun set over his balcony. Yeah, that was incredible. I need to give my body a few hours to recoup before a repeat. I'll never admit to Grayson that I'm a bit sore, but it was totally worth it.

"Why are you in here and not in our bed? I need to devour that body one more time before we both have to go back into the real world," Grayson whispers in my ear as he wraps his arms around me, nibbling his way up my neck as he reaches over and turns off the burner.

Smacking his hand away, I say, "No sir. I remember quite well being woken up by my out of control sex-crazed boyfriend less than an hour ago, and after a very energizing sexual release, he passed out cold while I couldn't go back to sleep. I decided to get up and get ready for my day."

Tugging on my earlobe with his teeth and continuing his assault on my neck, his warm breath whispers, "Well, you could say you wore me out, but I've got my second wind now and you have on far too many clothes."

I try to move myself away from his hold and turn the burner back on. "Nope, that is not happening. I've already showered and gotten ready for work. Now I'm just being a loving girlfriend and making you breakfast before heading out to my office."

Pulling me back into his arms, he rubs his very erect cock into the crack of my bum. "I'd rather have you for breakfast."

"Sorry babe, that isn't going to happen. Looks like you'll have to either take a cold shower or take care of 'Sir' yourself because I am making you breakfast and heading to work. I have too much to do today before meeting up with Stevens and Jackson tonight at your headquarters to work with them in the gym."

"Really?! You're turning me down? You are actually telling me to whack off in the shower instead of making love to you again? Come on, babe, you know you want him as much as he wants your little snug box."

"You're giving my va-jay-jay pet names now?" I snicker.

"So, what if I am?"

"Hmm, maybe I should name her. I mean all of you have named your thingies..."

Grayson cracks up, his deep laughter vibrating against my back as he squeezes my boobs, trying to distract me with his nibbling and fondling. "Come on, baby. I can get these leggings off you in second and throw you onto the table and make love to you really fast while you watch this time."

As I reach over for a couple of paper towels to drain the bacon on, I shake my head no, even though I can't help but smile at his persistence. I'm trying everything humanly possible to slow down my rapidly accelerating sexual craving for everything Grayson is offering, but my body needs some time. Geez, this man's sexual drive is unquenchable. "Have you never been turned down? No means no, Grayson," I say with a giggle.

"Well, fine. But I'm telling you now, once we're married, you aren't allowed to tell me to go whack off in the shower. As my wife, you'll have to help satisfy me," he teases, giving a slightly harder bite to my earlobe.

Unable to control my shock with that reply, I hide it behind my laughter, before informing him, "Since you put it that way, if we were married, I'd be able to... shall we say, satisfy 'Sir' in other ways."

"Fuck! That is not nice, teasing me like that."

"Sorry sweetie. But you need to get into the shower now or your breakfast is going to get cold."

Grayson finally releases me with a heavy sigh. "I never thought you'd be such a mean tease... making me think of you giving me head when I have to go take a cold shower. Evil... Evil... woman."

Grayson is still mumbling as he walks out of the kitchen, head down all dejected-like, and I can't help but laugh at his antics. I also can't help myself from watching his amazing ass flex as he goes up the stairs. Damn, that ass is perfection. "Hey!" I call up to him. "I never said you had to take a cold shower, I just said I would not be handling 'Sir' this time. I promise he won't die. Oh, and when we get married, that never leaving the other unsatisfied goes both ways buddy," I say teasingly while still laughing.

"Stop staring at my ass. If you aren't going to help me out in the shower, you don't get to watch my ass," Grayson calls out looking over his shoulder, catching me staring at said ass with a big smile on his face.

"Fine, take your shower." I poke my tongue out at him, making him laugh harder.

"I will. But if you change your mind, I'll be waiting. You have less than five minutes before I finish him off myself." I hear him yelling as he walks into his bedroom.

Once we finished breakfast, Grayson had to go and grab his phone that wouldn't stop ringing. I'm pretty sure it was Hawkins that was calling over and over again. On Friday night, Grayson sent out a mass text message to all the Brothers telling them that he was planning on staying home all weekend with me and *did not want to be disturbed.* Hawkins doesn't like Grayson not touching base with him for almost three days.

As for me, I've missed a couple of calls from Uncle Louie, so I had to send him a text telling him that I'd talk to him this morning once I got to work. I'm also sure my roomies will have one hundred and one questions for me when I come home tonight too. That is if they don't show up at work, demanding we have lunch to catch up on every detail. They sent me at least four texts each.

As I'm putting the last of the dishes into the dishwasher, I realize Grayson is off the phone when I hear the piano intro to John Legend's song 'All of Me'. Now that just starts my heart pounding. I quickly close the dishwasher and head into the living room. Come on, what girl on the planet wouldn't want to be serenaded by their hot boyfriend? This is a dream come true.

"What would I do without your smart mouth drawing me in, and you kicking me out,"

Oh my God. His voice is incredible. He just continues to sing, looking right into my eyes as I try to walk over casually and sit beside him on the piano bench. I can barely hide the fact that I'm as giddy as a pre-teen girl being sung to by some pop star. He has his head turned to face me, still looking deep into my eyes, just melting my very being.

"My head's under water, but I'm breathing fine,"

I honestly think I'm going to die of happiness right here, just as Grayson smiles and shakes his head, while rolling his eyes singing,

"You're crazy and I'm out of my mind."

And I can't even be mad he just called me crazy, because of the chorus. Oh, I'd give this man anything he wanted. I would kill for him. I would even die for him. My life without him in it is worthless. He could destroy me so easily, and he has no clue. This is so beautiful. I can feel my eyes filling with tears. God, no one has ever been able to control my emotions like he can. Every word of this song is also so true for us. Geez, we've become the best ever 'living chick flick'.

Each word is packed with power and truth as he sings, *"You're my downfall, you're my muse. My worst distraction, my rhythm and blues."*

Our souls are completely entwined. They can never be separated, or we may not survive. What else could explain how fast and hard we've fallen under each other's spell? This is love, without question or reservation. There is no slowing it down or stopping it. We both feel it, there is no going back. This is it, no matter how scared I am at times, we have to figure out a way to make it work.

I can't stop myself as I join in and sing every word back to him. Because it has such meaning, I know I'll never hear this song again and not think back to this moment. If anyone was to see this, Lord only knows what they think of the two of us.

By the time we reach the last verse I have to shut up and just allow him to sing it to me. *"I give you all, all of me. And you'll give me all, all of you..."*

"I love you so much, Grayson." I pull him into a brief sweet kiss. Pulling away and looking up at him through my lashes, I ask. "Do you think you can make me a couple of videos of you serenading me like this? I could watch them when I'm having a bad day at work, or just need to feel your love."

"Anything for you, babe," he replies with a little chuckle, as he slowly leans in to kiss me, just as my phone starts playing 'Not All Heroes Wear Caps' by Owl City.

"Oh God, that's Uncle Louie. I've ignored him all weekend, so if I don't get that, he's going to get on a plane to kick my ass. It's time for introductions anyway," I say as I make a mad dash to grab my cell and answer it.

"Good morning, Uncle Louie."

"You don't answer your phone all weekend, then send me a text saying you'd call me when you got to your office? What the fuck is going on, Alessandra?" Uncle Louie asks firmly.

Shit! He's mad. Maybe I should take him off of speaker-phone. Grayson looks to be going into shock, making me to want to laugh.

"First, it's Lexy, remember? And relax Uncle Louie. Everything is fine. Grayson finally got to come home. He's walking without a crutch. He's almost a hundred percent, so I spent the weekend with him."

"Excuse me? You did what?! I've heard nothing about a wedding or even an engagement!"

That comment makes Grayson mumble, "Shit!"

I can't help but laugh. "Come on, Uncle Louie. What year is it? We are not living in the Stone Ages. Geez."

"Little One, I am being serious."

"Well, I should tell you I have you on speakerphone and Grayson is sitting right here with me."

"Sorry Sir, I... I... love Lexy. She's the only woman for me, I swear it. So believe me, one day soon I will ask you for her hand in marriage. I have the deepest respect for her, and you," Grayson says nervously, practically stumbling over his words.

"Well son, you and I will talk very soon, without Lexy listening to our every word."

"Hey! We don't keep secrets, we tell each other everything. Why do you need to talk to Grayson alone? Uncle Louie, do you have any information about the Russians? You better not be keeping that shit from me."

"Alessandra!"

"My name is not Alessandra!"

"Fine, Alexa Sophia Rogers, you watch your mouth. I am not keeping anything to do with the Russians from you, not after everything that went down a few weeks ago. I've been keeping up to date with both Tony and the Benassi Family. But I should warn you, your Papa got wind of all of this business with the Russians, and he is thinking you might be a part of it. Don't worry, everyone is denying it and not telling him jack shit."

"Good. Keep it that way. I will try not to swear, but why do you want to talk to Grayson?"

"Little One, I'm practically your Papa, and my talking to Grayson is a man-to-man thing. And as much as you like to swing your imaginary dick around, this time it will not work."

"Fine!" I say, rolling my eyes. I put my phone on the top of the piano and cross my arms over my chest. I can feel Grayson trying to hold back his snickering.

"So Grayson, I do hope that this relationship is completely exclusive."

"It is sir, completely exclusive. I haven't even looked at another woman since the day Lexy fell back into my life. There will never be anyone else for me but her."

"Good to know. I haven't killed anyone in a while and I'd rather keep my hands clean," Uncle Louie says with a deep chuckle.

"Come on Uncle Louie! I trust Grayson with my heart. He'd never do that," I say, as I feel Grayson put his arm around my waist, pulling me closer to him as we sit on his piano bench.

"Okay, since we're being adults and you two are involved in a... shall we say intimate relationship, I am only saying this once: so help the both of you if you pop up pregnant before I walk you down the aisle. There will be hell to pay for that one. I'll kick your ass for sure Grayson, and believe me, I can and will do it. And Lexy, you can forget about that big church wedding as well if that happens. So, you better suit up young man. Do I make myself clear?" Uncle Louie says, once again sounding every inch the father giving the new guy the ground rules.

I can actually hear Grayson swallowing beside me. I cannot help myself as I bust out laughing. "Oh, my God! Uncle Louie, you are scaring the crap out of Grayson. Don't worry, I've been getting the shots since I moved to America. The last thing I want is a baby right now so that will not be a problem. And a little FYI, don't go planning my wedding yet as no one has even asked me."

"Well, I was just making sure. Glad to hear you want to wait till you're married. But I do hope that after you say 'I do', you don't keep me waiting too long to become a Nonno."

"Are you kidding me?! You have two small kids of your own to finish raising. Don't even think about being a grandpa yet. Give me a break!"

Grayson starts coughing beside me as Uncle Louie joins in the chuckling.

"Aren't you supposed to be at work, young lady? I've never known you to hide for a weekend and then be late to work."

Rolling my eyes and looking over at Grayson, I say "See?! Controlling men. Always! I can't escape it."

"Do not give me any more of your sass, Little One. I'll be seeing you this Sunday. Grayson's father and mother have invited the family over for dinner. That means me and Camilla, along with Luigi, Sandy, Rocco and Lucca."

341

Both Grayson and I whip our heads to look at each other. He is so wide-eyed I can tell this is just as much of a surprise to him as it is to me. "What? When did you talk to his parents?"

"Well young lady, if you would have answered your phone this weekend, I would have talked to you both about it first. But since you both decided to hide out at Grayson's home and not talk to a soul, I was not about to be rude when Dick called. He thinks it's time we all meet."

"I have to kick Tony ass again! Why didn't he talk to me about this? Shit!"

"Babe, it'll be okay. I'll talk to Mom and make sure Grandma Piedmont is there. Dad'll be on his best behavior with Mom's mom there," Grayson says giving me another sideways squeeze.

"Language Lexy! And no, you do not have to kick Tony's ass. Did you not see several texts from him as well as voice-mails when you turned your phone back on?"

"Well yeah, but this is different."

"No, it is not. He handled it fine. I gave Tony permission to give my number to Dick, so you have no right to be angry with him. It's time I meet this man of yours face to face. And meeting his family will be a good thing. We'll all be on our best behavior."

"Well, I guess it'll be okay. And I am very excited about seeing you. When does everyone get into to town?"

"We're all arriving at different times and staying in different places. Tony gave us all everyone's phone numbers as well as addresses. But we are coming prepared, just in case you need us. We'd also like to meet and see all the Brothers, if that's alright?"

"That can easily be arranged sir, but not at dinner with my folks. We can either meet at my place or I can gladly show you our headquarters if that is what interests you?"

"Yes. That is something we'll talk about in a couple of

minutes after I send Lexy to work so we can talk man-to-man."

"Excuse me? Send me to work?! Why can I not hear this conversation?"

"Alexa! I will not repeat this to you again. This is man-to-man, father to potential son-in-law. And yes, I am talking about you behind your back. I think the boy needs a few warnings."

"*Warnings?!*"

"Yes, warnings. Now get up off that ass of yours and be the responsible leader I trained you to be and get to work. Grayson, I'll be calling you in less than five minutes, so kiss her goodbye and show her the door. Consider this test number one."

"Test number one?! What the hell is that supposed to mean?!" I ask, but Uncle Louie has already hung up.

"Babe, I'm sure that was meant for me, testing to see if I can get you to leave before he calls."

"Well, fuck that! I'm not going anywhere. You can just answer the phone on speaker and I'll sit here quiet as a church mouse."

Grayson starts laughing in my face. "You?! Quiet as a church mouse? Tell me another. Your uncle will think I am the biggest pussy because he will say something you don't agree with and you will call him out on it."

"So, you really want me to fucking leave?!"

Grayson tries to control his snickering with the biggest smirk on his face. "So, in all the times you've been alone with my mom, you have never talked about me? Can you look me in the eye and tell me you and my mom don't have a few secrets? Remember, we don't lie to each other. Think about that *before* you jump to say no, because I will call my mom and ask."

"Shit! You do not play fair." Grayson helps me up from the piano bench, grabbing my satchel and putting it over my head while walking me to the door as we continue our little chat.

"Now you wouldn't want me to look like I'm pussy-whipped to your uncle, would you?" he asks with one eyebrow raised.

"Fine! I'll go but I am not happy about it. And I do want you to share *some* of what he says."

Grayson bends down and starts to kiss me and all laughter stops as I reach around and squeeze his ass, deepening our kiss. He pushes me back into the door. God, now I don't want to go to work today. As Grayson cups my ass and starts to lift me off the floor, his phone starts to ring. He pulls away abruptly, pulling his phone from his back pocket and looking at the screen.

"Yeah, this is him. No caller ID." He bends down again and gives me a quick peck before opening the door, right before he swipes his phone, answering, "Riggs!" As he turns to walk back into his living room.

23

MEETING FAMILY

Grayson

I've never been more nervous in my life. Lexy's uncle wants to talk to me privately. Jesus, I can only hope he also wants her to wait at Hawkins' castle when we go into battle with the Russians. Walking into the living room, I hear her uncle ask,

"Were you able to get her to go to work, son?"

"Yes, sir. I just walked her to the door."

"You sure about that?" he asks, so I turn to look at the door, only to see Lexy trying to sneak back in. I shake my head at her, smiling. She's such a sneaky little thing. You can tell by the look on her face she isn't happy as she flips me off.

"You know her very well. She is trying to sneak back in," I say as I hear her uncle start laughing in my ear.

"You big mouth," Lexy says from the door, now flipping me off with both hands.

"Let me guess, she is trying to manipulate you. Has she flipped you off yet?"

"Yup, nailed it," Lexy turns that fine ass of hers in my direction, wiggling and swatting it, motioning me to kiss it with oversized duck lips. All I can do is shake my head at her antics, as I turn and walk out onto my balcony, locking the door behind me. I wave bye-bye to her, with a big smile on my face. She flips me off again.

"Has the brat left yet, or has she resorted to flirting with you?"

"Well, maybe. Because she has turned that fin... butt to me, smacking it and motioning for me to kiss it." Fuck I have to watch what I say. This is like talking to her father. "But I put an end to her antics. I came out to my balcony and locked the door."

"You do know she is used to always getting her way, right? You are the first real relationship she has ever had. She was as innocent and inexperienced as can be before coming to America. She *always* had chaperones and was never allowed to be alone with any boys before you."

Humm... well he doesn't know everything about her because he is acting like she was a virgin, and I know for sure she wasn't. So, she had at least one secret relationship he doesn't know about, and I am not going to be the one to tell him any different. Nope, not going there.

"She has told me how strict her upbringing was," I inform him, turning to look over my shoulder to see she has finally left. I walk over and lean over the banister, wondering where this conversation is going.

"She was brought up as royalty, because in our Family, she was. No one ever turned their back to her. That would be disrespectful. She was trained since she could walk to demand respect, to protect herself, and that she was better than everyone else as well. She never had to want for anything."

"I understand that. She can be a bit bossy but I do not believe for a minute she thinks she is better than anyone else."

"I said she was trained to think those things, but she has a heart of gold and fought them since day one. Even as a very little girl, she'd want to share and give a lot of her toys and clothes to children within the Family that didn't have as much. Her dream has always been to be a normal girl, but I do not think that is possible for her. She was born a leader. She is not used to taking orders. She could get in a man's face that is easily twice her size and tell him what to do, and if he questioned her, she wouldn't hesitate to grab him by the balls, literally, and show him who's boss."

"Shit!"

"Yeah, that is my concern. I want to know if you have big enough balls not to break her spirit but to help control and guide her. That's an awful big job, son. She will butt heads with you, and you have to learn when to bend and when to stand by her side, strong and firm."

"I love her. I'd never break her spirit. I'll protect her with my dying breath."

"I believe you. But can you walk beside her and try not to control her? She will kick your ass and hand you your balls if you try to dominate her."

"Lexy and I haven't really butted heads yet, but I'm sure it will happen at some point. I think we'll be able to deal with it and talk it out like two reasonable adults."

"Ha! Are you ready to fight with Lexy beside you?"

"I was hoping you'd be willing to help me talk to her about staying with the other women and Hawkins at his castle. I'm sure she has told you how much she loves it up there. I think she'll be safer with them. She can be the boss there and I'd be able to concentrate a lot better knowing she is safe."

Now I hear him bust out into a deep belly laugh that keeps going on and on. Finally, he says, "Son, you have a lot to learn. I think the two of you are in for some really ugly and painful arguments. I can only hope you are man enough to survive because I do believe she is deeply in love with you, and I do not know how she will deal with losing you."

"She is not going to lose me! Why would you say that?"

"Son, let me warn you. She is not going to let another

man dictate what she can and cannot do. Once she discovered her gift and abilities, there was no stopping her. She will not go to Hawkins' castle with the ladies. She will be on the front lines. That is who you fell in love with. She is known as the Warrior Princess. Little girls dream of being like her. I am sure Hawkins can tell you, that on the Dark Web she's known as the Mafia Assassin. Plenty of men fear her. You should take that to heart before she hands you your balls."

"And what if she gets shot again, or killed? I can't live with that."

"Look, who saved your ass just a few weeks ago? And from what I've heard, it wasn't the first time. You need to learn to figure out a way to deal with this or you could lose her. I know her. She will never hide. Maybe after this Russian ordeal passes you can figure a way to talk her into starting a family, because that is the only way she'll ever lay down her sword. She told me that many years ago."

"Those were flukes."

"You can't be that much of a dumbass."

"Hey! I am highly qualified and I trained for years. I can protect her. She doesn't need to fight anymore."

"I don't doubt that, but when was the first time you shot a gun? When did you start your training? How many men have you killed? I don't know how much Lexy has told you about herself and her battle scars, but she has been training since before she was old enough to attend primary school. She was shooting a gun when most little girls were playing with dolls. She had her first kill at fifteen, and her hands weren't even shaking. She never shed a tear. It was instinct for her."

"She has told me a lot about her life and upbringing. But she doesn't have to do that anymore. The Brothers and I will protect her."

"Fuck, you're not listening to a word I'm saying. There is not one man in her life that she hasn't taken down, myself included. Obviously, she is handling you with kid gloves. This worries me, son. We have a battle coming with the Russians, and if you think for a second that you can lock her away somewhere and go into battle without her, you may be kissing her goodbye."

"No, I refuse to accept that. Lexy and I belong together. We are truly soulmates."

"Well if you really believe that, you need to take a long look at her skills and stop thinking with your dick. Stop seeing her as a helpless little girl. You need to think with your heart and mind. Because when that switch in her flips, there is no turning it off. Are you aware she has already warned the Benassi Family all of you are under *her* protection? None of you ever have to worry about anyone in that Family because they know her and fear her. They know not to cross her. I can promise you, when she is headed into battle, you'll see it in her eyes and in her mannerisms. You better wake up before she hands you your ass."

"We'll work this out. You'll see."

"I hope so son, because I'd never give my blessing to a man who wants to control her and refuses to accept her for who and what she is. To love her, is to accept *all* of her, even the parts you don't particularly care for, not try to make her into something she is not."

"I do. I just... I just... want her safe."

"Believe me, I do too. But I also know her better than you do. So, I'm telling you to watch her. Pay attention to her skills and abilities. Take her to the range and challenge her yourself. Put a wager on it. She'll never bet unless she is confident she can take you, and she will. Open your eyes and see her as the strong warrior she is, not the little woman you'd rather her be."

"I don't want to change her."

"Don't you? You just said you wanted her to stand down and hide with the women."

"That's different."

349

"Is it? Really? The Lexy I've known since she was born would never hide."

"*Fuck!* Sorry sir, I know you don't like swearing."

"You do not have to watch your language around me, but you do need to take a minute to think about what I have shared with you. Maybe you two need to slow this down, get to know each other better. I can make a few calls and we can handle this Russian issue ourselves. You don't know Lexy at all son. She has already made it known that no one in the Osokina Family will survive. She doesn't make that statement flippantly. She means it, and will see it carried out personally. They threaten the ones she loves, which is you and the Brothers. She's made an oath. Why do you think we're coming now? We know our girl. You won't have to worry about her in battle. We can handle this."

"*No!* Those Russians have put a price on my head as well as hers. We will do this together. Maybe you are right. I've been watching her train with the Brothers while I've been recouping, and she is good. But I know my men, and other than the tricks she can do with her grappling hooks, they are taking it easy on her. Maybe I should challenge my men more. If she wants to fight with us, we'll treat her like one of us. No kid gloves."

"Good. That is what she wants and needs. She talks highly of all of you. I am aware that any one of you, after you have watched her and learned her tricks, could probably take her in hand to hand combat. Remember, she doesn't fight by any rules, and if she knows you are being soft on her, she will not be gentle either. She'll bite, scratch, kick and use anything she can get her hands on to beat you. So be warned. But you also have to realize she's very wise and will not go into a battle alone. She knows her limitations. That is why she stays in the rafters, because of her incredible upper body strength and ability with a gun."

"I know, but maybe we can figure this out together. I

meant it when I told you that one day I plan on asking you for her hand in marriage. I just want to get past this threat first."

"Understood, but like you said, we will see. I wish you luck. I think you'll need it. But that isn't the only reason I wanted to talk to you. I needed to ask you how much do you think your family really knows about Little One's past life? I don't want to cross any lines. I am out of the Family business. I'm not involved in any of their criminal activities, not unless they are under direct attack or if Lexy needs me. But Luigi is still very much a part of the Family, and so are Rocco and Lucca. They have been informed not to mention anything. They are trying to clean up the businesses and make them more legit, but it isn't an easy task."

"I'm sure my mom has figured out a little, but my father is just doing web searches and I know you keep all that cleaned up. Neither of them know her real last name. Did you tell them yours?"

"No. I just introduced myself as her Uncle Louie, who basically raised her."

"I think after my dad meets you, hopefully we can get him to drop all of this. But even if he doesn't, his approval means nothing to me. My mom loves Lexy dearly. In fact, I think she'd take Lexy's side over mine," I inform him with a chuckle. I really believe that.

"I think that will be good for her. Lexy had Camilla and my mama in her life growing up, but they weren't her mother. Lexy needs some good motherly examples in her life. I don't know how much she told you about her own mother. Sophia loved Lexy with everything in her, but she had her own demons, and that is not my story to tell."

"I know about her mom battling depression all Lexy's life, and why. She told me some of it when we first met."

"Really? Hmm. Okay. It's nice to know she trusted you even back then because she usually doesn't talk about her mother, at all, with anyone. From what she has told me, there are a lot of mother figures she has gotten close to, and I'm glad for that."

"You can say that once the Camelot Brothers bring you into the fold, you will instantly get a lot of parental figures, whether you want them or not." Now I'm the one laughing, and Uncle Louie joins in.

"Glad to know. Let me wish you luck once again with Lexy, because you are going to need a lot of it. You'll figure it out, hopefully before it's too late. I'll text you a couple of different numbers in case you need me. Tony can always get in touch with me too. We'll talk again real soon. I will let you get to work yourself. It's been nice talking to you son. Oh, and please feel free to call me Lou."

"Thank you, sir, I mean Lou. I look forward to meeting you on Sunday. If you get to town sooner, please feel free to give me a call. We could meet up for coffee or something."

"Sounds nice." And with that, he disconnects.

Well shit. I've got all kinds of things racing in my mind. I've got to figure out a way to deal with this information and see if I can actually feel comfortable fighting with Lexy beside me. Damn. I know she is good, but... I've got a lot to think about on my drive to headquarters, because I am not going to lose her.

After checking on some clients, I call all the Brothers in for an emergency meeting at headquarters. I need to update them about Lexy's family heading this way. They need to know what to expect. Before I even realize it, most of the day has flown right past us. I think we all could use a full workout so I recommended we all hit the gym. We need to be ready and stay on top of our game. I do love the fact we don't have to go anywhere to work out. There isn't anything our headquarters lacks. When we build something, we build it right.

At times, a good workout can really help to clear my head. All the Brothers pair up and start different workouts. Stevens and Jackson begin working on their rope skills: climbing, swinging and jumping to the other ropes we have tied to the rafters. Some Brothers hit the machines or other equipment, while some spot each other with free weights.

Hawkins and I always prefer to start our workout by hitting the track at the top of the gym, where we can watch everyone. After our brisk forth lap, he gives me a head nod towards the inside. Sometimes Hawk can be a man of few words. I know his mind is wandering and worried as well. No need to question him. I know he's heading back to hit the web and see if he can find out anything about Lexy's family.

Walking out onto the training floor, I grab a weighted jump rope and try to build up my jumping speed. I'm still building the strength up in my leg, and I can feel the burn quickly. My leg is far from a hundred percent, but it is getting better every day.

I turn my head to see Lexy walk in. She puts her finger over her lips to make sure no one says anything. Then she slowly walks over to where Jackson and Stevens are being idiots, swearing and insulting each other, all while they're trying to kick or punch each other, determined to knock the other down from their rope to the protective nets we have hooked up to catch them.

Before I know it, Lexy grabs one of the climbing ropes and is up it before I can blink. Shaking my head, I can't believe her speed, or the fact that the guys haven't seen her. I'm wondering what she's up to. They are at least five feet from her, swinging around and completely oblivious. Shit! She leaps off the top of her rope like she's a damn chimpanzee and grabs ahold of Jackson's back. I watch as everyone stops their workouts and watches the show before us.

"Shit Lexy! Are you trying to kill me?" Jackson yells, grabbing the rope tightly and trying not to slip off.

"Come on Jackson, are you telling me you can't hold my weight, and yours? Are you such a weak-ass pussy! You couldn't climb and rescue someone like this?" Lexy teases him.

"I'm not a pussy! I just wasn't ready for you to jump my ass like that. See? I've got a good hold of the rope now. Want me to grab the next rope and hand you off to Stevens?"

Stevens starts swinging his rope towards them. "Come on Lexy, jump over here. I can catch you and take you to the floor. I wouldn't want that pussy to drop you," Stevens calls out.

"Nope, I know Jackson won't drop me. But I do want to see how well he can actually defend his rope while under personal attack," Lexy says, as she moves quickly, partially climbing up his body. Damn, my girl is fast and strong. I watch as she grabs ahold of the rope over his head and pushes the side of his face backward, hard. Oh shit, she isn't playing around. She's trying to make him lose his hold. Now I've gotta watch the show to see what she can do.

"Fuck! That hurt."

"It's called training Jackson! Suck it up and fight like a man, or do I have bigger balls than you do?" Lexy yells as she continues her assault on him.

Before you know it, she is actually punching him and Jackson is trying to block her hits, leaving him hanging onto the rope with just one hand, while he still has some of her weight on him. Lexy continues to climb over him, once she is holding on to the rope above his head, she uses her feet to kick and push on his shoulder. Damn. He leans back to dodge a foot to the face, causing him to lose his grip and he drops to the net below yelling "Mother fucker! You don't play fair."

"In battle, nothing is fair Jackson. You just have to be smarter than your opponent. Strength and size has nothing to do with it," Lexy calls down as all the Brothers are cheering for her, and the teasing begins on Jackson. Thank God we put those nets up.

"Haha Jackson, you just got schooled by a little girl. Again," Stevens taunts.

"You ready for this Stevens? You think you can knock me down?" Lexy calls out, as she starts swinging from one rope to the next like a goddamn monkey. Fuck! It makes me so nervous every time I watch her do this shit.

We have nine ropes tied to the rafters that they practice on. They are all spaced about six feet apart. Even with the net below them, it still doesn't stop my heart from racing. My girl does have incredible arm strength, but that knowledge doesn't calm me down one bit.

"Yeah, I do! How good do you think you can support my weight when I jump on your back?" Stevens calls back to her as he chases her from one rope to the other.

"You have to catch me first," she says, as she does an occasional spinning stunt to switch direction as she travels between the ropes. She's swinging way higher and faster than Stevens. You can tell he's a bit nervous and doesn't have the confidence she does, because his eyes are so focused on each rope as he transfers, to the next rope, unlike Lexy who isn't even looking at the ropes. Her eyes are on Stevens. She is that confident of each rope's placement. Shit.

"Oh, I'll catch you bitch, because I definitely have bigger balls than you do!" Stevens says just as Lexy lets go of her rope, spins in the air and grabs ahold of the top of Stevens' rope, about four feet above his head. She instantly kicks him hard in the arm and shoulder with both feet, pushing him backwards. That catches him completely off guard, causing him to release the rope and drop to the net, screaming, "Ooohhh, shit!"

"What was that you were saying about the bigger balls?" Lexy slows her swinging and starts laughing, watching Stevens bounce up and down in the nets below.

"Fuck you!" Stevens calls out, flipping her off as everyone starts barking insults at him and laughing. He quickly crawls over to the edge of the net and does a flip off of it as several Brothers greet him with punches and more insults.

Lexy looks over to me and throws me a kiss before releasing her rope and doing a double back flip before she hits the net bouncing, making me smile ear to ear. As scary as that shit is, damn that was beautiful and graceful. I walk over to her as she's crawling across the net to get down. I see a shocked look cover her face, before it breaks into a huge smile that makes me turn around to see what caused such a reaction. I see Tony and three other guys I've never seen before walking in, with Tiffany right beside them.

The second Lexy's feet hit the ground she runs right past me and leaps into the arms of the guy right beside Tony. He's smiling so big that one dimple shows on the side of his face. He's got messy black hair and is about 6'3 or so and a bit over two hundred pounds. I'm pulled out of my examination of this dude when Tony says, "Lex, I don't know if your old man wants you jumping into Luigi's arms like that," Tony continues to chuckle as he walks towards me.

"Riggs, Tony said both you and Lexy knew these guys were coming. They told me they were Lexy's family and wanted to meet you before her uncle arrives this weekend. Looks like you two forgot to tell me you were expecting guests," Tiffany says in a scolding tone with one eyebrow raised.

"Sorry Tiffany. I didn't know when they'd show, but thanks for letting them back."

"I was going to warn you, but Tony wanted to surprise Lexy," Tiffany says.

Tiffany really doesn't like surprises. My bad. I'll have to be better with this. Hoping to defuse this with her I say, "It's okay. You can see Lexy is thrilled they're here. Thanks for handling it like a champ. I'll be more understanding next time and make sure you know what's going down," I say with a chuckle.

So, these guys must be her old bodyguards, I think to myself. They start talking in Italian to each other so fast I can barely catch what they're saying. Lexy literally has her legs wrapped around Luigi's waist. He kisses her hard on the lips as he squeezes her ass.

Lexy pulls away and a smile spreads across Luigi's face as she says, "Smettila stronzo."

I watch as all three of the men just laugh, and even I know she just called him an asshole.

"Presentami al tuo ragazza," Luigi says, as he puts Lexy down and rolls his tongue under his bottom lip as he looks me right in the eyes and walks over to me. Oh shit, he just told Lexy he wants to meet me.

"Grayson, I'd like you to meet one of my best friends and old bodyguards. This is Luigi."

I smile at him and stick my hand out, and before I know what's happening, he punches me in the side of the jaw, causing me to bite my lower lip. Fuck! I didn't even have time to block him.

Lexy instantly attacks him, pushing him hard in the chest, "Per cosa cazza era?"

"Yeah, what the fuck was that for?" I repeat her.

"Well, well, your boy can speak a little Italian," Luigi says with a very heavy Italian accent.

"Come on Luigi, I'd hate to have to kick your ass here and now," Lexy says pushing him again.

I reach out grabbing her, pulling her away from him and into my arms. The two guys in the back are still laughing at the show.

"Did you really think I'd not punch this asshole of yours in the face when I met him? You were fucking fifteen when he made his move on you. I'm not blind. He wasn't a boy back

357

then. He was a hell of a lot older. What was he then, nineteen or twenty?" Luigi says looking between me and Lexy. Shit.

"Look, she was at our sister's high school graduation party, and as much as I like giving Riggs the perv shit for her being fifteen, you know damn well she didn't look fifteen back then. Yeah, I was there too but I didn't touch her or Lisa, so my ass is safe. Just stating the facts, bro." Stevens comes to my defense now, standing beside us. I'm pretty sure all the Brothers are slowly gathering around.

"That I can agree with. She didn't look fifteen. She didn't even look fifteen when she was twelve. I punched him on principle. And besides, I had to see Aless, rather Lexy, get pissed, knowing I busted his lip," he says looking between us, while I'm licking the blood from my lower lip. "Awww, will that make kissing a bit tough for you, Princess?" Luigi says sarcastically.

Lexy's head whips around to look at me. "He did bust your lip," she says as she lightly touches it before turning back around, fairly sparking in anger. "Luigi, do you want me to ruin your vacation? Because I'm halfway tempted to kick you in the balls, so you won't be able to have fun with your wife while you're here."

"Now, now Princess, you wouldn't want to do that. Sandy is ripe with my bambino and really enjoys messing around with her husband right now. That wouldn't be nice at all, and you'd have to explain it to her because I am sure she would also fully support me punching Grayson. In fact, she'd probably be a little pissed I didn't kick him in the nuts for making a move on you when you were just fifteen," he says with a big boyish smile.

"Fine. I'll let you slide for now. Let me introduce you to the Brothers real fast," Lexy says, stepping away from me and pointing to everyone individually as she says their name and they all respond with a chin lift. Then she says to the Brothers, "This is Luigi. He used to be my personal bodyguard but is now more like a brother to me. And these two big guys have been Family guards for as long as I can remember. This is Rocco and Lucca," she says with the biggest smile on her face as she walks over and throws her arms around each of them. They lift her off the floor and kiss her on the forehead, each cheek and then on the lips. I'm guessing that's a pure Italian thing.

I walk over to both them, hoping not to get punched this time. "It's very nice to meet you. I've heard a lot about you. You guarded her mother as well as her grandmother and helped her run the Villa in Northern Italy."

Rocco starts to shake my hand, but quickly acts like he might punch me, causing me to dodge and flinch before he slaps me on the back and shakes my hand with a deep chuckle. "Don't worry son, I'm not going to punch you. Luigi already showed you how we felt. You'd better treat Little One like the Princess she is."

Shaking his hand, I reassure him, "There is nothing you have to worry about. I'm madly in love with her. She's my world. There is nothing I wouldn't do for her."

Lucca sticks out his hand to shake mine. "Well, you better mean that, or you'll answer to us. And not many men live who have to answer to us. Just saying," he says with a smirk on his face. I have a feeling he isn't joking about that.

"Be nice you two. He's the love of my life, so you have to love him too. One day we'll all be family," Lexy says putting her arm around me.

"Well, that better wait until you walk down the aisle," Rocco says, looking between me and Lexy. Shit.

"Lexy, don't answer that," Tony says walking up to us. "Okay big guys, let's not go there. We aren't in the Stone Ages anymore, nor are we under Family law. Let's leave it at that. Let's live in our make-believe world when it comes to their relationship. You're wearing white when you and Grayson walk down the aisle, aren't you Lexy?" Tony puts his arm around the other side of her, letting them know he has her back too.

"Uncle Louie wouldn't have it any other way," she quickly responds, covering our asses.

The three of them, along with the Brothers, crack up laughing.

"Shit, this is going to be fun. You guys are easy to mess with. Uncle Louie already told us we couldn't kick your ass over taking her virtue. We have to save that for him," Rocco says and they start laughing again.

Oh fuck! They are clueless she has been with someone before me too. But shit, I'm not going to deny taking her virtue, because I'd never do something like that to her. Let them think whatever they want about us because I am sleeping with her now and there will never be another.

Lexy turns to me, "Don't worry baby, I can control Uncle Louie. He won't do anything. I'll just threaten him that I'll have a baby outside of wedlock and not be married by a priest if he touches you. That's his worst nightmare," she says with a giggle of her own.

I can't help but join in all the laughter around me as I pull her into my arms, lifting her off the ground. "Do you know how much I love you? And a little FYI, I can handle your uncle."

Then I start kissing her in front of her family, not giving a rat's ass about them or my busted lip.

"Okay, knock it off you two," Luigi says. Lexy pulls away and turns to him as he continues, "Lexy, we're going to leave and see you on Sunday night for dinner at the Riggs' home. I've made plans to take Sandy around to see the sights. Rocca and Lucca have Family business to handle. We don't need anyone to know we're all here together. They're going to make plans to start training with the Benassi Family starting next Monday."

"The Benassi Family? You battle with me and the Brothers," Lexy makes the statement quite firmly. They look between each other and smiles spread on their faces.

"Piccolo, non ti vendono da pari a pari. Non hai mostrato lora chi sei," Luigi says looking Lexy in the eye.

"They know me, I've been training with them the last few weeks. We can train with them."

"Stai giocando con loro. Hai davvero combattuto con loro?"

"Stop being rude. Several of the Brothers speak Italian. Speak to me in English. I have nothing to hide from them. And yes, I have fought with them and you know that. We fought in Italy years ago. I also just handed both Stevens and Jackson their asses on the ropes."

"Piccolo, Lou just talked with us moments ago, and he thinks your man has reservations about fighting with you. He'd rather hide you with the women. We need to be ready just in case. We cannot let yours or his emotions get in the way. We are not going to allow the Russians to get the upper hand. Are you standing down? Have you put away your training and become his piccola donna mantenuta?"

"I will never stand down. It is in my blood, and you know it. I am not now, nor will I ever be someone's little woman to hide," Lexy says looking between me and Luigi. Shit! I watch a smile spread across his face as he bumps Lexy hard in the shoulder with his own, knocking her back a bit as she stands her ground and returns his bump and shove with one of her own. She also gives him a fast punch in the gut that causes him to instantly double over and start coughing. The dude is chuckling.

"Good to see your fire. You need to show these men who you really are this week, no more of this figa merda. You take them down and show them the principessa guerriera della mafia."

Both Lucca and Rocca are standing at attention, nodding

in agreement. Lucca adds, "Yes, show them who the Warrior Princess is."

Then both him and Rocco pound the center of their chest over their heart with their fist, their heads practically bowed to Lexy. I think this must be some kind of honor salute or something. Then Luigi steps back away from her and all three of them do it again.

Lexy just nods at them, standing at attention too. "I vow to you, I will not stand down. No man will ever control me again. If a battle comes, we fight together, as we are Family." Lexy looks over to me as she says that, and I can hear a low rumble from the Brothers behind me.

"Okay... Okay enough of this. All of you put your dicks away. You too Lexy. We aren't in Italy anymore," Tony says, walking over to the center of them as he continues. "Luigi, don't you have to get back to your little woman yourself?"

"Yes, I do. I was hoping Lexy would come back with me and join us for a glass of wine. Sandy is pissed at me already because I wouldn't allow her to come with me now. She'd really like to see you before we head out," Luigi says, giving Lexy that boyish smile again and showing off his dimple. That really gets under my skin. I know he's married, but still.

"Oh, I'd love to. Can Grayson come with me? I'd love for Sandy to meet him," Lexy instantly replies. Her whole being is now relaxed like I didn't just see this little 'solemn vow' thing moments ago. My mind is racing, and I'm saved by Tony.

"Sorry Lexy, their meeting will have to wait till Sunday. Your man is needed with Hawkins and me. We found a little situation between Ginger and one of her Johns that needs his attention. I'll explain later if that is okay with you."

"Sure, fine. But I'm going to walk all of them out then run home and change really fast so I can meet up with Luigi and Sandy at their hotel. I'll see you tonight, and we'll talk then." Then Lexy throws her arms around me, leaping into my arms and wrapping her legs around my waist. She gives me a quick kiss then rests her forehead on mine, looking into my eyes. I can't help but squeeze her ass, as she whispers, "We talk seriously tonight. I need to explain things and make sure you and I are in agreement. I'll text you when I leave to see if you're here or at your home. Okay?"

"Sounds good, babe. I love you. Don't ever forget that."

"I love you too. Always!" she says as she jumps down and runs off towards her family. I watch as they head to the door, following Tiffany. They all seem so close, chatting up a storm. Luigi lets everyone walk out the door in front of him, where he pauses for a second just looking at me. He gives me a chin lift and leaves. Jesus, what just happened? I'm pulled out of my thoughts again by Tony.

"Shit. It's like stepping back in time. I don't really want to go back to that kind of Family life either. I thoroughly love my freedom. Fuck!" Tony says from beside me.

"Tony, I think it's time we talk. Let's head to the office."

"Yeah, I think so too."

And with that, Tony and I head inside to join Hawkins in the office. I don't know if I'm ready for this, but I got a gut feeling that shit just got real.

24

SECRETS YOU WOULD NEVER HAVE GUESSED

Grayson

*W*alking to the office with Tony beside me, I think this is the only time I've been with him that he hasn't been running his mouth. His quietness makes it obvious that he's nervous about something, and I get the feeling it's more than just a situation with Ginger. In reality, I'm glad he's quiet because I've got a lot of shit on my mind right now.

"I hope you don't screw this up with Lexy, 'cause I don't know if I'll be able to put her back together again. She's been living off a fantasy of you forever," Tony says softly as we reach the office door.

"Same goes for me, Tony. She's always been my fantasy." Placing my hand on the scanner, the door opens. I stand aside so Tony can walk in first. "After we go over this Ginger issue, I'd really like it if we could talk honestly. Man to Man."

"I was hoping you were willing to talk openly and honestly with me," Tony says pausing at the door for a second, looking me in the eye before walking in.

"We both need to be open and honest."

"I just hope you can handle it," Tony says before calling

out to Hawk, "I got the intel you wanted about Ginger's 'John'."

"Is he for real Tony?" Hawk says, looking up from his computer at our round table. He gives the wall monitors a quick glance to see what's going on all over the compound before looking back at us.

Tony grabs a chair, sitting down and putting his feet up on the table, making himself right at home as he starts talking. "Yup, this man is as serious as can be. He's willing to give Ginger one million dollars to have his baby and give him full custody of it. He will cover medical expenses on top of that. He doesn't care if it's a boy or a girl, he just wants it to be conceived the old-fashioned way. But come on, who can blame him there? He's got some bizarre hang ups about artificial insemination."

"What the fuck?!" I ask, whipping my head to Hawk.

"Yeah, Riggs, that is just what I thought at first. But we've done a thorough background check on the guy. He's legit. No skeletons in his closet that I could find."

"Why does he want Ginger to have his baby? And doesn't this fall under the… you know, selling a baby category?" Shit!

"He wants to hire her as a surrogate. It happens every day all over the place. We're just making sure it's all above board and legal. That's why I have an appointment with Mom Spencer and Ginger tomorrow, to go over all the family law shit. She is really thinking about it. What chick wouldn't give it a lot of thought?"

"But why Ginger?"

"She has the same coloring as his late wife. She died over three years ago of an aneurysm. They had been trying to have a baby for over five years without any luck. Ginger has already been tested and the doctors are confident if she does decide to do this, there shouldn't be a problem."

"Damn! Do you think she could have a baby and give it

away? It would be half her. It's not like she's carrying his wife's eggs."

"Well, there would be a lot of testing she would still have to go through, and naturally a contract, but we'll have to wait and see."

"I'll have to add my two cents in here," Tony says from his relaxed seat at the other side of the table. "This is one of those stories you just have to hear how it goes. I mean come on, a rich John wants her to have his baby for him to raise alone? It's a romance novel in the making. Dayum, as the ladies would say."

We all crack up laughing for a minute before I turn to Tony and our eyes lock. The laughter ends all of a sudden. Hawkins looks between us.

"Okay, what else are you two wanting to talk about? Because by the look on both your faces, I'd say it doesn't have anything to do with Ginger," Hawkins says.

"Yeah, I'm hoping Tony can help enlighten me with a few things about Lexy and her family." Tony doesn't respond, he just studies me very intently.

"Don't hold your breath on Tony telling you anything we don't already know. I've been trying to find out about them for months and you know I come up with jack shit, so unless Tony is willing to tell us who he is and share their secrets, we're up shit creek without a paddle," Hawkins says, swaying his chair back and forth.

Chuckling, Tony says, "Glad to know you aren't as good as I am in your research. I knew all about the twelve of you and your families before Lexy even got here."

"That's because we can't erase ourselves from the World Wide Web like you can. Our families have businesses and are members in country clubs and shit. I can't erase all that. But believe me, there is still a lot the Brothers of Camelot security have done you know nothing about," Hawkins defends.

"I wouldn't be sure about that, because there is a good chance, I know it. Come on, you know I'm better than you."

"Fuck you! And for your information, I knew who Lexy was before she told Riggs. But you, on the other hand… are the real mystery. Your real name is no more Tony Jarvis than mine is Santa Claus, and everywhere I search, I come up with a dead end."

"Will you ever trust us enough to tell us who you really are?" I ask.

Tony takes his feet off the table and runs his fingers through his messy black and white tipped hair, tilting his head to the side and biting his lip before he finally speaks. Turning to Hawkins, he asks, "Can you lock that door to where no one, not even another Brother can come in?"

"Yeah, easily." Hawkins quickly looks down at his computer, clicking away like a fiend, and within five seconds, clicking fills the room and metal doors slide out from the walls, covering each of the exits and locking into place. "See, I have a lot of cool toys here. Nothing can get through those doors, not even plastic explosives. You should know me by now. We've gotta have plenty of safe rooms, just in case."

"Lexy and I have them everywhere too. I completely understand," Tony replies.

"Now, why such privacy?" Hawkins asks.

"Because I want a vow, a solemn oath from both of you that anything I say in here will not be repeated to anyone, and that includes the rest of the Brothers. If you can't make that pledge, then I tell you nothing. I know you are both men of your word. I also know, even if there is no real leader of the Brothers of Camelot, you two are really the brains behind a lot of it."

Hawkins and I look to each other and he gives me a head nod. "Okay Tony, we both swear an oath, just as solemn as the oath you share with Lexy," I tell him, looking straight into his eyes.

"First of all, you need to really understand that Lexy and I were raised completely different than any of you. We were brought up knowing what was expected of us. We were both, as you would call, it 'Mafia Royalty'."

"So, you belong to a different crime Family in Italy?" Hawkins interrupts him to ask.

"Yes, I did, but not anymore. You could say the Canzano Family… no, I take that back. You can say Alessandra Sophia Canzano ended my Family's reign and took it over completely by killing most of them, including my father."

"Holy Shit! Did you just imply Lexy killed your father?" I ask. He has got to be kidding!

"Nothing to imply. She did, and I'm very glad of it."

"Fuck!!" Hawkins and I both say in unison, glancing over at each other as Tony continues.

"I know that's a bit shocking, knowing how close Lexy and I are now, but my father was an evil, evil man." Tony leans forward, resting his forearms on the table and inhaling deeply before looking over at me with his head cocked. "Riggs, you met Lexy's Papa when you were in Italy. Lexy has told you how much of a controlling dickhead he was over her. He looks nice compared to mine. Let me back this up and tell you a little about my life and Family growing up. But remember this never gets repeated, especially to Lexy. *Do I make myself clear?!* Capisce?!" Tony says with a heavier Italian accent then I've ever heard from him.

"My word is as good as yours. I will take the things shared in this room to the grave," I reassure him.

"Me too man. I swear it, and I'll even go a step further. After today, I'll be as open and honest with you too. I'll personally tell you everything about my life story because I have a gut feeling your life was as fucked up as mine, but in a different way. I've never told this shit to anyone outside of the Brothers, but they were there beside me during all of it. If you're baring your soul like this, I think I can trust you too."

"You're damn straight I can be trusted. Like I said before, I've never told this to anyone. Not even my mother or sisters know all I've been through. And before you ask," Tony says looking over to me again, "I have only told your sister bits and pieces, not my whole life story. And honestly, I don't know if I will ever tell her."

I just nod, not knowing what else to say about that. I know how different Lexy's life was from mine, but Tony? So many questions are rushing into my head. How much does he love my sister? If he tells me something, I think is important, can I keep it from her? I need to hear him out, either way. Maybe it can help me figure more out about Lexy and how to keep her safe too. A rush of emotions and a bit of fear about what he's about to share hits me. I hear Hawkins continue.

"And Tony, if I believe you are being honest and answer any questions we have, you and I will be equals going forth. No secrets. We'll work and help each other, together," Hawkins says and my head whips to him. Jesus, is he for real? He's practically bringing Tony on board without even talking to us about it. What the hell am I in for? Shit! This oath just got real.

"When you're the oldest male in an Italian Family and your Papa is the Capo, like mine, from my earliest memory, I've known my place. You must learn, train and be ready to take over for your Papa when he is ready to hand over the reins, or should he get killed. That is just how things are done. Here's a great example. Let me guess, you two got bb guns for Christmas when you were what, seven or eight?"

Hawkins and I look over at each other chuckling, remembering our childhood before I answer, saying, "Well, Stevens' dad got us bb guns when we were eight and made sure we went through all the safety training and precautions. How old were you?" I ask, hoping we have something in common.

"I was only five when my Papa took me out and taught me how to shoot my Nonno's little Beretta 950. I mean my grandpa's gun. By six, I got my first Beretta Tomcat, and by seven, I was ordered to shoot my uncle, because he was gay. He was the only man in my Family I ever loved. He'd always sneak into my room and play with me. From my youngest memories, my only happy times were with him. I can still remember all the Lego Star Wars sets we built together. We'd play for hours on end, pretending to be superheroes with capes in the woods behind our home. As long as none of the men saw us, we were fine. I could play around him and be an average boy." Tony looks at the ground and rubs his face.

"Fuck, are you serious? Seven? Shooting your uncle?" I'm just blown away. Jesus. Was Lexy's life like this as well? He was just a boy! Thinking back to our childhood, we couldn't even go hunting until we were thirteen and had proven we were mature enough to even handle a real gun.

Tony lifts his head and looks on the verge of losing it, "Come on Grayson, in most crime Families, being homosexual is unforgivable. If your own blood Family doesn't handle you, when you're caught by another member of the Family, not only you, but your lover as well, will be tortured and killed. That is why most Families kill their child first, wanting to spare them some of the pain."

"I still remember walking into the house with my Papa after my daily training and shooting practice on the Family range, when we saw my Uncle Augusto kissing a Family guard. My Papa instantly shot and killed the guard. Then he started beating the shit out of his youngest brother, calling him a fag and such. Then he turned and ordered me to my room, telling me not to say a word about what I saw.

"The next night, my Papa took me behind the Family mausoleum, where my beaten and naked uncle was being held up by two guards. Once they saw us, they released him and walked away, leaving him barely standing, trembling uncontrollably by a fresh-dug grave. My father started yelling at him and said how he disgraced the Family and deserved to die. I watched my uncle weep and beg for us to kill him and put him out of his suffering, since his brother had already murdered the only man he'd ever loved.

"After that, all I remember is my Papa handing me my gun and telling me to shoot on the count of three." Tony hangs his head once again, running his fingers through his hair. Hawkins and I just sit there listening, occasionally looking at each other in horror.

"I did as I was told, in fear of my own life. I purposely aimed for his feet. But what could I do? I was seven and had to obey. I still miss him today." Tony just hangs his head. God, what do I do? What can I say after that? He was fucking seven years old.

"You could say I shot my first person at seven, when you and the Brothers hadn't even shot a bb gun yet," he says in a soft voice, looking between both of us, I'm sure trying to hold his shit together and change the subject. His eyes are watery from unshed tears that he is determined to hold back, as he continues.

"Lexy's whole life was like mine. Nothing but preparation to take over as Capo Donna, but much harder because she was a girl. She started formal training at six and had her first kill at fifteen. The first person she took out was one of my Family members. His goal was to sneak onto the Canzano shooting range dressed as one of their Family and take out the Capo. But he didn't have a chance. Once Lexy saw him, that switch in her flipped and she dropped him with only two bullets. Rumor has it, her hands weren't even shaking, and she never shed a tear. Not like any typical teen girl you knew growing up, huh?"

Tony just looks between Hawk and me. We're both just shaking our heads, not saying a word. God, I honestly couldn't imagine a life like theirs. It's so hard to believe that the stunning beauty with those enthralling eyes that altered my life forever, killed someone mere months after we met.

I'm pulled back into the now, when Tony starts speaking again.

"On my thirteenth birthday, my father sent my mother and sisters away for the weekend. He told them I was a man now and needed to celebrate with the men in the Family. We all had a fabulous dinner and all the men treated me with honor. They saw me as a man, not a boy. Wine flowed freely. After dinner, I watched as lots of women came in, all of them barely dressed. Before my eyes, it rapidly became an all-out orgy. What thirteen year old boy wouldn't want to watch that?

"My father had two very beautiful Family whores take me to my bedroom, where they both seduced me. They spent the rest of the weekend in my bedroom, doing everything for me, and to me. There was a constant flow of wine and pot. They kept getting me aroused as often as they could and then encouraging me to have sex with them, every way you could think of. Just how every guy wants to lose his virginity, right?

"Occasionally, even my Papa would come in to make sure I was having fun. He'd gloat at how much of a man I was now. Sometimes he'd grab a chair in my room and watch us as he'd whack off. Yeah, I bet your thirteenth birthday wasn't as fun filled as that now was it? Didn't I have a great father? And that's only part of it." Tony's accent is still heavy, and even though he spoke sarcastically, I notice his hands shaking as he would randomly tap his fingers on the table. Damn, his life was fucked up. I can tell this is difficult for him to talk about. I need to lighten the mood.

"Hell, no. My mom took all of the Brothers to play laser tag at a gaming center. Yeah, you could say our lives were very different growing up. Stevens' dad finally took us older boys hunting for my actual thirteenth birthday. It was a fun filled weekend of camping and hunting, but it was more like shooting coke cans off rocks. But according to him and Jackson's dad, we were finally becoming young men, worthy enough to shoot a real gun. That was a lot different from yours for sure," I say, hoping to get Tony to relax some.

"That's nothing. When I was fifteen and wanted to start dating, my Papa refused to allow me to get into any real relationship with a girl close to my own age. He said since I was quiet and on the sensitive side, he was afraid I'd fall for one of them. I grew tired of fucking club whores and was finding it difficult to just get it up and randomly perform when my Papa felt I needed to fuck someone. So, my wonderful Papa had the shit beat out of me and then I was raped by his two personal guards. He said he had to make sure I would never get turned on by a man and become a fag like his little brother whom we'd had to kill. Great parenting, huh?"

Hawkins and I just sit there in complete and utter shock. Tony is sitting there with his head lowered, taking slow deep breaths. One of his legs is bouncing with nerves. What father has his own son raped at fifteen, by two men that work for him? *Fuck!* This is some messed up shit. I could have never imagined this. Now I can understand why he wanted his father dead.

Hearing Hawkins clearing his throat, I look over to him as he asks, "Can I ask what your old name used to be? Was it Caza?"

Tony chuckles and lifts his head to look at Hawkins, "Yeah man, you're looking at the man who used to be Pietro Caza. It wasn't just my life my father fucked with, he also screwed around on my mom and planned on marrying off my older sister when she was eighteen to a forty five year old man, one of the guards that raped me. Thank God Lexy killed him before that happened. He would have regularly beaten and raped her into submission with my Papa's blessing. See, in my Family, marriages were always arranged by my Papa and my Nonno before him. That is one of the jobs of the Capo.

"Did you know I hacked into Al Canzano's computer and let Lexy know every man that was on his short list of men he was considering as her possible husband? Not only was I on there, but Luigi, who you just met was, and a couple of other guys who were far from worthy of her. Oh, and a few times he had Rocco and Lucca on his little list of potential husbands for her. But once he mentioned it to them, they refused and demanded to be removed. Lexy and I used to laugh about it all the time. That was when she told me about you, and that no way in hell would she ever marry any of them. She'd kill her own papa first she said, and I believe she would have."

Thank fuck he never married her off to any of them. But it does make me wonder, did Tony and Luigi crush on her, knowing her father wanted one of them to marry her? I shake my head, none of that matters now. Lexy is mine. That life is far behind her and she's never going back to it. Hearing Tony's voice again, it pulls me out of my thoughts.

"Let me take you back a little bit into why our Families were at war. You see, her papa was supposed to marry my aunt, so when Al fell in love with and married Sophia, war was on. That marriage went against all our principles. Sophia wasn't Italian and his marriage to my aunt was arranged when they were children. You are never to go against something arranged like that, especially with an outsider. That rarely ever happens, even today.

"The first battle left my Nonno dead, along with half the family. My father instantly became Capo. At that moment, he made a vow to the Family that he would not rest until he disgraced Al Canzano and made him suffer. His goal was to kill Sophia, but my family missed and killed her sister, Elena, at her engagement party to Lou, years later. Sophia watched her sister die, which put her into labor early, causing her to lose her baby, Al Junior, days later. That is how Sophia was broken. After that, Al was obsessed with his revenge to kill even more of my Family. The hatred went deep. Their family grew bigger and stronger while mine rapidly faded."

Now I interrupt him, "So under your Family's orders, not

only did Elena get murdered, but years later, they murdered Lexy's mother?"

"Yeah, on Lexy's sixteenth birthday. That is why she hates celebrating them. Remember, she was shot for the first time at her Family's celebration of crowning her Princess at six. That was the day Al announced she'd be taking over from him one day, being the first female Capo Donna. Oh, and don't forget, she got the shit beat out of her by her papa at her fifteenth birthday celebration. But let's first talk about that sixteenth birthday party. That is more important. Has she told you about it?"

"She told me she killed a lot of men that day, because they shot and killed her mother who died in her arms. I'm assuming now that the Capo she killed was your father?"

"Well, she told you more than I thought she would. But let me tell you how we met. I'm sure Lexy doesn't even know what happened a month before her birthday, and I'd rather we all take this to our graves, because it would serve no purpose for her to know this now.

"Like I said before, my papa was a dumbass, and I knew Al would never go along with this. He actually called a meeting with all of Italy's Family Capos and requested that the Capo of the Canzano Family hear him out. He talked about ending the war and forgiving Al for the humiliation he caused my Family, if he'd agree to marry me and Lexy. Naturally, Lexy's papa laughed in my father's face in front of all the other Capos. Al said he'd rather see my father dead, that he would never forgive him for Sophia losing their son and for mentally destroying the first woman he ever loved. He blamed my father and rightfully so.

"That was it, my father told every man in the Family to prepare for war. He demanded I stay with the women and children in one of our warehouse's safe rooms with over a dozen men to guard us. He completely underestimated the Princess of the Canzano Family, your Lexy. Al had bragged about her abilities for years, but no one believed him until that day.

"I have no idea how many men Lexy killed before she got to the warehouse, but I'm sure it was a lot. She only brought four men with her: Luigi, Lou and two other Family members. They annihilated us. As I told you before, my father was a dumbass. He sent close to a hundred men to attack and kill as many as possible in the Canzano Family. Women, children, he didn't care. He even put a million dollar reward on Lexy and her mom's head. Our men didn't stand a chance against hers.

"But let me tell you, I've never experienced fear in my life like I did that day. It started when Lexy burst into the downstairs safe room. I pulled my gun on her with shaking hands. She just stood there and told us all to be quiet, and no one would be hurt. I don't know how she heard him over the women and children's cries and screams, but she suddenly turned around and shot and killed my personal guard who appeared behind her in the hallway. It was unbelievable to see. Perfect accuracy, right between the eyes. When she turned back and looked at me with those piercing blue eyes, I asked her, 'You're the Canzano Princess aren't you?' All she said was, 'Yes. Now, do you want to die today? Put down your gun before I'm forced to do something I'll regret in front of your mother and little sister.' She spoke in such a calm tone. She wasn't shaking or anything, and she was covered in blood. And I mean *covered*."

"Holy Hell! I need a drink and I'm sure as fuck you do too. What's your poison?" Hawkins asks, running his fingers through his hair before standing up and walking over to the bar.

"I'd love a glass and a bottle of grappa," Tony says looking over at me, giving a head nod.

"Sounds good. Grab me a glass as well."

"Can you handle your grappa?" Tony asks with a smirk on his face.

"Yes, I can, and right now I need it," I quickly respond. Shit. I think I may need this more than he does. My gut is tied in knots just imagining all of this.

Hawkins walks over with a whiskey on the rocks in one hand and a bottle of grappa in the other, which he puts in front of Tony. Tony opens the bottle and quickly pours himself a glass, downing it instantly before pouring me one and sliding it over to me. He sets the bottle between us. I can see his hand is still shaking, and I'll be damned if mine aren't shaking as well.

"As I was saying, she started telling all of us how horrible my Family was, shooting women and children. Then she told us that one of our men killed her mother, and she had died in her arms." Tony looks me right in the eye. "She wasn't crying. Her hands were steady. She was calm and cool like nothing had happened, even though her mother had just died in her arms. Realization hit me that she was no typical teenaged girl. She was a woman, a true warrior. Once she told me that, I put my gun down and kicked it over to her. I knew she was invincible in that moment. She was on a mission and nothing would stop her." Then he pauses and slowly takes another drink before turning away from me and continuing.

"Anyway, she ended up getting my mother to take her to my father. Within moments of her leaving, the shooting upstairs ended. That is when I really got scared. I didn't know what to expect when her men came down to us. I knew I was as good as dead because that's the rule of the Family. You are supposed to eliminate the bloodline, and that was me, and her men knew it. When the door busted open, this time it was Lou, Luigi, Antonio and Vito, Al Canzano's first guard. I knew protocol. I was about to be executed in front of everyone, proving they were the ones in control. So, I got on my knees and bowed my head, showing my submission."

"Fuck, this is worse than a goddamned Mafia movie because this is your fucking life. Jesus. I would have pissed myself for sure," Hawkins says getting up to get himself a refill. He just grabs the whole bottle and comes back to the table. "Sorry, Tony. Please go on."

"It's okay man," Tony says chuckling, as he pours himself another glass of grappa and drinks it down like a man dying of thirst. I grab the bottle and pour myself another as well. Shit, this grappa is affecting me more than Tony, that's for sure. I've been so busy today that I've only had protein drinks. No real food, since Lexy's fixed me breakfast this morning. Fuck it, I think as Tony continues.

"As I'm on my knees, I know Vito, Antonio and Luigi have their guns aimed at me, as my little sister wraps her arms around me crying *'Please don't! Get up Pete! Get Up!'* but I stayed there as I heard my Aunt Olga call to her, *'Come here sweetheart. Come to Auntie,'* Lou's strong voice called out *'Stand down'.*

Vito instantly replied, *'He must die!'* But Lou said *'No! I'm in charge. I'm second in command under the Princess, not you. You answer to Al. Now shut the fuck up and stand down before I put a bullet in you.'* And Vito, to my surprise, did as Lou ordered.

Then I watched out of the corner of my eye as every bone in my body shook. Lou squatted down to my little sister and asked her, *'Is this your brother Pietro?'*

She just nodded her head as tears fell from her eyes. I didn't want her to be scarred for life by seeing me murdered in front of her. Then Lou asked her, *'Is Pietro a good big brother? Does he play with you? Does he read your stories?'* as he wiped away her tears.

Viviana nodded her head as her little quivering voice burst out, *'Yes! He's the bestest brother. He plays with me all the time. He plays Barbie too. He even made my Barbie a royal cape so she could be a real Princess too.'*

'Is he like your Papa?' Lou asked her.

"*No! My Papa is a mean, mean man. He likes to hit all of us. If you want to kill somebody, go kill him.'*

I could hear some of the women snickering, as well as his men's deep chuckle. '*What is your name?*'

'*Viviana*'

'*Well Viviana, I don't think you have to worry about that, because our Princess Alessandra will take care of your Papa. He will not be around to hurt you or anyone else. You can keep playing with your big brother, and I hope he stays your best friend for many years to come.*'

I felt tears run from my eyes as I watched my little sister run over and hug him. You know you have to be one bad son of a bitch when even your youngest daughter, who's just shy of six, doesn't even care if you're killed.

Then Lou stood back up beside me and told me, '*Stand up son*.*"* Tony looks between me and Hawk a couple of times before he says, "He called me son. My heart was breaking. He looked me in the eye and said, '*You know as of now, all of you are a part of the Canzano Family, not quite the way your Papa and Capo wanted, but that's okay. None of you women have to worry about anything. Give yourselves time to heal, because odds are, your husbands aren't coming home. You won't live lavishly but your bills will be paid. If you have jobs, keep them, if you want one, that will be arranged for you. You all know how this goes. If you want no part of this Family, I recommend you disappear within the next forty eight hours.*'

"Then I was never more shocked in all my life, when he flipped around his gun and handed it to me saying, '*If Little One doesn't call me in the next twenty minutes I'm asking you to put a bullet in my head, because that young lady is my sole reason for living and I do not want to live a day without her.*' I could not believe any of this. I never thought my life would be spared, nor did I ever think I'd see the powerful Lou Canzano look like a broken man, asking me to end his life if Aless didn't call him. I could hear my heart pounding in my ears as we all just waited quietly for his phone to ring.

"It seemed like eternity before it did. It felt like the weight of the world was lifted off my shoulders the moment his cell phone rang. For the first time in my life, I knew I was *free*. All the gray clouds rolled away and it felt like the sun was shining on me for the first time in my life, as I heard Lou's voice talking, *'Princess, are you okay?'* I knew she was okay and had completed her mission. My father was dead. Then I heard Lou say, *'Don't hyperventilate on me, okay? I need you.'* He was pacing back and forth as he spoke to her, then he yelled at Luigi to get my home address, and within seconds, they were all running out the door to get to her.

"Once they were gone, I told the women to take their children and get home, and that if they knew what was best for them and their children, they would submit to the Canzano Family. I explained to them how to get out from the underground exit. I didn't want them going upstairs and seeing all the carnage of the dead men. I made my little sister leave with my aunt and reassured her I'd be there shortly.

"The moment they were all gone, I rushed out of there and up to the main office. I had to get on the computer and get that camera feed. You know what that's like Hawkins. I watched Aless from cameras she didn't know were there. I could see her very clearly. As the adrenalin rush of the battle left her, she just sat there on the side of our garage. She still wasn't crying. When Lou pulled up, he leapt from the SUV with a blanket in hand and swept her up and into his arms like a small child. I got a good look at her face, and still no tears.

"Grayson, she is a true warrior. You have to believe me. She can handle this battle and whatever else may come before her, but I don't think she can survive losing you, nor will she be able to submit and stand down to you. That giving up of power is not in her DNA. When that internal switch is flipped, there is no turning it off till the battle is over."

"I believe you Tony, but she doesn't have to be like that anymore. She has me, and she isn't losing me either. She has the Brothers. We'll take care of her. Both of you, your lives have been living hell. You don't have to do this anymore," I stress to him, hoping he realizes he doesn't have to fight anymore either. He's a free man. He can stay with the IT shit and not actually fight.

"You don't get it. It is *who she is!* It's in her blood. It's in her every fiber," Tony stresses shaking his head, his eyes filled with tears. "She will not stand down. I saw it when we went to the Benassi Family. She isn't Lexy right now, she is the Warrior Princess preparing for battle. Don't push her or that switch will flip, and if it does, God help you because I will stand by her."

"I can handle Lexy. Don't worry about that."

"Do you still have the tapes? Of course, you do. You're just like me," Hawkins states.

"Yeah, I have them all. No one but me has ever seen them. But believe me, I've watched her shoot those two raping assholes over and over again, blowing the backs of their fucking heads off. And for your information, I felt damn good seeing that happen. I've even watched her rid the world of my evil father more than once, and I felt no remorse or guilt there either. Go ahead and think I'm a sick mother fucker all you want, but it gives me peace. I have no fear of anything because all of them are dead. I'll forever be in debt to Lexy. I owe her my life. She will forever be my hero. My salvation," Tony says as he wipes a tear from his cheek. "Fuck it! She has a bigger dick than I do. I'm the emotional pussy right now. But it does feel good to tell someone else the secrets I've kept to myself all these years."

"Can I see them?" Hawkins asks. My head whips to him, shocked as shit he wants to see them. I think to myself that Tony should destroy them so he never has to relive any of it and can begin to heal. Shit.

"Hawk, Brother, why the hell do you want to see them? Maybe Tony is beginning to heal and that could open his wounds all over again," I say, stressing to Hawkins.

"No. We aren't wired like you are," Hawk says just staring at Tony.

"Later, as you said before. Today puts us on equal ground," Tony says with a chin lift to Hawkins.

"Thanks Brother," Hawk says with another head nod to him, as they both polish off another glass. Geesh. I could use another myself, so I pour myself one.

"I really think you need to listen to me, Riggs. She has handed many a man their balls. She knows no bounds, and when challenged, she does not obey any rules. When we battle, I have her back and she has mine. We learned from our first encounter with the Russians. We never separate from each other anymore. She leads and I am always right behind her, making sure no one is at her back. Trust us. They'd have to take me out first. She's not stupid. She leads. She's not busting in the front doors, she comes in the back, eliminating anyone trying to escape and herds everyone to the men on the front line for them to take care of. She knows what she is doing. You need to figure out a way to deal and be an equal."

"Tony, I don't know if I can do that."

Both Tony and Hawkins say together, "Figure it out."

"What the hell? You two are thinking alike now? Hawk, you know I can protect her."

"Riggs, I've known you all my life, and I'm going to tell you, in all honesty, that sometimes you can be a stubborn asshole. If you love her, don't fuck this up."

"I won't. She's my forever. I could not continue life without her. She's the reason my heart beats. I have to guard and protect her."

"Riggs, listen to me," Tony says, leaning forward and resting his forearms on the table again. "Let me tell you how intense her training was. There was nothing in her life that wasn't centered around training. Not only is she a marksman, she's also is incredible with a knife, sword or any form of blade. She has trained in, and mastered, several martial arts. She was taught that anytime she walks into a room, she needs to be prepared for battle. Her eyes will scan the room, looking for exits, who's the weakest and who's the strongest in the room, and what she can turn into a weapon."

He throws his head back into the chair and looks up to the ceiling, running his fingers through his hair again before looking back at me. "I can't believe I'm about to tell you this. She'd hand me my balls for sure. Okay, the first time I've ever seen Lexy let her guard down was when she performed at your club. She was relaxed, smiling freely. Her eyes never searched the room once. She even had on shoes that had a strap around her ankles."

"What the fuck? What do you mean, straps around her ankles?" I'm completely lost.

"Her eyes didn't scan the room, looking for an escape route, or what she could use as a weapon. She wore shoes that had straps around her ankles, something her uncle would never allow. You see, Lexy had to train for months in high heels before she was allowed to wear them off the compound. She had to be able to run, fight and climb in them. If she couldn't preform the challenges, she had to kick the shoes off. You cannot kick off shoes strapped around your ankles. She knows when she is with you, she is safe. For the first time in her life, she trusts someone else with her safety, and you don't even know it."

"I would never let anything happen to her. I'd take a bullet for her in a heartbeat."

"She would do the same for you, and she has proven it over and over again."

"Riggs, Brother. I really think you should think about this. We've seen how good she is the last few weeks. She's worked with every one of the Brothers. Look how good both Stevens and Jackson are with the ropes now. She's kick-boxed with us. Hand to hand combat as well. I worked out with her more than any of you. She knows her shit. You're going to hate to hear this, but you need to listen to what Tony has to say. Brother, he's warning you. You might not want to push her."

"Hawk, I can handle Lexy. I'll talk reasonably with her. And be honest, you weren't given it your all. None of you were. You were being soft on her because she's my woman. Every one of us could hand her her ass and you know it. Come on. Do you mean to tell me Lexy can really kick your ass?" I ask Hawk, rolling my eyes as I finish off my glass of grappa and putting it down a little harder than I should have.

"I honestly don't know. She was an excellent, sparring partner. She gave me a damn good workout and kept me on my toes, caught me off guard a couple of times too. But we weren't really fighting to kill each other. With her mixed training, I'll admit that she might be able to take me. I don't know. And guess what - I don't really want to go there."

Shaking my head, I cannot believe Hawkins thinks Lexy might be able to take him. He's got at least fifty pounds on her. The thought of her beating him makes me want to laugh. Just then, all our phones chime. That is never a good thing. Saying a fast prayer and hoping it isn't the Russians, I pull my phone out of the pocket of my lose gym shorts. Shit, I was going to take a shower and get dressed and here I am, still in these nasty shorts and tank top. Looking at my cell, I see a mass text to all the Brothers from Lexy. Hell, she has called a meeting in the gym in thirty minutes. What the fuck is she up to?

"Oh, fuck! She's been with Luigi all this time. He has probably got her questioning your guys' abilities about going into battle beside her against the Russians," Tony says, shaking his head now.

"Do you really think she'd go after the Russians without us?"

"If she thinks for a minute that you don't trust her and continue to think of her as anything but your equal, hell yeah. As she said earlier, all she'd have to do is make a couple of phone calls and we could handle them without you guys, and she knows it."

"Shit, that can't happen."

"Grayson, I mean it, stop thinking with your dick and heart. Think with your mind. Don't destroy what the two of you have over your male ego. She's better than you give her credit for," Hawkins stresses to me.

What the fuck! Is Hawk really turning on me? Lexy is a little thing. Yeah, she is good, but... but... damn, I should have eaten something. All this grappa is beginning to mess with my head. I'm getting pissed. Turning to Tony, I have to ask, "Dude, what do you think this meeting is for?"

"What do you think? She's going to challenge you. She has to make you see," Tony says, standing up, continuing to shake his head. Damn, that boy can put away his grappa like no other. I guess it is an Italian thing. I've got to grab some water and a bite to eat so I can clear my head.

"Tony, I can handle Lexy and her challenge. If I have to hand her, her ass and humiliate her in front of the Brothers, I will. You've all been handling her with kid gloves, and you know it."

"Riggs... Brother... I don't think you want to go there," Hawk says as he starts typing on his computer. Seconds later, we hear the doors unlocking and sliding back into the wall.

We all get up and start heading towards the meet up with Lexy and the Brothers in the gym. The grappa has gone to my head, all kinds of things are rushing around in it. I need to decide how I should handle this with Lexy. Should I just grab her and toss her to the ground and show her how easily I can take her down and make her cry uncle? Shit!

I overhear Hawk talking to Tony, "Thanks Ton, for sharing and giving us insight into both of your lives. It does answer a lot of questions. We'll talk more later. I promise, all of this stays between us."

"Thanks Brother. And Grayson, think first and make sure every move is worth it," Tony says to me.

"I got this." And I sure hope like hell I do.

25

THE PRINCESS WARRIOR RETURNS
WITH REGRETS

Lexy

"*H*ello, I have a meeting with the Brothers..." I barely finish my sentence before Tiffany interrupts me.

"Damn Lexy, I would never think that was you. You do look like a stout man in that. Shit, it hides all your curves, and your voice is different too. Thank God Sarah warned me, or I would have pushed the security button so the Brothers would know someone unknown was here," Tiffany says looking me up and down from over the counter at the entrance of the Brothers of Camelot headquarters.

Out of the corner of my eye, I notice the hidden separation panel slide open. Walking in, I see Sarah, who quickly walks up beside me and we make our way past several desks. Heads turn and look my way. Tiffany is telling Brenda something as we pass her and head down a long hallway and up some stairs to the gym.

Sarah has been such a good friend. We've become very close over the last few months. She helped Tony update my uniform to make it look more like the Brothers and less like the Family now. Sarah and her designing skills have come in so handy in helping Tony. They really are a good combination. She has a big smile on her face, I'm sure from being proud of her work. I'll never understand why the Brothers keep the women in the family out of everything. They could be such a good asset for them if they'd just get over their outdated male dominant way of thinking that they should rule the world.

"Come on, Tiffany, you know you'll be the one to get us in the gym. Sarah is still banned from the area for some insane macho reason," I call behind us through my mask, still a little shocked at how much of a man I sound like wearing this. Tiffany picks up her long gypsy skirt and runs to catch up with us.

"I'm coming. I just had to make sure Brenda took over the front end for me. She was asking who you were, and naturally, I told her nothing for now. We'll explain everything to them later. You completely fooled everyone down here," Tiffany says as she makes her way towards us.

I can't help but be thankful for Tony's pure genius abilities. He's done such a wonderful job with all the battling toys he's made for me over the years, and tonight I'm going to show them all off. I'm really looking forward to this too. We stand to the side for Tiffany to get in front of us.

"I personally think Tony did a fantastic job with your outfit and gear. I think Hawkins is going to be a tad bit jealous. But I'm sure after you show off, those two will be huddled in a corner somewhere talking techno-geek shit." Sarah says as Tiffany finally makes it past us.

"I can't wait to examine it myself and see how heavy it is. I mean, I've felt the guys' bulletproof vests and they aren't that heavy, but they are kind of bulky. I can tell when they have it on," Tiffany adds as we reach the door.

Tony designed mine to cover more of my body parts. With Sarah's help, this time he made my clothes look like one of the

Brothers, but its way more stretchy so I can perform all my moves with ease. As Tiffany places her hand on the scanner I say, "Just remember to gather up all my stuff and stash it in your office. I'll get it later. I am sure the Brothers will have tons of questions, but that is up to Tony to share or not."

"You've got it Lexy. I can't wait to watch this. I've got my phone ready to go as well. I'm sure the other Wenches will be excited to see it too. It's about time Grayson is taken down a notch or two, and believe me, I can't wait for you to hand him his balls. I always knew he had a little of his father in him, but Jesus, come on, after everything he knows about you, he still thinks of you as some helpless female. It's such bullshit. If I were you, I would have kicked his ass a long time ago. I can't wait to get a better myself so I can put one of these guys in their place," Tiffany says with a giggle.

"And I am sure that one day you will take a title away from one of them, just like I did. We just have to find the right event."

"Tony says I'm getting really good with my throwing. We've been practicing at his place too," Sarah adds.

"Tony is an excellent teacher, and he will not go easy on you just because you two are involved. He knows that doesn't help anything. So, if he says you're getting good, you really are."

"I really want one. Just one title, and I swear to God I'd never accept a challenge on it again. Nope, no way. I'd be just like you and hold on to it forever," Sarah says with such determination.

"And I am sure as time goes on and we continue to work hard with our training, slowly us Wenches will be taking more and more titles from those overconfident assholes," I add in.

Both of them are chuckling as we walk into the gym to see the guys gathered around two long tables in the back, shoving pizza in their faces and drinking beer. Geesh, I didn't realize they'd think I was calling this meeting just to be their dinner entertainment. Well, fuck it! Let the fun begin.

"Oh Lexy, I forgot to tell you, I ordered them pizza, because they were complaining about not having dinner. It'll also slow them down a bit, just in case," Tiffany says, just as I see Spencer and Clausen turn and look in our direction. They instantly start elbowing the other Brothers and within seconds, all eyes are on me as I walk into the middle of the gym floor. I'm kind of thrilled they haven't taken up the mats all over the floor.

"Hey, look! See? That's Lexy. Doesn't she look like a short fat Italian man? Go ahead, say something Lexy," Steven calls out, shoving a huge piece of folded crust into his mouth."

"I wanted all of you to see how I dress to go to battle," I say, slowly turning around and holding my arms out for them to check me out. "I can see perfectly fine through this hooded mask I have on. It disguises my voice to sound like a man. I have on added padding as well as a much larger bulletproof vest under all of this too."

"Shit! You had us totally fooled back then. That's a damn good disguise if you ask me," Jackson gives his input.

"Fuck, you could have never convinced me it was a chick back then. You should have seen her! She saved my ass shooting those Russians while flying around those rafters in Italy. She played a typical dick Italian boss too, just like their Capo. We tried to say thank you and she wouldn't give us anything more than a head nod before she went flying on her way," Drake says, tipping his beer to me. "Thank you by the way. I wouldn't be standing here today if it wasn't for you back there."

I reach up and pull the mask off, looking over to him. "Nothing to thank me for. I only did what any of you would do. We worked together as a team." I toss my mask over to Tiffany.

"Okay, now let me tell you a little about this outfit. Tony,

Sarah and I have done a few modifications since Italy. Back
then I had to dress like the Family, in what looked more like
nice black dress slacks and a dress shirt. You've all seen my
men. They are rarely seen together without looking the same.
Even in battle, their uniform doesn't change."

"She isn't shitting you. Some of her men even had on a tie
while fighting the Russians. Could you imagine that?"
Carpenter says laughing, and several of the Brothers join in.
That's when I look over to Grayson, who is just standing there
in some very loose fitting gym shorts and tank top, watching
me with a small smile on his face. He looks more curious than
anything, as he continues to eat his pizza. I look away not
wanting to be distracted and hoping he can figure out a way
to trust me or I will have to kick his ass tonight.

"That is so true Carpenter. Some of the Family I have
never even seen in street clothes. But things are different here.
Like these pants I have on, they look very close to the cargo
style pants you all wear, but mine are made from a completely
different fabric that doesn't inhibit my movement. Do any of
you think you could do this in your pants and protective
gear?" I instantly do multiple back flips, while grabbing my
small hidden paintball gun from the back of my pants before I
land softly in the Chinese splits, with my body lying flat on the
floor holding both hands in front of me pointing my gun at
them, and say, "Bang, bang."

"Damn, girl. That's fucking impressive. Not a one of us
could do the splits like that. I didn't even know a body could
move like that. By the way, how did you grab that gun flipping
around like that?" Stevens asks as he applauds me. A couple
of the Brothers join in, cheering me on.

Quickly popping back up and onto my feet, I leave my gun
laying on the floor for later, hoping they don't notice. As I start
unbuttoning my padded men's shirt exposing the front of my
bulletproof vest, I explain, "You can see that this shirt has
padding in the arms to make me more bulky like a man. It

also adds a bit more protection and hides my vest quite nicely." I hand it to Tiffany, who has come over to take my clothes for me. She gives a small head nod and stays close, knowing not to walk too far away from me as I'll be handing her more stuff.

"That's a bulletproof vest underneath your clothes? I've never seen one that looks like that. What surprises me, even more, is your mobility and how you could do all those flips. How safe is that vest, if it is that flexible?" Spencer asks.

"Now those are Tony's secrets. He's the one who designs them for me and puts several angled layers of Kevlar in them. They are as hot as hell, and heavy, but as he would say, they protect all the major parts." I start undoing my pants to take them off to show the Brothers my full vest, when I hear Grayson's voice.

"What the fuck are you doing?"

"Taking off my pants. Geesh, get over yourself, Grayson. Everyone has seen me in my workout clothes. What did you think I was doing? Stripping down to my thong in front of all of them?" Shaking my head and cutting my eyes to him, I can see he doesn't look pleased and it is pissing me off. I can hear some of the Brothers chuckling.

"Riggs, take another drink of your beer and chill. She called this meeting for a reason, and I for one, want to see what else Lexy has in store for us," Clausen says, handing Grayson a beer.

Grayson takes the beer and downs half of it. Yeah, he is getting worked up and right now I don't give a shit. That just increases my odds of taking him down fast. But right now, I have to stay focused and convince the rest of the Brothers I am worthy to fight beside them. I'm pretty confident I have more than half of them willing to stand with me now. Reaching back, I hand my pants over to Tiffany.

"I'd like you all to take a closer look at the vest Tony made for me. I meant it when I said it covers all the major parts. He has lengthened it to cover more of my female organs too. That is why it goes down into more of a V-shape. It also replicates the male body and his package when in slacks." That causes them to chuckle again. I take it off and hand it over to Tiffany and say, "Thank you."

"I'll keep it safe, but I will be examining all this stuff myself," Tiffany says as she heads for the door to put all of my stuff away.

I turn, looking at all of them as I slowly walk in Stevens' direction, continuing my talk. "All of you Brothers like to tease me about my size. But being compact makes it easier to catch my attacker off guard. One reason is that you aren't used to fighting someone my size, and your overconfident male ego tells you that you can take me out in seconds if you want to. Am I correct?"

Hearing them mumble to themselves and each other, I walk over to stand directly in front of Stevens with my feet less than twelve inches in front of his and ask, "Do you think in this position I can disarm you and kick you in the head without moving my left foot?" I look him in the eyes and raise my eyebrow, then I look down to my grappling pipe sticking out of the side of his high top basketball shoe. Looking back up at him, I cannot resist rolling my eyes.

"Fuck no! You can't do that," he says with a smirk on his face as he continues, "But hey, give it your best shot." He crosses his arms over his chest with sickening male confidence.

I instantly reach up and pat his cheek. Looking down at his shoe, I slightly twist and throw my right leg up sideways, bending at the waist and not moving my left foot, I grab my grappling pipe out of his shoe. I do the Chinese splits again, standing this time, just as my right foot kicks him in the side of the head. Geesh, they just saw me do the splits, when will these guys learn? Just as quickly as I started, I'm standing back up laughing and throwing my grappling pipe around like it was a nun-chuck, up and over my head, dropping it behind me, catching it over and over again.

"Hey! Give that back to me. It's my souvenir from Italy."

"And who do you think accidentally dropped it on you? Duh! It was mine. I'll give it back to you once I show you what you've been playing with all this time." I walk about ten feet away from him and continue my demonstration. "Let me tell you guys something. I have several weapons on me at all times. Have you ever noticed I always wear thick belts with amazing buckles? It's more than just a fashion statement," I say as I throw the grappling hook up towards the rafters and push the center button on my belt, watching all the hooks pop out and the rope uncoil towards me. Hearing their gasps, I can't help but smile.

"Whoa! Fuck! How did you make it do that?" Stevens asks.

As I reach up and grab the coiled end of the rope, I click the carabiner onto my belt and as Stevens gets closer to me, I slide the button on my belt to the left and I start rising to the rafters faster. "See Stevens? I don't always have to climb, a little push of this jewel on my buckle and I have the ability to go as fast or as slow as I need to, and you can't hear a thing. All my grappling hooks have razor sharp hooks and can be used as a weapon or will attach themselves to practically anything I throw them at. I've been telling you guys Tony's a badass at this."

"Woohoo! That's my boyfriend everyone!" Sarah calls out, as she takes off running across the gym to where Tony is standing with a shit-eating grin on his face beside Hawkins. Once she reaches him, she leaps into his arms wrapping her legs around him, kissing him smack on the lips.

"Tony, buddy, shit, you gotta help a Brother out. I want a set of those," Jackson says still looking up at me.

"So that hook, how much can it lift?" Carpenter asks.

"You aren't getting a set fucker. You haven't been training like Stevens and I have," Jackson barks at him.

Tony sets Sarah back down and keeps his arm around her, looking towards Carpenter and Jackson. "We've tested it to lift at least 350 pounds easily. That was with Lexy and one of her guards hanging onto her. And Jackson, Lexy already had me make you and Stevens a set. I'll work with both of you, training you on how to use them properly."

"Riggs, you're awful quiet. You've got a real badass as a girlfriend. What do you think? With toys like this, you're dating a female Batman," Stevens teases Grayson, who just smiles shaking his head, still not saying a word.

The second my feet touch the ground, I push the button on my belt and my grappling hook recoils its rope and drops from the rafters. I casually reach out and catch it. Tossing it to Stevens, I say, "Catch! And a little FYI, I'm not Batman. He doesn't kill people and I don't believe he even carries a gun." I glance over to see Grayson's face. He is watching my every move, but his face is as expressionless as stone.

Stevens catches it, and within seconds starts examining it. "I still can't figure out how you did that." He looks up at me, "It's never accidentally opened before has it?"

"No, it hasn't. I've watched you twirl it and bang it like it was a drum and it never opened. Let's say you were our test dummy," I say, giving him a wink.

"Ha ha. But really."

"I'm being serious. Unless you have the controller, it's just a lead pipe."

"Cool."

"Oh, and Stevens, I've got more toys than just those grappling hooks."

"Like what? Show me."

"I need to tell you a little more before I share. First, I've told all of this to Grayson and I don't know how much he has shared with all of you. But I killed my first person before I was sixteen. I've been training all my life."

Once again, I hear the Brothers mumbling to each other. I slide my hands one at a time over my belt, releasing a mini dagger into each hand. I watch the Brothers looking amongst themselves, all but Grayson who is still just staring at me like he has x-ray vision.

"Who did you kill before you were sixteen?" Spencer asks.

"A rival Family had sent a man into one of our Family shooting ranges. He thought he could slip in and wouldn't be noticed, and he could kill my Papa, our Family Capo. He was sadly mistaken. I saw him and took him out before he could kill him."

"Have you killed anyone else?" Clausen asks. You can hear a pin drop, all of the Brothers seeming to hold their breath as they wait for my answer.

"Yes. I probably have more kills under my belt than all of you put together. I've mastered all weapons, from guns to knives and even swords. I'm extremely quiet and accurate. Usually, they don't even hear me coming. There are plenty advantages to being small, and a woman. I've been trained to always scope out exits the moment I walk into a room, then to recognize everything I can turn into a weapon if I need to. I also analyze every person in the room to figure out who is the weakest and who'd be the biggest challenge," I say looking around at all of them before locking eyes with Grayson for a few seconds before looking away.

"Shit, I believe you, and I wouldn't want to mess with you. You might be a little thing, but I've seen you in action with a gun in hand, and I've watched you closely as you work out the past few weeks. The things you can do with Stevens and Jackson is mind blowing. You're one badass for sure. I definitely would want you on our side," Bishop says with a head nod towards me.

"Thanks, Bishop. That means a lot to know that some of you trust me."

"Come on Lexy, forget Bishop's kiss up. I still wanna see your other toys."

"Okay Stevens, how good are you with a knife?" And before he can reply, I toss one of my little daggers into the heavy rubber tip of the toe of his basketball shoes. Hearing the gasps of all the Brothers makes showing off a little so worth it. I hold back the smile that wants so badly to form on my face.

"Shit! Where the fuck did that come from?!" Stevens asks as he bends down and pulls the dagger out of the tip of his shoe.

"Oh, there is more where that came from. I always have at least two, and sometimes as many as four daggers on me any time I have one of my belts on." Then I toss the second one into the toe of Jackson's boot.

"Fuck, girl! You could have gotten my toe with that." He reaches down and pulls it out of his shoe, as I slowly walk towards Grayson. Before I can say anything, I watch as Jackson rubs his thumb over the blade testing to see how sharp it is. "Shit! What the fuck? I just took a hunk out of my finger! Gregory, get over here and look to see if I need stitches. Fuck!"

"Jackson, never handle any of my knives like that. They are surgically sharp. I can throw one into the wall and it'd take gloves and pliers to get it out."

"Fuck, you could have said that before I almost cut my thumb off." Jackson is wide eyed and losing the color in his face as he continues his whining, "I think I'm going to be sick. I've never been able to handle the sight of my own blood. Anyone else's blood I'm fine with, just not my own goddamn blood I can't handle."

"Stop being a pussy," Brenden says as he looks at his finger, as he calls out, "Tiffany, go get me some butterfly bandages and a big Band-Aid before Jackson here passes out on us. Jackson, it isn't that bad, and you're an idiot for running your finger over the blade. How stupid does someone have to be?"

"Come on, we've all run our finger over a blade before. I just wasn't expecting it to almost take off my thumb. Oh, Dr. Gregory, seeing your blood wouldn't affect me at all. In fact, it sounds pretty good right about now," Jackson says, leaning into Brenden.

"Knock it off," Grayson and I say in unison, surprising both of us. I turn around now to realize I'm standing less than a foot away from Grayson, looking into his deep blue eyes and hoping to be able to read him and figure out what he is thinking. But I can't. Grayson's eyes look me up and down, spending a couple of seconds longer on my cleavage peeking out of my sports bra.

"Good minds think alike in correcting our men." How will he respond if I take partial control over his men?

"You mean my men?" Grayson says softly, looking up from my chest and locking eyes with me again.

"Well, I think in leadership we're a bit on equal footing. I'm not trying to take your men Grayson. I just want to be a part of the team. I think my skills could help with the Brothers, and I've proven myself worthy," I say as Grayson's eyes roam back to my chest for a second before they quickly return back to my eyes.

"I just don't know about that," Grayson says with a smirk slowly appearing on his face.

While we are locked into a staring competition, I slide my hand up my chest and into my bra, as I quickly release one of my throwing stars into my fingers, Grayson's eyes go back to my chest.

"I think we need to make the playing field a little more equal, and since you continue to check out my tits, I think it's only fair I check out yours." On that note, I quickly slide my fingers upward with my throwing star between them, cutting Grayson's very loose fitting tank top completely open, not taking my eyes off of his.

Grayson quickly steps back and looks down at his chest, his cut tank top split wide open, exposing his muscular chest. Unable to control my smile, I wave the throwing star in between my fingers, flicking my hand down quickly, releasing the star to stick into the mat right between his legs.

"Fuck, Lexy! You could have really cut me with that."

"Oh please. If I wanted to cut you, I could have. I don't have accidents. Oh, and my bras are custom made. They all have hidden pockets that conceal my throwing stars. I've even walked through airline security with them and they were never discovered." Stepping away from Grayson and getting more pissed off by the second, I look around at the Brothers and say, "Now I ask you. How many of you Brothers think I am worthy to fight with you?"

"It isn't their decision. It's mine," Grayson says firmly, stepping up beside me as he tosses his ruined tank top to the floor flexing his chest muscles, distracting me for a brief second.

"I thought no one was a leader within the Brothers? Isn't every decision made by the group as a whole? Okay," I say as I walk away from Grayson, my anger continuing to grow. I slowly look into the eyes of each of the Brothers, wondering where they stand. "You guys have seen me practice and train with all of you. Who thinks they can actually take me down?" I look over to Grayson, seeing his brows draw together.

"Lexy, I speak for more than half of the Brothers when I say we trust your abilities completely. There is no need to challenge any of us," Clay says looking over at Grayson.

"Thank you, Clay. But there are still some, or at least one, that thinks because they are taller, heavier and have a dick swinging between their legs that they are better than me. They believe that because I have tits, they can take me out. Let me remind you all, unlike you, I do not play fair or follow any rules. As your mothers, sisters, and female friends might have told you, I've literally handed many a man their balls before and I'm not afraid to prove myself to any of you. Just be warned, if you take this challenge, there are no rules. Nothing is off limits," I say as I pop my knuckles and rotate my neck around, bouncing on my toes loosening myself up more.

"Stevens, you've dicked around and played with her long enough. Show her how easy it is to take her out," Grayson orders.

"Nope. Not happening. Have you been watching everything your batman woman can do? I'm not getting the shit kicked out of me, or getting my balls cut off."

"When did all of you become such pussies? Are you going to be like Hawkins and think Lexy can actually kick your ass? Fight like a man and not a pussy. Don't go light on her. Come on Jackson, it'd take you less than two minutes to pin her ass to the floor till she screams uncle."

"What the hell does my Uncle have to do with this? He's one hundred percent be on my side, knowing full well I can hand you your balls in less than two minutes," I say looking at Grayson. Yeah, I'm going to have to take him out and show him. I think one good kick to his leg, and he'll be down for the count. It's not like it'll permanently damage it. It's healed, just weak.

"Riggs, I hate to tell you this, but you need to stand down and accept this. None of us will fight your woman. I've been in the ring with her and she doesn't play well with others, just like me," Jackson warns.

"You have got to be fucking with me! I have not spent years working and training all of you for you all to grow a pussy. If I have to do this myself, I will," Grayson says, looking over at me.

"Riggs, you don't want to go there. I'm warning you. Look at her eyes, she's not playing," Tony warns.

"And neither am I," Grayson says as he walks towards me. "Okay Lexy, first one to pin the other gets to control the next mission."

"Music to my ears." I punch him full force in his stomach and I watch as he instantly folds and steps back for a second. I know he wasn't ready for that at all. He hadn't flexed his stomach muscles to help ease the force of my punch. As I step back and ask, "You okay big guy?"

"Yeah, I'm fine," Grayson says as he coughs and stands up, swinging his open hand towards me like he is trying to grab me.

"Come on Riggs, you think you can just grab me or are you trying to smack me like a little girl? Gonna try and pull my hair next? I don't think so. What do you think you're going to do? Slowly grab me and lay me on the floor? That's pretty funny. Show me what you got!" I move into him again, swinging. This time he at least puts his hands up and blocks, before he actually swings and tries to grab me again. That move causes me to instantly turn and get out of his reach.

"Lexy, I'm not going to hurt you like that. But I will grab your ass and throw it to the ground pinning it until you say uncle," Grayson says as he reaches for me again, as I continue to dodge him.

"You can't hurt me you overgrown chauvinistic asshole." Once Grayson gets closer to me, I spin, jump and kick him in the side of his shoulder and tap his head. "Fight like a man and pull that big dick of yours out of that pussy you got it tucked in," I say as I land.

"Damn, Lexy. Okay, you really want a taste of this?" Grayson finally puts his open hands into fists and swings in my direction. Now we're talking. I dodge his fists as they come flying my way. This is where me being short comes in handy. Since Grayson is more than a foot taller than me, I can more easily dodge. I can tell he's probably had more than just the two beers I saw him drinking earlier because his balance gets thrown off with every swing.

"Wow Grayson, you can't even hit a moving woman. I bet you can't hit a moving target with a gun either." I get closer, and punch him again in his stomach, but this time he is ready, and he returns my strike with a punch of his own to my side. Damn, that hurt like a bitch.

As I try to spin out of his way, he successfully grabs my upper arm tightly. I try to pull away by twisting and turning, but he grabs my shoulder with his other hand and holds me a bit of a distance from him. I know I could end this in two seconds by kicking him in the balls, but I'll wait to see what his next move is.

Looking me in the eyes, I can see the vein on the side of his forehead protruding, something I've never noticed before. I know he is mad as hell and wants me to surrender as he says, "See how fast I got you? Now say uncle so I don't have to humiliate you by throwing your ass on the floor and pinning you. Because I will do it, don't think for a second I won't."

"Not so easy asshole," I inform him, as I lift my foot with a little jump and press it into his chest, as I tuck myself inward and then push off his chest, throwing myself backwards and into a flip, twisting both of his hands causing him to release me.

I notice the Brothers are cheering me on, with whoops and applause, and shouts of 'YEAH, kick his ass.' A few are yelling for Grayson not to make an ass of himself, wanting him to stop. No way will I let him end this by being a pussy.

Just then I hear a roar, and I look back to see Grayson as he full-on lunges at me in a football tackle roaring all the way, taking me to the ground briefly knocking the breath out of me. "Say uncle! See? Less than two minutes and I have you pinned. I win," Grayson claims victory, releasing me and standing up, leaving me on the floor as I catch my breath, and all I see is red.

"All of you are pussies. It didn't take me two minutes to pin her ass. Now, this is over," Grayson says. As he steps forward, I throw my hands over my head and pop back up, looking right at his leg. As I chamber my leg in position to kick it and knock him back on his ass, he moves, and I kick him in the dick. SHIT!

Instantly I hear all the Brothers moan and grab their own dicks, while everything seems to be moving in slow motion as Grayson drops to the ground, cupping his family jewels. I watch as he curls into a ball, his eyes rolling upward as I stand there shaking in anger. I'm still seeing red and beyond pissed. I walk over to him and put my foot on his shoulder as he continues to cough.

"Lesson number one. *Never* turn your back on the enemy, unless you know without question they are dead. And as you can see, I'm not dead, nor am I down for the count." I reach up and take off one ruby stud earring at a time, dropping them on him. They cannot track me now. "I can't do this. I have to take some time to think. I'm pissed beyond belief and mad as hell at you. I am a warrior, not a typical girl, and you do not respect me or who I am. I cannot be near you right now. It only makes me more angry. I never surrendered, and why the fuck you wanted me to say uncle is beyond me."

Turning, I see a look of disbelief on all the Brothers faces, as they just stand there staring at me. I can feel tears beginning to form in my eyes as reality hits me. I've got to get out of here. I look over and see Hawkins wiping his hand down his face, and a look of shock covers Sarah's face. Tony is just looking at me as I yell, "Tony! Let's go. I've gotta get the hell out of here. *Now!*" I turn and run for the door.

"Babe, I gotta go. I'll call you in a little while. I've got to go with Lexy. You may need to call an ambulance for your brother. I warned him. Sorry." Then I hear Tony running after me.

Tears start to run down my face, as I hear Grayson

coughing and taking deep breaths trying not to throw up, as he finally calls out, "Stop her!"

I bust out of the doors not looking at anyone, until I am out in the parking lot. I hear Tony right behind me as he clicks his car remote, unlocking the doors to his sports car. I quickly get in and curl into myself, feeling like I'm going to hyperventilate. I try without luck to slow my breathing.

"Don't you dare throw up in my car. Where to, Lexy?"

"Take me to your underground compound. Do not tell anyone where I am, and that includes Sarah. I need time to think. You'd better have some goddamn grappa at your house because I'm going to need it," I say over my tears.

Tony starts his car and we take off. My mind is racing, and the tears keep falling. Did I just break up with Grayson? No! I just told him, 'I need time'. I've got to figure this out. How can I be with him if he doesn't see me as an equal? I can't ever be under a man's control again. What the fuck am I going to do?

26

INTERNAL BATTLES

Grayson

"Goddamn! Look at this, I got the best view. Watch closely as I zoom in. Grayson was getting turned on while fighting with Lexy," I hear Stevens telling the Brothers.

I can barely catch my breath. I feel like I'm going to die. I've already thrown up everything all over the place. I think she kicked my dick off. I can't move and I can't even bring myself to tell Stevens to shut up.

"Look right here! See? His shorts are sporting a good sized tent. But wait, let me slow it down. Now look as Lexy's foot makes full contact with his dick and the kick spins him around as he collapses on the floor. *Damn!* That has to hurt like a mother fucker. I'm sure she broke it," I hear Stevens giving a blow by blow of the death of my dick.

"Riggs, are you bleeding? Is Sir-Vula-Ate-Her still attached? Hey, if he never works again at least, your dick has the right name. 'Sir' may not be able to bang again, but at least you can eat pussy." Steven calls out to me, chuckling. Does my good friend have no mercy in his heart for me?

"Stevens, shut the fuck up. Our Brother is really hurt," Gregory yells at him.

Thank God someone cares enough to shut him up. "Riggs, seriously, I need to take a look to see if we need to call an ambulance or if we'll be able to take you to the hospital ourselves."

"Hey, we've all been kicked in the balls at some point in our lives. Is getting your dick kicked worse? I was just joking around. You think he's seriously hurt? Fucking shit," Stevens says, finally sounding a bit concerned.

"No... ambulance," I mumble, barely above a whisper. Shit, I'm still seeing stars and my body is just trembling.

"Dick Jr. I've got you a bag of frozen peas," I hear Tiffany say, sarcastically.

I slowly open up my eyes to see Gregory, Tiffany and Bishop kneeling beside me, while several Brothers are looking over Stevens' shoulder watching his video. The others are just staring at me with painful expressions on their faces, cupping their own balls in sympathy. I slowly reach up to grab the large bag of peas and put it on my dick. I've never been more thankful to not see blood on my hand. That means my dick is still attached to my body, even if it'd rather drop off right now.

Sensing movement beside me, I peek through my eyelashes to see Bishop throwing towels over the areas where I barfed, and he begins to clean it up. Jesus. I am really going to owe these guys.

"Come on, buddy, let's roll you over on your back. As crazy as this sounds, I need to see your dick," Gregory says as he puts his hands on my shoulders.

"Give me a second. I want to see if the peas help first. I can't move yet," I say slowly, sounding very breathy. I think I'd pass out if I tried to move right now or speak any louder.

"Riggs, you could have a serious injury here. The sooner you let me take a look, the better your odds," Gregory pleads.

"Should I call mom?" I hear Sarah, and realize she is somewhere behind them.

"No! Don't call mom. Give me five goddamn minutes and get someone to go after Lexy. I need to talk to her."

"No one is going to do that. You've already proved you're a dumbass for not listening to us. She needs some time. You heard her just as well as we did. The only thing you should be thinking about is getting your dick looked at, Brother," I hear Hawkins say from over my head.

My heart is pounding. I feel like I'm going to pass out. My chest hurts. Oh GOD! What am I going to do without her? I won't be able to survive. I am an asshole. I can't control my breathing. Fuck! How the hell did I lose control like this? I deserve every bit of this pain and anguish. Fingers snap in front of my face, making me try and open my eyes.

"Okay Riggs, open your eyes and look at me." As I slowly manage to open my eyes, I look up at Gregory as he continues. "Your breathing is getting very erratic. I'm getting worried about you and I'm about to call an ambulance."

"No, don't call an ambulance. My mind is racing, going over everything. I'm just freaking out about what I did. I can't lose Lexy. She's everything, and I fucked up badly."

"Yeah, I'd say you fucked up, you dumbass. You're as big of an asshole as dad. Mom's liable to hand you yours on a silver platter when she finds out about this," Sarah says, chewing me out.

"Sarah that can wait. We need to see how bad his injury is. I'm sure Mom Riggs will be the first to meet us at the hospital. I don't care if I call an ambulance or we take him ourselves, your brother is going to the hospital for an injury like this."

Looking around, I force myself to slow my breathing. I see all the Brothers are gathered around me, finally putting their phones away. I'm sure they'd all like to join in with Sarah and start cussing me out. God, what was I thinking? I actually punched Lexy. I punched her! Oh God, I have to fix this.

Shit, I drank way too much grappa today without eating, and then I had several beers. Fuck. After throwing everything up, I feel like shit. What a shitty way to sober up. Man, I've never fucked up this badly in my life. The sooner I get this over with the faster I can find Lexy. I slowly roll over on my back.

"Bishop, toss me some of those towels. There is still a shit load of barf over here," Stevens says, I turn my head in his direction, "You going to barf again? You do know you owe all of us for this. Damn, this is just gross." I watch as Stevens gets on his hands and knees and cleans up my mess, making sure I don't have barf on me either.

Lying on my back with my knees bent up and with the frozen peas on my dick, I'm wondering is 'Sir' ever going to work again? My dick has never hurt like this before. Well, if I can't fix this with Lexy, I probably won't need him. I'll never want anyone but her. The pain in my chest is just as bad, if not worse, than my dick. It keeps building and is becoming unbearable. My heart is breaking without her. I've got to persuade someone to go and find her and talk to her. They need to make sure she's okay and tell her I love her and how sorry I am. I need to apologize and beg for forgiveness. God! I have to get her back.

"Riggs, it's time to let me take a look," Gregory says as he slowly lowers my legs. I can barely handle the pain rushing through my body as I remove the frozen peas. Within seconds I feel him lifting the waistband of my shorts to take a look.

"Fuck! Yeah, we're taking you to the hospital now. Clausen go pull the SUV around to the front doors. Hunter, go and get us a gurney from the medical center downstairs. Your penis is going to be severely bruised if not worse. It's already swelling and very discolored. She could have damaged your urethra with a kick like that. It could be fractured or broken. And yes, you can break your dick. We'll need to run tests. Once we're in the SUV, I'll call ahead and let them know we're on our way and to get a specialist to meet us in the ER."

"Come on, Brother you gotta show us. Can you visually tell if it's broken? Is it bent out of shape? I've got his stomach juice on my hands, I earned the right to see it," Steven teases.

Closing my eyes and concentrating on my breathing, I hear the Brothers shuffling around to take a peek at my injured dick. Gregory pulls my shorts down further looking at my dick more closely, before moving out of the way and exposing me to them. Those perverts. Hearing all of their moans makes me even more worried, and I'm sure they're imagining what I'm feeling. Now I have to listen to all of them as they add their own two cents. In all honesty, I'm too scared to open my eyes and look down to see the damage to my favorite appendage.

"Shit!!! Is that blood or a bruise?"

"Dayuumm, that's kind of a deep purply color. Is it going to turn black and fall off? I hear that can happen to dick injuries."

"That's gonna put 'Sir' out of commission for a long time. It takes a broken bone six to eight weeks to heal. How long does it take a broken boner?"

"Fuck! I'll never challenge Lexy at anything. That's gotta hurt like a son of a bitch."

"Did you see her eyes? You could see it in those eyes. She was out for blood. I'm fucking never challenging that woman. Those eyes put the fear of God in me for sure."

"Well, I'm glad it hurts. Maybe it'll make him finally believe in her. She took his big ass down in seconds." Now that was Sarah adding her comments. Did she just check my dick out too?! GAWD…

"That's enough. I don't want to hear any more talk about my wounded appendage. I need you guys to be good Brothers and go find Lexy for me." All I hear is mumbling surrounding me. That just lets me know no one is going to help me.

"Riggs, listen to me. We're giving Lexy the time she requested. I got the earrings she tossed on you and I'll see if she'll answer my call in a little while. I'm sure Sarah will be seeing Tony later tonight and I bet Lexy will be with him. We know he can't live without your sister, if you didn't know that already. She'll be able to get us an update. Now put this new bag of peas on your dick. That's where I draw the line. I'm not touching your junk," Tiffany says, sticking out another bag of frozen peas.

Gregory takes them from her and places them between my shorts and boxers, more directly on my dick, before covering me back up. I inhale sharply because that hurts like hell and causes me to see stars. God, everyone in this room, including my sister and Tiffany, just saw my dick. I still have no desire to see the damage. I can still barely move. How long has it been? Man, I've been kicked in the balls a few times in my life playing sports, but this hurts a hell of a lot worse. I don't even know if I can sit up.

"Okay, you ready to go to the hospital?"

"If I say no, will you all just leave and let me die right here?"

"We're not letting you die anywhere. This isn't going to kill you. You will live another day, but it'll be a while before 'Sir' is working like he used to."

"Be honest with me Gregory, what's the worst case here? I mean, will 'Sir' be okay? How long does it take dick injuries to heal? He will heal, won't he?" I have to know.

"Well, I'm not a urologist, but I have dealt with some pretty bad penis injuries in the ER and this doesn't look good. But I've also seen worse. I mean, your dick is still attached to your body after all," he says with a chuckle before continuing, "We'll have to run tests and those will not be fun either. Sorry Brother, I don't know if that makes you feel any better."

"It doesn't," I reply, getting pissed at the Brothers for

laughing at his joke. God, how I wish I could wake up and have all this be a nightmare. I don't think I'm that lucky. As the Brothers chuckle and continue to joke between each other about my dick, I look at Gregory and tell him, "I don't know if I'm ready to try and sit up yet, and I sure as hell can't walk. I think if I try, it'll make me throw up again, or just pass out."

"Don't worry big guy, we'll have Carpenter and Jackson carefully pick you up and get you on the gurney to wheel you out to the SUV."

"Geesh, I can't believe after all the times you've had to put me back together again here, a broken dick is what actually gets me to the hospital."

"I could give you something for pain," Gregory offers.

"No, I deserve to feel this."

"I'm running ahead and will meet you in the ER. I'll call Tony from my car and see if he'll tell me how Lexy is doing. I can't believe I'm even offering to tell you shit." Sarah says as she takes off running.

"Maybe Jackson and Carpenter can just help me stand up and walk on each side of me to get out of here? Maybe we don't need a gurney."

"Grayson, you are going out of here on a gurney. I do not have a clue what the damage to your dick is so walking and going downstairs all the way to the SUV is not happening," Gregory says in full-on doctor mode.

Right on cue, Hunter comes in the door, pushing the gurney over to me. I slowly try to lift myself up off the floor. Shit, I feel this all the way deep down in my balls and down into both thighs before it rushes up and floods into my abdomen.

"We got you Brother," Carpenter says from behind me, slowly putting his hands under my arms. Trying to lift myself a bit to help, I see Jackson eyes glaring at me. Damn, I can tell he is still pissed at me as he puts his hands under my legs. I should have guessed Jackson would be on Lexy's side all the way with this. He'd probably even like to work with her in charge. Shit.

Then I hear Carpenter call to him, "On my count. 1, 2, 3." Stars appear in my vision as they move me. On the gurney, I turn to my side, pulling my legs in some. Damn, lying on my side feels a hell of a lot better than lying on my back. Shit. I'll probably be facing Mom before I see the doctor. Can my life get any worse?

"Dr. Gregory, would you like to give me an update and explain what happened?"

A doctor asks as he walks into my ER room. Gregory is still barking orders at the nurses. He made everyone else, but Hawkins wait in the waiting room until he got me settled.

"Cut his shorts off of him. Get him an IV, he's been throwing up due to his penis injury and we need to push fluids. He's also been drinking. Get a full blood workup, too, A-SAP." Then he turns and says to the doctor. "This is Grayson Riggs, twenty eight, and one of the Brothers of Camelot. He was sparring and got his penis kicked pretty hard. It's already swollen and very discolored. No lacerations. One of the Brothers has a good video of the injury actually occurring. It was more penile impact than testicles."

Thank God he didn't say I pissed off my girlfriend and she tried to kick my dick off. The doctor walks closer to me, "Hello there, Grayson. You're Diana's, rather Dr. Riggs' son, aren't you?"

"Yes, sir I am, but please, there is no need to call her."

Chuckling, he responds, "Well, too late for that. I guess your sister called ahead and she called me before Dr. Gregory did, asking me to greet you when you arrived. She'll be down once she finishes up delivering a baby. So, you are spared a worrisome mother for a little bit. Now, let's take a look at this injury."

Inhaling deeply, I blink my eyes. Fuck, this hurts like a mother fucker and he's barely touched my dick.

"How much have you had to drink, and when? And it's not wise to be fighting while under the influence."

"I don't think I have any alcohol left in me. I barfed my guts up to the point of dry heaves after getting hurt. And believe me, this is not something I've ever done before, nor will I ever do it again."

"Well, with all the swelling not only in your penis but testicles too, and the massive amount of bruising already appearing, that had to be one hell of a kick. We're going to give you something for the pain and to help you relax, but we don't usually sedate for these tests. We'll talk about that after a complete blood work up. I will definitely be performing two different tests. I'll be placing a fiber optic camera into your urethra to check for damage, then the more intense test will be the retrograde urethrogram. That is where I inject special dye through the urethra and x-ray your penis. If anything looks questionable, there are a few other tests we can follow up with. Let's make sure we don't have any rips or tears in your shaft or urethra first."

I hear Hawkins gasping in the chair on the other side of the room. Any man would be uncomfortable hearing this. "So, you aren't thinking he, I mean it, is broken? I mean, the guys were saying I could have a broken dick, uh, penis."

As the doctor lightly moves my dick around and applies light pressure, I honestly think I might be crying. God does this hurts so bad. Drugs do sound good right about now, as I can no longer contain a high pitch moan of pain. Over a sharp inhale of air, I can feel my eyes watering.

"With this swelling and discoloration due to the bruising, it is tough to tell, but I don't think so. We'll know more once we have some test results. Have you been able to urinate since the injury?"

"I have barely moved since the injury. I haven't passed out, but I've come close and seen stars a few times. I don't know if I can pee right now."

"Well, let me put it this way, if you can't urinate that's okay. We'll be able to empty your bladder when we start the procedure."

"No, no. I'll try on my own first. Thanks."

"Okay, I'll be back in a few minutes after we get the blood work and I'll go set up the room for testing." Then with a head nod, he leaves, just as Mom Stevens and Mom Gregory walk in.

"What happened? Noah texted me and told me you were here with a really bad penis injury, but he refused to tell me how it happened," Mom Stevens says, walking right over and lifting the sheet the doctor placed over me taking a close look at my dick with Mom Gregory right beside her. Yikes! I cannot believe this.

"Oh, that looks bad Grayson. How on the earth did this happen? And is Dr. Hansen doing a retrograde urethrogram?" Mom Gregory asks coming over to me and giving me a hug, followed by Mom Stevens.

"Yeah, he said he's going to run a couple of tests. I'm hoping I'm knocked out for them. Just the thought of tubes jammed up my dick is enough to make me want to..."

"Well, after watching several of the videos that your sister and Brothers sent to me, I'm kind of hoping the kind doctor doesn't sedate you. Maybe it'll help remind you that you aren't as much of a badass as you think you are," Mom interrupts me as she walks in, "What were you thinking? Gawd, I'm going to start calling you Richard. You are so much your father's son," she says as she walks over and like everyone else, lifts the sheets and takes a close up look at my dick. Jesus. Maybe they should just take a close-up dick-pic and send it to all our family and friends. Let's not leave anyone out now. Shit.

"Nice to see you too Mom. It's also nice how you instantly take Lexy's side over your own son. Thanks."

"Well I saw how you hit her. You could have broken or cracked her ribs, you brutal ox. That was an asshole move, if I say so myself. What were you thinking? The both of you, fighting like that!"

"Mom, come on, I was just trying to show her she doesn't have to fight anymore. I can take care of her." Fuck, what am I saying? I'm telling my Mom way too much.

She smacks my head. "What do you think we are? Stupid? Why did you think your father fought so hard about you all forming this 'Brothers of Camelot Security Team'? Because we knew damn well, you'd be putting yourself in danger. Come on, Grayson! You think we didn't know when you were 'out of town on business' you were healing somewhere?!" She does air quotes and looks over at Gregory.

"I'll let you talk with the Moms and go give the Brothers an update." Gregory turns and exits before anyone can say anything to stop him.

"Gregory, you pussy! Never knew you were such a chicken shit!" I yell towards the door as Stevens walks in.

"Oh… now I see why Gregory was hustling down the hall so fast. Hi Moms, well? Is his dick going to make it, or will they have to amputate it?" Stevens says, giving his mom a hug.

"They haven't told him yet. They're going to have to run some tests first," Hawkins says from his chair on the other side of the room, where he's busy typing away on his computer in his lap. I can only pray he is trying to find Lexy for me.

"I need to tell you something young man," Mom says, looking over to Moms Stevens and Gregory, who both give her a nod. "Okay, us Moms have personal experience of how well trained your girlfriend is. Let's hope she's still your girlfriend. I was hoping for an engagement in the coming months, you asshole."

"Believe me Mom, so was I. You do not need to lecture me. I know how bad I screwed up. You need to help me out. I don't think she'll talk to me right now. She's really pissed. But she'll answer her phone if you call. Please help your son out and call her, tell her how sorry I am, and how badly I need to see her."

"No. I will try to talk to her myself, for myself, to make sure she's okay, but I will not be your messenger. Lexy is like me. She will be too mad to talk to you right now. You do not need to make this worse. Give her some time to calm down and realize how much of a true asshole she fell in love with."

"Fine. I'm sure Hawkins is looking for her for me," I say looking over to Hawk, who just sighs shaking his head. Yeah, he is looking, but obviously not having much luck.

"Did she not take off her tracking earrings?"

"Yeah, she did, but Hawkins has other ways."

"Grayson take a few minutes and listen to me. You will not find her. I'm confident Lexy will be with Tony. No one knows where his main house is. Yeah, he has a condo close to Lexy, but he also has his own house and compound. She'll be there with him. Let me tell you a little secret, your sister doesn't even know where it is because she wears a blindfold every time they go to his place."

"Fuck. Well, once they put my dick back together, I'll find her."

"Do you think of her as an equal yet? Forget about wanting to protect her, do you trust her enough to take care of herself and those you love?"

"Mom, I don't know how much you know about Lexy's life before she came to America..."

"We know more than you think. You boys do know you have awful smart parents, right"? Mom Gregory asks.

"Grayson, us Moms have all talked to, and spent months

training and getting to know your girl. We're more than aware she probably ran from an Italian crime family," Mom Stevens says, shocking the hell out of me.

"Son, let me tell you a little story." Then Mom tells us how Lexy saved Mom Stevens' from a psych patient that was holding her hostage with a scalp to her neck. The three of them share how Lexy went into full protective warrior mode. Saving Barbara and getting them to help her take this man out. Jesus, Lexy, really does have a gift, even if it scares the shit out of me.

"Mom, why didn't you tell any of this to us before now?"

"Because she asked us not to. She wanted to tell you herself who she really is first. We're only assuming, after everything we've learned about her and what that elderly woman told us in Italy all those years ago. We're assuming she's, what do you call it? A Mafia Princess?"

"Yeah, she was, but not anymore."

"Grayson, look at me," Mom Stevens says.

Turning to look at her, I see Hawkins is now standing between Mom Stevens and Mom Gregory with Stevens on the other side of his mom, still with his arm around her. Hawkins looks a bit freaked out as well. Mom Gregory wraps her arm around him, as he does the same to her.

"I would not be standing here today if it wasn't for Lexy. But she's very smart and knew a man that was bi-polar and having a manic schizophrenic episode is stronger than a wild animal. She didn't try to take him on, on her own. She sent us a signal that we were doing this as a group, and we did. None of us got hurt, or worse, because of her abilities and quick thinking. I will forever be in debt to her."

"So will we," Hawkins says, putting his other arm around Mom Stevens.

"You're damn right there," Stevens iterates, as he looks as me and asks, "How many times does that girl of yours have to save our asses, and now my Mom too, for you to finally believe she is as good as you are, if not better? At least she knows when to ask for help."

"You're right. She is, and she has. But it doesn't stop my fear. She isn't bulletproof."

Mom pulls the sheet to the side off my leg and touches the newest scar on my upper thigh, as she looks me in the eyes. "And neither are you. But I trust you. Do I worry? Every goddamn day. But I have to trust you and put my faith in the fact that the Brothers and God are watching over you. And going by what Stevens just said, I think you are keeping some stories from us of Lexy saving you too."

Closing my eyes, it feels like a ton of bricks are resting on my chest at the realization that everyone is right. I have to figure out a way to live with this and allow Lexy to stand beside me and not try to stand in front of her. I have to believe if she needs me, she'll let me know. She is a smart fighter and very wise. She is training my two best men to fight beside her, knowing that it will be easier for me to let her lead, knowing they have her back. I can always lead the other team. She started this years ago when she chose Stevens to fight with her in Italy. God, I'm such a dumbass.

I can barely concentrate with all the pain from my dick, but at least I've figured this much out. Now I just have to find Lexy and talk to her. I've got some major ass-kissing to do, and I have to prove to her that I do trust her and her abilities. We'll make this work.

"Grayson, I love you, and if I hear from Lexy, I'll let you know. I didn't mean it when I said I didn't want the doctor to drug you for this. But in reality, they usually don't completely knock you out for these tests. They will numb the head of your penis to relax is before inserting the catheters. I'll go in with you and hold your hand. You just close your eyes and try to think of something else."

Well shit. I did this to myself. I just pray I don't have a broken dick. I need 'Sir', he just has to be okay. I want those clear blue eyed babies too. Hearing the door open again, I open my eyes to see Dr. Hanson walk in.

"Okay Grayson, time to get you into the procedure room. I'll explain everything in there."

Oh God, I am so not ready for this…

27

CONFRONTED WITH REALITY

Lexy

"*T*ony, you'd better have brought me some chocolate strawberries or know how to make them, because I need them with my wine," I call out as the front door opens to Tony's underground compound house, where I've been hiding out the last three days, drowning my sorrows and broken heart in alcohol and sweets.

Shit, not only does Tony walk in, but so does every one of the Wenches plus Joyce, that really shy girl Brenda has been bringing to our training. I barely even know her. Fuck. I'm not in the mood for this. What the hell are they planning? A damn intervention or something? I think Tony needs an ass kicking, and since I've already broken his kick boxing dummy, I think he'll do just fine.

"Well Lex, I couldn't find any chocolate strawberries in the store and no, I don't know how to make them, but I know someone who'd just love to help," Tony says, carrying in several large grocery store bags, as he nods his head towards Tiffany and Isabella.

"And guess what Lexy? We all wore blindfolds over here so

419

you don't have to worry about us telling Grayson where to find you, even if it is driving the poor guy insane not being able to see or talk to you," Isabella says as she walks over and gives me a hug.

"Sweetie, you need to stop the drinking and take a shower. You'll feel a lot better I promise," she whispers, being motherly.

"I second that. You look like shit," Sarah says insultingly.

"Well Sarah, for your information I didn't ask for your damn opinion, and I also didn't invite any of you over here," I can't help but bitch.

"Wow, when Tony warned us about you being a bitch, I really didn't think he was being honest. But he's right, you are a bitch," Britney informs me

"Well, fuck you too." I am not used to anyone talking to me like this.

"Okay Lexy, we're here to help you figure things out because that's what *real* friends do and us Wenches are your real friends, like it or not, so get used to it. You aren't getting rid of us. I don't give a shit if you dump Grayson or not, that's your decision. I've known him all my life and don't want to see him hurt, but believe me, I'd be pissed off too after I saw all the videos of your fight," Brenda adds her two cents.

"What videos of the fight? Who has videos? I haven't seen any of those. I've only seen the ones Grayson sent me." I need to see the fighting videos. I can't break down and watch Grayson sing to me again. I've finally stopped crying. I know my eyes are red and swollen and I'm thankful the Wenches didn't mention that.

"What videos did my brother send you? We aren't showing you shit till you answer some of our questions. We're here to help you figure all this crap out, but that comes with you being open and honest. We'll share all of our videos, but you have to share too," Sarah demands.

"Babe, I told you Lexy is only used to everyone agreeing

with her and doing as she requests. That is why I brought you all over here. After three days of having to deal with the ex-Princess by myself, I figure she needs to learn how real friends behave and treat the people they love. Let's remember that no one was even allowed to show her their back."

"Tony! What the fuck?!" Now I'm getting pissed.

"Well ladies, let's all show her our asses and let her know we don't play like that." And as instructed, every one of the Wenches turn their asses to me and whacks them saying, "Kiss it bitch! We aren't going anywhere."

As they all walk into the living room, making themselves at home, I just curl up in my corner of the couch. Tony, Tiffany and Isabella head to the kitchen. Damn, I know she's carrying twins, but she is huge already.

"Lexy, would you like to come into the kitchen and see how simple it is to make chocolate covered strawberries?" Isabella asks while standing in the doorway, caressing her large baby bump. "These little guys can't wait for some themselves."

"I'd really rather not right now. I'm not in the mood for a cooking lesson. I'd rather just eat and drink myself to death. Thanks."

"I can see you've been doing a good job of that already. I don't want to see you spiral into a deep depression. I spent years in therapy after my mom moved me away from Drake as a teenager, and neither of us would have had to suffer through all of that if we'd have just put our pride aside and really talked to each other. I'm just saying."

Tiffany interrupts saying, "Isabella, we don't need the two of us to make these. It's just melting chocolate and dipping the strawberries in it. I've got this. You take those babies in there and see if you can get them fighting with each other again. Lexy hasn't seen that yet. And wait for me to join you before you all start talking about Grayson and her relationship. Trying cheering her up with baby news first."

"I can hear you, Tiffany. Nothing will cheer me up. I

broke Grayson's dick. Now I'll never have babies of my own,"
I cry out. I am not ready to talk to anyone about Grayson's
and my shit. I just don't know what to do. I just hurt all over.
My soul feels lost without him. What I'd give just to rest my
forehead on his.

"Look Lexy, I was at the hospital and the doctor told him
you didn't break it. It's just severely bruised and will take a
week or two before it's all better. Believe me, Mom was doing
the hallelujah dance in the hallway with the other moms,"
Sarah informs me with relief, as all the girl start laughing. "I'm
not shitting you. They went out in the hallway saying
HALLELUJAH!!! THANK YOU JESUS!!! With hands lifted
in the air, dancing around in the hallway. You'd think we were
at one of Joyce and Isabella's church services."

"Sarah, that isn't nice!" Isabella scolds as she turns her
head towards the kitchen calling out, "Tiffany, have Tony and
Thomas help you out by washing the strawberries and getting
them ready. Give me a holler when the chocolate is melted so
I can grab the first batch, we can just dip them into melted
chocolate and start eating them like fondue. We're friends for
life, we can share cooties." She comes over and joins me in my
corner of the couch when she's done yelling instructions.

"Thomas? He came too? Where is he?"

Right on cue, Thomas walks in yelling, "Ton, I backed the
SUV in just like you like it. I followed your instructions to the
letter. All the girls' blindfolds are hanging on the rearview
mirror." Anissa, Shelly and Dana come in behind him.

Fuck! You have got to be kidding me! I'm ready to kill
Tony. Nine people are here now. This is not helping. I need to
think. I need to be alone. I do not need everyone over here
telling me what I should do. I need to figure this out myself.

"Look at you. Come on, do you really think a five minute
phone call would be enough? We had to see you for
ourselves," Anissa says, coming over and pulling me into a big

hug. "Sweetie, you need to eat. Do you need chocolate? What's your poison for a crushed heart? I'll get it for you."

"Thanks, Nissa. I'd love another glass of red wine."

"I'll get it for you sweetie," she says as she walks over to the bar to get me a glass. "Anyone else want something while I'm over here?" Anissa calls out. She's always such a dear friend.

Everyone starts yelling out their orders as Shelly and Dana head over to help her. Shelly turns to me, "Go ahead Lexy, bitch and moan about how bad he hurt you and how you want his dick on a silver platter, and then we'll all get lost in a couple of bottles of Tony's expensive wine and figure your shit out. And let me be the first to say that if you are seriously wanting to plot cutting his dick off, I've got your back on that mission."

"Yeah, that's what having your own pack of Wenches is all about. Not only sorting your shit, but letting you know we got your back," Dana says from her spot beside Anissa.

"I've got the best idea! Just bring over several bottles and ten glasses, and some sparkling apple cider for the momma. That way we don't have to get up for refills," Thomas says, as he looks around the room, his eyes settling on me. "Girl, you look like shit. Get that fat ass of yours in the shower and wash your hair, and I'll get you some cut up cucumbers for those crazy swollen eyes. Jesus! Have you looked in a mirror the last three days you've been hiding out here?" Thomas says with his hand on his hip pointing towards the bedrooms.

"Fuck you! Nobody tells me what the fuck to do or when to do it. I'll easily kick your ass if you even try. And I don't want to take a goddamn shower. As I said before, none of you were invited over here. So, you don't have to look at me or smell me for that matter. And for your information, I don't smell that bad." I lift my arm in front of them and smell my pit. Not the best smelling, but I've smelled way worse.

"Dayummm. You are a royal bitch. You need your ass spanked. Badly," Thomas continues his verbal attack.

"No one is touching my ass."

"Well, that's just what I'm going to tell your Neanderthal boyfriend the next time he threatens me with bodily harm. Instead of the blow job I originally requested, I'll throw your ass under the bus and tell him where you're at if he'll spank that big ass of yours and let me watch," Thomas says making everyone laugh and yell that they want to watch too. My sick-ass friends, where is their love and support now?

"You did not tell him you wanted a blow job! Nor would you."

"You wanna bet, bitch? He sent over a couple of Brothers and threatened to kick my ass. I told them I call bullshit because I'm his sister's BFF and too many of my newly found pack of Wenches would protect me. But if he wanted me to tell him where you are, one of them would have to blow me," Thomas says, snapping his fingers with a big smile and a wink. Now everyone is laughing. Oh gawd, would I have liked to have seen that.

"Okay, both of you. You've woken up the babies. Now hush," Isabella says from beside me as she grabs my hand and places it on her stomach. Oh My God. I can feel the little ones kicking me.

"Wow! Those two little munchkins can really kick. That is so strong you can probably even see it."

"Oh, you can. You need to see this for yourself. I can only imagine what it's going to look like as they get bigger. I feel like my stomach is a scene from that old horror movie Alien," Isabella says as she lifts her shirt and shows us her tight stomach. We can see rounded areas lift for a second, poking up, like it's a foot or a knee maybe. God, how I pray Grayson and I can still have babies. I sooo want that one day.

Thomas comes running over and practically puts his face in Isabella's stomach. "Watching this is like the most magical thing ever. You ladies are so lucky to be able to carry the miracle of life in you. Oh, how I'd love to be a part of this one day. I told Sarah just the other day that once Tony knocks her up, I'm going to wear one of those fake baby bumps so we can do it together."

My head immediately snaps to Sarah as I blurt out, "You aren't trying to get pregnant, are you?"

"Lord, no. Not right now, anyway. But we've talked about one day. Give me at least a year or two, three at most. But I do believe Tony is my forever. He's perfect. He not only loves me unconditionally, he's great with my best friend. You don't understand how important that is to me. Not one boyfriend in my past has been able to deal with mine and Thomas's relationship. They've always been jealous and accused me of screwing him because of our closeness."

I'm thinking it's because Tony may be crushing on him too. What the fuck has Tony gotten himself into? He needs to tell Sarah everything. He should have told her months ago.

"I always see the three of you together, but damn girl, I didn't realize you were that serious," Britney says with a surprised look on her face.

"So, is this your way of telling your best girlfriends' since you were born, that none of us should expect to be your Maid of Honor?" Brenda asks.

"Not happening. Sarah and I promised one another years ago that we'd be each other Best Woman and Man of Honor, and none of you bitches are changing that. And besides, it'll be perfect because when it happens, Tony will be having Lexy as his Best Woman so I can walk her down the aisle. Watching Riggs squirm the whole time will give me such joy. He has to know I'll look a hell of a lot better in a fucking tux then he would. And besides, I'm the better man. I'd never punch a woman the way he did."

Laughing at him I say, "Thomas, don't go holding your breath. Tony has to ask me, and I might say no, after he brought all of you over here while I'm trying to deal with my broken heart."

"You must think I'm stupid. You love Tony as much as I do Sarah."

"Wait a minute, how did you drive here? Tony told you where this place is?"

Shaking his head and looking up to the ceiling like I'm some twit, he admits, "Duh, I work here with Tony. He hired me months ago. He knows I'd never tell the Brothers shit. I'm not joking when I told you about sucking my dick. You should see how rapidly they turn green at just the suggestion. It's a shame those boys are straighter than a 2x4. Life just isn't fair sometimes. They look too damn good to all be straight," he says, batting his wrist around and shaking his head. All the girls bust up laughing.

"Oh, my gawd, how I would have loved to have seen that. But come on, some of the Brothers could never pull off being gay. Not even joking around," Brenda says, still laughing. Her poor friend, Joyce, is bright red and giggling beside her.

"Yeah, Jackson, Grayson, and Drake and probably Carpenter could never pull off being gay. They are way too big and would make some damn ugly girls. I saw pictures that Tiffany had taken of Stevens when he lost a bet with Lexy, and damn, he could make a big girl jealous," Britney adds, laughing.

"Oh my gosh, do you remember back in high school when they all dressed up like cheerleaders? I bet Mom Gregory still has pictures of that. They *all* made ugly girls, believe me," Sarah tells us.

Now I have to ask Mom Riggs to show me his high school pictures. I really want to see Grayson's pictures, all the way back to when he was born. Thinking about this stuff makes my heart hurt worse.

"We weren't talking cross dressing, we're talking dicks. Lexy, is that massive eggplant dick of Grayson's always so massive? I mean, is he a grower or just a shower - when it isn't all swollen and purple? 'Cause if he is always like that, damn girl, how does that thing fit? You're just a little thing!" Thomas teases as Anissa hands me a nice big glass of wine

I look at the almost empty bottle of grappa on the table and hope Tony got me more of that, because after I get rid of all my friends, I'm going to need it. I miss Grayson's big dick. I miss everything about him. His eyes, his lips, his hair, his massive arms that give the best hugs. My heart aches to rest my forehead on his. What have I done? I need him. My body, my soul, need him to survive. I can't sleep more than a few hours before I wake up crying. I've cried more in the last three days than I have in my whole life.

"Look at her, she is thinking of that massive dick of his," Thomas teases, from his spot on the floor by Isabella's feet, resting a hand on her baby bump. Everyone starts laughing again.

"Thomas, you can be a real bitch yourself. Asshole," I tell him, pushing him with my foot.

"Well, thank you. I love being called a bitch. I take it as a compliment," he shoots back at me, pushing my foot away.

"Thanks for all the help, Thomas. Tiffany and I got it. You just stay there chatting like a bitch with all the girls. Don't worry about us, we're being the perfect hostesses without you, asshole," Tony says walking in with a massive amount of strawberries on a tray with Tiffany next to him carrying two big bowls of melted chocolate and a basket over her arm full of paper bowls and plastic wear for us to use.

"Well, sweetheart, I didn't hear you ask me for help," Thomas grouses, getting up to assist them.

"Lexy, don't answer that. We do not need more details about my brother's dick. We've all seen the pictures, or the real thing. I need to bleach my brain. Gross!" Sarah says, acting like she's gagging.

"Pictures? You guys have pictures of 'Sir'?"

"You call his dick, 'Sir'? Oh Lord, you got it bad," Brenda says, rolling her eyes.

Handing me a bowl of strawberries covered in thick chocolate and a plastic fork, Tiffany says, "Okay, that's enough dick talk for a minute."

"But she never answered my question. Is he a grower or a shower?" Thomas asks again.

"Fine, Thomas, he's both. You happy now? And can someone answer my question? Do you have pictures of a wounded 'Sir'?"

"Come on Lexy, you do not want to see those. It'll just make you feel worse. Just remember he deserved it. You did no permanent damage so let's leave it at that. And it's obvious you still love the guy so why the fuck are you still hiding out here? As you would say, did you lose your balls in that fight? Why aren't you talking to him?" Tiffany asks.

"Yeah, the longer you hide out, the tougher it's going to be," Sarah adds.

"I know he's been calling and sending you texts, why aren't you just answering those? You know, start the conversation you need to be having," Brenda adds her two cents now as well.

"Sweetie, she's right. The longer you wait, the harder it'll be. What are you having trouble deciding? Do you think your relationship might not work out now?" Isabella asks, patting my leg.

I feel my eyes filling with tears again as I finish off my glass of wine and grab the grappa bottle.

"Honey, staying in a constant state of drunkenness, isn't going to help the pain either. You really need to do some soul-searching. Do you want to talk it out?" Anissa asks, as I can hear the girls agree with her.

"Fine!" I put the grappa back on the coffee table. "You all want to know why I can't see him for a couple more days? It's because of this." I stand up and pull off Tony's oversized sweatshirt that I've been wearing since I got here. I instantly hear gasps and swears.

"Grayson did that to you?" Sarah demands.

"No, the tooth fairy did while I was sleeping. Yes, Grayson did this! How do you think he'll feel when he sees it? After talking to Tony, I learned Grayson had been drinking before our little fight and he was unaware of how hard he was grabbing me."

"Dang, all those bruises have to hurt. I suddenly feel like kicking him in the family jewels myself. Injured or not, that just boils my blood," Isabella says pulling out her phone and taking a picture of me.

Both my upper arms are so purple you can actually see the definition of where Grayson's hands had grabbed me several times, and my side has even a bigger purple bruise where he punched me. Pulling the sweatshirt back on, I sit down on the couch, looking around at all of them. I don't want their pity.

"Excuse me Lexy, have you tried cold herbal tea compresses on them? If you have any dried chamomile and lavender flowers, those work great too. You'd just need to brew them together and soak a towel in the mixture then wrap your arms. It could really help. Arnica salve with lavender oil is another option. You need to be eating things loaded with Vitamin K, like spinach and broccoli, or take supplements. That to would help a lot," Joyce informs me a little above a whisper.

"I thought you were a vet," I ask.

"Well, I am a vet now, but before that, I did a lot of other things. When I was a young girl, I used to help my mother care for people within our church community. She was like a midwife, pediatrician and doctor. Since we didn't use Western medicine, I learned a lot of homeopathic tricks that really work," Joyce adds.

"Thank you so much for sharing. I love the idea. Tony, do

you have any of those things we can prepare for Lexy?" Isabella asks.

"No, but I'm texting one of my men downstairs in the office to go out and get them. We can give it a try," Tony says while looking at his phone, texting away.

"Really, thank you, Joyce. I'd try anything to get rid of them more quickly. They don't really hurt. They were sore until yesterday, but today they are just really ugly. I know Grayson didn't mean to hurt me. I egged him on, and my arms got bruised because he was holding my arms so tightly when I kicked off his chest into a backflip. I don't want you to think badly of him. I helped cause these injuries with my own behavior."

"I saw the videos as well. I can see both of your sides. He didn't need to hold your arms so tightly and could have released them sooner. But hindsight is always 20/20. You do have ample skills to defend yourself and you proved that to him. He needs to trust and believe in you," Joyce adds.

"I know. I just don't know if I can handle it if he doesn't respect my abilities. I don't want to boss him around, I just want him to see me as his equal. I want to stand beside him in life, not behind him where he thinks I belong."

"That sounds beautiful. I hope that for you too. Where I come from that is unheard of. What I have seen since I gained my freedom is that several of the Brothers of Camelot families have that. The moms have just as much say as the dads. I even think at times one or the other will take the lead, depending on the situation. They don't always have to be dominant over the other, and that is what I admire the most. I think you could have that with Grayson too." Joyce says with a blush on her cheeks as she looks back down.

"Thank you, Joyce. I hope so."

"You totally can. Grayson is an emotional mess. He knows he screwed up. And yeah, he'd be so upset if he knew he caused so much damage to your arms. He just wants to talk to you so he can apologize to you himself. I swear, if he ever does anything like this to you again, all us Wenches will kick his ass for you," Sarah says, and everyone lifts their glasses saying, "Here, Here!"

"Thanks, Wenches. I'm sorry for being a bitch earlier. I miss Grayson and this separation is killing me. My chest hurts to breathe, but I can't see him until my arms are better, or makeup can hide it some. I have never felt physical pain like I am feeling right now and it's not from the bruises on my body. My heart hurts. It feels like it's literally broken." I can feel my eyes filling with tears once again, "I've never cried this much in my life. I am not a crier at all. I think I may have cried like three times in my whole life and I'm not kidding. This is unbearable," I say, wiping away a tear as it rolls down my cheek.

"What is Grayson saying in his texts? Is he apologizing or just begging to see you?" Anissa asks.

"He keeps telling me he loves me and that we need to talk. But the music videos are what's killing me. I can't call or text after those."

"What music videos? Please don't tell me he is sending you Ed Sheeran videos," Sarah says, sitting in Tony's lap and rolling her eyes. Those two are inseparable.

"No, not Ed Sheeran videos. He sent me videos of himself playing the piano or guitar singing the song 'Perfect' and several other Ed Sheeran songs. But the one that crushed me the most is 'You Are The Reason' by Calum Scott. That one makes me ugly cry every time."

"I wanna see them," Sarah says

"Me too!" says everyone but Tony.

"Oh God, I might scream and go insane if I have to listen to Grayson serenading her one more time," Tony whines.

"Well, I'll get you some earplugs then because I've never heard my brother serenade any girl and I have to hear this. Is he any good?"

"Yes, very. Here, watch it on my iPad."

"Gawd, I can't believe I'm even offering you this, but hand me that thing. I'll make it play on the TV so everyone can see it," Tony says, lifting Sarah off his lap and putting her in their chair before coming over and taking my iPad. With a couple of clicks, Tony has Grayson's video cued up on the big screen TV. Thank God I didn't know he could do this, or I would have been sitting in here all day yesterday, just hitting replay.

"Don't get any ideas Lexy. I'm blocking this after they play once each because I am not sitting here listening to Grayson 24/7 while you cry. That shit ain't happening," Tony says, and I flip him off. "Yeah, you love me, and you know you do. Here goes my torture." He hits play and cringes.

The big screen TV shows Grayson sitting at his piano. As he looks into his phone, he says. *"I love you, Lexy. Every word of this song is us right now. Listen to the words, I'm singing it just for you."* Then he starts playing the piano, looking down at the keys as he begins to sing.

'There goes my heart beating
Cause you are the reason
I'm losing sleep
Please come back now'

No one is saying a word, they're just staring at the screen as tears begin to fall from my eyes all over again. God! I miss my man. How will I survive without him? We have to make it, we belong together. As he reaches the chorus, I notice several other Wenches are crying with me. Isabella puts her arm around me and whispers "I'm not a crier either, but dang, this just rips your heart out."

"I know. I love him so much. I find it hard to breathe

without him. I'll never make it without him in my life. I need him. He's the other half of my soul."

"I feel your pain. Drake and I share that same bond. We're lucky women. You'll work it out. I'm sure of it now," Isabella says, cuddled up next to me, crying along with me as we watch.

'I'd climb every mountain
And swim every ocean
Just to be with you
And fix what I've broken
Oh, cause I need you to see
That you are the reason.'

"Yeah, that's enough. We aren't watching anymore. I can't even handle it. Man, I'd never guess my brother had that much heart, or that he was so good. Damn Tony, you need to send me something not so sad, but I want to be serenaded too." Sarah speaks up at the end of the song.

"First, I never said I could sing. I can do a lot of things baby, but singing isn't one of them," Tony responds with a chuckle, picking Sarah back up and putting her in his lap as she giggles along with him.

"So, you aren't even gonna try? Come on Ton, you and I'll work on one for her, even if you have to lip sync. Our girl deserves to be serenaded too," Thomas adds, moving over to sit on the floor by their feet. "I'll make you a list of a few songs."

Tony just chuckles shaking his head before looking over at me, "See what you and Grayson started? Fine, I'll think about it. But no one sees this other than you," he says to Sarah just before he kisses her. Thomas just looks up at them with a sigh. I cannot help but to roll my eyes. Yeah, Thomas is for sure crushing on Tony. I have to talk to him about this situation he's got himself tangled up in. Oh, I can see the rocky roads ahead of us all. Shit. Anissa's voice pulls me out of my thoughts.

"Oh, you are so blessed, even if you don't see it now Lexy. Any girl would love for a guy to send them videos like this. Damn, your man is talented. You are one lucky bitch. If I say so myself."

"I have to agree with you to Anissa. Lexy girl, get those herbal tea wraps on your body and get your ass in gear. You need to work this out with your man," Shelly adds.

"I second that," Dana adds as well.

"Well now that we all agree, they'll work it out. Come on Wenches, we all know these two belong together. Let's enjoy these strawberries. I have more junk food cooking in the kitchen. We'll go in there and enjoy the treats and drown our sorrow of not finding a man like that for ourselves yet," Tiffany calls out, picking up her glass and a bottle and heading towards the kitchen. All the girls and Thomas start getting up to follow.

Anissa pauses for a second and comes over to hug me again, whispering, "You got this girlie. Love you. I'm going to join Tiffany and the other girls in the kitchen. If you need anything, just holler."

"Thanks, Nissa. I'm okay. I'm just going to watch the other videos while you guys are in there. I'll be fine." I watch as Anissa heads into the kitchen.

Then I turn to see Tony and Sarah sucking face like they are alone without me still in here watching. I'm not having this, nope. I do not need the reminder of what I'm missing out on by being separated from Grayson.

"Tony! Time for you to get out of here and stop doing that where I can see you. Take it upstairs to your bedroom. I don't want to see it. I'm about to turn on Grayson singing 'Perfect' again, and this time Tony, I swear to God I'll turn it up so loud everyone working in the lower levels of the compound will hear it," I inform them, tossing pillows at them as I cue up Grayson with my free hand.

"Fuck Lexy! Excuse me," Tony says, abruptly pulling away and blocking the pillows. "You do know this is my house and compound, not yours, right?"

"We share everything. And I'm your best friend suffering from a broken heart. I don't need you rubbing your happiness in my face."

"Fine, we're going," he says, picking Sarah up and throwing her over his shoulder, swatting her ass hard. Damn, that had to hurt, but all she's doing is giggling. "You want some more of that, sweetie? Thomas is having the time of his life with the Wenches. Let's go get our nasty on for a while."

"Yes, please. I want it hard and the nastier, the better."

"Your fantasy is my command. I got some new toys too," Tony says, heading towards the stairs and squeezing her ass cheek even harder. Damn, those two are into the kinky shit. I just know it.

"I don't want to hear that! Sarah, don't mention having to bleach your brain of what Grayson's dick looks like and then talk to my bestie like that in front of me. Gross."

As they head up the stairs, Sarah calls out, "You sound jealous to me. Grayson must be boring in bed. You two only trying the ol' missionary position? Sounds about right for my stiff old-school chauvinistic brother. My condolences." She cracks up laughing and Tony joins in as they disappear from my view.

Geesh, shaking my head, trying to clear it, I hit play and I watch Grayson singing 'Perfect' to me. Grabbing the bottle of grappa from the table, I take a long drink. Feeling tears fall from my eyes, I wonder who ever knew love could be so painful. We've got to work it out.

Am I pissed at Grayson? Yes! Why does he have to always have to feel like I need protecting? Will we end up in a full blown fight, yelling and arguing about it all over again? If he cannot love me for who and what I am, I'm gonna have to figure a way to walk away from him. I really don't think I can have a man control me like that. My life under my father's finger was hell. I'm not going back to a controlling man. NO! I've got to be strong. I've got to stay free. But can I live without him?

I finish off the bottle of grappa and curl up into a ball on the couch and silently cry. How can I go on without him? If we can't figure this out, I'll have to learn. I must.

28

PARENTS

Grayson

"Stevens, you do know that when he wakes up, he's going to kick your ass, right? You've completely trashed Mr. OCD's house," I can hear Jackson telling Stevens. I can't even open my eyes yet. I'm so fucking hammered. I don't give a shit what he does. He can burn down the place for all I care, just don't ask me to move. Let me be like a pirate going down with his ship, except it's a house and not a ship. God, I'm so drunk even my thoughts aren't making sense.

"Hey, I didn't do all this myself. All you asses have been coming and going the last five days. This isn't just my food containers and boxes. And all you heard him yell, "Leave them!" All I did was follow orders."

"He's drunker than I've ever seen him. You know he didn't mean it," I hear Hawkins correct him. But I really don't give a rat's ass. Without Lexy, I'm as good as a dead man.

"You missed your calling Stevens. You could have been an architect with the Clay family, or even a part of Camelot Construction with your skills. You do a damn good job of building crap out of take out boxes," I hear Carpenter kissing Stevens' ass.

"I have to admit that I agree with Carpenter. Who would have thought you could do such a great job making Pizza boxes and Chinese food containers look like castle walls? That's a damn good wall. I would have never thought to use those take out boxes as castle towers." What the hell is Clay talking about?

Slowly I roll over on my faux bear skin rug that covers part of living room floor, blinking and squinting my eyes as light pours in from my balcony windows. Shit, I hate the sun right now. What the fuck is all around me?!

"Oh, Stevens, you better get ready to run again. It looks like the dragon is stirring," I hear Hunter say.

"Hey Riggs, good buddy. You waking up again?" Stevens asks as he stands up, waving his hands at a shitload of boxes around me that resemble the cardboard and duct tape castles we used to make at Mom Gregory's house when we were kids. Jesus, how much shit have I eaten this week? "While you were passed out this time, I took you back to your childhood and surrounded you in castle walls and we decided you were the angry dragon. What do you think? Look, I even made a draw-bridge by your head so we can stick your food and beer in there with you. I only used boxes that delivery services brought here," Stevens says with such enthusiasm that I am so not ready for.

"You're cleaning this shit up, you do know that right? Has anyone found Lexy yet?" I ask rubbing my bearded face, trying to sit up a bit. Thank God it's only castle walls all around me, and not a full-blown castle. Hell, I haven't done shit to myself since I got home from the hospital five days ago. I refuse to go into my room because it smells like Lexy, and that is where we made love the last time she was here, before I fucked up our lives and relationship.

"Well, we do know she's in the same shape you are, and

she's still hiding at Tony's underground compound. The Moms are getting pissed and going to talk to Tony, so we might get some intel from them later today." Hawkins gives me an update as I reach over and grab a warm beer off the coffee table.

"And dude, none of us are willing to give Thomas a blow job for information for you. Sorry Brother, but we all draw the line there. But on our last go round with him, he did say he'd lead us to the underground hideaway if you'd agree and I quote, 'to spank Lexy's fat ass and let him and some of the Wenches watch,'" he says, chuckling as he continues, "But I guess the Wenches are getting pissed at her too."

Realization of the mess of everything hits me, as I watch Jackson walking around the outside of my castle walls, playing my guitar as he starts singing. I don't really listen to him as my thoughts continue to race. Wait up, what the fuck is he singing? My head is buzzing but starts to clear, the harder I try to listen.

I know you love her, but it's over mate
It doesn't matter, put your phone away
It's never easy to walk away, let her go
It'll be okay

"Jackson! What the fuck?! That's low even for you. 'Be Alright'? You asshole. I'm not losing Lexy. I won't let her break up with me. There will never be another. SHE'S MY FUCKING SOUL!!! MY LIFE!! And by the way, you sound nothing like 'Dean Lewis'. Fuck you 'mate'," I yell at him. Oh God, my head! I realize I shouldn't have yelled as I grab my head with both hands in agony, hoping the ringing of the bass drums banging in my head will stop.

"Oh, well how about this song instead? Is this more what

you're feeling?" Jackson starts playing my guitar again and belting out the last chorus of 'In My Blood' by Shawn Medes:

Help me, it's like the walls are caving in
    Sometimes I feel like giving up
    No medicine is strong enough
    Someone help me,
    I'm crawling in my skin
    Sometimes I feel like giving up
    But I just can't
    It isn't in my blood.

Then all the damn Brothers start singing backup for him. Fuck 'em all. At least this song's words are more true. I know they're just getting me back for them having to listen to me sing love songs to Lexy. As my alcohol buzz continues to fade, the haze beginning to lift, I look around at these cardboard castle walls. It does look pretty good. I think I'll stay in it. At least Stevens left the coffee table in here with me so I can put my shit on it. Needing to return to my numb world, I take a long swig of my beer.

"Dude, don't drink that. That beer has to be warm. Here, take this cold one." Stevens reaches over, pulling my beer out of my hand as I take his cold one.

"Hunter, did you bring me more grappa and whiskey from the club?"

"Yeah, Brother I did. I also brought you a French dip sandwich and fries. It's still warm. You should eat some real food."

"What are you now, Hunter, my father? Hand me a bottle of grappa before I kick your ass, dad!" I demand. I don't want to lose my buzz. I'd rather be drunk off my ass. I can barely sit up. The room is spinning, and I don't give a shit.

I grab the bottle of grappa from Hunter and open it, taking a long drink, thinking about my dick for a second. It is a bit better. At least I can piss without wanting to cry. 'Sir' will live on for another day. He's still a bit sore, but the Brothers have been great at getting me frozen peas. I even think a couple of them have switched out my peas when I've been passed out for a couple of hours. But man is he purple. You can practically see the imprint of Lexy's shoe on him. I'm one lucky son of a bitch. It supposedly doesn't have any permanent damage, but it'll be a while before Sir will be up for playing. I can't help but snicker at my own joke.

Hearing a commotion, I turn to look towards the door. It must be more Brothers coming to check on me, but Madame didn't announce their arrival. Hawkins must have turned her off so I wouldn't get all bitchy every time she announced one of them.

"No Grayson, he isn't your father, but I am," I hear my dad's voice. Oh shit! He must have been in the hallway for a while and I didn't even notice.

Trying to open my eyes, I see several of the dads walking in. Hawkins has a relieved expression on his face. Oh, fuck! He called the dads and threw me under the bus. Goddamn him. I want to kick his ass.

"Hey, Dad. What are you doing here?" I say, trying to act sober and normal, knowing I'm doing a shitty job of it.

"What the fuck do you think? How old are you? You didn't do this shit when you were a kid, are you making up for it now? You call yourself a responsible man? You haven't gone to work one day this week. Yes, I've been checking up on you and I called Tiffany."

"Sam, what the hell is this shit all over the place? Did all of you boys regress to childhood? Duct tape castles?" Pop Carpenter yells.

"No sir. That was all Stevens doing."

"And you sat there like a dumbass drinking beer and didn't

441

do anything to stop him. All you boys get up and clean all this shit up. NOW!"

I hear all the Brothers hustling around. I want to laugh because it reminds me of when we were kids. God, I miss being a kid. Being a grown up hurts like hell. Adulting sucks rotten ass.

"Please tell me none of you called women over here?" I hear Pop Gregory bark.

"No sir. There hasn't been one chick over here. Not a one," Clay quickly replies.

"Thank god. You did one thing right at least."

"Grayson, it's time for you to grow the fuck up and handle this like a man. This pity party shit ends today. You are better than this. When was the last time you've eaten?"

"Sorry, Dad. I'm on a liquid diet for life. It helps with the pain of my dying heart," I say lifting my bottle of grappa up in a salute before taking another big drink.

"I don't think so, son," Dad says, stepping into my castle and reaching to take my grappa from me. I wrap my arms around it tucking it into my side like it's a football as I turn my body, trying to protect it.

Dad huffs in annoyance and then he starts ripping apart the wonderful castle my good buddy built to protect me. The room is still spinning, but at least I'm still able to protect my grappa.

I hear Pop Spencer talking on his phone, "Harris, stop off and get Grayson one of our special burritos. The boy needs it in a big way. Yeah, let me check. Have all you boys been drinking as much as Grayson here?"

"No sir. Everyone's had a few beers, but no one else is really drunk. Maybe a little buzzed but that's it. We aren't dumbasses like Grayson is. Well, right now anyway. We've been rotating and going to work, and we've been eating too," Hawkins squeals on all of us. Fuck, I always knew he'd turn us over to the parents even as a kid. The goodie-two-shoes ass kisser. Him and Bishop, always the first to squeal.

"Grayson, do you think you're going to get Lexy back being so drunk off your ass you can't even sit up? What the hell would you even do if your mom brought her over here now? You're in no shape to see her. You think she'd stick around and look at you like this?" My dad says.

He may have a point there. His words penetrate my alcohol fog enough for me to try to think. I'm I sober enough to talk to Lexy. Where's my phone? I twist and turn till I see it on the coffee table. I reach over and nab it, watching the screen turn on. I don't see any calls or texts from Lexy, and my heart falls out of my chest.

My dad grabs my phone out of my hand. "Noah, keep this. Do not let him talk to Lexy right now. We have to sober his ass up."

"You're a bit late for that. He's been sending texts and leaving a voicemail, and even videos since she ran out of headquarters," Hawkins squeals again.

"I don't wanna sober my ass up!"

Hearing more voices coming from the entryway, some I don't even recognize, but one voice stands out above the others and it's the one I wish I wasn't hearing. My mom. Oh shit!

"Grayson Richard Riggs! Look at you. What in the hell? I would never expect such behavior from you."

"Grayson Riggs! I thought you were a man. Not some drunken University kid!" I hear a deep, heavily Italian accented voice. FUCK! "I'm supposed to entrust Lexy with the likes of you?"

Looking up, I see a massive man in a black suit and a white shirt, no tie. He's got black hair with graying sides. He looks so familiar, but the grappa in my system won't let me place him. I can see he's about my size as he walks closer to me. I try and sit up.

Shit, Shit, Shit!!! This is Lexy's uncle. What the fuck do I say?! I watch him look around the room before he continues, "And all of you, you're supposed to be men! You call yourselves 'The Brothers of Camelot'? I think my brother Al may have been right all those years ago calling you 'boys'. This shit's been going on for five fucking days I hear, and you boys keep letting him wallow around in self-pity and alcohol?"

The Brothers hang their heads, not saying anything. Being reamed out by an angry Italian man is no picnic. I sit up more, trying to hold my shoulders back, but the room spins more and more. Oh gawd, I've seriously screwed up.

"I'm sorry sir. I'll get my shi... I mean, myself, together. I swear it."

"You're damn right, you'll get your shit together. Why the fuck haven't you gone to Lexy and straightened this shit out yet? I hear she's being a stubborn little shit and not answering your calls, so you just gave up and got lost in a bottle?"

Getting pissed at his assumption, I say a bit louder than I probably should, "NO! I've been calling her and texting her every few hours. Look at my phone if you don't believe me. She won't answer me. Hawkins has been trying to find her as well, but Tony has her hiding underground somewhere and our tracking system isn't as good as his."

"I know he's been coming out of his hidey-hole, and if I still know my Lexy, she's turned him into her little errand boy. Why haven't any of you kicked his ass and forced him to take you to Lexy?"

"Did you hear what she did to Grayson's dick? She almost kicked it off his body. And Tony is her boy: you mess with him and you answer to her, and there isn't a man in here stupid enough to do that."

"Fuck, you are a bunch of pussies." He leans into my face and grabs my bottle of grappa, looking at it before handing it to my father. "I do not want to see you in this shape again. How the hell can *you*, not your techno boy, but *you*, find Lexy in the shape you're in? What if those Russians attack your family today? What kind of condition would you be in? I can promise you that no matter what little heartache happened to one of the members of the Benassi or the Canzano Families, they wouldn't all be drunk off their asses when they know an attack is imminent. I thought you were the leader!"

"I am, sir. I fucked up. I'm sorry. It'll never happen again. I swear it."

"If this is how you handle Lexy after your first real fight, I don't know if you have the balls to deal with my daughter, and there's no way in hell that I'll let her be with a man who doesn't know how to handle her." His face is inches from mine. Shit.

"I agree. I've never responded to a situation like this. It was our first fight and she hid from me. I've been trying to find her, I swear it. I love her more than life itself. I respect her. I admit she is one hell of a warrior and it scares the ever loving shit out of me. I'll figure out a way to deal with that. I'll stand by her side, but I'll not let her boss me around. I promise I will not boss her around unless she acts like this again and shuts me the fuck out. I will not stand for that."

"Sounds like you might have some little balls after all. You man enough to tell her that?"

"Yes, sir."

"Then get your shit together, because I'm going to find Lexy with your mother's help. She *will* be talking to you within the next twenty-four hours or I'll kick her ass myself. I refuse to let her act like a spoiled brat and not talk to you. I'll deal with her first. You two better figure your shit out before Sunday when I bring my wife and the rest of her family over to your parents' house. Do you understand me?"

"Yes, sir."

"Now, no more drinking! Eat some goddamn food and clean your ass up. Do I make myself clear?"

"Crystal clear, sir."

He turns and looks at all the Brothers as they all look down, trying to look busy cleaning up my trashed house. I watch as he walks over to my father. "I hope you don't mind me talking to your son like that."

"No, go right ahead. You could probably kick his ass right now and we'd all be fine with it. I cannot believe his behavior myself."

"Is this the first time he's been in love?"

"Yeah. I've never seen him like this. He's been like a protective lovesick puppy since she came back into his life."

Lou laughs before he says, "I did some crazy shit myself the first time I was in love and I'm sure you did too. And I'll put an end to this once I get to my daughter. If these kids work this out, I'm sure we'll be seeing you Sunday night on much better terms." He sticks his hand out and shakes my dad's hand before he looks back to me and just shakes his head.

"Okay Lou, we have less than fifteen minutes to meet Thomas over at the club. He'll get us to Lexy. Follow me," Mom says to him, before turning to me. "Young man I swear to God, if I ever see you like this again, I am liable to kick your ass myself. Now eat something and get in the damn shower," she says as she turns and walks out, with Lou following right behind her.

Once they are out the door, I'm the first to call out. "FUCK!!!!" followed by several Brothers.

"Goddamn, I thought I was going to piss myself. Jesus," Stevens says.

"You and me both Brother. Grayson, you want to answer to him as a future father-in-law? Shhhiiiittt," Jackson replies.

I'm so disappointed in myself. I cannot believe I humiliated myself so badly in front of Lexy's uncle. Damn. I have some major ass kissing to do. And if another goddamn person tells me to take a fucking shower, I'm going to scream. Gawd, I don't stink that badly.

"Take this burrito and eat it, Grayson. You've been officially cut off. That goes for all of you boys," Pop Bishop announces, always the drill sergeant. "Liam, get a vacuum cleaner in here. Noah, you Sam and Gabe get some large trash bags and clean this shit up. I want it all sorted too: paper in one bag, cans and bottles in another. Hunter and Clay, you two gather up all the glasses and anything else that goes in the dishwasher and run it." Everyone stands around for a second looking at each other. Pop Bishop's ex-military life kicks in as he yells, "BOYS! HOP TO IT. MOVE IT! MOVE IT! NOW!"

"Yes, sir!" they quickly respond, and they all get up and start running around to do the chore that was assigned to them. I'm sitting here wanting to laugh again, remembering the time we had a party at my house as teens when Mom and Dad were out of town. Somehow Pop Bishop found out and did the exact same thing to us that he's doing now. We had my house cleaner than it was before my parents left.

"Grayson, you are not supposed to be daydreaming! EAT!" Pop Bishop yells at me.

"Ah, yes sir," I instantly reply. The burrito in my hand does look really good, so I open it and take a big bite. Chewing it up I hear my stomach grumble. I think yesterday we had pizza, but I haven't eaten anything other than liquid stupidity since then. My drunken self takes another big bite. FUCK, I need something to drink, fast. I yell out, "Someone get me some milk. Shit! this is as hot as fuck."

"Here you go, Grayson." I grab the glass from Pop Gregory, drinking it all. As the cold liquid hits my stomach, it starts churning. I've never been so drunk or hung over. I threw up, but shit, I'm not feeling so hot. Maybe I ate the burrito to fast. I try to slow my breathing, wondering how Pop Gregory knew I was going to ask for milk.

I feel all the liquor, the burrito and milk battling in my

stomach. Oh shit! I'm going to be sick. I look around in pure terror for a garbage can.

"Richard, Sammy, grab Grayson's arms and help lift him up. We need to get him to the bathroom before he spews or we're going to have one hell of a mess on our hands," I hear Pop Spencer call out as he moves everyone out of the way.

I feel the dads lift me to my feet and help drag/walk me into the hallway bathroom. I barely make it to the toilet before I start to hurl. I can't stop. I think I just threw up my balls. My dick is hurting like hell all over again. Who knew my stomach was so connected to my dick? I keep throwing up, for what feels like forever, before the dads finally lower me to the floor, letting me cling to the porcelain god. Oh fuck, I feel like royal shit right now.

My dad puts a cold washcloth on the back of my neck and says, "Here son. I'm sure you're not done yet." He hands me another washcloth and a glass of water.

Rinsing my mouth out, and spitting it into the toilet, I try to battle the urge to throw up again. I hear someone else throwing up in the distance. Then I realize it's gotta be Jackson or Stevens. Neither of them can handle hearing anyone barf.

"I cannot believe my eyes. You two assholes are barfing just because Riggs is? What is this, sympathy barf?" I hear Bishop yelling at the same time as the garbage disposal turns on.

"Shut the fuck up 'Liam'. I've never been able to listen to some one barf," Stevens whines as he throws up again.

"Stop it, Stevens! You're going to make me hurl too," I hear Jackson's shaky voice complain. He sounds like he's pacing somewhere, breathing heavily.

"Both of you, get out of the house. Go for a fucking run. That'll sober your asses up. This sympathy barfing has to stop. We've got enough on our hands with Grayson. Give me a mile. NOW!" Once again, I hear Pop Bishop barking out orders.

"I don't know if I can make it to the door," Stevens whines as Carpenter and Hunter laugh.

"Richard, I'll be back in a bit. I'm taking Noah, Gabe, Sam and Zack for a couple of miles run on the beach to clear their heads," Pop Bishop yells down the hall to Dad.

"Why the heck do we have to go? We weren't barfing!" Hunter grumbles.

"You giving me lip, boy?"

"No, sir."

"Both of you were standing there with your thumbs up your asses watching your Brothers barf, and all the help you could give was to laugh at them. At least Liam was helping them out by turning on the garbage disposal and cleaning up the counter. Where's the camaraderie for your Brother? You boys were brought up better than this. Now move your asses!" All I hear is running feet as Pop Bishop shouts, "Move IT! Move IT!"

You think you're finished barfing, son?" My Dad asks, pulling me back to the fact my face in the toilet.

"I feel worse than shit. All I want to do is go to sleep and hope I'll wake up and the last five days would have been a horrible nightmare. Dad, I fucked up bad. What does Lexy's Uncle think of me?"

"Well Grayson, all I can say is that you'll just have to prove to him you're better than this. You're a good kid. So, you fucked up once, we have all made mistakes. Let us help you to your bed. No more sleeping on the floor."

"But... but my bed smells like Lexy."

"You want us to go change your sheets?"

Just the thought of getting rid of Lexy's smell hurts me to my core. "No. Just help me up. The room is still spinning."

Pop Carpenter and Dad help me up off the floor and guide

me upstairs to my room, sitting me on the corner of my bed. Turning, I collapse in on myself as I look around the room and see Lexy's things scattered here and there. Neat and orderly is not one of her strong points, but I love her all the same. God, I miss her. I've got to sleep this off and sober up. Once I wake up, I'm fixing this, but right now, all I can think of is holding Lexy's pillow and breathing her sweet floral fragrance in.

"Okay Grayson, we're going to leave. I trust you to get some sleep. I'm making all the Brothers leave and give you some silence. I know Nicholas will probably want to stick around, but I know he'll give you your space. Love you, son, it'll all work out, I promise."

"Love you, too dad. Thanks for not continuing to lecture me. I'm fully aware of my screw-ups. I learn from my mistakes, and I don't want to make them again."

"I know son. Get some sleep."

"Grayson I just want you to know that there isn't a father in the room that didn't fuck up at least once. One day, we'll all share our own screw-ups with you. It'll help you learn from our mistakes as well. You probably won't screw up like this and get drunk over it again, but you will screw up in other ways. Love and marriage aren't easy, but they're the best things in life. Get some sleep. I'm going to join Harris and the kids on their run so I can kick Sam's ass myself," Pop Carpenter says.

And on that note, both of them leave the room and close the door behind them. I reach over and grab Lexy's pillow, clinging to it like it's my life preserver and I'm drowning in an ocean of heartbreak and pain. I break down and start weeping into the pillow, realizing what a hard-headed asshole I've been and all the mistakes I've made. I've got to win Lexy back. Inhaling her wonderful scent, I let go and cry myself to sleep.

29
CONFRONTED WITH REALITY

Lexy

*I*f anyone else shows up at this house, I swear I'm going to explode. The Wenches have been coming and going like they fucking own the place. I just want to be alone. I need to figure out what the hell I am going to do. I've had enough of everyone telling me what *they* think I should do. I have to live with whatever I decide, and I know I can't live without Grayson in my life. I reach over and grab the bottle of grappa I've been nursing since yesterday. At least I've cut back on that for now. I need to clear my head some so I can think, but I can't handle the pain in my heart.

I feel like shit. My eyes are still swollen, and my knuckles are bruised from pounding the punching bag in Tony's gym. I've spent an average of three hours minimum, twice a day, working out or dancing. My frustration leads me to training and punching, but my love of music and Grayson pulls me to my favorite escape which is dancing. At least when I'm doing that, everyone leaves me alone. Some will come in and peek on me and they actually seem to enjoy watching me. I wish they wouldn't watch, I prefer it when I'm alone. I enjoy getting lost in my dancing while singing a love song straight from my heart, until it causes me to break down and cry more. I can't wait for these tears to go away. I hope they never return.

Enough is enough. It's time. I've got to get my shit together, suck it up and talk to Grayson. I need to apologize. Sarah is convinced that if I just talk to him, we can work this out. But can we? What if he still doesn't want me to battle with the Brothers? What then?

I've got a meeting with the Benassi Family on Saturday to go over my plan once I know the Russians are here. They called me yesterday, wanting to know what was going on. I told them I was sick. I've turned into a lying pussy. To cover my ass, I sent Tony to train with them. They need to be ready at a second's notice. If the Russians attack, we all need to be prepared.

"Lexy, come on, it has been long enough. I just got a text from Hawkins and the Dads went over there to kick Grayson's ass and make him sober up. I guess he's been drunk the last five days too." Sarah stands up and walks over to me, actually pointing her long finger at me, demanding, "You have to call him today or I'll kick your ass myself."

Jumping to my feet, I look down at her finger then into her eyes. "So, you're ready for me to hand you your ass? It's awful brave of you to point your finger at me!"

"Lexy, chill," Tony says, walking over to protect Sarah.

What the fuck? He's backing her? Turning my head, I watch as several of the Wenches get up and stand beside them as well. Oh, hell no! This cannot be happening. I'm instantly being made aware of how short I am compared to these Amazon women. I leap up on the chair behind me so I can look down on all of them.

"I see how it is. Now you'll turn your back on me and protect your girlfriend, Tony? What the hell? She is the one yelling and pointing her finger at me."

"Get over yourself, Lexy. We're your friends. How many times do we need to tell you that? You've been holed up here long enough. As Isabella would say, 'time to put your big girl panties on and deal with it.' I love you Lex, but it's time."

"Fuck you, Tony. I need time to think. I need to be alone. None of you will give me any time to figure out what the hell I'm going to do."

"I beg to differ with you Lexy, but we've given you plenty of time and space. We've all been here to support you all the way. Yes, we've added our two cents, but that's just what we do," Brenda adds.

"Well, I never asked any of you for your two cents."

"Lexy, sweetheart, everyone in this room loves you, but how long are you planning on hiding? It isn't making things easier, that's for damn sure," Anissa says, walking over and joining the crowd in front of me.

"Come on, what the hell?! Are you all going to jump on me when I'm down?"

Sarah takes a step closer to me, while still pointing that finger at me. She has no idea how badly I want to grab it and break it. I can see her anger building as she yells at me. "I've had it with your 'woe-is-me' attitude. I didn't realize you were so immature that you'd toy with my brother's heart and feelings. If you love him, like you claim you do, talk to him. Gawd, what the fuck are you, a teenager? The man has left you hundreds of texts, voicemails and even sent you music videos of himself singing. Stuff that any normal girl would kill for. He's been trying to get you to send him a text saying *something*. If I were Grayson, I'd dump your ass. He deserves better than this! He deserves a woman, not a little girl."

"FUCK YOU!" I yell right back at her. "I am a goddamn woman! I'm just…"

"Sarah! What the hell is going on in here? I can hear you both yelling all the way in the other room," Mom Riggs yells as she walks in, interrupting my shouting match with Sarah and looking around the room at all of us.

Oh shit. Now I've got all the moms walking in. GAWD! I should have just escaped and gone into hiding and not told a damn soul where I was.

"Mom, you cannot tell me you agree with the way she's been handling this! We've all talked to her till we're blue in the face. Jesus!" Sarah yells back at her mom.

"Alessandra! What the hell are you doing, standing on the furniture like an uncontrollable bratty child, yelling at your friends? I raised you better than this."

Fuck! Uncle Louie is here. I watch him look around the room and march over to me. I'm so pissed I cannot control my tongue as I blurt out, "My name is not Alessandra anymore." Instantly I regret that. Maybe I should have put down the grappa bottle sooner, as I'm still holding on to it for dear life. Thank God I'm still standing in the chair because now I am at least as tall as he is.

"Alright then, if that is how you'd like to play this. Alexa Sophia Rogers, would you like for me to call your grandmother and tell her how you are behaving? Because I will. I just had lunch with her a few hours ago. Now get off of that goddamn chair and act like the young lady I raised and not the bratty child your friend just said you were. Because I completely agree with her."

"No! I am not having all these Amazons looking down at me, disrespecting me."

Uncle Louie puts his hands under my armpits and lifts me up like I weigh nothing and puts me on the floor. Then he takes the bottle of grappa from my hand and looks between me and the bottle as he says, "You are officially cut off too. For someone who isn't talking to your boyfriend you both have the same problem with making grappa your best friend."

"What do you mean by that?"

A smirk appears on Uncle Louie's face and I feel my heart

drop to my feet. "Well, I just left your boyfriend's house after handing him his ass. I will never bless a relationship to a boy that cannot handle you. He was laying on the floor, surrounded by a cardboard wall, drunk off his ass with a bottle of grappa in his hand as well. He's behaving like an immature university boy, not like the man I spoke to days ago over the phone. That is what you've turned him into."

"Grayson is a man! He's perfect. We just had a fight. I love him and I'm an adult and don't need your blessing!"

"I cannot believe that mouth of yours, nor the way you are treating your friends. Guess what young lady - you are no longer the Capo Donna of Northern Italy. You gave up the right to boss people around. All you wanted was to be a normal girl, remember that? Well, looking at you now, I don't think you're prepared to be a typical girl, nor are you mature enough. You definitely aren't ready for a *real* relationship with a man, if this is how you act when you have a disagreement. I cannot believe the behavior I've just witnessed," Uncle Louie says firmly, looking down at me.

"I am mature enough! And I'm a damn good friend. I've taught everyone in this room how to defend themselves. I've been there for them because I love them and never want them to feel vulnerable. I'm here for them always and they know it," I yell right back at him.

"Really?! By jumping on chairs and yelling at your friends who just want to help you? I think I'll have to disagree with you. I may have screwed up raising you by not allowing you to make friends of your own, because obviously, you do not know how to treat them."

"I do, too. I'm a good friend. Ask them yourself!"

"At this second, all I see is a little girl, throwing a childish fit. You're treating a man that supposedly loves you like dirt. That man looked like shit. Not only did you almost kick his dick off, but you've broken his spirit, stomping on his heart. I would have never thought you could be so immature and cruel. If you want to break up with him, be a grown ass woman and call him to tell him you're done. Don't lead him on like this. You respond to that man."

Ripping off my oversized t-shirt, I hear the moms gasp as I yell right back at him, "I'm a goddamn woman who doesn't want to hurt the man she can't imagine life without. Look at me! Take a close look at me! How do you think Grayson would react if he saw the bruises he caused? Huh?" I extend my arms where you can still see the light purple finger marks and the fading bruise on my side where he punched me.

"Damn him, I raised him better than this too. Now I want to slap the shit out of my son. What the hell was he thinking? It's been five days! I can only imagine what you looked like when this first happened," Mom Riggs says, examining my arms.

"No! I egged him on. I wanted him to treat me as an equal, not a fragile, dainty little girl. I've had way worse bruises than this before. It happens. I am a woman. I bruise easily," I try to explain.

"You finally said something that is right. You are a female and you can, and do, get hurt more easily, whether you want to believe it or not. Now that's the girl I raised, speaking with respect, but defending yourself. But I am not pleased with these marks," Uncle Louie says while lifting my arm and looking at them. I watch his Adams apple bob up and down. I can tell he is getting pissed. He reaches over and feels my ribs.

"Uncle Louie, I'm fine. Yeah, he bruised my ribs a bit but today they barely hurt. You've seen me hurt worse than this too."

"That is true, but it still doesn't make me happy." He looks over to Tony. "Why the hell didn't you call me when this went down?"

"Hey, I was just following orders. I was told not to tell a soul where she was, but I couldn't keep the Wenches away. Look how many are here now, and that isn't all of them. They threatened to cut my dick off if I didn't bring them over, and I believed them. She's been teaching them!" Tony says, pointing my way.

"Unless she is giving you orders in battle, you do not have to obey her. She's supposed to be your friend too, not your boss. You're just as much to blame for all of this shit as she is. She is not your Capo Donna anymore. You do know that, right? I didn't realize you are as screwed up as she is, or I might not have agreed to let her come out here with you."

"I am not screwed up like that!" Tony barks back.

Uncle Louie cocks his head and his eyes widen, looking directly at Tony. I watch and a smile slowly creeps on my face as Tony looks down and away from Uncle Louie's powerful stare that he still can crush us both with. "Doesn't look that way to me, son. Now get on your phone or computer or whatever you prefer and let those Camelot boys know where this place is. If we're working together with them, you aren't allowed to have a hideout. Who do you think you are, Batman now? With your own Batcave?" Uncle Louie says with a chuckle.

"Yes, sir. I mean no, sir. I don't think I am Batman. I'll send the intel over to Hawkins now, but I will inform him not to send anyone over for a bit because you are handling things, if that is alright with you?" Tony replies.

"Sounds good. Inform him not to tell Grayson her location until he has slept it off. I wouldn't want these two to deal with this shit until they are both *completely* sober."

"I am sober," I say and several of my so-called friends snicker and look away, covering their faces.

"Why do I not believe you, Little One? Okay then, if you're sober answer me this - what are you going to tell your boyfriend if he tells you he doesn't want you fighting and going into battle with them? What if he wants you to be his stay-at-home wife and mother to his babies? What then? What will you tell him?" Uncle Louie says looking into my eyes. I can feel my eyes filling with unshed tears, and my heart starts racing because deep down, that is my biggest fear. If that's what he wants, I know I'll have to walk away. I can't let him take away who I am and force me to be something I am not.

"Excuse me, but I know my son. There is no way Grayson would want Lexy home barefoot and pregnant. That is not how he was brought up. Every woman in my family is strong, independent and powerful in their own right. Even my daughter, his sister Sarah, doesn't take shit from men. She's kicked many to the curb for not accepting her the way she is. Tony has been the first man to really ever win her heart and she trusts him. Grayson could have had dozens of weak-minded submissive girls my mother in law has pushed on him, if he wanted a spineless woman, but he doesn't. He wants Lexy. He just has to figure a way to deal with the warrior side of her. These two just need to sit down and talk. They are both leaders, like my husband and I are. It's rough, but they love each other and will work it out. Or they'd better," Mom Riggs says, walking over to me and giving me a genuine smile and a wink.

"Sarah is Tony's girlfriend?" Uncle Louie asks, looking very surprised as he looks between me and Tony. Sarah wraps her arms around him, and he returns the gesture by wrapping his around her.

"Yes, Tony is my boyfriend. We've been seeing each other in a committed relationship for months now." Sarah says proudly, and Tony smiles ear to ear, giving Uncle Louie a pleading look.

"Well, congratulations. That is good news to me. I wish you both the best of luck," Uncle Louie says, giving me a questioning look.

"Oh, you don't worry that big ol' heart of yours, Mr. Louie. Tony worships her. We're all the bestest of friends. Can't you just tell? Look at them, they're just adorable together," Thomas says as he walks towards Sarah and Tony with a big smile on his face. I know exactly what Uncle Louie is thinking, because he knows Tony. Jesus, I hope he doesn't blurt out anything.

"And you are?" Uncle Louie asks with one eyebrow raised.

"Oh, let me introduce you. This is Thomas. He's been Sarah's best friend since elementary school. He's like my adopted son, or daughter at times," Mom Riggs says with a smile.

"Okay. I see how it is. Nice to meet you, Thomas," Uncle Louie says, looking between me and Tony. Yeah, I've got a gut feeling Tony and I are going to be getting a lecture in the very near future.

"Nice to meet you too, Mr. Louie," Thomas says, sticking his hand out to shake Uncle Louie's as he teasingly checks out Uncle Louie with a smirk on his face. Several of the Wenches start giggling, egging Thomas on.

Thank God Uncle Louie doesn't fall for his joking. He turns back to me and asks, "Well, Lexy? You didn't answer my question. If you're so sober, can your mind come up with an answer if Diana happens to be wrong and Grayson does want you to give up your independence?"

I feel a tear run down my cheek, unable to control it. "Why do you think I'm still hiding out? I don't want to hurt Grayson, and I know if I talk to him, I'll lose it and break down. I'll never love another, but I refuse to allow another man to control me and take away my freedom. If that means I walk away from him, as much as it kills me, I will." I lower my face into my hands and sob. I feel both Mom Riggs and Uncle Louie's arms around me in a group hug.

"Oh, my sweet fearless Lexy, Grayson loves you with all his heart. As I've told you before, you are the only girl he has ever given roses to. The only one he ever brought home. You remind me of myself, strong and fearless. He just needs to figure a way to handle you and control that the idiotic part of himself he inherited from his father. I feel it in my heart that you two are meant for each other," Mom Riggs says as she kisses my forehead before stepping away, leaving me to fall into Uncle Louie's warm and comforting embrace.

Oh God, I needed this so much. No human brings me as much comfort with an embrace as Uncle Louie and Grayson do, but it is in such different ways. But I always find comfort and safety in Uncle Louie's arms.

"I know this is a tough one for you Little One, but deep down, you are the strong warrior I raised. You can handle this and anything else that comes your way. You just have to get rid of that inner bitch that wants to boss everyone around. I love you, and I always will. You two kids will figure this out. Now you go and take a shower to freshen up, while me and these moms fix you your favorite meal."

Wiping away my tears, I look up at him asking, "My favorite meal?"

"Yes dear, I'm going to teach these moms how to make real Italian Pesto. We got the supplies before we came here, and I'm sure one of them knows how to make that American strawberry cake of yours," Uncle Louie says, kissing my forehead and pushing the hair that has fallen out of my braid from my face.

"American strawberry cake?" I question.

"Yes, American strawberry cake. That was your Grandma Rogers' recipe that your mom and Elena loved, and she taught it to cook way back then."

"Really?! I never knew that. Wow, you do learn something new every day. Why did you never tell me?"

"You have to ask?" he says disbelievingly.

Rolling my eyes, I reply, "No. My evil Papa, who has lied to me my whole life probably wouldn't have allowed it. But it is you, as always, I need to thank. Uncle Louie, you're right. I need to handle this, and I will, I swear. Grayson and I will work it out, but not until all this alcohol is out of my system and I've eaten my favorite meal. By the way, where is Camilla?"

"She is at the hotel. The kids were completely worn out after an afternoon with the Rogers family, just like you used to be when you were younger than both of them. You know how they all can be. Now, you go get showered and we'll talk more later. And no, I did not tell them how you screwed up your relationship with your boyfriend. I think you owe your friends an apology as well."

"Yeah, you're right. Thank you for not telling them. By this time tomorrow, I swear I will have talked to Grayson. I just have to figure out for myself the best way to do that. I'll deal with it."

"I believe you. Do what is right in your heart, and always remember I'm here for you too, you know. You can always talk with me about anything. This is the life you always dreamed of, don't screw it up by being a bossy bitch. Be a friend. Try understanding them and respect them. They saw your pain and just wanted to help."

"I know. You're the greatest Uncle Louie. I'm sorry for screwing up." Turning and looking at my friends, I say, "Sorry Wenches. I've been a horrible bitch and a sucky-ass friend, talking down to all of you. Please forgive me. I'll work on it." I walk around the room, hugging each one of them. I'm so lucky that they are all loving and wonderful.

Grabbing my phone, I jog into my bedroom and send Grayson a text before getting in the shower.

'*I love you, ALWAYS. You are My One Love. We'll work this out. Talk soon.*' I couldn't resist adding a kissy-face emoji. I press send, and just stand here, hoping I get an instant response. When I don't, I remember Uncle Louie says he's probably passed out, but I smile knowing that'll be the first thing he sees when he wakes up.

I'm already feeling better, my spirits are lifting. Mom Riggs is right. Every woman in Grayson's life is strong and works hard. None of them are the quiet, submissive type. Every one of the moms has strength and spunk, and I love each one of them. I'm beginning to get a good feeling. Gosh, this is really Grayson's and my first fight. I get into the shower, thinking that we both handled this horribly. Being honest is the best way to deal with this. I'm just going to lay out the facts: if he cannot love me the way I am and stand beside me instead of in front of me, he needs to tell me now.

Deep in my heart, I know he loves me, my strength and power. He was getting turned on fighting with me. Yeah, it's time to get my man back. I cannot wait to experience make-up sex with him. I've been told it's supposed to be amazing. Yeah, after I eat and everyone goes home, I'm taking one of Tony's cars over to Grayson's. We're talking tonight, enough wasting time. It's been five days without Sir filling me to completion. My core contracts at the thought. Now I'm thinking maybe I should just sneak into bed with him and we can talk after I attack him. I need him. My body and soul craves him. I'm hours away from an incredible release, I just know it. Time can't rush by fast enough. I've got to get to my man.

After my power nap, something I am a pro at, I'm fully rejuvenated. I know I'm taking a chance, but I can't just sit here at Tony's any longer. No matter how deep down I shudder in nervousness, I still can't wait to see Grayson.

It's been eight hours since I sent him that text, and still no response. Gawd, I hope he's just sleeping. My mind won't stop racing. What if he is really pissed at me for being so stupid and not responding to him? Do I have a bad case of the dumbass-ness or what? I'm practically scared shitless.

As I pull into Grayson's driveway, I can feel my heart pounding like it is about to burst out of my chest. This just has to work out. I keep repeating to myself, 'Think positive…. Think Positive.' I can't lose him. I hope Tony isn't pissed in the morning when he realizes I borrowed his sports car. The thought makes me giggle. It is what could get me here the fastest, which is why I chose it. Getting out of the car, I pause for a second to admire all the stars and remember... Oh, I hope Grayson is ready for a surprise. As I head for the door, I take a deep breath, this is it. I'm going to knock on the door in hopes he is the one who opens it and not one of the Brothers.

30

MEETING IN THE MIDDLE

Grayson

"Sir, Ms. Lexy is at the front door."

Holy Shit! I jump out of the shower and grab a towel, quickly wrapping it around my waist before grabbing another to rub on my head and the rest of my body as I make a mad dash for the door. Why the hell didn't she just let herself in? Oh, Fuck! Is she here to dump my stupid ass? No…. no… no… I cannot think that way.

"Coming!" I yell as I run down the stairs, hoping not to slip and break my neck. As I reach the door and grab the knob, I take a deep breath and slowly let it out before I pull the door open. As I look at the woman of my dreams, my heart starts racing. She's so beautiful and she's here. Oh God, I've missed her. She slowly looks up at me and our eyes lock. Those spectacular clear blue eyes of hers see straight into my soul and make me ache with longing. She controls my world, even if she doesn't realize it.

Damn, my heart hurts even more knowing the pain I've caused her by being such a stubborn jackass. We just stand in my doorway, taking each other in. I watch as she bites her lower lip, checking out my chest. Uncontrollably, it flexes on its own. I can tell she is nervous, and I blurt out, "Are you here to dump my stupid ass?"

"God, no. I love you, Grayson. Didn't you read my text?"

"No, I didn't see it. They took my phone away hours ago, before I passed out. When I woke up, all I wanted was a shower. Then Madame announced you were here, and I haven't had a chance to go looking for it. What did it say?"

"Emm," She slowly looks up my body, causing my dick to swell which makes it hurt again. I try to clear my thoughts so my dick won't explode as she says, "I just told you I loved you and we needed to work this out, or something like that," she says as a blush spreads across her cheeks. I can't help but smile. I love the way she blushes so easily around me. I'll make doubly sure to find my phone. I'm sure that text said more than just that.

"So, you're here to talk?" The way she is looking at my body makes me think she wants more than just to talk. She looks as hungry for me as I am for her.

"Well, we do need to talk," she replies just above a whisper, still checking me out, slowly. Well, I am standing here in nothing but a towel, still a little damp from my shower. Her gaze is so hot it feels like an actual caress, and I'm beginning to sport some major wood. Fuck, the harder I get, the more pain rushes to my balls and gut. Shit, this can't be happening.

Noticing she's wearing an oversize black t-shirt with 'Stark Security' printed on it makes my jealously rage. Fuck that! That's Tony's shirt. "Call me jealous, I don't give a shit, but you have to take that shirt off. Yeah, I know Tony supposedly has a thing going on with my sister, but you always turn to him. He's your best friend, but that's what I wanna be. Call me immature and a jealous asshole, that's fine, but I don't like seeing another guy's name on your chest. I'll give you a dozen of my 'Camelot Security' t-shirts to keep over at Tony's. Just take that fucker off."

A huge smile spreads across her face and she tilts her head and licks her lips. "Sounds good to me. I'll gladly take it off if we can talk after you let me have my wild wicked way with you. Crazy hard makeup sex sounds really good right now."

"Hell yeah!" I reach and grab her, pulling her into the house as she leaps into my arms and wraps her legs around my waist. My towel falls to the floor as I pin her to the wall beside the door, closing it with my foot.

Passionately, I start kissing her like my life depends on it and my dick turns to granite. I think I'm going to die from the pain ripping into my dick and balls. The harder I get, the worse the pain. God, this can't be happening. I'm trying not to think about the pain and just hope it passes. With one hand I reach down, grabbing the hem of the offensive t-shirt and ripping it upwards, breaking our kiss just long enough to rip it off of her and toss it to the floor.

I devour her mouth again, grabbing that scrumptious ass and giving it a good squeeze. I'd love to throw her over my knee and rip these leggings off and bite one of her ass cheeks right now. Lifting her away from the wall, I walk us into my living room and rub her hungry pussy up and down my cock on the way. Oh shit. It hurts like hell but still feels damn good at the same time. Oh shit! I sit down on the couch with her continuing to moan and ride my cock. I don't think I can take it. It hurts so damn bad, but I'm so fucking close to blowing my load. Pulling away from Lexy's kiss, I throw my head back and call out, "FUCK! This hurts like hell, but I'm so goddamn close. Give me a minute." I breathe heavily, trying to catch my breath and manage the pain.

"Baby, what is it? Did I hurt you?" Lexy asks as she leaps off me, dropping to the floor on her knees between my legs. "Oh God! Look what I did to Sir! I am sooo sorry Grayson," Lexy says as she leans forward and lightly kisses the side of my cock that is still purple with bruises. Damn, at any other time

I'd love to see her mouth that close to my dick, but right now it hurts so badly I can feel tears fill my eyes.

"Babe, don't. I can't take it. I'm so fucking close to blowing, but my dick hurts so fucking bad I can barely breathe right now," I whisper, still trying to breathe slowly and get Sir to stand down.

"But baby, he's leaking! I know he's close so let me help you. What can I do?" she asks as she wraps her hand around the base of my dick and firmly squeezes him. It feels so fucking good it causes me to see stars. Lexy leans forward and licks the head of my dick. Fuck! Sooo good... I spread my arms across the back of the couch, squeezing the cushions, breathing through my open mouth, trying to figure out what the hell to do.

"Babe, I... I just don't know what to tell you. It hurts like a mother fucker. But you're right, I'm so damn close. I've missed you so badly. I just can't handle the friction. Seeing 'Sir' that close to your mouth is causing him to leak pre-cum. He wants that hungry pussy of yours so badly, but he hasn't healed enough for that. Shit!"

"I can handle this, baby. Just relax and enjoy."

Lexy starts slowly using that sweet tongue of hers, licking around the head of my dick. I'm trying so desperately to control my breathing and praying the shooting pain goes away. I fight the tears, rushing to my eyes as my cock gets harder. Oh God, I watch as she flattens her tongue over the tip as she lightly squeezes, then sucks just the head between those full lips of hers.

My hands release the back of the couch of their own accord and I grab her head, holding her in place. "Oh God Lexy, I'm .... I'm going to cum." She gives the head of my cock a quick, firm suck before she pulls away with a pop, and my dick starts exploding, shooting cum straight up my abs and chest. She smiles again before dropping her head back to my dick and licking me clean. I'm seeing stars and I close my eyes for a brief second, escaping into paradise with a mind-blowing orgasm.

"For your information, that was not a real blow job. It was just a little over-the-top foreplay to help you to get your release since I wounded 'Sir' so badly," Lexy says apologetically as I catch my breath. I open my eyes to see her sitting on her heels between my legs. God, what a beautiful sight.

"Okay, if that's your story I'll let you call it whatever you want to call it. Feel free to suck the head of 'Sir' anytime you want to. Can I return the favor now?" I say as I reach forward to unzip her sports bra and toss it on the coffee table, pulling her into my lap. Leaning down, I suck on her nipple, making her moan.

"Nope, you do not need to return the favor. That can wait. We need to talk."

"What? Come on, baby. It's time to let me have *my* wicked way with your body. I will not stick my tongue in that hungry pussy. I'll just nibble and tug on that hard clit until you scream out my name... and your undying love for me."

She pushes away from me, sitting further back on my thighs, looking at her left hand. "I do not see a ring on this finger, and I sure as hell do not remember you even asking me to marry your sorry ass." She tilts her head to the side and starts dramatically tapping her temple. "You'd think I'd remember something that should have been pretty damn earth-shattering, something that I'd always look back on thinking 'No woman is as lucky as I am to have such a wonderful man make a proposal so romantic.' Nope, I don't remember anything like that."

I cannot help but laugh at her antics. "Is this your way of shutting me down once again and not allowing me to go down on you and show you how 'Sir' earned his name?"

"I meant it, Grayson. I am saving that for our honeymoon after we have a wedding fit for the history books. I can see it now: arriving at the front of Camelot's Chapel in a carriage, pulled by two of Hawkins' Clydesdale horses. Tony and Thomas will help me get out of the carriage, and I'll be dressed in my incredible vintage cream wedding dress with a ten foot long train. I'll stand beside Uncle Louie, waiting to go into the church."

"I can see it too. But all you said before was that you were saving that until after you are married. You never said *anything* about the honeymoon. So, moments after you say I do, I'm throwing that luscious ass of yours over my shoulder and running out of the chapel to the bridal chambers, where I'll be eating that fine hungry pussy of your till you scream my name," I say as I pull her onto my chest, laughing.

As she starts giggling herself, she adds, "I don't think so 'Sir'. That will not happen. You are not doing a Drake and Isabella. We all know he probably took her back into the bridal chambers to consummate their marriage vows. We aren't stupid."

"Well, Drake started a Brothers Tradition I have to continue." As she lies on my chest, we both continue to laugh. I tug at her leggings and add, "Someone has on to many clothes. I want to feel all of you, skin to skin. Let's continue this in the bedroom."

She lifts up and kisses me really quickly, before saying, "Fine, but we talk first, before any more fooling around. Agreed?"

Reluctantly and with a deep sigh, I agree. "Fine, I'll agree, if you insist. But your clothes stay down here."

"Okay." She stands up and turns around, bending over and putting that fine ass of hers in my face. She wiggles and removes her leggings before I watch her pull that thong from her tantalizing ass. I cannot resist a temptation like that, so I grab hold of her hips and quickly lick the crease of her ass before lightly biting her ass cheek. Lexy pulls away from me and tries to act like she is scolding me, but she's failing horribly. "Grayson, knock that off. None of that till we talk. I mean it," she says as she giggles and takes off running butt-naked up the stairs.

Goddamn, we better make this talking shit fast, because I have other ideas for that delicious woman of mine. I take off after her, yelling, "Madame, lock down the house and scramble my passwords so the Brothers can't get in easily."

"Yes Sir. Access codes put on scrambled status. House locked and secured. Have a good evening, Sir. Signing off." Nice, if Hawkins shows up, he'll know Lexy is here and will not bother me. Walking into our bedroom, I find Lexy looking breathtaking. She's lying on her side with one leg bent forward covering the sweetness between her legs that I'm sure is wet for me. Her head rests on her bent arm, which is wrapped around an over-stuffed pillow. She looks at me, licking her lips.

"Okay, let's talk," she says, looking at my hardening cock. Damn, that woman can break me. I know she wants me, but if she is determined to talk, we will talk.

"Okay, what would you like to say? I'm finding it hard to stay focused on anything other than hearing you breathing heavy and calling out my name a time or two as I watch you cum."

"Like I said, that can wait Grayson. Do I need to get dressed?"

"No, you don't, but if you're serious about only talking right now, let's get under the covers and let me wrap my arms around you so I can feel your skin against mine."

I watch as she quickly pulls down the covers and crawls in, and as I climb in, she moves over beside me without hesitation. I wrap my arms around her, pulling her tight to my chest. She rests her head just under my chin and I inhale her clean floral freshness. It feels like home. Safe and secure, like everything will be alright.

"I need you to be honest with me, Grayson. What do you expect of me? If you want me to stand down, I cannot and will not do that. Not with these Russians. But I can swear to you that the only time I will go into battle is if it is a direct attack on my family or yours. Or for that matter, any of the Wenches, Brothers or our friends. Otherwise, I'll not interfere in any of Camelot or Stark Security issues unless I'm asked. Can you live with that? Tell me now, because if you can't, as tough as it is, and as much as I love you, I'll have to walk away. I cannot allow another man to control me or dictate my life in any way."

"You don't waste any time, do you? You go straight to the tough questions."

"No, I don't waste time because we both know I'm good at what I do. But that is not the daily life I want. Look, I was offered jobs by the CIA and FBI, as well as other government agencies in this country. I turned them all down. They all know who I am and what I'm capable of. I don't want to live that life. I have my clubs and nonprofit programs that I want to dedicate myself to. Look Grayson, that life was forced on me as a child. Yes, I'm good. I'm damn good. But I've always wanted to be normal. It's hard, because when things like this happen, that built-in switch goes off and I will follow through. Especially if it involves you or those we love."

"You would really be okay doing that? Or are you doing it for me? Are you sure that's the life you really want? You'd be happy not being a part of our day to day security issues?"

"Look, when I left Italy, I was never so thrilled and relieved to have that part of my life over. I haven't murdered anyone since I left, well, except for those Russians. But in all honesty, I have beat the shit out of a couple of guys I saw with their girlfriends who wouldn't take no for an answer or being physically aggressive with them. I rescued the girls and got them away from those asses. But no one knows it was me. I keep that part of my life well hidden. It's yet another reason I wear brown contacts or dark sunglasses. Grayson, I could have easily accepted any of those job offers from those agencies, if I wanted to live my life that way. They had all heard about my skill, but it didn't even cross my mind to accept."

"Really? Were those offers made here or in New York?"

"New York, but none of that matters. They know about me here too. Come on, I know they watch me just to make sure I don't have any illegal connections, which I don't by the way. But Grayson, no one threatens my family or yours and lives to talk about it. I will kill every last member of the Osokina family myself. I've already made plans to do so and have been working with the Benassi family. I'd like to include you and the Brothers, but if you cannot handle it, I'll do it alone."

"Hell no! We do this together. You're one of us now. We can work with the Benassi Family, but the Brothers take the lead. I don't think I can fight beside you because I'm an over-protective asshole, and I'm afraid you'll get hurt. I know you're good, no, you are the best at what you do. I couldn't swing around on a fucking rope and be as accurate as you are, not with a gun or any other weapon. We can divide and conquer. I'll take the lead with the front end attack, and you can do what you do best - come in the back and hit the air with Tony, Stevens and Jackson. The Benassi Family will have your ass from the ground. I will learn to live with that."

"I've been so afraid you wanted me to be your little woman and that you'd never trust me. I know what I'm doing, I swear. It all comes naturally to me. I know my limitations and I am fully aware that I am a woman, a small one at that and do not have your strength and size. But I make up for it in knowledge and other abilities."

"I know you do baby. I'm ... I'm just scared. You aren't bulletproof."

"And neither are you."

"True, but…"

"Grayson, like I said before, I'll only fight when it is people we know and love dearly that are in danger. Your day today work I want no part of. Nobody messes with my family or friends and lives to talk about it. When that switch is flipped, you do not have the power or ability to turn it off. I just go on autopilot and there is no stopping me."

"I don't like it, but I can live with it."

"Good. And besides, I think you kind of like the fact I can kick ass and take names."

Chuckling, I roll my eyes and admit, "Well, since we're being honest, it is a major turn on to see how badass you are and how you can kick ass and take names with ease. 'Cause when we were fighting, that's what got me hurt in the first place. I knew I was getting turned on, but I was unaware how much wood I was sporting until I saw Stevens' video of you practically kicking my dick off. If I would have had my hormones under control, that never would have happened."

Giggling, she replies, "Yeah, you moved at just the wrong time. In all honesty, I was aiming low. I was going to kick your injured leg."

"What? That is a low blow, even for you. My leg's not 100% yet."

"Yeah, I know. But I warned you I do not fight fair. I fight to win, and I did."

"True that," I say as I lightly run my fingers up her bruised arm. "I did this by grabbing you, didn't I?"

"Yes, but they don't hurt, I swear. I'll admit the first couple of days I was a bit sore, but believe me, I've been bruised a lot worse."

Pulling back the covers, I look at her ribs. "Shit! Baby, I'm really sorry. I was practically drunk. It had been a rough morning, or I would have never allowed myself to have fallen for your taunting."

"What made your day so rough? Meeting my family wasn't that bad."

Snickering, "No, it wasn't. That was very interesting,

meeting your bodyguards. I am a bit relieved Luigi is married. You two seem a bit too close for my comfort."

She lifts her head up off my chest and rolls her eyes at me before giving me her sass. "Really?! You're jealous of my old bodyguard, who, by the way, married his childhood sweetheart who is very pregnant?"

"Hey, I saw the way he looked at you, and the way you looked at him. I understand that he's married, but I also know he was on your dad's list of potential husbands," I inform her, not believing I went there and brought it up.

"Oh brother. My Papa considered Lucca and Rocco, which would never happen, as well as Orlando and Dante from the Benassi Family. Are you jealous of them? You already admitted your issues with Tony."

"You're beautiful and I love you, so naturally I'd be a bit nervous and jealous of people your own father wanted you to marry."

"Well, I would have *never* married *anyone* my Papa picked for me. Oh, and here's an FYI: Orlando and Dante are both married to dear friends of mine, so you have nothing to be jealous about. You're the only one I've ever wanted or needed."

Flipping her onto her back, I kiss her passionately, making both of us breathless. "Now, can we be done with talking for tonight? I've missed you and I need to make up for lost time."

"No, you don't. I love you too. But you're wounded, and I'm not doing what I did earlier again tonight. Besides, we've also lost a lot of sleep and there is nothing I want more than to fall asleep in your arms. Where I belong."

Pulling her even closer to me, she wraps herself around me. Damn, this is paradise. "You're right, I am very sleep deprived. I don't sleep nearly as good without you in my bed."

"I love you Grayson Richard "Dickie" Riggs, and I'm so glad you could meet me in the middle and not try to control me."

"Dickie?"

"Yeah, your mom calls your father 'Dick' when he's being one, so I decided your new nickname will be 'Dickie'.

"Ah, no!"

"Emm, you don't have a choice. The Wenches agree. You act like a dick again, and we'll call you on it. So, suck it up and deal, 'Dickie'," she says with a giggle, cuddling into me so close I don't think air could get between us.

Fuck it. She can call me anything she wants as long as she snuggles this close to me. I feel completely at peace. We're going to make it. I've got my forever woman back in my bed and in my life to stay. I'm confident I can handle all of this. Now I just have to figure a way to kiss up to her uncle and prove to him that I am worthy of his 'daughter' so I can ask for his blessing and make this official. She was right with her teasing earlier, I do need to put a ring on her. Now I just have to think about that perfect, earth-shattering proposal she wants, and she completely deserves it.

Kissing the top of her head, I whisper, "I love you baby and I'll always try to meet you in the middle. I'm sure there will be times when I'll give into to what you want, just like I am sure there will be times you'll give in to me."

"I'm sure you are correct, but don't hold your breath for me to give in a lot. I'm spoiled with getting my way. It's only fair I should warn you about that," she says with a snicker. "And I love you for now and for always."

Yeah, I got my paradise, and I know there will not be a boring minute with her around. I close my eyes, just breathing her in. This, right here, is everything.

31

OPENNESS WITH FAMILY

Lexy

*S*lowly sliding out of bed, I try to be really quiet because I don't want to wake up Grayson. Once my feet hit the floor, I make a silent dash to the bathroom, and then to his closet to grab a 'Camelot Security' t-shirt. It wasn't very smart of me to listen to him and leave all my clothes downstairs. Oh well. Knowing how he feels about me wearing something of Tony's gives me a little thrill, so my choice of shirt should please him.

God, I've been so stupid. I should have come over days ago and saved us a lot of heartache. Oh, making up was nice though. After a couple of hours of sleep, I was awakened by Grayson ever so slowly making love to me. It was the longest, slowest, most romantic, passionate lovemaking we've ever done. I think he made me come three times. He was so determined to make it work. He had to take it slow because every time he started to speed up, the friction got too painful for him. I contracted my muscles around him a lot to help him cum on his own. Damn it was worth it. Just thinking about it causes my va-jay-jay to tingle all over again.

Dashing out of the closet and towards the door, I cannot stop myself from taking one fast glance at Grayson. He looks so good stretched out across the bed with his ass showing. What perfection. Yummylicious. I should go over there and bite his ass cheek like he did mine, but I know where that will lead, and I seriously need my fix. There is nothing better than that first sip of coffee in the morning, so as much as it kills me, I leave Mr. Fine Ass alone and leave the room.

When I get to the kitchen, I walk around the massive island, grabbing a mug to start my coffee. I'm startled by a noise behind me, and without thinking, I grab two of the largest knives out of the knife block in front of me, spinning around, ready to attack.

"Jesus, Lexy! Shit! It's just me!" My eyes focus on Hawkins, who has fallen into a defensive stance.

"Well, fuck. Why the hell don't you announce yourself? Do you have a death wish? I could have killed you. God!" My heart is racing. "Now is not the time to test me. I have the Russian's imminent attack on my brain."

"Well, excuse me! I thought when you walked out of your room and saw your clothes folded by the door, you would have realized I was here."

Putting the knives back in the block, I reply, "Hawkins, learn something about me. First thing in the morning, my brain does not function correctly until I have had my caffeine fix. I heard Grayson scramble the codes to get in here last night, so I wasn't expecting anyone to show up here this early in the morning. And by the way, what are you doing here anyway?" I ask, grabbing my coffee and quickly adding some sugar before taking a nice long drink, my senses waking up with the blessed taste. Now that my brain is beginning to focus, I notice that the only thing Hawkins has on is a pair of Docker-type shorts and a hoodie tied around his waist.

Not able to help myself, I start watching his every step, wondering what's going on with him. He makes his way to the coffee machine, ignoring my question. When he turns the corner of the island, I notice he has a massive tattoo covering his back. Wow, it's beautiful and very scenic. There's a huge hawk perched on a branch in a tree that has the Brothers of Camelot shield hanging from it. The hawk has its wings partially spread, like it's thinking of taking off as it looks into the cloudy sky. Hmm, there seems to be some doves flying in the clouds. I want to get a closer look, but he turns around too quickly. I've gotta say something and not give away that I was staring at his back.

Luckily as Hawkins turns around, he starts talking. "You and I have something in common. I'm not worth shit until I've had my coffee, and I've only been here for a couple of hours. It's not very easy to crack my own fucking security system with just my phone."

"Where's your satchel? You're like Tony - you never go anywhere without your computer."

"Well, let's say sometimes shit happens and I leave it at the club."

Grayson walks into the kitchen and around the island to me, pushing Hawkins out of the way. "Why the hell are you out of bed so fucking early?" He leans down and kisses me briefly on the lips before he pulls me into his arms and starts kissing his way up my neck to my ear, whispering, "This isn't the first time you've woken up and snuck out of bed before me. Looks like I'm going to have to really pick up my bedding skills to fuck you to the point of exhaustion so you can sleep in with me, instead of it just giving you energy to get up so damn early."

I can't help but giggle. I look over at Hawkins to see he has both hands wrapped around his mug, studying the countertop. Reaching around Grayson, I smack his fine ass that is covered in nothing but a nice tight pair of black boxer briefs. "Behave yourself. I'm not coming back to bed if that's what you're trying to talk me into."

"You can't blame a man for trying," he says as he steps away with a wink, grabbing himself a cup of coffee before turning to Hawkins. "Spill! What happened at the club? It must have been big for you to forget your satchel and jog more than five miles over here."

"Nothing happened at the club. Well, other than a bunch of rowdy girls having a bachelorette party, screaming and giggling at everything. You know me. I can't deal with that kind of scene. I needed to get away from that, so I just stepped out and walked down to the beach. My mind wouldn't turn off, going over the events of the past week, and before I knew it, I was jogging, and that's when it happened," Hawkins tells us. He puts down his coffee mug and starts running both hands through his hair, looking up to the ceiling. His eyes are glossed over, like he's a million miles away. I've never seen him like this.

"What happened on the beach? Do I need to call Spencer or the Brothers? Or have you already handled that?"

"Emm, it's okay Brother. I just beat the shit out of two guys. I haven't slept good for days, and last night was bad. Both stories got screwed in my head, everything we learned about earlier this week, you know." He pauses and looks over to Grayson, receiving a head shaking 'no', from him. He returns a head nod before he continues, "And I kept hearing those noises in my head, when suddenly they turned into real screams this time. When I stopped, the realization hit me that someone was screaming for help and that mixed with what was going on in my mind, pulling me into the now. By then I figured I was miles away from the club."

"Who was it?" Grayson asks.

"There were these two guys, I'd say in their late twenties beating the shit out of a much younger pretty boy. They were yelling gay slurs at him and I noticed one of the guys was trying to take his pants off. But with our earlier conversation with... you know... that guy, and memories of Thomas in

479

high school ran into my brain. I had to stop it. You know my triggers. I got the guy away from them telling him to run. I don't remember much after that, other than I left the two guys on the beach, bloody and unconscious.

"Don't worry, after I jogged a bit further down the beach, I ran up to the main road making sure no security cameras could catch me and flagged down a young couple. I told them I didn't have my cell phone and I found two guys beat up pretty badly on the beach while I was jogging and asked if they could call for help. They asked me where and I pointed them in the right direction. They said they were nursing students and called as they ran off. They were so eager to go help, they didn't even ask my name."

"Shit, Hawk! One of these days you're..." Grayson starts but I interrupt.

"I would have done the same thing. You can call it a trigger, I call mine a switch, but when it gets flipped, shit happens. Do you think you could have killed them? I know your skill level, remember?"

"They aren't dead. Both were breathing when I left them, but definitely not in the best of shape. I came straight here afterwards and had to break in which wasn't easy. Thanks for switching the codes onto scramble mode. You asshole!"

"Hey, don't blame me. Lexy just came back and I didn't want to be disturbed. You can't be pissed because of that. And I knew it'd only slow you down, not stop you because you're standing in my kitchen now. I figured with me scrambling the codes, you'd know for sure Lexy was here."

"Yeah, but you're still an asshole. Anyway, within minutes of hacking into Madame, I was in and on the computer. Both the fuckers were taken, alive, to county hospital. They're in stable condition, last time I checked."

I reach over and give Hawkins a side hug, "Don't listen to this guy," I say, throwing my thumb over my shoulder, pointing at Grayson. "What you did was great. It probably saved that young kid's life."

"Well the fuckers won't be able to identify me anyway. I zipped up my hoodie and tied it so the only thing they could see was my eyes. That's how I usually jog when I know my mind is having issues. And by the time I got to the road, I had taken it off and tied it around my waist. The young couple never saw it."

"You're one lucky fool, you know that right? One day Hawkins, you're going to screw something up so bad we won't be able to figure a way to get you out of it," Grayson bites out.

"Whatever. Well, your parents are here," Hawkins says as we hear Darth Vader's theme music coming from his cell phone as he pulls it from his pocket.

"How the fuck do you know that? Grayson asks, his brow crinkled.

"Because everyone's gate has 'Auto ID', so if a parent is getting close, I know about it. Let's be honest here. Sometimes a warning can be a blessing."

"Yeah, but don't you think *all* our phones should be fitted with that ID app so *we* would know when they're coming too?"

"Nope. They're your parents. I'm the one needing the mental warning."

"Oh shit. I need to get dressed. I've got nothing on but this t-shirt."

"Sir! Your parents have arrived. I'm letting them in," Madame announces.

"Double shit. Madame! Delay them!" Grayson calls out as Hawkins starts typing on his phone. As we're headed out of the kitchen, the front door opens. Grayson reaches around me and smacks Hawkins on the head. "You little fucker. You did this."

"You're damn right I did. Scrambling the code! Locking my ass out! It's not like you were banging on the coffee table.

Well, I take that back. Maybe you were. I did find a towel and pieces of Lexy's clothes all over the house."

"Oh, look Richard, they finally made up," I hear Mom Riggs call out as she runs over to us, sweeping me into a big hug. "Well look at you two! Still not dressed at almost nine o'clock in the morning, and everyone knows how much of an early riser Grayson is." She looks between us wiggling her eyebrows. "And what in the heck are you doing over here this early in the morning Nicholas? I know it's not because Grayson and Lexy wanted you to join them in some hot make-up sex. That just isn't my son's style. Sarah, on the other hand, is a whole other story," Mom Riggs says with a little chuckle, as she walks us back into the kitchen with her arms around us.

"Grayson, I've been shopping with your mother since six a.m. I need some strong coffee with a little shot of courage," Pop Riggs says, as he pushes past us and walks into the kitchen.

"Come on, quit looking so shell shocked," she says as she looks between us, before turning her attention to Grayson. "It is not like I haven't seen you in your underwear son. It was only days ago that we were all looking at your penis."

Now with that comment, I cannot stop myself from cracking up laughing. As we walk back into the kitchen, I watch as Pop Riggs goes straight for the coffee machine, something I'm sure he has done dozens of times. Grayson opens up an upper cabinet and pulls out a bottle of bourbon. I'm pulled away from watching their coffee prep as I see Mom Riggs walk over to Hawkins, checking on him as he looks down and hops onto a bar stool.

Feeling the need to help Hawkins out, I ask, "Mom Riggs, what are you two doing here so early? I thought the dinner wasn't until tomorrow night."

"Well once everyone found out your family was coming over Lexy, the Camelot family wanted to see how they all reacted to seeing you and Grayson together, so they invited themselves to dinner. We had to turn our nice little Sunday night family dinner into a massive family early Saturday afternoon barbeque. I've already talked to your family, and they loved that idea as well. This way, they can just meet everyone at once."

Grayson speaks up a little louder than I expected. "WHAT! You're just going to do this without even talking to me first? What if Lexy hadn't shown up here last night? What then?"

Pop Riggs speaks up, "Well son, Lou and I decided last night that we were giving you kids till this afternoon to get together on your own, or we were going to lock your asses in a room at our house till you worked it out."

"You're shitting me! So Lexy and I don't get to spend the day together, alone, to figure out a way for me to win back her uncle's trust after I made an idiot of myself?"

"Grayson, it's only nine! You have a good five plus hours to talk or whatever. But I do expect the two of you to get there no later than three. We've already met Lou and it'll be nice to meet Camilla and their kids as well as the rest of her family. It'll be fine if we have some time with them before you two get there. Now back to the original question. Nicholas, what are you doing over here?"

Mom Riggs walks over and sits down on the stool beside him. Putting her hand under his chin and turning it to her, she says softly, "Sweet boy of ours, you look awfully tired. Have you not been sleeping well? When was the last time you talked with Monica? I mean Mom Gregory?"

Hawkins shrugs his shoulders and I can barely hear him mumble, "About a month ago, and no, I'm not sleeping that good. I've just had a bad week is all."

Mom Riggs lightly rubs her finger over his knuckles as she says, "Have you had another blackout and possibly been fighting someone again?"

"Not really a complete blackout. I got pulled out of my spell jogging on the beach, and kind of beat these two guys up, but they deserved it. I didn't hurt them that bad. I promise," Hawkins says, hanging his head as Mom Riggs pulls him into a sideways hug.

"Richard, text Monica and tell her to make Nicholas', I mean Hawkins, his favorites. We're bringing him over to take a power nap before the barbeque."

"You got it dear," Pop Riggs says as he starts texting away.

As I observe more of Hawkins tattoo from my position at the cupboards behind him, I can see the Hawk on his back more clearly. It is beautiful, its face and chest are very colorful. That is when I notice each Brother's name is written inside of the feathers on its wings. Then I look at the tree he's perched in and can easily see every parent's name on a leaf within the tree, along with the other siblings of the original Brothers. Wait… is that Bella's name? It's on Drake's feather, yet within the leaves, you can clearly see Isabella's name because she is a sibling, so I guess that since she's now married to Drake, she's been added to his feather.

That's when I notice Grayson's wing. It has his full name of Grayson Richard Riggs, and then you can make out Aless – Lexy. Oh, my ever-loving God, the 'Lexy' is still red, which means he just added that. That's the most touching thing I think I've ever seen. Hawkins' back tells quite a story. God, would I love to take a picture of it to study it all later. Maybe it would help explain Hawkins better.

Then I notice the Hawk has a heart on its chest, with the word 'Family' and K-W… something. But at this distance I can't make it out the other small letters, nor can I read the names on the flying doves. Unlike all the other Brothers, this tattoo explains why I haven't seen Hawkins' back before, not even at his castle when we first met. I'm sure this is a sacred part of him.

Shit, I'm busted. I look up and see Grayson watching me

checking out Hawkins' back. He just shakes his head with a smirk on his face. I just roll my eyes as he walks over to me.

"Okay, you lovebirds. I'm taking Hawkins with me, and we'll see you two no later than three. Understood?"

"Capisce, I mean, yes ma'am," I reply, cuddling into Grayson's big arms.

"Okay Mom, we didn't get much sleep last night either, so a power nap sounds good to me too," Grayson says as he snuggles his face into my neck. "Doesn't it, Lex?"

"Excuse him. We have a lot of talking to do," I tease as we watch everyone get up and head towards the door.

"'Talking' is your code word for sex I'm guessing," Hawkins jokes, rolling his eyes at us. He does look really tired. I hope he gets some well-earned sleep over at Mom Gregory's.

"They aren't fooling anyone. I'll send a message to all the Brothers, demanding they leave you alone until tonight, once I get in the car," Mom Riggs says as she wraps her arm around Hawkins.

"Brothers?! You invited all of them too? Jesus Mom! Is there anyone you didn't invite?" Grayson gripes releasing me and standing up straight, semi-glaring at his mom.

"Well, if I think of anyone, I'll let you know. Get over yourself, Grayson. This is happening, with or without your blessing." Then she looks over to Hawkins and says, "Let me guess, you lost your shoes and shirt somewhere?"

He just hangs his head and nods. Poor guy, I've never seen him like this. I wonder how often this happens. I'm going to have to drill Grayson about this. I can't help it. I care too, and if there is any way I can help, I need to. Once they're out the door, the questioning will start.

"We'll see you before three, not one minute after. If you want to win points with Lou, you might want to keep that in mind," Pop Riggs adds as he follows Hawkins and Mom Riggs out the door.

"Don't worry Dad. I got this, or I better," Grayson adds.

Pop Riggs gives him a smile and a head nod before closing the door.

"Okay, start talking. What's going on with Hawkins? What's the full meaning behind his tattoo? I'm sure you know it," I fire off my questions one after another.

Chuckling Grayson says, "Really? They barely close the door and you start drilling me about Hawkins?"

"You're damn right, I do. I need to know."

"Need to? I don't think you *need to*, *want to* is more like it. But as far as the tattoo goes, yes, it holds a lot of meaning to Hawkins. He started it the moment he turned eighteen, but that is his story and his life and I'm not telling you anymore."

"Fine, you meanie! Did you know he added my name to your leaf?"

"He added 'Aless' to it the moment I told him I thought you were my soulmate, my forever."

"He's added 'Lexy' to it now."

"Wow, now you found out something I didn't know," Grayson says as he leans down and starts kissing his way up my neck again. "I think we've talked enough about Hawkins, don't you? I'm thinking that power nap sounds awful good. I think it's time to wear you out. What do you say?"

"Grayson, you know you have to take it easy. You need to be careful, so you don't re-injure yourself, rather, 'Sir'. "

Well, 'Sir' and I both really enjoyed our nice slow, passionate lovemaking session in the wee hours of this morning, and going by your multiple orgasms, I'd say you did too," he says between kisses.

"Ooohh, that was incredible," I reply, as I turn into his arms and start kissing his chest, my hand slowly feeling up 'Sir' with a gentle squeeze. I hear Grayson's quick intake of air. "Yeah, I think you talked me into round two."

Grayson reaches down and puts his hands under my t-shirt and cups my ass, lifting me up and onto the kitchen counter. "How about we start right here?" Grayson says as he pulls my t-shirt off over my head and tosses it to the floor. "This counter is the perfect height for me to watch as I make you cum. Not only can I watch your face, but our connection."

"Ahhh Grayson, we eat on this counter," I can't resist teasing.

"I'd like to eat you on this counter."

"No! There hasn't been any 'I do's' exchanged, remember?"

"Hey, I'll always keep trying."

Slowly leaning back on my elbows, I watch as Grayson steps back and takes off his boxers, tossing them on my t-shirt. God, I'm lucky to have such a Greek God of perfection standing in front of me, completely nude. He turns every morsel of my body into an inferno of lust and desire. He takes 'Sir' into his hand and slowly strokes himself as he says, "How about I make you cum first here, before I carry you upstairs to continue this? I think we'll both enjoy watching."

Pulling my legs up to the edge of the counter, I allow them both to drop apart, making myself completely open and on display for his lustful eye. Grayson steps up and looks as he eases his hands on my knees, pushing them up a little more and pulling my hips to the edge of the counter as he oh so slowly caresses up my thighs. With one hand, he gets 'Sir' in place and slowly slides into me. Damn, it feels so incredible. I've got a feeling both of us aren't going to get any talking done in the next five hours or so. Making love till I pass out sounds damn fun. As I continue to watch Grayson sliding in and out of me ever so slowly, I escape into a level of paradise most people only dream of.

The Barbecue

Walking out onto the deck at the Riggs house, this place already feels like home. This is what I missed all my life, genuine family and friends that'll be honest with you, and love you unconditionally. I walk over to the banister and lean over, looking out into the yard. Seeing everyone huddled in little groups, talking like old friends makes me smile. I wish it could be like this always.

All the dads are talking with Uncle Louie, Rocco and Lucca, drinking their beers and liquors like they're all old friends. Uncle Louie even brought over cigars for the men to smoke after lunch. Watching several of the dads coughing like teenage boys when they try the cigars is funny. My family bursts out laughing, and they jokingly pound them on the back.

The moms made Camilla and the kids feel so welcome. They're sharing recipes and sharing childhood stories about the Brothers, and Camilla is sharing stories about me. I think she really likes them too. Isabella and Sandy hit it off in a matter of seconds with them both being pregnant. Sandy isn't due for another month, but I think Isabella is bigger than she is, and she has a lot longer to go. Today couldn't have gone any better.

Feeling Grayson's big arms wrap around me from behind, he asks, "What are you thinking that has put such a big grin on your face? Let me guess, are you thinking about the last time I had you pinned against a banister on the Stevens' deck back in New Jersey?"

Turning in his arms and running my hands up his incredible chest, I reply, "No, but now that you mention it, what a great memory. Do you know that was my first kiss?"

"Are you shitting me?" Grayson asks as he laughs out loud, getting Luigi, Tony, Hawkins, and Stevens attention.

Hawkins looks so much better after he spent a few hours over at the Gregory's. He must have gotten a really good power nap. He looks more calm and at peace. He even has a smile on his face. "What are you laughing at Riggs?" Hawkins calls out.

"Mind your own damn business!" Grayson teases, as he looks down into my eyes. "So, you're telling me I was your first kiss? Well, do you know your Uncle thinks I was first at something else too?"

Rolling my eyes at him and his jealousy, I say, "Give me a break. Who I chose to be my first is not important, and neither is yours as far as I am concerned. That's my business, and I don't give a damn who my uncle or anyone else for that matter thinks was my first. I was the one that picked, not my Papa, and that is all I ever cared about. As long as we are each other's lasts, that is all that is important, and you, Grayson Richard Riggs, will be my last. I can promise you that. No other man will ever touch me. And here is a little FYI: No other man has ever had my heart."

He smiles so big both his dimples pop, and he leans down and kisses me. Cupping my ass, he lifts me up and turns me around, sitting me on the edge of the banister, like he did so many years ago. My heart explodes with emotions and some of my favorite memories. Oh God, I finally have the man of my dreams.

"Okay you two, knock it off. You are in public, you know. You two aren't alone on my deck like you were back in New Jersey. Grayson, you're real, dumbass! All her family is right here. Are you wanting to get punched again?" We are pulled out of our passionate moment by Stevens' rudeness once again. Geez, his timing sucks ass.

"You know what Stevens? I think I need to kick your ass again. What do you think about that?" Grayson turns and calls back to Stevens.

"You made out with Aless, I mean Lexy, on the deck of that house in New Jersey? You're damn lucky I didn't find out about that back then or I would have had to have shot you. Kissing a fifteen year old Princess! You were a sick fucker back then weren't you?!" Luigi teases, as the guys walk over to us.

"Luigi!" I hear Sandy, his wife, call out from beside Isabella. "Be nice. They obviously had chemistry back then, and they still do today."

I watch as Luigi rolls his eyes, shaking his head with a smile, showing off that one dimple as he says, "Amore, lei era solo una bambina."

"Luigi, I was not a child!" I fire back at him.

"Come on Luigi, we already talked about this. She did not look fifteen, and you already punched me for that," Grayson replies with a chuckle.

"Luigi Fanucci! Tell me you didn't really punch Grayson!" Sandy stands up and walks over to us with Isabella, Brenda and Joyce right behind her.

Luigi tries to control his laughter as a very serious Sandy walks over with her cute little baby bump poking out. God, I bet I'll hate Sandy when I get pregnant. She is the kind of woman that hasn't put on an ounce of weight anywhere but her tummy, whereas I will no doubt look like a beached whale. I watch as she pops both fisted hands up on her narrow hips.

I cannot stop myself from egging this on. "He really did Sandy. He walked right up and punched Grayson without any kind of warning or anything. I was completely shocked myself. I mean come on, that was years ago," I say so sweetly, looking over Sandy's shoulder to Luigi, sticking my tongue out at him in teasing.

"Baby, come on. Lexy knew I couldn't pass it by. You knew I'd have to do it. I beat Lou to the punch. Literally," Luigi says, pulling her into his arms, just as the moms and dads join us on the deck.

"Now Sandy, Luigi didn't mean any real harm. He was just determined to be the one to punch him. He knew we all wanted to do it," Uncle Louie joins in the teasing.

"Believe me Sandy, if Luigi hadn't punched him, I was

planning on it," Rocco says, punching his right fist into left palm a couple of times. I make sure to stand in front of Grayson, so none of these assholes get any macho ideas.

"Men are so childish. Did that accomplish anything? Did it change the fact Grayson kissed her over seven years ago? No, it didn't," Sandy teases, finally relaxing as she realizes every one of the men are enjoying the moment.

"If it makes you feel any better Sandy, all of us dads would have probably have kicked his ass ourselves back then if we knew he was making moves on a fifteen year old girl when he was nineteen. We taught him better than that. But that is water under the bridge, and Lexy has grown on all of us. You can say we're kind of glad my son's a bit of a perv," Pop Riggs says with a bit of a chuckle, patting Uncle Louie on the shoulder, receiving a head nod in response.

"Thank you, I guess. If that is your way of saying you finally approve of my relationship with Grayson," I reply looking over at Pop Riggs with a shy smile. Grayson wraps his arms around me, pulling me into his front, causing me to blush even more. "You were the only one I was worried about."

"Sweet Lexy, you never had anything to worry about with Richard. I know just how to get Dick here in line," Mom Riggs says as she throws her thumb over her shoulder, pointing at him. "Give yourself some time and you'll figure out some womanly ways of your own to get your point of view better understood by your man," she adds with a wink to me, as several of the men and women start laughing.

Suddenly we all hear these weird alarms go off. Looking around, I see Tony and Hawkins grab their phones almost in unison.

"Fuck!" Tony says with a serious look on his face as he scrolls through his phone.

"Holy shit!" Hawkins adds, doing the same as Tony. They both look up briefly, locking eyes with a head nod to each other. This is not good. Tony looks over to me with the light of battle in his eyes. Without another word, I know the Russians have arrived. Hawkins locks eyes with Grayson and begins to walk over to us.

"Okay, I hate to cut this party short, but something has come up and Hawkins and several of us have to leave and get to headquarters," Grayson announces, as several of the Brothers instantly stand up and begin to move towards each other, serious looks on each of their faces. Yeah, they know a battle is coming.

Uncle Louie looks between me and Tony as his phone goes off as well. He pulls it out of his pocket as Camilla walks over to him, putting her arm around him. "Mother fucker! I'm going to kick his ass," Uncle Louie says, shaking his head. I can tell he's getting very angry.

"Who is it, Uncle Louie?" I ask, but before he can answer, Mom Riggs interrupts me.

"Grayson Richard Riggs, I am not buying any of that shit. What is going on? We're family, and I am tired of you boys acting like we are helpless and defenseless children. We need to know what is going down. I do not want to see more bruises and scars appear on any of you without explanation."

"Mom, just give us a few hours to figure things out for ourselves and we'll let you know if this is something we need to put the family on lockdown for."

Tony whispers something to Sarah and her face pales and looks sad. She gives him a quick kiss before he locks eyes with me and heads over in my direction. This is not good.

"Grayson, we are doing no such thing. You need to let us in on the danger, if there are any," Mom Riggs continues.

Everyone is making their way up and onto the deck. The silence is deafening. The parents look around at each other and then the Brothers, I'm sure trying to figure out what is going on. Some get closer to their loved ones, pulling them into their arms, clinging to them.

No, this shit is not going to happen this way. It isn't going to be kept a secret. They need to know, so I speak up. "Tony, is it the Russians?"

"Lexy, not now! We'll compare notes and see what's going down when we get to headquarters. We have no reason yet to get our parents worried."

Uncle Louie looks around the huge gathering on the deck as he speaks up, "Grayson, I think you are mistaken. Are you not all family? They don't need to be kept in the dark. They need all the information necessary to stay safe. I do not want anything to happen to your family, so unless you are going to put them in a safe house or compound, they need to be informed."

"Yeah, I agree. If we need to go up to Hawkins castle, give me the word and me and some of the Wenches will head up there now. I don't like the way all of you look, and my number one priority is keeping my babies safe," Isabella says as she wraps her arms around her big baby bump, Drake right behind her, wrapping his arms around Bella and the bump, whispering something in her ear.

"You are right Isabella. You know you'll always be safe at my place. I'd feel a lot better with you at the castle anyway. Go and take whoever you can persuade to go with you up there," Hawkins says, looking up from his phone for a second in her direction. "Don't you agree Fitz?"

"Agreed. I just told her I'd feel better if she headed up there myself. Thanks Hawk," Drake replies, giving Isabella's belly a rub and kissing the top of her head.

"That does it for me. Tony, start talking. I want intel now!"

Without hesitation, he starts telling everyone. "You are correct, the Russians are here. Several got here last night, but I know they mean war because Ivan Osokina himself landed just a few moments ago."

"Shit!" I say looking over at Grayson, and then to Hawkins.

"How do you know it's really him?" Hawkins asks, looking over at Tony.

"Because my man at the airport knows him. What's your intel telling you, Hawk?"

Interrupting them, Grayson says more strongly this time, "I really think we should just take this to headquarters."

"No! We're all family and I am telling everyone." Turning away from Grayson, I stand up on a bench, looking over at all my family and friends. "Okay, the days of you all being in the dark is over. This is a direct threat against everyone. The Russians are known to go after family if they can't get their targets, which last we heard is Grayson and me."

"Lexy!" Grayson says more firmly.

"Grayson, shut it and let Lexy finish," Mom Riggs scolds.

"I agree. I think everyone needs to know this. I'd feel a hell of a lot better with all of them going up to the Castle. That is what it was built for: a safe haven for all our family. No one will get to any of them there," Hawkins says, looking straight at Grayson.

Grayson just stands there shaking his head. I know he's nervous but keeping our loved ones in the dark is not the best way to protect them. "Fine. Go ahead Lexy, but please just tell them the basics of what they need to know," he says with a pleading look.

"Okay. Camilla, take the kids and Sandy with you. I definitely want you heading up to Hawkins' place. The kids will have the time of their life there. That is the safest place for you. You are officially on lockdown. Follow Isabella. She'll give you the address. Pace yourselves a bit so it won't look like a caravan."

"Consider it done," Camilla responds, pulling Marta and Dino close to her.

Looking around the deck at everyone else, I say, "You may all be perfectly fine. I do not know how much the Russians know about all of you, but they do know everything about

Grayson and I that they could pull off the internet and pay for on the Dark Web."

"Lexy you need to know that it was the Benassi Family that texted, telling me your Papa and Vito are here. They are having a sit down with Nero and Renzo as we speak. You don't know how badly I want to kick my brother's ass right now. I'm letting you know if he causes any shit, he might not be going back home alive."

"That is if I don't beat you to it. Now is not the time. We'll deal with him later. Do you think he knows about the Russians and me being here?"

"Yes. That is what Nero texted me about," Uncle Louie replies.

"Holy fuck. Lex, maybe you should go up to the castle as well. I don't need to be worrying about your father being out there trying to kidnap you and take you back to Italy too," Grayson suggests, the worry clear in his voice.

"Baby, I can handle my Papa. He's scared shitless of me, and for good cause. He will not try anything so stupid. I've got this. We have a plan, and I'm sticking to it." Looking over to the moms, I say, "Ladies, I'm serious here. I do not want *anyone* to go *anywhere alone!* Not even to the bathroom at a restaurant. You go with two other people everywhere. Do not wear any form of shoes you cannot run or fight in, and I mean that. If you aren't working, maybe now is a great time for a mini vacation. We'd all feel a lot better dealing with this issue knowing you are safe. If the castle is too far away, go to headquarters." Looking over to Mom Carpenter, I add, "That means you and your kids too. Ethan and Benny can easily get you and Rachel into either location. Do what you think is best."

"Samuel and I will talk once you're finished and see what location he wants us to head to. Rachel and I do really enjoy going up to the Castle, so we'll probably join Isabella there," Mom Carpenter replies, wrapping her arms around her husband, who pulls Rachel under his other arm.

"I'm just letting you know that Barbara, Monica, and I have an important hospital meeting late tonight, and then we're supposed to meet Ivy for cocktails. I promise it'll only be one, then after that, we'll check in with you and go from there," Mom Riggs informs me.

"Okay, that sounds good. Dads, I know you all have carry permits, so I suggest you make use of them. The same applies to all of you: please try not to travel alone, and I'd feel a lot better if you touch base and let us know where you are at all times."

"Do you really think anyone would try something with one of us?" Pop Gregory asks.

"You are probably safe, but the Russians love to grab family members, thinking they can use our love for you to help them catch us, so keep that in mind. We're probably just being overly cautious."

"Lexy, come on. I don't want them all roaming around carrying guns while they're scared," Grayson pleads again.

"Son, most of us, because of what we do in life, carry a gun with us at some point, so it isn't asking us to do anything we don't already do. Lexy's warning and advice will just make us stay more alert. We will be fine. You boys take extra precautions yourself," Pop Riggs says, as he walks over and gives Grayson a hug. "I mean that! Keep your mind on the job and nothing else," he adds, looking over to me.

Uncle Louie picks me up and stands me back on the ground. Rocca, Lucca, Luigi and Tony gather around me. "Okay men, we're all headed over to Tony's underground compound to get ready and touch base with the Benassi Family." Turning to Tony, I add, "I want you to get Sarah and any of the Wenches that would rather stay at your place to head over there. I'll call my roommates and have them meet us at Camelot headquarters later. We both know they will be safe at the townhouse for now."

"I was hoping you'd be okay with Sarah and some of the

Wenches coming to the compound. I think they'll be safer there. It's also better to divide them up," Tony says, sounding relieved.

"I agree."

Uncle Louie puts his hands on my shoulders and looks deep into my eyes as he says, "Okay Little One, are you mentally prepared for this? I do not want you leading us into battle with your mind anywhere else but on the mission. I'll deal with your Papa."

"My mind is on killing every last one of those mother fuckers. Ivan Osokina just signed his death certificate. He'll be going back to the Motherland in a body bag. That is unless the Benassi's handle the situation like they did with his son," I say with a smile. Feeding him to the pigs would be quite nice, I think. "As for my father, we will deal with him after this is over."

Uncle Louie's smile is beaming, "Capisce. Glad to have you back, Little One. I knew you were in there somewhere."

A smile overtakes me for a second as the warmth of hearing Uncle Louie calling me 'Little One' again, fills me with love and brings me peace.

Suddenly feeling Grayson's presence behind me, he wraps me up in his arms as he asks in a tender voice that pulls on my heartstring, "Lex, do you want to come with us to headquarters? I think Tony can link into Hawkins' system and we can figure this out together. I'd rather you stay close to me and the rest of the Brothers with your father in town."

"Riggs, listen to me," Luigi interrupts, before I can say anything. "Al thinks he has Rocca, Lucca and I to help him get Lexy back. He's sadly mistaken. We have Lexy's back. Al can go fuck himself. He will not get anywhere near her. I swear it," Luigi says, pounding his chest before putting his hand on Grayson's shoulder, giving it a squeeze.

Luigi handled that perfectly. My heart is bursting with pride. He truly became a leader in my absence. I lean into

Grayson's arms saying, "Baby, we'll all be over to headquarters once we get changed and grab our gear. We'll be bringing some of the Benassi Family with us. We'll go over our plan there. Trust me, okay? That's very important."

"I trust you, 'Little One'. I really do," Grayson says with a smile, resting his forehead to mine for a brief second so we can just look into each other's eyes, before giving me a quick kiss. Then he looks at my family. "As for you men, I'll see you soon. Anything happens to her while in your care, you answer to me. No excuses. Understood?"

Watching a smile spread across Luigi's face, I know he's about to say something smartassed. "Nice to see you have some balls after all. Threatening us! Bah! That's pretty impressive coming from you. After this is over, I want to challenge you at anything, you name it. Hand to hand combat? What about guns? You think you can beat me?" Luigi questions, before throwing his head back, laughing.

"Challenge accepted. Name it, I'll hand you your ass, mother…" I put my hand over Grayson's mouth before he can finish what he was going to say.

"Okay, enough of this. No more swinging your dicks around till after this is over or I'll rip them off and feed them to you. Capisce?!"

They both start chuckling while still giving each other the eye, as Luigi continues, "We've been watching her since before you ever got a stiffie for her. We got this." Luigi bumps shoulders with Grayson a bit too hard for my liking, being a dick. I might need to warm up before the battle and go a few rounds with my good buddy.

Throwing my arms around Grayson's neck gets his eyes off Luigi and focused on me. I allow my eyes to soften on him, hoping he can see my reassurance that all will be okay. Then I continue to pull him down for a passionate kiss, before pulling away breathlessly, touching our foreheads together as I tell him, "I love you."

"I love you more than anything in this world. Don't ever forget that."

"I won't, it's ingrained in my soul. I'll be okay, I swear it. I'm so ready to end this and get back to where we were. We'll be at headquarters very soon." Receiving a head nod from Grayson, my Family and I head for the door.

Once outside in the Riggs' driveway, I watch as everyone staggers their leaving, and all go in different directions. Some have long goodbyes, whispering to each other that all will be well. It's reassuring to see they really are prepared for this, just in case we're being watched.

It is time to mentally prepare for this battle, to stay focused on my goal of killing every last one of these mother fuckers. Ivan Osokina is going to join his sons today. He will not leave this warehouse alive. This has to go well. Then it's time to deal with my father for the very last time.

32

PREPARING FOR BATTLE

Lexy

"*W*ho's ready to kick ass and get this show on the road? We'll wait until nightfall to attack. I already checked in with Hawkins. The Brothers are all ready and waiting for us. Lexy, did you send a text to your roomies to meet us at Camelot headquarters? If not, I'll send it," Tony shoots off as he gets in the SUV and closes the door. It is barely closed before he's opening up his laptop. Times like this, he can't disconnect from the cyber world. I'm sure his brain is running nonstop.

I can't help but smile. It feels like old times with Luigi driving and Uncle Louie in the front beside him. How many times have we gone to battle just like this? All we're missing is Antonio and Stephen in the back seat. Oh, the memories. Those days are far behind me now, and hopefully, these battling days will be few and far between.

"No Tony, I didn't. Can you send it, please? My cell phone is somewhere buried in my bag. I forgot all about it. My concentration was on changing and getting prepared, which led to going a few rounds with Luigi. You missed it while you were working out your 'anxiety' with Sarah," I can't help but tease, rolling my eyes at him when he looks my way, knowing they snuck in a quickie.

"You're just jealous you couldn't sneak in a quick bang with Grayson yourself," Tony teases right back, before Luigi interrupts.

"Tony, I'd rather not think of Lexy having sex with anyone, or I might have to beat the shit out of you for shits and giggles. That might relieve my own anxiety," Luigi fires back at him with a chuckle and a quick glance into the rearview mirror.

"Do we know where they are yet?"

"Yeah, they're at the waterfront in their warehouse. But Ivan Osokina isn't there yet, so we wait. They have taken a few hostages in, we think through the back. ID's are unknown, they had their heads bagged."

"Shit! Is all the family accounted for?"

"Checking now," Tony answers, his full attention is back at on his laptop. Man, his typing speed always blown my mind.

Looking out the window, my mind is rushing every which way. What the hell is my Papa here for? There is no way he can be thinking I'll go home. Just wait till I tell him I am aware of all his lies. The look on his face will be priceless when he finds out that Mom and Nonna tricked him all those years ago. I'm American and he can't do jack-shit about it.

In no time, we're pulling into the Camelot headquarters, as the sun is beginning to set. We pass a kid on a skateboard headed in the same direction. That seems odd and gives me a bad feeling. I wonder where the hell that kid is going. I didn't recognize him. There are no homes in this direction either. My senses tell me something is up and I need to get Luigi to check this out because something isn't right.

Once we've parked the SUV, we all get out in unison and

Tony takes the lead, briskly headed for the door. I grab Luigi by the arm, "Did you see that kid when we drove up?"

"Yeah, I noticed him and wondered if there were homes close by or if someone here has a kid. Not a good thing to have a kid around here right now."

"That is just what I was thinking. I don't have a good feeling about this. Hang back and talk to the kid. I'll meet you inside."

"You got it, Boss," Luigi says with a head nod, just like old times.

"Luigi, don't hurt the kid."

"Hey... what do you think I am? I wouldn't hurt the kid unless I knew without question, he was here to hurt you."

I almost want to chuckle at that one. "Come on, it's a kid! Maybe he has a bit of a hero worship thing for the Brothers. They are very popular around here. He definitely isn't a threat to me, just send him on his way."

"Done," Luigi replies, leisurely walking through the parking lot towards the rapidly approaching kid.

Uncle Louie's holding the door open for me. "Good call. I don't have a good feeling either," Uncle Louie says as I pass him.

Looking around inside, I see all the Brothers gathered, preparing for battle. Damn, Grayson looks hot. I have to keep my mind off how nice those black cargo pants look on his sweet ass. Jesus, I'm better than this. Taking a deep cleansing breath, I shake my head clear of all thoughts not connected with what is ahead of us.

"Hello, men. Are all of you ready for this?"

Stevens and Jackson are going through the backpacks Tony gave them earlier, making sure their grappling hooks are stored correctly and checking the other supplies they might need. "We're ready. I've got plenty of clips and hooks in here. Our SUV is loaded as well. I've even got emergency medical supplies ready, just in case," Stevens calls out.

"Thanks Stevens. Good to know."

You can tell by the buzz that fills the air that these men are prepared and just waiting for the clock to show us it's time to go. They are just trying to stay busy. Grayson walks over to me, a serious expression on his face. I know just how he feels. You just get so antsy before a battle. The waiting is a killer. They all have on their bulletproof vests and have smeared black paint on their faces to help camouflage them.

"When will the Benassi Family be arriving? Do you think any of them need to warm up? We have the range downstairs available if you think they need it," Grayson says, checking me out as he pulls me into his arms for a quick kiss, rubbing his hand up my back. I don't think that was meant as a caress, I think he was making sure I had on my vest on too.

"They should be here any minute. By chance, do any of you know a kid about twelve who rides a skateboard? He was headed this way and I sent Luigi to talk to him, and hopefully shoo him away. Now is not a good time for a kid to be around here."

"Did he have messy brown hair, thin, and didn't look too well taken care of?" Grayson asks with wrinkled brow.

"Yeah, that's the kid."

"Tiffany, check the cameras and see if Dusty is headed this way," Grayson calls out.

"On it." Tiffany stops talking to Clausen and Spencer as she dashes over to her desk.

"Grayson, who is this kid?"

"He's a lonely kid. His parents are in jail. Drugs. He lives with his grandmother a few miles down the road. Some of us are in a mentoring program and he's one of the local kids we help out and try to be good examples for. But he isn't supposed to be down here this late at night."

"Riggs, it is him. Luigi is bringing him in the front door now. Not too nicely at that," Tiffany tells all of us, standing up from her computer.

"Shit! I told Luigi to be nice and not hurt the kid," I say as Grayson and I head towards the front office by Tiffany's area. We open up the security door just as Luigi opens up the front door, walking the kid in by the back of his shirt. What the…?

"I figured I'd better bring this kid to you. He just shoved a package into the front of his gym shorts and no way am I taking it out. He's been shaking it, so let's pray it isn't a bomb or this kid may be dickless at any moment."

"Dusty, what are you doing here?" Grayson quickly asks him as Luigi releases his shirt.

The kid sticks his chest out with pride. "I don't know this guy in the suit, and he sounds weird, so I wasn't telling him jack shit," Dusty replies stepping away from Luigi, pulling the package out of his pants. He looks at the small brown box and shakes it at Luigi. "See? I told you there is no bomb in here. I think it's probably a watch or something."

"Why didn't you open it and see? And what are you doing here? It's late and not a good time," Grayson adds, as several more Brothers surround us.

"There's a guy down the road who asked me to give you guys a message and give you this box. He had a weird accent too. It wasn't anything like that guy." He sticks his shaking finger out and points to Luigi, then turns back to Grayson. "But he wasn't Mexican or Korean either, because I have friends with parents from all over the place and I've never heard his accent," Dusty says still holding the box out with shaking hands. You can tell by the way he is babbling he's very nervous.

Oh shit! It could easily be the Russians. We need to get as much information out of him as we can. "What did the man tell you? And can you tell us anything else about him? Like was he old? Young? Is he still down the road?"

"Yeah. He gave me a fifty dollar bill to bring this down here, and said he'd give me fifty more if I came back down there and gave him a report."

"Jackson, Stevens!" Grayson barely gets their names out before they speak up.

"On it!" Jackson calls out, as he heads to the door.

"Dusty, where was he waiting for you?" Stevens asks, walking over and messing up his hair even more. Dusty pulls away and playfully punches Stevens, causing him to double over. "Good one, Little Brother."

"I'm not in trouble for talking to him, am I Stevens?"

"No. We need to talk to him ourselves is all." Stevens handles him perfectly, gaining the kid's trust.

"He was at the abandoned boathouse down the road. You know, the one you all told me I'm not supposed to hang out at and I wasn't, I swear! I was just skating by it."

"Thanks, we're on it," Stevens says, running out the door as Dusty continues.

"The dude wasn't by himself. He was there with another guy, just parked there. He called me over and asked if I knew where Camelot Security was. I told him I was good friends with all of you, so he told me this box needed to be delivered to a Princess ConZono, or something like that. It's something her father lost. I'm thinking it's his watch by the rattling noise." He sticks the box out again, shaking it, and I reach over and take it.

"Thank you. That would be me," I reply.

The kid looks me up and down, "You don't look like a Princess."

"Well I am, and you don't look like a hero, but you are, for bringing this to me. Now, what did the men look like?" I question.

"Emm, they were both wearing dark suits and ties. I think maybe a third guy was in the backseat of their fancy car, but I couldn't see real good. I knew they weren't kidnappers. You know, kidnappers wouldn't be dressed all nice like that and be in a fancy car. I thought maybe they were lost, but he waved a fifty dollar bill at me, and you know how badly Grandma

Smitty could use fifty bucks." He hangs his head and whispers, "You're not gonna let me go and get the other fifty bucks are you?"

"Shit no!" Spencer walks over and puts his arm around Dusty. "You know better than that. Those men were definitely dangerous. Jesus! What were you thinking? Come with me kid. Tiff has all kinds of treats downstairs. We'll call your Grandma and tell her you're hanging out with us for a while."

Dusty smiles really big, getting all excited. "You mean you'll give me another ride in your sports car? Shit, my buddies are never going to believe me. Can someone take my picture so I can show them?"

"You got it dude, but we're going to have a nice long talk about not talking to strangers again. You're all your grandma has left in this world, and we'd like to keep you alive."

Dramatically rolling his eyes, Dusty agrees. "Okay. I'll listen to your lecture. But can I have the treats first? You wouldn't want me to die bored and hungry, would you?"

Laughing, Spencer pushes Dusty into the Security department, headed for the elevators as he says, "Come on smartass. You're on lockdown with the rest of us and you better keep your mouth closed if you want to be a part of Little Brothers of Camelot."

"My lips are as good as sewn shut, zipped tight, locked and the key thrown away." Dusty acts like he zips his lips closed and throws away an imaginary key.

Once the doors of the elevator close, I open up the box. "Shit!" I lift up a cut off finger, examining it.

"What the fuck! Is that a goddamn finger?" Clausen says, putting his hand over his mouth like he might get sick. Uncle Louie and Luigi look over my shoulder.

"Yes, it's a finger. But it isn't my Papa's. It's probably Vito's, his personal guard."

"Shit Lexy, put that back in the box," Grayson adds, his face all crinkled up.

Babies! Rolling my eyes at them, I say, "It is just a finger. I'm thinking by the lean of it, it's his trigger finger. Fuck that sucks. Maybe it can be saved. Tiffany, can you put this on ice for now? Tony, I'm thinking those two hostages you saw earlier were Papa and Vito. Fucking assholes got themselves captured."

Brenden appears beside me. "Let me see it, Lexy." He takes it and looks at it closely. "Yeah, Tiffany and I'll take care of this to preserve it. The sooner we find the person it belongs to the better the odds of re-attaching it and it being functional." Brenden takes the finger and heads off with Tiffany.

Looking around the room, I see everyone is staring at me strangely. "What's the problem?"

"How do you know that wasn't your dad's finger you were holding like it was no big deal?" Clausen asks, obviously still bothered by what he just witnessed. Poor guy.

"Because my Papa gets a manicure every other week, and those nails were chewed off like Vito's."

"That's right, Vito has always been a nail biter all his life. Good call, Little One. That means the Osokina Family has both of them," Uncle Louie says, shaking his head.

"Mother fucking shit! Goddamit!" Tony cries out.

Everyone instantly goes silent and looks at him as he types away. Hawkins gets up from his computer and goes to look over Tony's shoulder. "Fuck, what is this tracking program? It shows whoever you're tracking is at the Russian's warehouse."

"Yeah," Tony says, looking up from his computer. "It's not good. Somehow the Russians have your moms Grayson, Fitz, and Stevens."

You hear a roar of 'Fucks', 'Goddamn its' and 'Mother fuckers' go through the room as Stevens and Jackson walk back in.

"The Russians were gone by the time we got there. I think when Dusty didn't come right back, they split. Now tell me what's wrong," Stevens says, looking around the room.

"Damn it all to hell! Tony, how the fuck do you know that? And Hawkins, do they have on their earrings? Are you tracking them too?" Grayson demands.

"That's just it. Their earrings transmission got scrambled about an hour ago. They were still having drinks at a club downtown. Then once they went to their car, the signal started getting scrambled. I've been working on it ever since," Hawkins says, running both hands through his hair, looking very stressed.

"Tony, don't leave us hanging. Explain!" Grayson pleads, the worry clear in his voice.

Tony looks over to me with a questioning look. Shit. "Okay. I'll explain. Let Tony do what he does best and see what intel he can find. See, if you get abducted, it's very possible the kidnapper will take all your jewelry, making your earrings useless. Tony microchipped my ass a very long time ago, and when I shared that with the Wenches months ago, I suggested they all consider it."

"So, you're telling me that not only has Tony seen your ass, but all of our mom's and sister's too?" Grayson asks, looking a bit upset.

"Are you shitting me right now? Your mom is missing, and Tony has found her and you're worried he's seen all our asses?" I respond, dumbfounded he's being a Neanderthal right now.

"No! I didn't mean it like that. Sorry, I'm just freaking out right now," Grayson says, walking over to look at Tony's computer.

"What the fuck did you just say? You lost me. Our Moms have a chip in their asses and they're missing? What the fuck! Is my mom one of them?" Stevens says, hurrying over to look at Tony's computer too.

"This shit is getting too real. Hawkins, where is my fucking sister? Tony, are you sure they are up at the castle?" Clausen demands.

"Yes, I am 110% sure they are up at the castle. The only ones at the warehouse are Moms Riggs, Gregory and Stevens. I've got my men sending out drones to see if we can see anything from windows or outside for that matter. I want to get some heat sensitive information on the warehouse too. That will let us know how many we're dealing with. Last count I got was around eighteen. What was your count, Hawkins?"

"You've got three more then I do, but that's to be expected. I trust your count. Lexy, you sure the Benassi Family is coming?" Hawkins asks, typing on his laptop from beside Tony.

"Hawk, I just sent you the program that tracks all the Wenches who've been chipped, so you can track them as well from now on. A couple of them were chicken shit and didn't get them, but we both know they are up at the castle and safe."

"Thanks Brother," Hawkins responds.

"Just got a text, the Benassi's just pulled up. I'm going to get them and fill them in on the way in," Luigi says heading to the door.

"I just got confirmation that Ivan Osokina is at the warehouse," Hawkins announces.

Were all distracted as not only the Benassi Family, but my friends as well, come busting into the room. Anissa is the first one in the door, instantly firing off loads of questions, "Shit balls Lexy, what's going on? We're all here as you requested. Why are we on lockdown? Look at how you're dressed. There has to be some big shit happening."

"Fuck! What the hell is going down?" Shelly asks looking around as well. "And who are the men in suits?"

"Start talking, Lexy," Dana doesn't stay quiet either.

Before I can respond, I watch as Luigi leads the Benassi Family over to Rocca, Lucca and Uncle Louie, and they all start whispering in a huddle. My family is probably updating them.

I bring my attention back to my friends. "I do not have time to explain, but you are safe here and that is all that matters. Follow Clausen downstairs. You've all been here before," I try to persuade my friends.

"Nissa," Jackson calls out walking over to her.

I watch as she lowers her head and looks up at him with just her eyes, before responding, "Yes, sir."

Shit! She is a fucking natural submissive, not what Jackson needs to see right now. He doesn't need to be thinking of taking one of my friends as his new pet. Man, I can't put off talking to him any longer.

Jackson walks right up to her, lifting her chin up as he looks down into her eyes. I watch as Anissa just blinks her eyes in return. "You are not going to ask any more questions. Things will be explained when we get back. A lot of shit is going down and you girls are safer here. You got me?"

Anissa softly responds once again with a, "Yes, sir."

"Now take your friends underground and do whatever Clausen or Spencer says. Also, help make sure the kid down there stays relaxed and has fun." Then I watch as Jackson puts both hands on each side of her face and plants a hard kiss right on her lips. Oh lord! I'm sure Anissa just had a spontaneous orgasm. What the hell kind of game is Jackson playing with my friend?

As Jackson pulls away, I see Anissa lift her hand and lightly touch her lips, mumbling "Yes, sir" again.

"Hot damn. I bet your panties just melted with that one," Shelly says as she puts her arm around Anissa.

"Come on ladies, let's head downstairs," Clausen says, shaking his head and looking over to Jackson who gives him his signature double bird-flip and mouthing 'fuck you'.

We barely hear Dana tease, "Why can't I ever get one of those? I just want you to know that I hate you right now

Anissa. Shelly is now my official bestie. You've been keeping secrets from us and now it's time for you to share."

Fuck. I'm making a mental note to talk to Jackson once this is over. As the elevator doors close, I watch Grayson pace back and forth between Hawkins' and Tony's computers. I can tell he's on the verge of blowing up. "Come on, Tony! Hawkins! What's the intel? What do we do? Can we head out yet? We have to get to our moms."

"They're in the back of the warehouse upstairs. Lexy and I'll be able to get them out once we attack. This is what we do best, so calm your shit down Riggs," Tony tells Grayson.

"Fuck you! That's my mother."

"And it's too fucking personal for you!" Tony fires back.

Grabbing Grayson by the hand, I leap up to sit on the edge of a counter so I can be eye to eye with him. I rest my forehead to his and look deep into his eyes. His breathing slows to match mine and I say, "Baby, I got this. I know you're freaking out. Your mom and the others are smart. They are not defenseless. Please trust me, and them. I swear to you, we'll get them out unharmed. We need to stick with the plan. Okay?"

Grayson closes his eyes briefly and inhales deeply, pulling me into a crushing embrace. "This is the hardest thing I've ever done in my life. I do trust you. Please be careful babe, because if anything happens to you, my life is over too."

"Back at you. Keep your mind on our end goal. We got this. We're ready, and we're a hell of a lot better than they are."

"Yeah, we are. I love you. See you once it's over so we can celebrate." Then he pulls me off the counter and kisses me hard and with such passion, I feel like I could melt into a puddle at his feet.

"Knock that shit off. Now is not the time," I hear Luigi call out.

"Lexy! Get your mind on the battle," Uncle Louie adds.

Grayson puts me on the ground before looking over to Uncle Louie and Luigi. "My apologies, but that was a kiss for luck. Our minds are on nothing except the battle ahead now," Grayson addresses the Benassi Family, "The majority of your men are charging the front of the building with us. Lexy will lead the attack on the back of the building. She's in charge of Stevens, Jackson, Tony, Lou and Luigi in one SUV. Rocco and Lucca, you take four of the Benassi men with you. We are leaving here at 2100 on the dot."

"Agreed, but we lead the way. We have a fully loaded Hummer, similar to what I'm sure you used in your military days. But it looks sweet, armor plated with tinted windows and all weapons concealed until we're ready to use them. We'll break our way in, and you follow with your SUV." Orlando steps up front to speak.

"Really? It's bulletproof? What kinds of weapons are hidden inside?" Stevens walks over asking.

"Yeah, we wanna see this. Is it parked out front?" Jackson adds.

"I got footage," Tony interrupts loudly. The conversation comes to a complete halt and silence fills the room as we all hurry over to his computer.

"Tony, put it on the big screen," Hawkins shouts.

Within seconds, a very grainy image appears on the massive big screen TV in the back of the office pit. You can tell it's a drone image peeking in a small open window. You can see shoulder length dark hair. Shit, I think that is Mom Gregory, with Mom Stevens beside her. Her hair is much lighter.

"Is that my mom?" Stevens asks.

"I think so. I don't have control of the drone. I've got one of my men on the rooftop of another building. But this lets us know for sure they are in that back upper office. If we can't get through the door, Lexy and I'll get in through these windows," Tony explains.

"Agreed. How many are in the office? I can't tell, can you? Are Papa and Vito with the moms?"

"Yes. They have them all locked in the same room. They must know the moms are doctors."

Watching the screen, we can see them walking around, even though the pictures aren't very clear. A man walks into view and he has an AR15 in his hands, waving it around and pointing it at the moms, wanting them to move out of view. Shit!

"Mother fuckers! They are all dead," I growl.

"You're damn straight on that one Lexy," Stevens agrees with me.

"Have you seen my mom?" Grayson asks.

"Look on the bottom of the screen. I think she's taking care of Vito. There's another woman's head in the bottom of the screen but I don't know who it is."

Looking closer, I can see Mom Riggs on her knees in front on someone lying on the floor. We really can't identify who, but with the finger from the box, odds are it's Vito. Holy Shit!! Mother Mary, that is Isabella's mom in there with them. The guy with the gun just points it at her, so she gets up and hurries over to the side of the room we saw the other woman go. Fuck!!! Now I can see Papa. I think someone has beat the shit out of him too. He's talking to the man pointing the gun and is kneeling beside Mom Riggs and Vito.

"Goddamn! That's Mom," Grayson calls out. As we watch, the camera comes into focus more, finally. I say a little prayer thanking all that is holy. The camera zooms in on Mom Gregory taking vitals on Vito. Papa is very unkept, his lip is busted, and one eye is black and swollen, but he doesn't look seriously injured. He is still talking to the man with the gun. We can now see he had the moms sit down against the side wall, across the room. They look scared as they huddle together.

"Stevens, Jackson, you'll never fit through that narrow

window. You're way too bulky. Once we get to the back of the building, just like in Italy, Tony and I will scale the building and take out that asshole with one shot. Then we'll take out that window and be in there within seconds. When our feet hit ground, we'll secure the area and get to the door to let you in. Once you get in, we get them the fuck out of there. Stevens, Mom Riggs may need you to go with them. That call is up to her but be prepared. Make sure the SUV has the proper medical supplies."

"Done," Stevens responds as he watches the screen.

"We go in there and eliminate every last one of these fuckers. Taking moms is just the lowest. If they harm one hair on their heads, they will regret the day they were born," Grayson says.

"Oh, fuck! Look at the second drone's camera!" Hawkins stands while typing on his computer and a view of the front of the building becomes clearer. We see an additional SUV pull up in front of the warehouse. The doors open and seven more men get out. These guys are all in jeans and fatigues, and I instantly think that these guys have to be locals. Two large doors swing open in the front of the warehouse, and we watch several Russians in suits greet them. Hawkins adds, "That brings the count up to over twenty. I'm not liking this one little bit."

"Look! That fat older man inside the warehouse is Ivan Osokina. He looks just like his son, the one I killed in the alley, but with gray hair."

"Aless, I mean Lexy, I've met him, and he isn't that fat. He's got on a vest. He isn't like your Papa. He stays active in his family. He wants to be the one to kill you. He's given the order for the men to either capture or wound you and bring you to him," Dante informs us.

"Dante, when the fuck were you planning on telling us this?" Uncle Louie asks, slapping him on the back of the head.

"Look, with all the shit that has gone down since we

walked in the door, I haven't had a second to tell you. He had a meeting with my Papa less than an hour ago. He upped the bounty on Lexy's head. He knows you killed all his sons."

"I'm not afraid of him. He's joining his sons today in hell, with a bullet between the eyes."

"Take a good look, men. Whoever sees him first, KILL HIM!" Grayson emphasizes.

You can hear all men agree as they stare at the screen.

"Not if I can find him first," I add, just to rile them up.

Both Grayson and Uncle Louie call my name at the same time. "Lexy!" Uncle Louie waves a hand at Grayson, letting him know he was speaking first.

"Your job is getting us into the back room and getting the mothers out. If Ivan happens to be in that upper office, I'm sure you will be the one to take him out, but you are not going to hunt him down. We have a battle plan and as our squad leader, you're sticking to it. Do I make myself clear?"

"I agree with your Uncle. You are not to focus on Osokina. Our plan is to end this. I'm leading the attack in the front and you in the back, and whoever finds him, kills him. Period!" Grayson says, just as we see Ivan Osokina lift his phone to his ear, and Grayson's cell phone rings. "FUCK!" Grayson curses as he pulls his phone out of the side pocket of his cargo pants. "It says 'UNKNOWN'". Everyone in the room goes silent and he puts it on speaker.

"We need to meet in person."

"Who is this?"

"You know who this is. We meet. We aren't standing down. We're opening our special brand of clubs very soon. We've paid off the people we need to and got some local boys that think we're funding them. But that just shows you how Americans are such stupid overconfident assholes. Just like you, thinking you're in charge," Ivan Osokina says with his heavy accent.

"I never said I was in charge. You just assumed. I told you, sex slaves and underage girls weren't coming to my town."

Ivan busts out with a deep belly laugh. "Boy, they're already here. You don't know what you're missing. There's nothing like fucking a frightened young girl and breaking her into the trade."

You hear a strong intake of air coming from everyone in the room. My blood is beginning to boil. I know they'll all agree that every last one of those fuckers is dead after hearing that.

"You sick fuck! If that is how you feel, what will this meeting accomplish?"

"I think I can persuade you to see things my way. We meet tomorrow night at eight on the waterfront. Oh, and after I play around with your Mama tonight, I'll trade you her for Alessandra. Yes, I know you're fucking the Capo Donna of the Canzano Family, but I think you'll gladly trade that cunt for your Mama."

Grayson walks over to the wall and punches it, putting his hand right through it. "Okay you mother fucker, you touch one goddamn hair on my mother, and I'll take my time killing you."

Laughing, he says, "You'd think you were Italian, being such a Mama's boy. You don't bring that cunt to the water-front tomorrow, your Mama is mine and I'll send you video of me playing with her real soon." Then he hangs up the phone, and we watch him on the screen, walking around the ware-house and laughing with his men.

Grayson throws his phone across the room, hitting a beam and breaking it into several pieces. He screams, "FUCK!!!" at the top of his lungs. Then he bends over and places both hands on his thighs taking deep breaths, before standing up and shouting, "That mother fucker dies tonight. Lexy, leave now and get into position. Get our mothers the hell out of there. I don't care who you need to kill to do it. Get my Mom NOW!"

"Done! They all die in that warehouse tonight," I say with my eyes locked to Grayson's. And with a head nod, my team heads for the door.

33

THE FINAL BATTLE

Lexy

*W*ith the battle before us, it's time to make sure all emotions are in check and that only one thing is on our minds: victory. We take the back roads over to the ocean side warehouse, giving them a little time to celebrate, knowing they'll be drinking their vodka. They think we will be easy to take down, but we're about to show them that *no one messes with our family and lives to talk about it.* There's nothing like catching the enemy completely off guard.

We're all sitting in the SUV in silence, with the lights off. Our eyes are fixed on the high back windows of the warehouse, just a short distance in front of us. As we ponder and just watch and mentally prepare ourselves, waiting for the clock to hit 2200 so we can attack. Victory *will* be ours.

I'm sure I'm not alone, wondering what is going on in there. Tony sent a message to his men running the drones, that if they saw anything happening to the moms to call him immediately, and we'd attack early. So far to our knowledge, nothing has happened to Mom Riggs. It better not either, or I swear on all that is holy, I'll personally cut Ivan Osokina's dick off and feed it to him, watching him die slowly as he chokes on it.

After we heard Grayson's conversation with Ivan, every one of the Brothers was very disturbed. I don't think they've ever had a direct attack on their family like this before. But I think it just feeds their anger and will make them more determined than ever to end this once and for all. Hearing how perverted Ivan is was all the Benassi's needed to hear to put their own worries aside that they were doing the right thing in joining forces with us.

I'm happy that Grayson agreed to let Orlando lead the way, driving his military style Hummer right into the warehouse. It reminds me of the old days with my Family. It does give me a bit of relief, knowing the first ones to be shot at will not be Grayson. But the Brothers will be seconds behind them. Grayson, Carpenter and Fitz, will lead the way. I'm still very surprised to see that Clay and Hunter insisted on taking part in this. Once they heard the moms were involved, they were changed and ready to fight within minutes. Nothing was keeping them behind.

It is comforting to know that Brenden has Bishop and Tiffany ready to go in the headquarters' surgery center. Oh, how I pray none of us need it, because they will have their hands full with Vito. Looking out the window and up to the heavens, I see a few stars in the night sky. I mentally call out to Mom and Nonna, saying a little prayer for protection.

'Mom, Nonna, hear my plea for strength \ and courage. Please protect each one of these men. Send down guardian angels to fight with us and protect us. Keep your hand on Grayson and let him come to no harm. Father, God, hear my prayers for mercy. We need your guidance and strength to help us kill these evil men and rid the earth of their wickedness. Amen' Mom, Nonna, I love and miss you every day. I hope I am making you proud.

Suddenly I'm pulled out of my mental prayer by a loud crash and gunfire.

"GO!!! The battle's begun. Head to the backdoor," I say as Tony and I pull our masks over our faces.

Luigi floors it and we rush down the back driveway to the warehouse. The second the SUV stops, all doors pop open and we all jump out. I start shouting orders, "Stevens, Jackson, I was right, your bodies will never fit through these windows. Be the first by the door, we'll get you in ASAP."

Jackson and Stevens look up, checking out the windows as Uncle Louie says, "Let's get in place men. Your fat asses won't fit up there any more than mine will. Trust Lexy and Tony, they are fast and quiet. They'll be at the door sooner than you think."

With a nod to Uncle Louie, I inform them, "Don't forget to keep an eye out for any of their men trying to escape. We're ready. Let's kick some ass and get the moms out of here." Tony and I dash over to the windows, and with a brief look at each other, we take off like synchronized swimmers, tossing our grappling hooks up in unison. Then with a nod to one another, we test our lines. We know if we try climbing up the side of the building, we could make noise, so we flip our switches and allow the pulley system to lift us quickly to the window. We both pull out our Beretta's, fitted with silencers for this special occasion.

Peeking into the window, the first thing I see is Mom Riggs and Mom Stevens applying pressure to the side of Vito's abdomen. His hand is also wrapped in what looks like a man's white shirt but is now covered in blood. Papa is sitting in a chair against the far wall. Both Mom Gregory and Isabella's mom are cuddled in the corner. I can tell Mom Gregory is trying to keep Ivy calm. None of them look injured. Thank God.

Hearing the door inside open up, Tony looks at me and I

hold up two fingers, pointing to the guards by the door. We can hear the gunfire and the loud noises of battle going on in the front of the building even louder with the door open.

The man calls out, "Do you want to kill them all? They just started a war by driving into the front of the building. I think all of them should die," he says, waving his AK47 at the moms.

Without thinking twice, Tony and I quickly take aim, firing our guns simultaneously, taking out both guards. There's an emotional cry and the scurry of feet below. Tony and I burst into the windows, pulling our grappling ropes inside and releasing them to drop to the floor. We're in. With a push of our buttons, we lower ourselves to the floor.

A smile spreads across my face as I see Mom Gregory standing with perfect form, pointing one of the dead guard's AK47 at us. "Identify yourself or die," Papa has the other guard's gun, but he is standing behind her. What a pussy.

Ripping off my mask and pointing my gun at Papa, I say, "We're here to rescue you, Moms. Tony, hit the door and let the men in." Looks like there's going to be a standoff with Papa and I still pointing guns at each other. "Drop your gun and kick it over here or you die."

Papa slowly lowers his gun. "I see you're still as big of a bitch as you were when you escaped. I am not here to kill you, just to take you home."

"I am home, and I'm an even bigger bitch. Don't push me Papa or I will shoot you. You are not in charge here." Glancing away from him, I ask the Mom's, "Is anyone hurt?"

Mom Riggs runs over and hugs me, "Thank God you're here. I knew you and Tony would show up at some point. I agree with you, your father is a truly an arrogant asshole. I can understand why you hate him so much. He's the reason Vito is hurt so badly. He continued to harass the guards and wouldn't shut up, so they took it out on Vito. We need to get him to the hospital ASAP. His finger has been cut off. I think they might have sent it to you, and he has had the shit beat out of him, as well as taken a couple of bullets. He's been conscious on and off, but we need to hurry," Mom Riggs informs me.

"You are correct, his finger is at headquarters. They have a full surgical room there. Brenden, Bishop and Tiffany are there to handle anyone who comes back hurt. Since Vito is my best friend in Italy's Papa, I'd rather not take him to a hospital, so the police don't find out and investigate this. Is that alright with you? Headquarters is also the closest medical center. You can at least get him stable and evaluate if he needs to be transferred to the hospital later."

"Agreed. If Brenden is there, that is where we will go. He's the hospital's best trauma doctor anyway. I'm going to have to give Grayson shit for not telling me they built a surgical center there. There are so many rules being broke by that. But now is not the time, I know," Mom Riggs is just being a concerned mom, but she is right, not now. I'm sure in time she'll understand why they need it.

Stevens busts through the door with Jackson right behind him, followed by Uncle Louie, Luigi, Rocco and Lucca. All have their weapons drawn. Stevens runs over to his mom, scooping her up and into a big hug. Turning to my men I order, "Rocco, Lucca, head into the warehouse. Jackson, hit the air. We'll join you in a few moments." With a head nod, they all take off, heading back and into the warehouse.

Jackson pauses and turns around looking at the moms. "Get your asses out of here. Do not stop. Go directly to headquarters. I'm sending a message you're all safe. Glad you're okay." And with that, he's out the door and we hear him reporting on his headset. "Mom's safe. Headed to headquarters. I'm in the air."

Uncle Louie and Luigi, rush over to Vito. Kneeling down beside him, Luigi pulls two large medical bags off his shoulder as Stevens rejoins them. He opens the first bag that turns into a collapsible stretcher. "Fuck! He doesn't look good," Uncle Louie comments with concern.

Mom Riggs takes charge. "He's alive. He just passed out moments ago. I need you guys to lift him in unison and place him on the stretcher. We need to get the hell out of here. Now."

Stevens takes over guiding the men with what to do. I glance over to Papa whose vein is popping out of his head, his neck and face bright red with fury. He looks ready to blow. "How long have you men known Alessandra was here in America? Tell me!" he yells over the gunfire we hear getting closer by the second.

"Shut the fuck up, Al! Vito is lying here, possibly dying. We're trying to get your asses out of here to safety," Uncle Louie says, walking over to Papa.

Papa lifts his gun and points it at Uncle Louie, and without thinking, I fire my gun, shooting Papa's gun out of his hand. "Do you want to die today, mother fucker? Do not *ever* point a gun at him or *any* of my goddamn men again. I will not think twice about taking you out."

Papa calls out, "Shit! You shot me."

"Consider yourself lucky that I didn't kill you. It's just a flesh wound. Now shut up and stop being a pussy and do as Mom Riggs says. You better not say anything rude to her either."

Papa reaches into the medical bag Stevens has open and grabs a roll of gauze, wrapping it around his hand as he gives me a death stare. "Fuck you, Alessandra. These are not your men. They are mine. You gave up that right when you ran away to America."

"We do not have the time for this right now. I will deal with you later."

"You will not deal with me later. You are coming with me. If I leave, you leave," Papa yells at me.

Uncle Louie grabs him by the shirt and throws him

against the wall, getting in his face as he says, "Not another goddamn word comes out of that mouth. Lexy has given you an order. Stand down or I'll be the one to either knock your ass out or shoot you," Uncle Louie demands, as he presses his Beretta against Papa's temple.

"Fine! But this is not over. I disown you as a brother. You are dead to me. All of you are a disgrace to the Family and will be handled accordingly. You all took an oath to *me*, pledging your life to this Family."

Uncle Louie cocks his gun, getting within inches of Papa's face. "Really Al, that's how you want to play this? Do you want to see your wife and children again? Keep talking and I'll enjoy sending your ashes back to Laura, if I don't have the Benassi's feed you to their pigs. Go ahead, say one more word. 'Make my day', as they would say in America."

Papa is breathing heavily like he just ran a marathon, but he finally shuts his mouth. I hear Stevens say, "On my count, one, two," and on three they lift Vito up as they head for the door.

"Princess, is that you?" I hear Vito's whisper of a voice, as his eyes flutter.

I quickly rush to his side and take his good hand in mine. "Yes Vito, it's me. We're taking you to get help."

"No hospital. They'll have me arrested."

"We're taking you to Camelot Headquarters. We have a full medical facility there. You'll get the best of care and we can hide you out there until you are stable enough to travel."

He looks at me with a small smile. "Oh, sweet Princess, I might have known you'd pick a strong man you can battle with. Alessandra, if I don't make it… let Gwen know how much I love her."

I place my finger over his lips making him hush as I lean down and look deep into his eyes, giving him orders. "I do not want to hear that kind of bullshit. You fight! You are a strong member of the Canzano Family. You are a good husband, father and soon to be Nonno. You fight, you stay alive. I refuse to let you die! You hear me?"

Vito's eyes open wider as he smiles, before he starts coughing, saying, "Fuck! That hurts like a mother fucker." Vito grabs my arm with his good hand and pulls me close to him as he whispers, "I'm fighting Alessandra, but I'm tired. I'm sorry, I couldn't talk your Papa out of coming here, trying to get you back. You deserve to be free, and I'm proud of you." Then his eyes fall closed.

Quickly looking to make sure he is still breathing, I thank God he is. I kiss him on both cheeks and then his forehead, before a swift kiss on the lips, whispering right back to him,

"Keep fighting, I'll be there when you wake up." The moment I stand up, I give Mom Riggs another hug. "I love you. Thank you for taking care of Vito. Now you are officially in charge the moment you get out this door. Stevens will drive you to headquarters. Hawkins will be talking to you the moment he sees you get into the SUV."

"Stevens is staying to help you. There are at least twenty five men in there, maybe more. No way. One of us will drive. I want all of you to come back to me in one piece. We have two doctors and a nurse in this room. We'll have plenty of medical staff at headquarters. Now go do what you do best, and kill that mother fucker," Mom Riggs says, kissing me on the cheek.

"Okay, if you're sure. Take this Berretta. I have others," I say with a smile and wink. "Oh, and if he gets out of line, shoot him," I hand her my Berretta, taking her AK47. I glare at Papa one last time, before I run over and give Mom Stevens and Mom Gregory a hug. Isabella's mom, for being such a verbal tough guy, is still crying, shaking, and looking like she may pass out at any minute. I lean in and give her a sideways hug. Mom Gregory helps her towards the door and to the waiting SUV. Looks like Mom Stevens will be the one to drive.

"Stevens, Luigi and Uncle Louie, you go and make sure

they get out of here safely then join us in the warehouse. Tony and I are hitting the air." With a head nod, they carry Vito out with Mom Riggs still pointing a gun at Papa, who is not happy at all. I pull my mask back on as Tony and I take off running out the door to the main part of the warehouse.

We need to make sure no one else is up here, so once we are out the door, we look all around and see no one. Knowing I need to let everyone know the moms are safe, I touch my left ear twice to access my communication device. "All moms are out and safe. Headed in to give you backup. And if Hawkins can hear this transmission, let Brenden know they're headed your way. Have the surgery team ready. Vito's in bad shape and heading there."

"Got it! Be safe. Keep me in the loop," Hawkins shaky voice comes into my ear.

Instantly Grayson's voice follows, "Jackson has been spotted flying around. Took out a Russian who spotted him, but I don't know if he got the word out or not, so be on the ready. Counts were off. There are over thirty men in here, both American gang members and Russians. That leads me to believe there are either weapons or drugs hidden in here. You're our eyes in the sky. See what you can find out. Over."

"On it! Be safe."

"Always and back at you. Out!" Grayson says. Man, I do love the way he kept it professional, like I was one of the men. That warms my heart. Okay, back to business.

As we get to the end of the hall, we discover another office door. Reaching out, I open it quickly with my AK47 ready to go. Looking around the office, all I see is a room filled with computers. The only thing that goes through my mind is the idea that these computers are filled with Russian Porn, of the children the Osokina Family have raped and sold into the sex trade. Before I can think twice, I take aim and blow every last one of the mother fuckers into pieces. Turning back around,

Tony is standing in the doorway with his mask off, looking angry.

"What the hell! I could have removed the hard drives and gotten good information we could have used."

"At this moment, all I want to do is destroy them. I can only imagine the perverted content on them. Come on Tony, this is a warehouse, not their headquarters. You might have been right, but it's too late now. Let's move." As I push past Tony, I know he is right. There could have been good intel on them, but I'll never admit to fucking up.

Opening the exit door and heading into the main part of the warehouse, we can see the battle raging. Shit! There aren't as many containers in this warehouse as there was in Italy. They must have already shipped a lot out. These two offices are the only second floor area, the rest is just open area. Looking around, I can see a maze of cargo containers below, and there are plenty of metal and wood support beams in the ceiling. Looking straight ahead, I see Jackson in the distance, lowering himself to the floor as he shoots Russians from behind, who are after Orlando and Dante.

"Let's move," I tell Tony as I throw my grappling hook onto the beams above us. Turning around, I see Tony point in the opposite direction as he heads to another row of containers across from me. Keeping low, we stay in each other's peripheral vision. Running to the end looking out at the battle, I can see Luigi and Uncle Louie standing behind the bulletproof doors of the hummer for protection. They're taking out anyone trying to escape. I watch as a couple of Russians run towards them, waving AK47's. Shit, is that the only weapon these people have? You don't need good aim to kill with those, just swing and pull the trigger. They are killing machines.

Fuck! I toss mine over my shoulder, pulling my Sig P226 out of my back holster. Looking over at Tony, I tap the center of my forehead between my eyes, letting him know we're on a direct kill mission. I toss another grappling hook up into the beams and swing over to another row of containers, looking over the edge. I see two Russians and an American opening up a container. Now I get to see what's inside of these. They pull away a fake wall of boxes to reveal a shit load of wooden crates. I'll bet you those will be the weapons. Trying to listen to their conversation, I turn on the magnification hearing aide in my mask.

"Who tipped off the Italians that we were making our weapons purchase tonight? Fuck! I'm half wasted from drinking all that vodka you gave us to celebrate us sealing this deal. You assholes took away our weapons when we got here, now I've already lost three men," an American says angrily.

"We told no one. It must have been your people. Here in this container is where we hid your weapons. Let's give your men some power." The two Russians start prying open a wooden crate.

Fuck that. Feeling Tony's presence beside me, I lay down on top of the container and touch the communication button on my headset and tell Tony, "We're taking all three out, you take the American. Then I'm down there to close up that container."

"Easy!"

"On my count," I hold up three fingers, then two, and then we both fire with perfect accuracy. The two Russians drop dead, with the American on top of them. We both re-holster our guns as we pop up to our feet, giving each other a high five.

Reaching out and grabbing my grappling rope, I lower myself in seconds with Tony beside me. Once our feet hit ground, we run over to the double doors, pushing them both closed. Then we lift the huge pole-like lever, locking the doors again.

Tony gives me a nod as he pulls out another grappling hook from his backpack, uncoiling it. Then with nimble fingers, he weaves it through the big heavy metal locking mechanism, climbing up the doors, continuing his weaving. Once he's on the top of the container, he wedges the grappling rod into the top. Standing up and removing his mask, he smiles down at me, looking very proud of himself. Then he flips the switch, causing the razor sharp hooks to spring open. Now that makes damn sure these doors will not be opening any time soon.

Motioning for him to head on to the next container, I grab my own grappling rope and start to lift myself, when out of nowhere a ballistic knife comes flying by my head, going straight through my left hand. SHIT!!! That causes me to release my rope and fall about six feet to the ground. The vibrations radiate up my legs from landing on my feet on the concrete floor. That hurt like a mother fucker. I pull the knife out of my hand as I'm grabbed from behind. Fuck this!

Twisting my body, I start stabbing the man holding me. He releases me as he clutches my mask in his hand. I turn around in a battle stance, with the knife in my right hand. The Russian is bleeding out badly from his side, as he yells, "FUCK! YOU'RE THE PRINCESS!"

My internal switch is flipped, and on pure instinct, I lunge forward, stabbing him in the heart and giving a twist. Goddamn, my hand hurts. Without pausing, I take the blade and cut the bottom half of my shirt off and wrap my hand tightly. Hearing what sounds like several people running in my direction, I wrap my right arm around my grappling rope and push the switch with my injured hand, causing more pain to rush up my arm. It lifts me to the top of the container.

Bent over clutching my hurt hand into my chest, I take off running to the front of the container. You can hear the battle is coming to an end, as there's barely any gunfire. I hear my Papa's voice call out, "Ivan, where the fuck is my daughter? If you have killed her, you will die a very slow, painful death."

"You are dying today Al, after I personally kill your daughter. I know she is still here, because none of my men have reported back to me. That is, unless she turned into a pussy and fled," Ivan says chuckling.

"Your men are all dead. My daughter is better than them. Didn't she already kill all your sons? No one left to carry on your Family name," Papa says, goading him right back.

Standing upright and looking over the edge of the container, I see a pallet full of open cases of military style fatigues. Here is my chance. I can only hope that all the boxes underneath them are clothes as well. Taking a deep breath, I grab another grappling hook from my backpack and toss it above their heads. I know I'll not make it far, but I do know now is my only shot to kill Ivan Osokina.

Hearing Tony calling and running up behind me, I take hold of the rope with both hands and swinging out as I scream, 'Die mother fucker!"

Instantly Papa and Ivan look up. I lock eyes with Ivan, and as he fires, so do I. Then everything goes black and I feel like I'm floating.

GRAYSON

Fuck! That was Lexy. Instantly I'm calling into my headgear, "Where is she? Does anyone have eyes?" I demand as I take off running, at the same time, I hear several guns fire.

Running to the end of this aisle of containers, I see Lou and Luigi running in front of me. Following them, I take the corner as I hear Tony say in my ear. "She's been hit! Down on a stack of boxes on the far left of the warehouse. She took out Osokina. He's dead."

Goddamn it! She better be okay. My heart is pounding so hard I'm sure my men can hear it too. As the pile of boxes comes into view, I see Tony and Luigi kneeling beside Lexy who's lying on top of the boxes. I can see blood. Shit, shit, shit!!

"Don't move her just yet. Let's check to see if anything is broken," Luigi says as he feels her legs.

Once I reach them, I carefully climb up onto the boxes as well, with Lou right beside me. Then I see her father, coming over right behind us. Shit. What the hell is he doing here?

Thank you, Jesus, I think to myself. She landed on a massive stack of fatigues. Then I notice half her black shirt has been cut away. Grabbing the front of it, I rip it open. I need to make sure she isn't bleeding. I can see the end of a bullet protruding from her bulletproof vest.

Leaning over her, I lightly caress her cheek, "Baby, can you hear me? It's over. You did it, Ivan Osokina is dead."

"Who the fuck are you, touching my daughter that way?" Al yells at me, grasping my arm and trying to pull me away.

"I'm her goddamn boyfriend," I yell right back as I notice Lexy's left hand is wrapped up with her shirt. Shit. Looking at it, I can see that is where the blood is coming from.

"Al, would you like to die today?" I hear Lou say as he cocks his gun.

I feel someone grab my gun and I turn my head to see that Lexy has taken it and is pointing it at her father. She shoots him in the shoulder, making him drop a gun I was unaware he had pointed at me. "Al, don't you ever touch Grayson again."

"Oh God, you're awake! Where are you hurt, baby?" I ask, un-velcroing her vest slowly.

"You fucking shot me twice today. I'm your father!"

"No, you the fuck aren't. Uncle Louie is my father. You were nothing to me but a sperm donor. You'd be dead already if it wasn't for your two children back in Italy. But if you ever come back to America, you're a dead man," Lexy, says still pointing my gun at him.

"You all took a pledge, a solemn oath to the Canzano Family. You all know the consequences for this betrayal," Al continues to yell at her as his neck turns red and a vein in his forehead starts protruding.

Lexy shoots him in the arm this time. "Getting closer to your heart, Al. You really ready to die today? I want to hear you release all of them by name from their Family pledge. Oh, I should probably tell you that I have a USB drive with a copy of all, and I mean *all* the Canzano Family files. If anything happens to any one of us, my lawyer knows to turn it over to both countries' government agencies. You ready to release us yet?"

"You fucking cunt!"

With that, I'm on my feet as all the Brothers, as well as a couple of men from the Benassi Family, stand with guns aimed at him. I take my gun out of Lexy's hand and walk over to Al, who is now bleeding from both his right shoulder and forearm. "Do you see all these men with guns aimed at you? Not a one of them are on your side. Now do as Lexy as told you release them. But first, apologize to her," I demand as I place the gun against his temple.

I watch his face gets redder by the second. Then Lou walks up to Al and punches him in the face, knocking him backwards, making him fall off the pile of boxes and hit the ground. Lou jumps down to him and grabs his bloody shirt, pulling him up and into his face. "It would bring me such joy to kill you. You already disowned me today, and believe me, the feeling is mutual. You are dead to me. I never want to hear your voice again." Then Lou spits to each side of Al. "If I ever see you after today, you are a dead man. Do I make myself clear? Now apologize to *my daughter!*"

He takes a deep breath, and stares right at Lou as he says, "My apologies Alessandra. You are all released from your oath to this Family."

"FREEZE! AFT! Drop your weapons!"

Fuck! Looking back over to Lexy, I see she has passed out

again. I drop my gun and raise my hands. announcing, "Grayson Riggs here, with the Brothers of Camelot."

"Riggs, what the fuck are you all here for? You should have notified us about this. We called the AFT when we realized what was going on with the Savage Hunter gang," Detective Franks says.

Lowering my hands, I'm honest with him, "We knew nothing about what was going down with them. Our business was with the Osokina Crime Family from Russia."

"Hey Detective, I can save you some time and show you which container has a shit ton of weapons. I'm Tony Jarvis, with Stark Enterprise. I think we met at Fitz's wedding." Tony jumps down from the boxes.

"Hey Tony, long time since I've seen you." An AFT agent walks over to him, shaking his hand.

"Good to see you too, Marcus. I've been a bit busy with a Russian Family thing."

"We caught a couple trying to escape. You coming down to the station with intel to help us lock them up?"

"Yeah, I can do that. But I'm going to need some help with some people you have connections with. You know, those secret ones upstairs that can help me with some family members staying here."

"I'm sure we can work something out. Do they have intel too?"

"Possibly. But do I have to call you Sergeant Collins, or will I still be on a first name basis there with you?"

Marcus chuckles and puts his hand on Tony's shoulder saying, "Lead us to the weapons, smartass and we'll talk."

"Hey, don't leave me in the cold here. And yes, you did meet me at Fitz and Isabella's wedding. I didn't know you were in tight with the Brothers," Detective Franks says.

As they walk off, I quickly turn my attention back to Lexy, who is still unconscious. Shit! I finally manage to remove her bulletproof vest completely And I can see where the bullet

533

almost pierced it. Her ribs have a nice sized bruise appearing, but I don't see any other blood. Thank God.

That is when I notice Luigi unwrapping her hand. He gives a deep gasp. "Fuck, this has to hurt like a mother fucker. It looks like a blade went straight through her hand," he says as he slowly flips it front to back.

Then I hear Detective Jerkins ask, "And who are you two?"

Quickly looking over to him, I see he is speaking to Lou and Al. Time to impress Lou with my quick thinking. "Let me introduce you to my future father in law. This is Lou Canzano. Lou Canzano, Detective Jerkins." Lou gives me a big smile, as he shakes the detective's hand.

"Oh, your Lexy's dad?"

"Yes, I am. We just moved here from Italy. This man on the ground is my ex-brother Al, the Capo of the Canzano Family of Italy. I have no part in the Family business and neither does Lexy. You might want to run him through your system though, you never know what you'll find. Now may I be excused and check on my daughter? She was hurt during this bat... er, I mean attack."

"Sure, sure, go ahead. We've already got ambulances and EMT's on standby."

With a nod, Lou rushes over here as Al yells, "You lying mother fucker! She is my daughter!"

"I think he might have hit his head when he fell because I've known Lexy and her family forever. She's the grand-daughter of Lexington and Sophia Rogers," Fitz explains as he walks over.

"I was thinking that was odd because I thought Lexy's last name is Rogers."

"Her mother passed away when she was very young, and when she moved here, she changed her last name to Rogers, in honor of her mother. Lou was completely okay with that because he had remarried and has adopted two more children. They're all a real tight bunch, that is, the American Canzano's and Rogers'. We've made them a part of our own now," Fitz tells him with a straight face, before putting his hand behind his back just for Al to see and he flips him off.

Al sits up and starts cussing under his breath, knowing full well he is fucked. "I'm bleeding. I've been shot twice, by her," he yells, pointing at Lexy, "And I might even have a bullet in my shoulder that'll match his gun."

Jerkins ignores him, lifts his arm and talks into his sleeve, "We have two back to the left of the warehouse that are wounded. One a civilian, the other a possible criminal. I want armed officers assigned to him until we can check things out. We need to see if he is involved in this."

"I'm okay. Just get me out of here," Lexy whispers, opening her eyes.

"Alexa Sophia Rogers, you are going to a goddamn hospital and that is not up for debate. Do I make myself clear?" Lou yells.

A smile spreads across her face as she says, "Yes, Dad. I heard everything. I just couldn't open my eyes. I think I've lost a bit of blood and the hit on my ribs knocked me out for a minute. I may have even hit my head with my crash landing."

Leaning over her and looking into those beautiful light blue eyes that are the reason my heart beats, I whisper, "I love you, beautiful. I'm not leaving your side. Thank God for your vest. You took a bullet that almost pierced it. You're going to have some fucked up ribs again." I rest my forehead to hers just for a second before I taste those full lips of hers.

"Knock that shit off," Luigi bellows, before whispering. "It's official you know, if Lou is now her dad, I'm her blood brother."

Lexy lifts her right hand and flips Luigi off, saying, "Fuck you, Bubba. I hope you like your new name. You're in America now, and isn't that what they call their brothers?"

We all start to chuckle as the EMT comes over. "Can I have all of you step back so we can get to the patient?"

"Do whatever the hell you want to her, but I am not leaving her side. I'm also riding in the ambulance, because neither of you are big enough to stop me. Oh, and I do have a gun and I'm not afraid to use it."

34

CELEBRATING WITH SHOCKS & SURPRISE

Lexy

*W*alking into Grayson's penthouse has become my home, since the moment I got out of the hospital two weeks ago. He has barely let me out of his sight. He has even been dropping me off and picking me up after work because he says I cannot drive using only one hand, which is nonsense. Even with one hand in a cast, I could easily drive myself. I hate to say it, but I kind of like his pampering. Today he surprised me. He actually allowed Stevens to pick me up and drop me off. He's up to something, I just know it, but what, I don't know. I feel it all the way down to my soul. He has been texting me all day like nothing is up, but he can't fool me.

Boy, my life has been a whirlwind the last couple of weeks. I had to have a minor surgery on my hand to repair the damage the knife caused. Well, at least it was a very clean cut, right through the bone, which they reassured me should heal nicely.

So much has happened with Vito. Grayson, Hawkins and Tony worked their magic to get Vito's family here to America.

That alone helped turn him around and helped him to fight to stay alive. I knew getting Gwen here would be the best thing for his recovery. He hasn't left headquarters since Mom Riggs brought him here. He's had Gwen and Annalisa by his side since his eyes opened. I've actually had so much fun catching up with them.

After the first week of Annalisa and Stephen being here and getting to know everyone, they fit right in. With Annalisa and Isabella both pregnant and due the same week, you can really tell how big Isabella is. The Brothers hung out with Stephen so he wouldn't go crazy being stuck at headquarters. We didn't want any outsiders to know they were here. We just didn't need the trouble.

It was so nice to figure out that Annalisa is truly my friend. Deep down, I'd always questioned it. I wondered if it was just because of who I was, and who our parents are. But we just clicked. On Sunday she went home to switch with Antonio and Gigi. Oh my gosh, having a little one running around was so much fun. It was good training to expose all the Brothers to toddlers since Isabella will be having two before we know it. But most of all, it has been great that they all hit it off with Grayson. They all congratulated me on finding my one true love.

Before I left, Brenden told us Vito will be okay to travel back to Italy very soon, so Tony and Hawkins are working on getting him out of the country by the weekend. But he'll be going back without Papa, rather Al. He is still being held in a federal jail, and I couldn't be happier. I think they have officially scared the shit out of him, and he will not be coming back to America again. Finally, I have closure, and the freedom from that feels marvelous. It also feels normal to call Uncle Louie 'Dad'. I've joked around about doing it for years, but after I called him that in front of Papa, I haven't called him anything else since. He truly is my Dad, and I love him for that.

There are still a few things up in the air, but they will settle soon, I'm confident. We're still waiting to see what will happen in the months to come with Rocco, Lucca and Luigi. They've been wearing ankle bracelets that the Feds put on them since the warehouse. I thank God they're here and are probably going to stay. They refuse to tell me anything other than, 'not to worry, they'll handle it'. This is one time I'm listening. I have to trust it'll all work out.

They are talking to some of the same agents I worked with when I came here. Who knows, maybe the Feds will not only help them to stay but give them jobs too. They would be better at it than me. I just want to be normal, and I'm glad this crisis is over. I've seen them smile more than I ever have, and they just look relaxed. It's a dream come true for me to have my adopted family here to stay. But that is —neither here nor there right now. I need to find out what Grayson is up to because it's driving me crazy.

"Well, don't you look as beautiful as always. How did your visit with Vito go? Brenden says he's doing a lot better and is ready to go home" Grayson says as he walks out of the kitchen looking hotter than hell. Wow. I'm speechless just checking him out. He's wearing a white dress shirt with the sleeves rolled up to his elbows, and he's holding a rose. But that isn't the best of it. He's barefoot and his very nicely fitted black dress slacks that emphasize his huge thighs and shows off his nice package. Dayum. I am going to have to check out that ass, just to make sure the back view is as nice as the front. "Babe, are you okay? You look frozen," he says, waving the long stem red rose under my nose with a smile on his face.

"Ah, I'm fine. You, you look incredibly handsome yourself, but I need to see the rest of you. Do you mind turning around, slowly?"

"Are you kidding?"

"Hell no, I'm not kidding! Turn around!" I say, spinning my finger in the air.

Grayson cracks up laughing and slowly turns around, and I'm thanking my lucky stars that this hella fine man is all mine. That ass… there are no words to describe sheer perfection.

"You going to tell me what that was all about?"

"Yeah. I had to check out your ass, which looks mighty fine by the way. You know I have a thing for your ass, just like you do for mine. You will just have to excuse my ogling. I'm used to seeing you in work clothes and not tight fitting dress slacks. I mean if you ever wanna get really lucky, just dress like this more often." I put both arms around his waist and slide them down, giving his bum a good squeeze.

"I can understand that. My Camelot Security fatigues, and t-shirt aren't nearly as sexy as your work outfit. But come on, what man wouldn't want to see his woman's scrumptious ass in those yoga pants on a daily basis?" Grayson says, putting his arms around me, squeezing my ass in return. He leans over and starts kissing up my neck.

"I'm just letting you know that I already wanna jump you. I'll race to the bedroom to see who can strip the fastest," I tease, knowing we already have plans to head over to the Camelot Bar and Club to meet up with everyone.

Grayson looks at his watch. "Well, in all reality, we're not on a time schedule so we could get a quickie in, but not until I show you something."

"What?! Showing me something is more important than a fast fuck?!" I really want him, bad.

Grayson starts nibbling my neck and rubs his hard-on against me, chuckling. "Babe, you're cheating. You know hearing you say 'fuck' turns me from semi-hard to granite in seconds. But I've worked a long time on this, and I'm hoping you'll want me a lot more after I show it to you."

"Fine!" I say, rolling my eyes and snapping my fingers to speed this up. "Okay, let's move, show me. Let's get this over with so I can have my wicked way with that body," I continue to tease.

Both of us start laughing as Grayson pulls away, releasing me and taking me by the hand. He leads me through the living room and out onto the deck. "Well, I hate to break your heart, but it's going to take more than a second."

"Where are we going?"

"The beach."

"The *beach!* It's nighttime Grayson, and remember, as much as I love a swim in the moonlight, we have a bit of a problem," I say waving my cast in front of him.

"Your arm will not be a problem. We aren't dressed for a swim either. I'm not going skinny dipping out there, you never know when someone will show up," he says with a chuckle as we begin our long way down his zigzag stairs from his penthouse to the beach.

"Okay then, can you give me a hint? What's on the beach?"

"Nope, you can wait. Doesn't the night sky look beautiful?"

"Yes, it does. Santa Monica is truly a piece of heaven. It even smells clean, the fresh salty air is bliss. It's not the typical fishy smell I'm used to around beaches. I love it here."

"So, you never want to go home, back to Italy?"

"Home to me is wherever you are. There is nothing there that being here with you doesn't beat," I say cuddling into his arm. As we get closer to the beach, I can see tons of tiki lights, starting at the bottom of the stairs.

"I feel the same way. There is no purpose in life without you in it," he says, kissing the top of my head as we reach the beach.

I kick off my slip on heels and really feel short now as my bare feet hit the sand. "Did you put all these tiki lights out here yourself?"

"I'll be honest, I had a little help. In reality, I needed the help because everything kept blowing away," he adds with a chuckle.

"Oh, Grayson, are we going to have a romantic dinner on the beach?"

"Nope. I need to talk to you for a minute and I thought there was no better place than on the beach underneath the stars," he says as we turn the corner and the tiki torches make a path to what looks like a giant odd circle. No, wait. The closer we get, I can see they make a heart. Oh my God! Grayson has made a giant heart shaped blanket with the edges surrounded with red and white roses. There must be close to a hundred roses.

"Grayson, this is beautiful. What do you want to talk about? If you're going to ask me to move in, I will. I've already told my roomies it was probably happening, and they said they wouldn't touch my room in case I ever need any 'me' time."

"Me time?! Your friends think you might want to escape my clutches sometimes? Do they think I was too overprotective, bringing you here instead of letting you go home after surgery?"

"Lord no. They're all jealous of how much you love me. They thought you were sweet taking care of me like that, and they had never seen that side of you. Come on, putting tight yoga pants on with one hand isn't easy."

Grayson chuckles, "Oh, but that was my favorite part," he says making his eyebrows dance as he pulls me into his arms just outside of the heart.

"Are you being a pervert again?"

"Always when it comes to you. Now listen to me for a minute."

"My lips are sealed. I'm all ears. So, it isn't about me moving in with you?"

Grayson shakes his head no then looks up to the stars as he begins to talk seriously, in a soft, deep tone that causes my blood to rush and my heart to pound. "Remember when I told you to always think of me when you looked up at the starlit sky, and know I'd be somewhere looking up at that same night sky?"

"Yes, and I still do to this day. It brings me peace, knowing you're out there somewhere thinking of me."

Grayson caresses the side of my face with the back of his hand as he looks into my eyes. "I love you, Alexa Sophia Rogers. You are my sun, moon and stars. There is nothing and no one that could ever take your place in my life, or in my heart. You're the one that fills my mind and soul with peace, love and a sense of completion, wholeness, that I've never felt before."

Then he takes my hand and leads me into the center of the heart and continues "Lexy, we've really gotten to know each other over the last few months, more so than I ever hoped after our chance encounter when we were both so young. I never gave up on that stunning beauty with those clear blue eyes that change my life forever. That feeling we shared was just the beginning. I have never, not once since then, looked at the stars and not said a wish or a prayer, wanting you to come back to see if what we felt was real. Lucky for us, you felt the same way. People may think we're crazy, but I don't give a shit. You're my soulmate."

Oh my God! Grayson steps back and gets on one knee in the center of the heart, looking up at me. I can feel myself begin to shake all over. I'm gonna faint. I touch my lips with my fingers, in total shock, to make sure my mouth isn't hanging open.

"Lexy, you are the center of my heart. Without you, there is no joy, no happiness, no love. You are My One Love. You make my heart complete. Will you do me the honor of spending the rest of your life with me?" Grayson asks as he opens a ring box, exposing my Mom's engagement ring.

"OH GOD YES!!!" I practically yell, dropping to my knees and wrapping both my hands around his, just looking at my Mom's ring. Feeling my eyes fill with tear, I ask, "When? How?"

"I'm a bit old fashioned and had to ask Lou for his blessing first. He gave me a bit of shit, but then he told me he couldn't have found a better match for you if he tried himself, and that it would mean the world to your family if I'd use this ring to propose. It's been in the Rogers' family for decades. Both your Mom, Grandma, and many more before them used this ring when they exchanged vows."

I stick my hand out for him to put it on me. "My mom used to show this to me in its box and tell me it was her moms and grandmas and one day it would be mine, but I never thought that day would come. She only wore it for the service and pictures, then Al gave her a massive Family ring to wear in front of everyone. Thank you," I say as Grayson slowly slides it onto my finger. It fits perfectly.

I throw my arms around his neck, kissing him, knocking him over. Grayson quickly continues one of the most passionate kisses ever, as he rolls me onto my back. We can't control ourselves, we're acting like we're starved for each other as we continue to kiss and caress each other. I feel Grayson pulling up my long skirt, and he briefly lifts his body just a bit so our bodies can touch more intimately. I bend one leg up at the knee, so I can get him where I need him the most. He begins to grind his hardness right into me, causing me to pull away from our passionate kiss to release a low moan.

"Baby, I've got to be inside of you." And with that, he rips the sides of my thong and I lift my hips allowing him to pull it off. He undoes his pants faster than I've ever seen and is in me within seconds. Oh God, he's so right. We're whole. We're complete.

"You are my forever, and always will be," I say as we make love like never before, quenching a hunger for each other in the best way possible.

As our climax builds, Grayson grabs my leg and puts it

over his shoulder, allowing him to take his possession of me deeper and harder. Our breathing matches the crashing waves of the ocean as we make love on the beach as the sunsets. We reach the precipice together, our emotions and love for each other are so strong I feel like they could burst into the sky, shooting across the heavens like fallen stars. I have my forever.

Rolling us to our sides, Grayson lightly kisses me before pulling away and looking into my eyes. He leans down and rests his forehead on mine with a smirk on his face, still catching his breath. "You're my happily ever after," he whispers.

"I do feel like I'm living a fairy tale."

"Me too, and I don't care what anyone else thinks either." Grayson rolls over on his back and screams at the top of his lungs, "SHE SAID YES!"

I cannot help but crack up laughing. That is so not Mr. Serious, Quiet Grayson. Once I'm composed, I pull my skirt back down and roll my eyes at him. "Like I'd say anything else."

"Hey, when you said that about moving in together, I thought I might be moving too fast for you."

"Hell no! I just never dreamed you'd ask me so soon, and so perfectly. Thank you for making my dreams come true."

"I hope to always make your dreams our reality," he says with a quick kiss before putting his pants back together. "I hate to say it, but if we don't show up tonight, everyone is going to harass us like there is no tomorrow, and I want to let the world know you are officially my fiancée."

"Well, so do I for that matter. I have to go flaunt this." I dangle my left hand in front of his face showing off my ring: an antique gold setting with a beautiful square cut diamond solitaire. "The Wenches are all going to have a fit. No one was expecting this to happen so soon. You haven't told anyone, have you?"

"No. I did have Sarah up here to help me set things up,

but she thinks it was for me to spring the fact that I got Steer and Roid to cover for you at the club so I could take you away for a 'WE-cation'."

Sitting up, I turn to face him, feeling really confused, "A 'We-cation'?" I ask, making air quotes.

"Yes, a 'WE-cation'. We've had no lengthy time by ourselves. This is going to be just the two of us, no family, no friends, no jobs. With Sarah's help, I planned for the two of us to escape everyone for a full week. Seven days with zero phone calls, texts, or emails. Just us. We need this. Your doctors said it's all good. As long as we don't get your cast wet, we should be fine."

"I love the idea of escaping with you for a week. Where are we going? Can I at least know that?"

"Nope. That is what Sarah helped me with. She packed for you. We have about," Grayson looks at his watch, "four hours before we are *free!*"

"Can I at least check what she packed? I'm afraid she could be faking you out just to get even with me for being a bitch a few weeks back. I could open it up and find it filled with nothing but paper...or something worse."

"Well, I don't plan on wearing many clothes myself on this trip. I plan on relaxing and making love to you endlessly, showing you how much I love you. Oh, and ordering lots and lots of room service," he says, standing up and taking my hand to pull me up. He surprises me by lifting me up like he's practicing for our honeymoon.

"Em, you know there are a lot of stairs over there, right? I can walk up them, you know. Oh, were you implying I eat a lot with that 'lots and lots of room service' comment?"

"We both love our food babe, even though mine has a tendency to be a bit healthier with less carbs than yours."

"Fuck less carbs. I'm Italian and I'm not giving up my bread or pasta. I have Marinara sauce in my veins. You can just enjoy watching me eat them."

"Oh, I do enjoy watching you eat," he teases, licking his lips, I'm sure referring to the time I helped him out with Sir, by kissing him.

"Hey buddy, that was not a blow job. Stop being a perv."

"I didn't say anything," he jokes, "But once you say, 'I do', all restrictions are off."

"True, but right now a *long* engagement sounds really nice."

"Not happening, babe. I made sure of that by telling your Dad we're living together until we get married now that we're engaged, and he wasn't too happy about that and said a short engagement sounded really nice. And come on, what do you think my Mom will do when she learns we're engaged? You think Ivy was bad, Mom and Grandma Piedmont? Lord help you."

Walking into the club almost two hours later, the elevator doors barely open to the Brother's private area when Grayson yells, once again, at the top of his lungs, "She said YES!!"

The Brothers just look at Grayson like he's lost his mind.

Sarah turns in her seat beside Tony at the bar, and yells back, "Yippy to the 'WE-cation'! Some of us have to work."

Grayson is smiling like a loon as he takes my cast hand and waves it at her as we walk out of the elevator. OH, MY GAWD. The instant stampede is crazy! Everyone comes running. The Wenches are literally screaming, and the Brothers are hooting and hollering with shouts of congratulations.

The Brothers slowly manage to pull Grayson in their direction and the Wenches pull me over in the other. The girls call me a bitch and tell me they utterly hate me because they are jealous of my ring and the perfect proposal, I'm only too happy to tell them about. I know it's all in fun and love. They're all thrilled for us.

It is so nice to have so many real friends and family in my life. Before we came here, we FaceTimed both sets of parents, and they had to come and celebrate with us. Both Mom Riggs and Mom Camilla are already talking wedding plans, and it hasn't even been three hours yet! They made a date to go have dinner up at Hawkins' so they can see the castle chapel and start making plans this weekend. I need a minute away from all this craziness before Grayson and I escape.

Perfect, I spot Isabella sitting at a table, rubbing her ever-growing baby bump. Tori, her best friend, is all smiles, just watching everything going on around her as she feels Isabella's babies moving. I walk over to them, hoping not to be followed by anyone else with more wedding questions. Maybe having a short engagement will be the best thing if this is a taste of what life will be like for me.

"Hi ladies. Mind if I join you, and hide away from all the wedding questions?"

"Oh sweetie, it's just begun. Have a seat," Bella says. Sitting in the chair beside her, she continues. "My mom had an actual photo album full of wedding themes and pictures of ideas less than twenty four hours after Drake and I told her we were getting married."

"I don't think that'll happen with Mom Camilla. Or at least, I hope not."

"Honey, it won't be your Mom you have to worry about. It's Mom Riggs and Grandma Piedmont. Lord only knows what Granny P will give you at your wedding shower. Brace yourself. I got a full leather crotchless catsuit with all kinds of lubes and toys," she whispers, turning bright red with embarrassment, putting her hand on my arm.

"Yeah, but admit it, they did come in handy, didn't they?" Tori teases her.

"Shhh, you aren't supposed to say anything! But yes, they

did," Isabella says breaking out in the cutest little giggle. I can't help but join in before she continues, whispering, "Have you and Grayson tried some of those toys at Nancy's Naughty's? Oh, they've got some good ones there, but that's a talk for another day."

"Shut it. You are not talking about hot sex in front of me. I'm the most sexually neglected person in this room, with the least experience so you're not going there. It's mean!" Tori says trying to look mad, crossing her arms under her breasts as she goes on. "Have I told you recently how much I hate you? If not, here's a reminder: I hate you. And I'll take it a step further right now, I hate you too," Tori teases and points at me.

"Why do you hate me?"

"*Oh please,* everyone knows your unreal love story. It's almost barfable," Tori says, pretending to stick her finger down her throat.

"Tori, your green-eyed monster is showing its horns," Isabella teases right back.

"Fuck it! I'll admit I'm jealous of every damn one of you. Look at all this fun." She waves her arm around the room. "What girl wouldn't be a tad bit jealous of you knowing *all* the Brothers of Camelot personally. You, and the Wenches, have known them since you were a kids. You're the closest to them and the only person I know who actually knows which Brother is wearing which helmet in the Brother's pictures. I've had to turn down bribes from girls trying to find out that information, thinking I know."

"Oh, I can tell you that," I say. Sometimes you gotta help a girl out.

Tori quickly sticks her fingers in her ears saying "LALALALA! Oh, gawd. See? Look at me acting like one of the kids we watch!" She laughs at herself. "See Lexy, I don't get to spend a lot of time with adults or the 'in crowd'." She does air quotes.

"Hey Tori, now that the crowds are on the other side of the room, I wanted to come over and get you registered here," Hawkins says, sitting down with an iPad in hand.

"What did you say?" she asks, looking very surprised, as she finishes off her glass of wine.

"You're Isabella's best friend, and things have been so crazy since the wedding that I haven't had the time to hunt you down and get this handled. But after tonight, you'll have easy access up here when you need an escape from life. You're always welcome. It will also get you into certain areas of my castle," Hawkins says with a hint of a smile.

"Okay Hawkins, were you eavesdropping on our conversation? Is this centerpiece bugged?" She lifts the centerpiece up and starts examining it. We all burst out laughing.

"Did I miss something?" Hawkins looks between us, with his brows drawn together. That does it and sets off another round of laughter.

Drake and Grayson walk over to join us, "Okay, what did we miss that was so funny?" Grayson asks picking me up making me feel light as a feather and taking my seat, putting me in his lap.

"Yup, I really hate you right now, even more than Isabella," Tori teases, shaking her head and pouring herself another glass of wine.

"Tori was just complaining she wasn't in the 'in crowd,' and then Hawkins walks up seconds later officially making her a part of the 'in crowd'" I do air quotes as well, making fun of Tori. Everyone continues to laugh. Hawkins ignores us and takes her hand, doing his programming stuff.

"Are those children of mine wrestling in your tummy again? Do I need to have a talk with them?" Drake says sitting on the other side of Isabella, bending over and kissing her baby bump before giving her a quick kiss on the lips.

"Nope, I take that back Lexy. My best friend gets all my hate, at least for the next two years, having to watch that."

Tori dramatically throws her head back, resting the back of her hand on her forehead, all Scarlett O'Hara like. Man, this woman is funny with the way she teases her best friend.

"Tori, why do you hate Isabella so much today? Is it me?" Drake joins in the fun, acting offended by placing his hand over his heart.

"Yes, it's all your fault. You don't have to be so damn perfect you know. Other than me, Isabella was the only one to talk to my baby bump. But I can't hate her for long, because she was my lifeline back then. I would have never made it through it all without her. She's the best adopted Auntie for JayJay too." She looks over to Isabella with a smile. "I guess I can't hate you for the next two years. Maybe just for the next two hours... having to watch the two of you acting all lovey-dovey and carrying on."

"How is Little JayJay anyway?"

"Oh, he's wonderful. Those tubes in his ears have been amazing. Hasn't had an ear infection since they were put in. He really is the love of my life. He's such a good little guy too." She practically sparkles when she talks about her son.

"How old is he?" I ask, thinking that since he didn't get to be Isabella's ringer bearer, maybe he could be ours.

"He's twenty two months, going on five," Tori says seriously.

"What?" Grayson asks.

"You haven't had the pleasure of meeting Little JayJay? Not only is he a cutie, but he is as smart as a whip. He always has some books with him wanting you to read to him, and if you try to hurry it along and skip parts, he'll point that little finger at you wrinkling his brow and tell you. 'No No'," Drake says, pointing his finger at Grayson.

"He isn't teasing. Sometimes he'll fall asleep holding 'Goodnight Moon'," Tori shares with us.

"Well, I've seen you with him on your hip a time or two, but we look forward to actually meeting him. Now I know what to get for him too," Grayson tells her with a wink, making Tori smile even bigger as she finishes off her wine.

"I've meet little JayJay several times and he's a cute kid. Isabella has told me a little about your story, and if you ever want help finding his father, I'd gladly help," Hawkins volunteers.

"Do I have to kill you, Isabella?" Tori mock glares at her then she smiles with a blush in Hawkins' direction and looks down, "Thanks Hawkins, but I literally don't know anything about him but his first name. There has been a time or two I thought I saw him driving around, but I was mistaken, and my dreams and fantasies are probably better than the real thing anyway. But thank you." Then she looks around the table at all of us asking, "Does anyone want anything from the bar? I'm going to get another bottle of wine."

"I can just yell and have one of the waitresses bring a couple of bottles over here. We still have clean glasses on the table," Drake adds.

"That's okay. This ass needs the exercise," Tori says, smacking herself on the bum. "And I was a waitress all through college," she adds as she heads to the bar.

"I hope that didn't offend her. I just wanted to help," Hawkins says.

"No, you're fine. She's been drinking and that usually makes her a little more sensitive. Drake honey, I'll drive her home and you can follow me when we're all ready to go," Isabella says to Drake, leaning back into his arms.

"I was going to suggest the same thing. Let her enjoy herself. She rarely gets out and I've only seen her drink one other time."

"Thank God it's the weekend. Otherwise, I'd be hearing her complain all day tomorrow about having to pump her breastmilk, because she doesn't want JayJay to get anything tainted," Isabella giggles again.

"Tori still breastfeeds?" I ask, because he is almost two.

"Only briefly in the morning when he first wakes up. Nighttime is the toughest because it helps to get him to sleep. But she is working on weaning him. It's going to be a struggle, but I'm hoping to breastfeed these two little peanuts, at least for the first six months if I can."

"I think it's great. I plan on breastfeeding the first year, but once they can talk and ask for it, they'll be cut off," I say with a laugh.

"Okay enough, talking about breasts. We're in public and my perverted mind is roaming where it shouldn't and you wouldn't want to wake up Henry now, would you?" Drake jokingly demands as he slams his hand down on the table playfully.

"You better keep your penis under control until we get home," Isabella shakes her finger at Drake.

Tori walks back up with two bottles of wine, asking, "Who wants white and who wants red? Let's see if I can still do this."

We all play along with her as she walks around the table, filling our glasses as she asks us, "Have you seen Jackson walking around with that guitar on his back? Please tell me the man can't sing."

"Oh, our moms made sure most of us could sing and play at least one instrument. We all had to take ballroom dancing as well. So yes, he can play it and sing. But he stole that guitar from my house a couple of weeks ago, and I can promise you I will get back after our 'WE-cation'," Grayson says.

Tori rolls her eyes, "Okay, now I get to hate on all you pampered boys." Then she shakes her head at me and Grayson. "A 'We-cation'? Okay, that's a bit too cute for a guy as hot as you to say. Sorry Lexy, just speaking the gospel truth here." We all start laughing.

The song has changed to 'Shallow' by Bradley Cooper and Lady Gaga, and all our attention is drawn to Jackson who is walking around and playing along with Bradley Cooper. He heads over to where Anissa is sitting on a bar stool, doing that thing with her head down and just looking up with her eyes, watching him. When he starts singing to her, even I feel a little giddy for her.

"Oh yeah, I hate your roomie now too. If she isn't banging Jackson yet, it's only a matter of time," Tori adds.

"Well as of earlier today, she swore the only time he kissed her was in front of all of us and he keeps telling me he isn't going to, but he likes having fun with her. But I've got a feeling that might not end well, and I'll be kicking his ass," I say.

"Lex you'll have to take a number, because I might beat you to it," Grayson says, shaking his head.

Now Jackson is behind Anissa, singing into her hair. She is as frozen as a statue with her eyes closed just enjoying the brief serenade. I'm sure she's on the verge of a spontaneous orgasm going by the look on her face. As he finishes his part, he tells Anissa to sing.

Her eyes pop open so fast and she practically screams, "No, nope I don't sing, and I sure as hell don't sing solos. No way. I have not had enough to drink to even think about it."

We cannot help but laugh at how fast she crashed from that climatic moment. That looked like someone just threw ice water on her. Sarah comes to the rescue. "Come on ladies, let's all sing." And just like that, every girl in the club starts bellowing Lady Gaga's part as I watch Jackson walk away from Anissa. Yup, it's time to talk to him again.

As the song ends, Tori finally pours herself another glass of wine. Then she reaches over and sits the bottles of wine in the middle of the table so we can all reach them. Everything happens so fast in the next few seconds that I can't believe my eyes.

Clausen walks up behind her and wraps one arm around her waist, pulling her into his front and whispers something into her ear. In a flash, Tori, grabs his hand from her waist and twists out of his hold and slaps Clausen across his face with such force, the noise draw's everyone's attention, even over the music. Everyone is on their feet in an instant, watching the drama between Tori and Clausen. Clausen has his hand on his already reddening face, and Tori seems to be on the verge of hyperventilating as she yells.

"CLAUSEN!"

"VICTORIA, what the hell? A simple no would work. Shit!" Clausen says. He removes his hand from his face and wow, you can see her handprint on the side of his face. He licks his lips cautiously. "Fuck! You busted my lip."

Isabella calls out, "Asher! What did you say to Tori?"

Spencer appears out of nowhere. "Okay, we're sorry for whatever Clausen did to cause this outburst, Ms. Cummings." He turns to Clausen and demands, "Apologize."

You can tell Clausen and Tori are both having trouble trying to figure out what just happened, when both of them look at each other and start talking at the same time.

"You first name is Asher? You told me it was Clausen!" Tori says, looking like she's completely confused.

"Oh, fuck." You hear both Isabella and Spencer call his name, probably not liking his language in the midst of this outburst. Clausen just stares at Tori saying, "You said your name was Victoria! But you're Tori Cummings, you're my sister's friend with the kid? That didn't take long," he says sarcastically.

And before anyone can say anything, she slaps him across the face again, this time on the verge of tears saying, "You're a fucking asshole. You don't know jack shit." And with that, she turns around and takes off running towards the elevator.

"Tori, honey, wait for me," Isabella calls out as she waddles as fast as she can after her. When she passes Clausen, she punches him hard in the shoulder and tells him, "Me and you are talking tomorrow. What did you say to her?" She doesn't wait for an answer as she storms off after Tori, with Drake right behind her.

"Holy shit, what just happened?" I ask Grayson and

Hawkins, who are still standing with me by our table. Everyone else is gathered around Clausen, trying to figure out what happened.

"I didn't know they even knew each other," Grayson says, pulling me back into his arms after standing us both up so we could see what was happening.

"I'm thinking they know each other a hell of a lot better than any of us would have even guessed," Hawkins adds.

"What are you talking about, Hawk?" Grayson asks.

"Don't worry about it. You have a full week to enjoy without any of us bothering you. Now is the best time to escape, while everyone's attention is on Clausen. See you in a week," Hawkins ends with a head nod as he walks away.

"Do you understand any of that?" Grayson asks me.

"I think I might have an idea, but I agree with Hawkins. Let's escape while we can."

"Okay. Let our 'WE-cation' begin." Grayson puts his arm around me and guides me against the back wall to the elevator. My, my, my, our lives will never be boring. Let the fun begin.

A NOTE FROM NECIE

Thank you for reading Book 2 in the Brother of Camelot series. There is more to come very soon. But which Brothers story do you think it'll be?

Be on the lookout for the 'Parents Story' and how the Brothers of Camelot came to be. I'll have to admit the number one question I'm asked, goes back to book one Drake and Isabella's story in "The Only One". Seems like everyone wants to know how Drake came to live with the Gregory's. Well, in the Parents Prequel to the series you'll meet ALL the parents and how it all came to be.

I hope you enjoyed the book and would love to hear from you.

73904961R00338

Made in the USA
Columbia, SC
10 September 2019